NEW SCIENCE FICTION
AND FANTASY
Eclipse
FOUR

**Also Edited by Jonathan Strahan:**

*Best Short Novels* (2004 through 2007)
*Fantasy: The Very Best of 2005*
*Science Fiction: The Very Best of 2005*
*The Best Science Fiction and Fantasy of the Year: Volumes 1–5*
*Eclipse One: New Science Fiction and Fantasy*
*Eclipse Two: New Science Fiction and Fantasy*
*Eclipse Three: New Science Fiction and Fantasy*
*The Starry Rift: Tales of New Tomorrows*

With Charles N. Brown
*The Locus Awards: Thirty Years of the Best in Fantasy and Science Fiction*

With Jeremy G. Byrne
*The Year's Best Australian Science Fiction and Fantasy: Volume 1*
*The Year's Best Australian Science Fiction and Fantasy: Volume 2*
*Eidolon 1*

With Terry Dowling
*The Jack Vance Treasury*
*The Jack Vance Reader*

With Gardner Dozois
*The New Space Opera*
*The New Space Opera 2*

With Karen Haber
*Science Fiction: Best of 2003*
*Science Fiction: Best of 2004*
*Fantasy: Best of 2004*

With Marianne S. Jablon
*Wings of Fire*

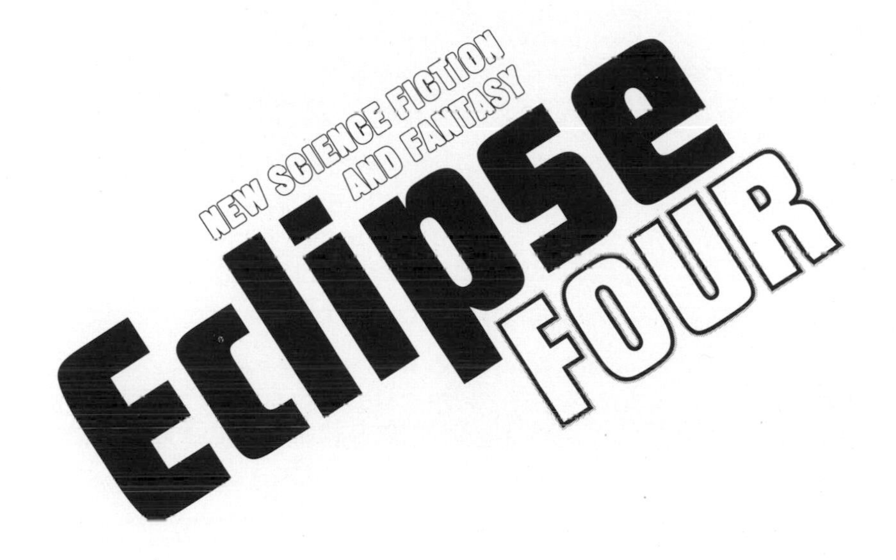


**EDITED BY JONATHAN STRAHAN**

**NIGHT SHADE BOOKS**
**SAN FRANCISCO**

Interior layout and design by Ross E. Lockhart



**First Edition**

**ISBN: 978-1-59780-197-3**

**Night Shade Books**
Please visit us on the web at
http://www.nightshadebooks.com

For Ross E. Lockhart, whose work behind the scenes has made each book we've worked on together better, with thanks.

# ACKNOWLEDGEMENTS

I doubt any book in this series has been more difficult to assemble than this one. My sincere thanks to Jason Williams, Jeremy Lassen, and Ross Lockhart at Night Shade Books for their confidence in this book and in the series; to Marty Halpern for his indefatigable, detailed copy editing on the series; to Alex, Alisa, and Tansy for their support when I felt a bit lost with this book; and to each and every writer who has been connected with the book, regardless of whether their stories appear here or not. I would especially like to thank those writers who came through under pressure when I'd begun to wonder is this book would happen at all, and to give an extra special nod to Gwyneth Jones, who waited so long for this to appear, and to Jim Kelly, who persevered long after anyone else might have given up.

Finally, as always, my deepest thanks to my wife Marianne and daughters Jessica and Sophie, from whom each and every moment spent working on this book was stolen.

# CONTENTS

# INTRODUCTION

## JONATHAN STRAHAN

Welcome to *Eclipse Four*. Five years ago, early in the Australian summer of 2007, I was hard at work on the first volume of what I hoped then would prove to be an annual series of unthemed science fiction and fantasy anthologies. It was, for me, a heady and exciting time.

The decision to launch the Eclipse series was an optimistic one, and it reflected a sense of optimism about science fiction and fantasy generally, and short fiction in particular, that was widely held at the time. Several other anthology series—Lou Anders's *Fast Forward*, George Mann's *The Solaris Book of Science Fiction* and *The Solaris Book of Fantasy*, and Ellen Datlow's *The Del Rey Book of Science Fiction and Fantasy*—were launched around the same time and all were received well. They were followed by Mike Ashley's *Clockwork Phoenix* series and many, many original anthologies.

That sense of optimism was, in many ways, well placed. As I wrote in the introduction to *Eclipse One*:

> "This is a good time for the short story in genre circles. Not maybe in business terms—we're yet to develop a twenty-first century business model that allows writers to make a living writing short stories—but in artistic terms, it's extraordinary. Whether in anthologies like this one, or in magazines or on websites, short stories are being published in staggering numbers. Thousands each year, millions of words, and in amongst this torrent of content is some extraordinary work."

That has continued to be true over the following years. Business models remained a problem. Print magazines didn't exactly flourish, but long-time campaigners like *Asimov's*, *Analog*, and *F&SF* continued to appear as they had for many decades, as did *Interzone*, *Realms of Fantasy* (though it did die twice), and many others. Online magazines evolved and became critical to the scene with *Clarkesworld*, *Subterranean*, *Tor.com*, *Strange Horizons*, and many, many, many more developing into important, well-paying markets that published some of our finest short fiction. It's easy to feel, in these days of the iPad and the Kindle, that a successful long-term business model is yet to emerge, but an honest observer would have to admit these are still good times for short fiction.

What does that mean for Eclipse? It was always intended to be a spiritual descendant of the classic anthology series of the 1960s and '70s like Knight's *Orbit*, Carr's *Universe*, and Silverberg's *New Dimensions*. With stories appearing on Hugo, Nebula, World Fantasy, Locus, Shirley Jackson, Sidewise, BSFA, Aurealis, Ditmar, and other ballots, and with volumes of the series itself winning the Aurealis Award, and being nominated for the World Fantasy and Locus awards, it's hard to not feel that it is meeting that goal.

That doesn't mean I'm any closer to knowing what a volume of *Eclipse* should be, or that I'm anywhere near done. Ever since Jetse de Vries named the series I've been taken by the idea that it was rare and unusual, a strange, dark eldritch thing where wonderful things might happen within its pages. I've tried, as much as I can, to make sure each volume was different, a place though where reality was eclipsed for a little while with something magical and new. And yet each volume has had its own personality. *Eclipse One* was very much a general beast, *Eclipse Two* much more science fiction-oriented, and *Eclipse Three* was the one with the broadest outlook.

What of *Eclipse Four*? In some ways it is the strangest and most eldritch volume yet. When I started work on it I intended it to be very much a sister volume to *Eclipse Three*, but like the wilful, living thing it is it insisted on being the book it would be, not an echo of its predecessor. During the nearly sixteen months I've been working on *Eclipse Four* writers have joined and left the book, have delivered and redelivered stories, and in some cases have moved from delivering one type of story to delivering another. In the end the fourteen stories here range from tall tales to coming-of-age stories, move from the deep South to the outer reaches of our solar system, and approach everything from how we find love and happiness to how we cope with death and grief.

Many of the writers here are new to *Eclipse*, but some, like Jeffrey Ford, are old friends and regulars to the series. All of them have outdone themselves and I'm deeply grateful to them all for letting me publish their work here. I would also like to express my gratitude here to my publishers, Night Shade, who have been wonderful to work with, and to my wife Marianne and daughters Jessica and Sophie, who have been endlessly patient. I would also like to thank you, the reader, for picking this book up and taking it home. I hope you enjoy it as much as I have, and that this is just the start of a beautiful friendship. As for me, I'm working on *Eclipse Five*. See you next year!

Jonathan Strahan
January 2011

# SLOW AS A BULLET

## ANDY DUNCAN

I ever tell you about the time Cliffert Corbett settled a bet by outrunning a bullet?

Oh.

Well, all right, Little Miss Smarty Ass, here it is again, but this time I'll stick to the truth, because I got enough sins to write out on St. Peter's blackboard as it is, thank you, and on the third go-round the truth is easiest to remember. So you just write down what I tell you, just *as* I tell you, and don't put in none of your women's embroidery this time.

You're too young to remember Cliffert Corbett, I reckon, but he was the kind that even if you did remember him, you wouldn't remember him, except for this one thing that I am going to tell you, the one remarkable thing he ever did in his life. It started one lazed-out, dragged-in Florida afternoon outside the gas station, when we were all passing around a sack of boiled peanuts and woofing about who was the fastest.

During all this, Cliffert hadn't said nothing, and he hadn't intended to say nothing, but Cliffert's mouth was just like your mouth and mine. Whenever it was shut it was only biding its time, just waiting for the mind to fall down on the job long enough for the mouth to jump into the gap and raise some hell. So when Cliffert squeezed one boiled peanut right into his eye and blinded himself, his mouth was ready. As he blinked away the juice, his mouth up and blabbed: "Any of you fast enough to outrun a bullet?"

They all turned and looked at him, and friend, he wasn't much to look at. Cliffert was built like a fence post, and a rickety post, too, maybe that last post standing of the old fence in back of the gas station, the one with the lone snipped rusty barbed-wire curl, the one the bobwhites wouldn't nest in, because the men liked to shoot at it for target practice. And everyone knew that if Cliffert, with his gimpy leg, was to race that fence post, their money would be elsewhere than on Cliffert.

And because what Cliffert had said wasn't joking like, but more angry, sort of a challenge, Isiah Bird asked, "You saying you can do that?"

And just before Cliffert got the last bit of salt out of his eyes, his mouth told Isiah, "I got five dollars says I can, Isiah Bird."

From there it didn't matter how shut Cliffert's mouth was, because before he knew what hit him Isiah had taken that bet, and the others had jumped in and put down money of their own, and they were hollering for other folks on the street to come get in on the action, and Dad Boykin made up a little register that showed enough money was riding on this to have Cliffert set for life if he just could outrun a bullet, which everyone in town knew he couldn't do, including Cliffert, plus he didn't have no five dollars to lose.

"We'll settle this right now," said Pump Jeffries, who ran the gas station. "I got my service pistol locked up in the office there, but it's well greased and ready to go."

"Hold on!" cried Cliffert, and they all studied him unfriendly like, knowing he was about to back out on the deal his mouth had made.

"I got to use my own gun," Cliffert said, "and my own bullets."

They all looked at each other, but when Isiah Bird nodded his head, the others nodded, too. "Fetch 'em, then," Dad Boykin said. "We'll wait right here."

"Now, boys," said Cliffert, thinking faster than he could run, "you got to give me some time to get ready. Because this ain't something you can just up and do, no matter how fast you are. You got to practice at it, work up to it. I need to get in shape."

"Listen at him now. He wants to go into training!"

"How long you need, then?"

"A year," Clifford said. "I'll outrun a bullet one year from this very day, the next twenty-first of July, right here in front of the gas station, at noon."

No one liked this very much, because they were all raring to go right then. But they talked it over and decided that Cliffert wasn't going to be any more able to outrun a bullet in a year than he was now.

"All right, Cliffert," they told him. "One year from today."

So then Cliffert limped on home, tearing his hair and moaning, cursing his fool mouth for getting him into this fix.

He was still moaning when he passed the hoodoo woman's house. You could tell it was the hoodoo woman's house because the holes in the cement blocks that held it up were full of charms, and the raked patterns in the dirt yard would move if you looked at them too hard, and the persimmon trees were heavy with blue bottles to catch spirits, and mainly because the hoodoo woman herself was always sitting on the porch, smoking a corncob pipe, at all hours and in all weathers, because her house was ideally situated to watch all the townsfolk going and coming, and she was afraid if she ever went inside she might miss something.

"What ails you, Cliffert Corbett, that you're carrying on such a way?"

So Cliffert limped into her yard, taking care not to step on any of the wiggly lines, and told her the whole thing.

"So you see, Miz Armetta, I won't be able to hold my head up in this town no more. I'll have to go live in Tallahassee with the rest of the liars."

The hoodoo woman snorted. "Just tell 'em you can't outrun a bullet, that you're sorry you stretched it any such a way. Isiah Bird keeps cattle and hogs both, and he'll let you work off that five dollars you owe him."

When he heard the word 'work,' Cliffert felt faint, and the sun went behind a cloud, and the dirt pattern in the yard looked like a big spider that crouched and waited.

"Oh, Miz Armetta, work is a harsh thing to say to a man! Ain't you got any other ideas for me than that?"

"Mmmph," she said, drawing on her pipe. "The holes men dig just to have a place to sit." She closed her eyes and rocked in her shuck chair and drummed her fingertips on her wrinkled forehead and asked, "They expecting you to use your own bullet?"

"Yes, and my own gun."

"Well, it's simple then," she said. "You need you some slow bullets."

"What you mean, slow bullets? I never heard tell of such a thing."

"I ain't, either," said the hoodoo woman, "but you got a year to find you some, or make you some."

Cliffert studied on this all the way home. There he lifted his daddy's old service pistol and gun belt out of the cedar chest and rummaged an old box of bullets out of the back corner of the Hoosier cabinet and set them both on the kitchen table and sat down before them. He rested his elbows on the oilcloth and rested his chin on his hands. He wasn't used to thinking, but now that first Isiah Bird and now the hoodoo woman had got him started in that direction, he was sort of beginning to enjoy it. He studied and studied, and by sunset he had his breakthrough.

"The *bullet* is just a lump of metal," he told the three-year-and-two-month-old Martha White calendar that twitched and tapped the wall in the evening breeze. "It's the powder in the cartridge that moves it along. So what I need is slow *powder*. But what would go into slow powder?"

He grabbed a stubby pencil, and on the topmost *Tallahassee Democrat* on a stack bound for the outhouse, he began to make a list of slow things.

For week after week, month after month, Cliffert messed at his kitchen table, and then in his back yard, with his gunpowder recipe, looking for the mix that gave a bullet the slowest start possible while still firing. First he ground up some snail shells and turtle shells and mixed that in. He drizzled a spoonful of molasses over it and made such a jommock that he had to start over, so from then on, he used only a dot of molasses in each batch, like the single roly-poly blob Aunt Berth put in the middle of her biscuit after the doctor told her to mind her sugar. For growing grass he had to visit a neighbor's yard, since his own yard was dirt and unraked dirt at that, but the flecks of dry paint were scraped from his own side porch and in the sun, too, which was one job of work. He tried recipe after recipe, a tad more of this and a teenchy bit less of that, and went through three boxes of bullets test-firing into a propped-up Sears, Roebuck catalog in the back yard, and even though the boxes emptied ever more slowly, he still was dissatisfied. Then one day he went to Fulmer's Hardware and told his problems to the man himself.

"You try any wet paint?" Mr. Fulmer asked.

"No," Cliffert said. "Just the flakings. How come you ask me that?"

"Well, I was just thinking," Mr. Fulmer said. He laid the edge of his left hand down on the counter, like it was slicing bread. "If wet paint is over *here*." He held his left hand still and laid down the edge of his right hand about ten inches away. "And dry paint is over *here*, and it goes from the one to the other, it stands to reason that the wet paint is slower than the dry, since it ain't caught up yet."

Cliffert studied Mr. Fulmer's hands for a spell. The store was silent, except for the *plip plip plip* from the next aisle. They couldn't see over the shelf but knew it was six-year-old Louvenia Parler, who liked to wait for her mama in the hardware store so she could play with the nails.

"That stands to reason," Cliffert finally said, "only if the wet paint is as old as the dry paint, so we know they started at the same time."

Mr. Fulmer folded his arms. "Now you talking sense. When you last paint your side porch?"

"I myself ain't never painted it, nor the front porch nor no other part of the house. It don't look like it's been painted since God laid down the dirt to make the mountains."

"That might be the original paint, sure enough, so you're out of luck. I don't stock no seventy-five-year-old paint."

"How old you got?"

Mr. Fulmer blew air between his lips like a noisemaker. "Ohh, let's see. I probably got paint about as old as Louvenia."

"Well, even Mr. Ford started somewhere. Let me have a gallon of the oldest you got."

Mr. Fulmer asked, "What color?" And before he even could regret asking, Cliffert said:

"Whatever color's the slowest, that's the one I want."

Mr. Fulmer laughed. "I know you chasing your tail now. The hell you goin' tell what color's slowest? I been pouring paint for thirty years, and it all pours and dries the same."

Cliffert opened his mouth to say he-didn't-know-what, but the sound they heard was a little-girl voice from the next aisle over, stretching out her "I" all sassy like.

"*I-I-I-I* know how," Louvenia said. "*I-I-I-I* know how to tell."

Cliffert looked at Mr. Fulmer, and Mr. Fulmer looked at Cliffert, and when they got tired of looking at each other, they looked over the top edge of the shelf and saw Louvenia sitting on the plank floor, calico skirt spread out like a lilypad, and all around her a briar-patch of nails, tenpenny and twopenny, dozens of them, all standing on their heads and ranged like soldiers.

"Tell us, Louvenia honey," Cliffert said.

"Watch for when a rainbow comes out," she said, "and see which color comes out the slowest." She scooped up a handful of twopennies and sifted them through her fingers back into the nail keg, *plip plip plip*.

"That's good thinking, Louvenia," Cliffert said. "I thank you kindly."

"You're welcome," she said.

"You put those back when you're done, now, Louvenia," Mr. Fulmer said as he and Cliffert pulled their heads back. "I swear, ever nail in this town will be handled by that child before she's done."

"It *is* a good idea," Cliffert said, "but my eyes ain't good enough to make it a practice."

"Mine, neither," Mr. Fulmer said. "I see a rainbow all at once, or I don't see it."

Cliffert opened his mouth again, but nothing came out. Mr. Fulmer waited. He wasn't in no hurry. If it hadn't been a slow day, he wouldn't have been standing there jawing about dry paint and rainbows. Finally Cliffert turned his hand edgewise and chopped the air seven times.

"They *are* the same order, ever time, in a rainbow," Cliffert said. "Read Out Your Good Book In Verse. Red the first, violet the last."

"Or the other way around," Mr. Fulmer said. "You going left to right or right to left?"

"Has to be one end or the other," Cliffert said. "Gimme a gallon of red and a gallon of violet."

"*I* call it purple," Mr. Fulmer said, "and paint don't come in purple. But I can sure mix you some red and blue to make purple."

"Well, I thank you," Cliffert said.

Mr. Fulmer whistled his way into the storage room, happy because he had helped solve a little hardware problem and because since the Crash he had about given up on ever moving another gallon of paint.

So Cliffert worked through Christmas adding dibs and dabs of paint to his mix, and after New Year's he threw in some January molasses 'cause those are the slowest, and then he shot off the results back of his house, *bang bang blim bang*. "It's the Battle of Atlanta," his neighbors cried, and beat the young'uns who walked too near Cliffert's fence. He didn't get close to satisfied till the first of June, and only then did he take his gun and his custom-made cartridges over to the hoodoo woman's house to show her what he had.

"Mmmph, mmmph, mmmph," said the hoodoo woman. The second "mmmph" meant she was impressed, and the third meant she was *flat* impressed.

"That's good, Cliffert Corbett," she said, "but hold on here, I got one more idea that might make her better still. Now, where'd I put that thing?" She rummaged her right hand through her apron pockets while holding her left hand out in the air stiff and flat, like she was drying her nails in the breeze, only there was no breeze and the nails were black and broken on her knobbed and ropy hand, and Cliffert didn't like the look of it. Then the hoodoo woman laughed a croupy laugh and pulled forth a corked bottle the size of her thumb, full of a pale green sloshy something. "If it was a snake it woulda bit me," said the hoodoo woman.

"What is it, Miz Armetta?"

"Money Stay With Me Oil. I reckon if it slows down the money, it might slow down your bullet, too. Here, unstop it for me while I reach out my dropper. Don't let none get on you, now! This is for fixing, not anointing."

Cliffert thought the bottle was powerful heavy for such a tee-ninchy dram of liquid, and was glad to hand it back to her when she was done plopping one sallow green blob onto the tip of each cartridge, then wiping them down with a bright red cloth. They should have gleamed brighter then, but instead they looked even duller, like their surface light was being sucked inside to die. "Don't just stand there," she said. "Get to writing. We need some name paper. Write your full name nine times in red ink."

"You got any red ink, Miz Armetta?"

She snorted. "Does Fulmer's have nails?"

Cliffert's hand hurt him by the time he was done—he couldn't make the Fs to suit her, and had to keep doing them over—but he had to admit, when they tried out the test bullet, that a little Money Stay With Me oil had gone a long way.

So on the appointed day, everybody in town who was interested in bets or guns or lies, or who was hanging around the gas station on that fateful day the year before, or who was related to any of those, all turned up at the gas station to see whether Cliffert actually would be there to admit to his lie and pay the man. Everyone was half surprised to see Cliffert limping across the lot, about five minutes to noon, and plumb surprised to see him wearing his daddy's gun belt. It was cinched to the last hole and still he had to hold it up with both hands, and the holster went down practically to his knee. But sticking out of the holster was a shiny silver gun butt that suggested Cliffert was open for business.

"Cliffert Corbett, you here to outrun a bullet today?" asked Isiah Bird.

"I will sure do that thing, Isiah Bird," said Cliffert in return.

"Do it, then," said Dad Boykin. "I got corn to shuck and chicken to pluck. I got obligations."

Cliffert planted his feet on the asphalt and looked down the side of the station toward the back of the lot, and hollered at the crowd, "Y'all make way so's a man can work!" But that little bantyweight holding up his belt looked just like a young'un playing gunfighter after a cowboy matinee, and we all just laughed at him. Lord, how we laughed! And didn't nobody budge an inch until he drew that gun—all slow and solemn-like—and pointed it at us with the steadiest hand you ever saw, and then we all found reasons to get behind him and beside him and up against the walls and otherwise out of the man's way. So in a few seconds there was nothing between Cliffert's gun and that shot-up old fence post at the back of the property, the last piece of the fence that separated the gas station from the woods behind. It was right splintered up, though not as much as you'd think, since the men of our town weren't the greatest shots in Florida, not even drunk.

"On three," Cliffert said, and he brought that gun up two-handed and squinted down the barrel, and without his hand on it, his gun belt slipped down to his knees. Nobody laughed, though, because that gun was steady, man, steady.

"One," Cliffert said.

We didn't say nothing.

"Two," Cliffert said.

We didn't breathe.

Then he fired, and we all jumped about a foot in the air. It wasn't just that the shot was three times as loud as any gunshot has any right to be. It also sounded... *wrong*. It sounded *interrupted*. It sounded like a scream that lasts only a half-second before someone claps a hand across your mouth. And the smoke coming out of the barrel was wrong, too. Instead of puffing away in an instant, it uncoiled slow in solid gray ropes, like baby snakes first poking their heads from a hidey-hole in springtime. And the fence post looked just the same as before.

"Misfire," someone said.

"Wait for it," Cliffert said, still sighting down the barrel and holding her steady.

The smoke kept on curling. And then, amid the smoke, something dark started pushing forth, like the gun itself was turning wrong side out. Lord have mercy, it was the tip of the bullet sliding into view, and nobody said a word as it eased on out of the barrel. It must have taken a solid minute just for that bullet to clear the gun. And just as we could see daylight between the bullet and the barrel, Cliffert stepped back a pace and raised the gun and blew across the tip. I never saw smoke so loath to be gone. A scrap of it snagged his lip and hung there awhile like a sorry gray mustache before it slid off into nothing.

"Move the gun too quick, you mess up the aim," Cliffert said. "I was days figuring that out."

Then I went back to watching the bullet, which was about a foot away and moving steady but no faster than before. In fact, I reckon it was moving even slower, since all its charge was blown, and from here on gravity takes over—in any normal Christian bullet, that is. You ever craned your neck to look up at an airplane that just seems to be making no progress at all? Watching that bullet was like watching that airplane, one about at the level of the tobacco pouch in my shirt pocket. Even Cliffert just stood there, gun still on his shoulder pointing at the top of the chinaberry tree, staring at the bullet he had made, as hypnotized as anyone.

Someone yelled, "Look at the shadow!"

The bullet's shadow was crawling along the ground, sliding in and out of every chip and crack in the asphalt, in no bigger hurry than the bullet it was tethered to above, and somehow that shadow was even worse than the bullet.

A shudder went through the crowd, and a few folks bust out crying, and they weren't all women neither, while some others started hollering for Jesus.

Cliffert sort of shook himself all over and said, "Look at me! I near forgot the bet." He holstered the gun and ambled forward. He was noways in a hurry, but in only a few steps he'd caught up to that bullet he had loosed, and in a few steps more he had walked past it, and as he walked he pulled a wrinkled paper from his pants pocket. He unfolded it and smoothed it out a little and turned around and held it up as he walked. Drawn on the paper in red ink was a bull's-eye target about six inches across, and Cliffert stumbled a little as he walked backwards, trying to gauge how high the target ought to be for the bullet to hit it square.

Now we had two things of wonderment to look at, Cliffert's bullet and Cliffert himself, and we all was so busy staring at one and then the other that we hadn't paid any mind at all to a third thing: Lou Lou Maddox's toothless mangy old collie dog, the one that was blind in one eye and couldn't see out the other, and had so much arthritis that she wouldn't have been walking if she hadn't been held up and jerked along by the fleas. That old dog had crawled out from under the Maddox porch next door and stood up all rickety and hitched her way across the side yard headed toward the gas station, maybe because she smelled the peanuts boiling, or because she wondered what all the fuss was about, and when we finally noticed her walking into the path of Cliffert's bullet, we all hollered at once—so loud that the damn dog stopped dead in her tracks and blinked at us with milky eyes, and that bullet not six inches from her shackly ribcage and inching closer.

"Salome!" screamed Lou Lou. "Get out of there, Salome!"

The dog blinked and looked sideways and saw that bullet a-coming. Salome yelped and hopped forward twice, so that the bullet just missed her hindquarters as it headed on.

Now Cliffert had finally got his target situated where he wanted it, by jamming it down on a splinter on that highest fence post at the back of the lot. And by the time the bullet was finally about a half-inch from the bull's-eye, everyone had had time to go get some supper and find a few more relations to tell about the marvel and bring them on back to the gas station, so the whole damn town was standing gathered around the target in a half-circle, all watching as the bullet nosed into the paper… and dented it a little… and then punched through (we all heard it)… and then kept on going, through the paper and into the fence post (we all heard a little grinding noise, *eckity eckity eckity eck*, like a mouse in the wall, but all continuous, not afeard of no cat or nothing else in this world, just doing its slow steady job of work)… and then the sawdust started sifting out of the back of the post… and here came the bullet, out the other side (we had flashlights and lanterns trained on it by then), and we all watched as the bullet went on into the brush and into the woods, and then it was so dark we couldn't see it no more. We thought about following it into the woods with our lights, but then we thought about getting all confused in the dark and getting ahead of it, and how it would be to have that bullet a-nosing into your side, so we decided not to hunt for it but say we did.

"Just imagine," said the hoodoo woman, the only person in town not at the gas station. Still a-sitting on her porch, she struck a match and fired her pipe and told the shapes gathering in the dirt, "Imagine having nothing better to do all day than watch a man shoot a fence post." She pointed her pipestem at a particularly lively patch of ground. "You stay down in that yard, Sonny Jim. I got my eyes on you."

What happened next?

Well, that was about when I left. So I ain't any too clear on the rest of it. I know Cliffert collected him some money, off of me and a lot of the others. It was enough to set him up for life in the style to which he was accustomed, not that he was accustomed to much. Someone told me he took the train to Pensacola that week and tried to sell the U.S. Army on what he had done, but the U.S. Army said thank you just the same, it couldn't see no point, no strategic advantage, in a bullet that even a colicky baby could crawl out of the way of. Not that the U.S. Army had any plans to actually shoot any colicky babies. That was just a for-example. They weren't aware in Pensacola of any immediate colicky baby threat, although they would continue to monitor the situation. So the U.S. Army hustled Cliffert out of the office, and he went on home and lived out his days a richer and more thoughtful man, but if he ever made any more slow bullets, the news ain't reached me yet. So that's more'n I know.

Except no one ever did see that bullet come out of them woods.

Maybe it finally come to rest in a tree, and maybe it didn't. Maybe it finally run out of juice, and dropped to the ground and died, and maybe it didn't. Maybe it's still in there someplace, a-looking around for something to shoot. Maybe it found its way out of them woods long ago. Could be anywhere by now. One day you might be going about your business, pestering the life out of some hopeful old man with that notebook of yourn, and his eyes might get wide and he might say, "Hey!" But it's too late, because you can't even get turned 'round good before *eckity, eckity, eck*, Cliffert Corbett's bullet is drilling into the back of your head, and next thing you know, there you is, dead as McKinley on the cooling board.

Why ain't you writing that down?

What? Call yourself educated and can't even spell *eckity, eckity, eck*? Shit. I could spell that myself, if I ever needed it done.

# TIDAL FORCES

## CAITLÍN R. KIERNAN

Charlotte says, "That's just it, Em. There wasn't any pain. I didn't feel anything much at all." She sips her coffee and stares out the kitchen window, squinting at the bright Monday morning sunlight. The sun melts like butter across her face. It catches in the strands of her brown hair, like a late summer afternoon tangling itself in dead cornstalks. It deepens the lines around her eyes and at the corners of her mouth. She takes another sip of coffee, then sets her cup down on the table. I've never once seen her use a saucer.

And the next minute seems to last longer than it ought to last, longer than the mere sum of the sixty seconds that compose it, the way time stretches out to fill in awkward pauses. She smiles for me, and so I smile back. I don't want to smile, but isn't that what you do? The person you love is frightened, but she smiles anyway. So you have to smile back, despite your own fear. I tell myself it isn't so much an act of reciprocation as an acknowledgement. I could be more honest with myself and say I only smiled back out of guilt.

"I *wish* it had hurt," she says, finally, on the other side of all that long, long moment. I don't have to ask what she means, though I wish that I did. I wish I didn't already know. She says the same words over again, but more quietly than before, and there's a subtle shift in emphasis. "I wish it *had* hurt."

I apologize and say I shouldn't have brought it up again, and she shrugs.

"No, don't be sorry, Em. Don't let's be sorry for anything."

I'm stacking days, building a house of cards made from nothing but days. Monday is the Ace of Hearts. Saturday is the Four of Spades.

Wednesday is the Seven of Clubs. Thursday night is, I suspect, the Seven of Diamonds, and it might be heavy enough to bring the whole precarious thing tumbling down around my ears. I would spend an entire hour watching cards fall, because time would stretch, the same way it stretches out to fill in awkward pauses, the way time is stretched thin in that thundering moment of a car crash. Or at the edges of a wound.

If it's Monday morning, I can lean across the breakfast table and kiss her, as if nothing has happened. And if we're lucky, that might be the moment that endures almost indefinitely. I can kiss her, taste her, savor her, drawing the moment out like a card drawn from a deck. But no, now it's Thursday night, instead of Monday morning. There's something playing on the television in the bedroom, but the sound is turned all the way down, so that whatever the something may be proceeds like a silent movie filmed in color and without intertitles. A movie for lip readers. There's no other light but the light from the television. She's lying next to me, almost undressed, asking me questions about the book I don't think I'm ever going to be able to finish. I understand she's not asking them because she needs to know the answers, which is the only reason I haven't tried to change the subject.

"The Age of Exploration was already long over with," I say. "For all intents and purposes, it ended early in the Seventeenth Century. Everything after that—reaching the north and south poles, for instance—is only a series of footnotes. There were no great blank spaces left for men to fill in. No more 'Here be monsters.'"

She's lying on top of the sheets. It's the middle of July and too hot for anything more than sheets. Clean white sheets and underwear. In the glow from the television, Charlotte looks less pale and less fragile than she would if the bedside lamp were on, and I'm grateful for the illusion. I want to stop talking, because it all sounds absurd, pedantic, all these unfinished, half-formed ideas that add up to nothing much at all. I want to stop talking and just lie here beside her.

"So writers made up stories about lost worlds," she says, having heard all this before and pretty much knowing it by heart. "But those made-up worlds weren't really *lost*. They just weren't *found* yet. They'd not yet been imagined."

"That's the point," I reply. "The value of those stories rests in their insistence that blank spaces still do exist on the map. They *have* to exist, even if it's necessary to twist and distort the map to make room for them. All those overlooked islands, inaccessible plateaus in South

American jungles, the sunken continents and the entrances to a hollow Earth, they were important psychological buffers against progress and certainty. It's no coincidence that they're usually places where time has stood still, to one degree or another."

"But not really so much time," she says, "as the processes of evolution, which require time."

"See? You understand this stuff better than I do," and I tell her she should write the book. I'm only half joking. That's something else Charlotte knows. I lay my hand on her exposed belly, just below the navel, and she flinches and pulls away.

"Don't do that," she says.

"All right. I won't. I wasn't thinking." I *was* thinking, but it's easier if I tell her that I wasn't.

Monday morning. Thursday night. This day or that. My own private house of cards, held together by nothing more substantial than balance and friction. And the loops I'd rather make than admit to the present. Connecting dot-to-dot, from here to there, from there to here. Here being half an hour before dawn on a Saturday, the sky growing lighter by slow degrees. Here, where I'm on my knees, and Charlotte is standing naked in front of me. Here, now, when the perfectly round hole above her left hip and below her ribcage has grown from a pinprick to the size of the saucers she never uses for her coffee cups.

"I don't think it will hurt," she tells me. And I can't see any point in asking whether she means, *I don't think it will hurt me*, or *I don't think it will hurt you.*

"Now?" I ask her, and she says, "No. Not yet. Wait."

So, handed that reprieve, I withdraw again to the relative safety of the Ace of Hearts—or Monday morning, call it what you will. In my mind's eye, I run back to the kitchen washed in warm yellow sunlight. Charlotte is telling me about the time, when she was ten years old, that she was shot with a BB gun, her brother's Red Ryder BB gun.

"It wasn't an accident," she's telling me. "He meant to do it. I still have the scar from where my mother had to dig the BB out of my ankle with tweezers and a sewing needle. It's very small, but it's a scar all the same."

"Is that what it felt like, like being hit with a BB?"

"No," she says, shaking her head and gazing down into her coffee cup. "It didn't. But when I think about the two things, it seems like there's a link between them, all these years apart. Like, somehow, this thing was an echo of the day he shot me with the BB gun."

"A meaningful coincidence," I suggest. "A sort of synchronicity."

"Maybe," Charlotte says. "But maybe not." She looks out the window again. From the kitchen, you can see the three oaks and her flower bed and the land running down to the rocks and the churning sea. "It's been an awfully long time since I read Jung. My memory's rusty. And, anyway, maybe it's not a coincidence. It could be something else. Just an echo."

"I don't understand, Charlotte. I really don't think I know what you mean."

"Never mind," she says, not taking her eyes off the window. "Whatever I do or don't mean, it isn't important."

The warm yellow light from the sun, the colorless light from a color television. A purplish sky fading towards the light of false dawn. The complete absence of light from the hole punched into her body by something that wasn't a BB. Something that also wasn't a shadow.

"What scares me most," she says (and I could draw *this* particular card from anywhere in the deck), "is that it didn't come back out the other side. So, it must still be lodged in there, *in* me."

I was watching when she was hit. I saw when she fell. I'm coming to that.

"Writers made up stories about *lost* worlds" she says again, after she's flinched, after I've pulled my hand back from the brink. "They did it because we were afraid of having found all there *was* to find. Accurate maps became more disturbing, at least unconsciously, than the idea of sailing off the edge of a flat world."

"I don't want to talk about the book."

"Maybe that's why you can't finish it."

"Maybe you don't know what you're talking about."

"Probably," she says, without the least bit of anger or impatience in her voice.

I roll over, turning my back on Charlotte and the silent television. Turning my back on what cannot be heard and doesn't want to be acknowledged. The sheets are damp with sweat, and there's the stink of ozone that's not *quite* the stink of ozone. The acrid smell that always follows her now, wherever she goes. No. That isn't true. The smell doesn't follow her, it comes *from* her. She *radiates* the stink that is almost, but not quite, the stink of ozone.

"Does *Alice's Adventures in Wonderland* count?" she asks me, even though I've said I don't want to talk about the goddamned book. I'm sure that she heard me, and I don't answer her.

Better not to linger too long on Thursday night.

Better if I return, instead, to Monday morning. Only Monday morning. Which I have carelessly, randomly, designated here as the Ace of Hearts, and hearts are cups, so Monday morning is the Ace of Cups. In four days more, Charlotte will ask me about Alice, and though I won't respond to the question (at least not aloud), I *will* recall that Lewis Carroll considered the *Queen* of Hearts—who rules over the Ace and is also the Queen of Cups—I will recollect that Lewis Carroll considered her the embodiment of a certain type of passion. That passion, he said, which is ungovernable, but which exists as an aimless, unseeing, furious thing. And he said, also, that the Queen of Cups, the Queen of Hearts, is not to be confused with the *Red* Queen, whom he named another brand of passion altogether.

Monday morning in the kitchen.

"My brother always claimed he was shooting at a blue jay and missed. He said he was aiming for the bird, and hit me. He said the sun was in his eyes."

"Did he make a habit of shooting songbirds?"

"Birds and squirrels," she says. "Once he shot a neighbor's cat, right between the eyes." And Charlotte presses the tip of an index finger to the spot between her brows. "The cat had to be taken to a vet to get the BB out, and my mom had to pay the bill. Of course, he said he wasn't shooting at the cat. He was shooting at a sparrow and missed."

"What a little bastard," I say.

"He was just a kid, only a year older than I was. Kids don't mean to be cruel, Em, they just are sometimes. From our perspectives, they appear cruel. They exist outside the boundaries of adult conceits of morality. Anyway, after the cat, my dad took the BB gun away from him. So, after that, he always kind of hated cats."

But here I am neglecting Wednesday, overlooking Wednesday, even though I went to the trouble of drawing a card for it. And it occurs to me now I didn't even draw one for Tuesday. Or Friday, for that matter. It occurs to me that I'm becoming lost in this ungainly metaphor, that the tail is wagging the dog. But Wednesday was of consequence. More so than was Thursday night, with its mute TV and the Seven of Diamonds and Charlotte shying away from my touch.

The Seven of Clubs. Wednesday, or the Seven of Pentacles, seen another way round. Charlotte, wrapped in her bathrobe, comes downstairs after taking a hot shower, and she finds me reading Kip Thorne's *Black Holes and Time Warps*, the book lying lewdly open in my lap.

I quickly close it, feeling like I'm a teenager again, and my mother's just barged into my room to find me masturbating to the *Hustler* centerfold. Yes, your daughter is a lesbian, and yes, your girlfriend is reading quantum theory behind your back.

Charlotte stares at me awhile, staring silently, and then she stares at the thick volume lying on the coffee table, *Principles of Physical Cosmology*. She sits down on the floor, not far from the sofa. Her hair is dripping, spattering the hardwood.

"I don't believe you're going to find anything in there," she says, meaning the books.

"I just thought..." I begin, but let the sentence die unfinished, because I'm not at all sure *what* I was thinking. Only that I've always turned to books for solace.

And here, on the afternoon of the Seven of Pentacles, this Wednesday weighted with those seven visionary chalices, she tells me what happened in the shower. How she stood in the steaming spray watching the water rolling down her breasts and *across* her stomach and *up* her buttocks before falling into the hole in her side. Not in defiance of gravity, but in perfect accord with gravity. She hardly speaks above a whisper. I sit quietly listening, wishing that I could suppose she'd only lost her mind. Recourse to wishful thinking, the seven visionary chalices of the Seven of Pentacles, of the Seven of Clubs, or Wednesday. Running away to hide in the comfort of insanity, or the authority of books, or the delusion of lost worlds.

"I'm sorry, but what the fuck do I say to that?" I ask her, and she laughs. It's a terrible sound, that laugh, a harrowing, forsaken sound. And then she stops laughing, and I feel relief spill over me, because now she's crying, instead. There's shame at the relief, of course, but even the shame is welcome. I couldn't have stood that terrible laughter much longer. I go to her and put my arms around her and hold her, as if holding her will make it all better. The sun's almost down by the time she finally stops crying.

I have a quote from Albert Einstein, from sometime in 1912, which I found in the book by Kip Thorne, the book Charlotte caught me reading on Wednesday: "Henceforth, space by itself, and time by itself, are doomed to fade away into mere shadows, and only a kind of union of the two will preserve an independent reality."

Space, time, shadows.

As I've said, I was watching when she was hit. I saw when she fell. That was Saturday last, two days before the yellow morning in the kitchen, and not to be confused with the *next* Saturday, which is the Four of Spades. I was sitting on the porch, and had been watching two noisy grey-white gulls wheeling far up against the blue summer sky. Charlotte had been working in her garden, pulling weeds. She called out to me, and I looked away from the birds. She was pointing towards the ocean, and at first I wasn't sure what it was she wanted me to see. I stared at the breakers shattering themselves against the granite boulders, and past that, to the horizon where the water was busy with its all but eternal task of shouldering the burden of the heavens. I was about to tell her that I didn't see anything. This wasn't true, of course. I just didn't see anything out of the ordinary, nothing special, nothing that ought not occupy that time and that space.

I saw nothing to give me pause.

But then I did.

Space, time, shadows.

I'll call it a shadow, because I'm at a loss for any more appropriate word. It was spread out like a shadow rushing across the waves, though, at first, I thought I was seeing something dark moving *beneath* the waves. A very big fish, perhaps. Possibly a large shark or a small whale. We've seen whales in the bay before. Or it might have been caused by a cloud passing in front of the sun, though there were no clouds that day. The truth is I knew it was none of these things. I can sit here all night long, composing a list of what it *wasn't*, and I'll never come any nearer to what it might have been.

"Emily," she shouted. "Do you *see* it?" And I called back that I did. Having noticed it, it was impossible *not* to see that grimy, indefinite smear sliding swiftly towards the shore. In a few seconds more, I realized, it would reach the boulders, and if it wasn't something beneath the water, the rocks wouldn't stop it. Part of my mind still insisted it was only a shadow, a freakish trick of the light, a mirage. Nothing substantial, certainly nothing malign, nothing that could do us any mischief or injury. No need to be alarmed, and yet I don't ever remember being as afraid I was then. I couldn't move, but I yelled for Charlotte to run. I don't think she heard me. Or if she heard me, she was also too mesmerized by the sight of the thing to move.

I was safe, there on the porch. It came no nearer to me than ten or twenty yards. But Charlotte, standing alone at the garden gate, was well within its circumference. It swept over her, and she screamed, and fell to the ground. It swept over her, and then was gone, vanishing into the tangle of green briars and poison ivy and wind-stunted evergreens behind our house. I stood there, smelling something that almost smelled like ozone. And maybe it's an awful cliché to put to paper, but my mind *reeled*. My heart raced, and my mind reeled. For a fraction of an instant I was seized by something that was neither *déjà vu* or vertigo, and I thought I might vomit.

But the sensation passed, like the shadow had, or the shadow of a shadow, and I dashed down the steps and across the grass to the place where Charlotte sat stunned among the clover and the dandelions. Her clothes and skin looked as though they'd been misted with the thinnest sheen of…what? Oil? No, no, no, not oil at all. But it's the closest I can come to describing that sticky brownish iridescence clinging to her dress and her face, her arms and the pickets of the garden fence and to every single blade of grass.

"It knocked me down," she said, sounding more amazed than hurt or frightened. Her eyes were filled with startled disbelief. "It wasn't *anything*, Em. It wasn't anything at all, but it knocked me right off my feet."

"Are you hurt?" I asked, and she shook her head.

I didn't ask her anything else, and she didn't say anything more. I helped her up and inside the house. I got her clothes off and led her into the downstairs shower. But the oily residue that the shadow had left behind had already begun to *evaporate*—and again, that's not the right word, but it's the best I can manage—before we began trying to scrub it away with soap and scalding clean water. By the next morning, there would be no sign of the stuff anywhere, inside the house or out of doors. Not so much as a stain.

"It knocked me down. It was just a shadow, but it knocked me down." I can't recall how many times she must have said that. She repeated it over and over again, as though repetition would render it less implausible, less inherently ludicrous. "A shadow knocked me down, Em. A shadow knocked me down."

But it wasn't until we were in the bedroom, and she was dressing, that I noticed the red welt above her left hip, just below her ribs. It almost looked like an insect bite, except the center was…well, when I bent down and examined it closely, I saw there *was* no center. There was only a hole. As I've said, a pinprick, but a hole all the same. There wasn't so much as a drop of blood, and she swore to me that it didn't hurt, that she was fine, and it was nothing to get excited about. She went to the medicine cabinet and found a Band-Aid to cover the welt. And I didn't see it again until the next day, which as yet has no playing card, the Sunday before the warm yellow Monday morning in the kitchen.

I'll call that Sunday by the Two of Spades.

It rains on the Two of Spades. It rains cats and dogs all the damn day long. I spend the afternoon sitting in my study, parked there in front of my computer, trying to find the end to Chapter Nine of the book I can't seem to finish. The rain beats at the windows, all rhythm and no melody. I write a line, then delete it. One step forward, two steps back. Zeno's "Achilles and the Tortoise" paradox played out at my keyboard—"That which is in locomotion must arrive at the halfway stage before it arrives at the goal," and each halfway stage has its own halfway stage, *ad infinitum*. These are the sorts of rationalizations that comfort me as I only pretend to be working. This is the *true* reward of my twelve years of college, these erudite excuses for not getting the job done. In the days to come, I will set the same apologetics and exculpations to work on the problem of how a shadow can possibly knock a woman down, and how a hole can be explained away as no more than a wound.

Sometime after seven o'clock, Charlotte raps on the door to ask me how it's going, and what I'd like for dinner. I haven't got a ready answer for either question, and she comes in and sits down on the futon near my desk. She has to move a stack of books to make a place to sit. We talk about the weather, which she tells me is supposed to improve after sunset, that the meteorologists are saying Monday will be sunny and hot. We talk about the book—my exploration of the phenomenon of the literary *Terrae Anachronismorum*, from 1714 and Simon Tyssot de Patot's *Voyages et Aventures de Jacques Massé* to 1918 and Edgar Rice Burroughs's *Out of Time's Abyss* (and beyond; see Aristotle on Zeno, above). I close Microsoft Word, accepting that nothing more will be written until at least tomorrow.

"I took off the Band-Aid," she says, reminding me of what I've spent the day trying to forget.

"When you fell, you probably jabbed yourself on a stick or something," I tell her, which doesn't explain *why* she fell, but seeks to dismiss the result of the fall.

"I don't think it was a stick."

"Well, whatever it was, you hardly got more than a scratch."

And that's when she asks me to look. I would have said no, if saying no were an option.

She stands and pulls up her t-shirt, just on the left side, and points at the hole, though there's no way I could ever miss it. On the rainy Two of Spades, hardly twenty-four hours after Charlotte was knocked off her feet by a shadow, it's already grown to the diameter of a dime. I've never seen anything so black in all my life, a black so complete I'm almost certain I would go blind if I stared into it too long. I don't say these things. I don't remember what I say, so maybe I say nothing at all. At first, I think the skin at the edges of the hole is puckered, drawn tight like the skin at the edges of a scab. Then I see that's not the case at all. The skin around the periphery of the hole in her flesh is *moving*, rotating, swirling about that preposterous and undeniable blackness.

"I'm scared," she whispers. "I mean, I'm *really* fucking scared, Emily."

I start to touch the wound, and she stops me. She grabs hold of my hand and stops me.

"Don't," she says, and so I don't.

"You *know* that it can't be what it looks like," I tell her, and I think maybe I even laugh.

"Em, I don't know anything at all."

"You damn well know *that* much, Charlotte. It's some sort of infection, that's all, and—"

She releases my hand, only to cover my mouth before I can finish. Three fingers to still my lips, and she asks me if we can go upstairs, if I'll please make love to her.

"Right now, that's all I want," she says. "In all the world, there's nothing I want more."

I almost make her promise that she'll see our doctor the next day, but already some part of me has admitted to myself this is nothing a physician can diagnose or treat. We have moved out beyond medicine. We have been pushed out into these nether regions by the shadow of a shadow. I have stared directly into that hole, and already I understand it's not merely a hole in Charlotte's skin, but a hole in the cosmos. I could parade her before any number of physicians and physicists, psychologists and priests, and not a one would have the means to seal that breach. In fact, I suspect they would deny the evidence, even if it meant denying all their science and technology and faith. There are things worse than blank spaces on maps. There are moments when certitude becomes the greatest enemy of sanity. Denial becomes an antidote.

Unlike those other days and those other cards, I haven't chosen the

Two of Spades at random. I've chosen it because on Thursday she asks me if Alice counts. And I have begun to assume that everything counts, just as everything is claimed by that infinitely small, infinitely dense point beyond the event horizon.

*"Would you tell me, please," said Alice, a little timidly, "why you are painting those roses?"*

*Five and Seven said nothing, but looked at Two. Two began, in a low voice, "Why, the fact is, you see, Miss, this here ought to have been a* red *rose-tree, and we put a white one in by mistake..."*

On that rainy Saturday, that Two of Spades with an incriminating red brush concealed behind its back, I do as she asks. I cannot do otherwise. I bed her. I fuck her. I am tender and violent by turns, as is she. On that stormy evening, that Two of Pentacles, that Two of *Coins* (a dime, in this case), we both futilely turn to sex looking for surcease from dread. We try to go *back* to our lives before she fell, and this is not so very different from all those "lost worlds" I've belabored in my unfinished manuscript: Maple White Land, Caprona, Skull Island, Symzonia, Pellucidar, the Mines of King Solomon. In our bed, we struggle to fashion a refuge from the present, populated by the reassuring, dependable past. And I am talking in circles within circles within circles, spiraling inward or out, it doesn't matter which.

I am arriving, very soon now, at the end of it, at the Saturday night—or more precisely, just before dawn on the Saturday morning—when the story I am writing here ends. And begins. I've taken too long to get to the point, if I assume the validity of a linear narrative. If I assume any one moment can take precedence over any other or assume the generally assumed (but unproven) inequity of relevance.

*A large rose-tree stood near the entrance of the garden; the roses growing on it were white, but there were three gardeners at it, busily painting them red.*

We are as intimate in those moments as two women can be, when one is forbidden to touch a dime-sized hole in the other's body. At some point, after dark, the rain stops falling, and we lie naked and still, listening to owls and whippoorwills beyond the bedroom walls.

On Wednesday, she comes downstairs and catches me reading the dry pornography of mathematics and relativity. Wednesday is the Seven of Clubs. She tells me there's nothing to be found in those books, nothing that will change what has happened, what may happen.

She says, "I don't know what will be left of me when it's done. I don't even know if I'll be enough to satisfy it, or if it will just keep getting bigger and bigger and bigger. I think it might be insatiable."

On Monday morning, she sips her coffee. We talk about eleven-year-old boys and BB guns.

But here, at last, it is shortly before sunup on a Saturday. Saturday, the Four of Spades. It's been an hour since Charlotte woke screaming, and I've sat and listened while she tried to make sense of the nightmare. The hole in her side is as wide as a softball (and, were this more obviously a comedy, I would list the objects that, by accident, have fallen into it the last few days). Besides the not-quite-ozone smell, there's now a faint but constant whistling sound, which is air being pulled into the hole. In the dream, she tells me, she knew exactly what was on the other side of the hole, but then she forgot most of it as soon as she awoke. In the dream, she says, she wasn't afraid, and that we were sitting out on the porch watching the sea while she explained it all to me. We were drinking Cokes, she said, and it was hot, and the air smelled like dog roses.

"You know I don't like Coke," I say.

"In the dream you did."

She says we were sitting on the porch, and that awful shadow came across the sea again, only this time it didn't frighten her. This time I saw it first and pointed it out to her, and we watched together as it moved rapidly towards the shore. This time, when it swept over the garden, she wasn't standing there to be knocked down.

"But you said you saw what was on the other side."

"That was later on. And I would tell you what I saw, if I could remember. But there was the sound of pipes, or a flute," she says. "I can recall that much of it, and I knew, in the dream, that the hole runs all the way to the middle, to the very center."

"The very center of what?" I ask, and she looks at me like she thinks I'm intentionally being slow-witted.

"The center of everything that ever was and is and ever will be, Em. The center. Only, somehow the center is both empty and filled with…" She trails off and stares at the floor.

"Filled with what?"

"I can't *say*. I don't *know*. But whatever it is, it's been there since before there was time. It's been there alone since before the universe was born."

I look up, catching our reflections in the mirror on the dressing table across the room. We're sitting on the edge of the bed, both of us naked, and I look a decade older than I am. Charlotte, though, she looks *so* young, younger than when we met. Never mind that yawning black mouth in her abdomen. In the half light before dawn, she seems to shine, a preface to the coming day, and I'm reminded of what I read about Hawking radiation and the quasar jet streams that escape some singularities. But this isn't the place or time for theories and equations. Here, there are only the two of us, and morning coming on, and what Charlotte can and cannot remember about her dream.

"Eons ago," she says, "it lost its mind. Though I don't think it ever really *had* a mind, not like a human mind. But still, it went insane, from the knowledge of what it is and what it can't ever stop being."

"You said you'd forgotten what was on the other side."

"I have. Almost all of it. This is *nothing*. If I went on a trip to Antarctica and came back and all I could tell you about my trip was that it was very white, that would be like what I'm telling you now about the dream."

The Four of Spades. The Four of Swords, which cartomancers read as stillness, peace, withdrawal, the act of turning sight back upon itself. They say nothing of the attendant perils of introspection or the damnation that would be visited upon an intelligence that could never look *away*.

"It's blind," she says. "It's blind, and insane, and the music from the pipes never ends."

This is when I ask her to stand up, and she only stares at me a moment or two before doing as I've asked. This is when I kneel in front of her, and I'm dimly aware that I'm kneeling before the inadvertent avatar of a god, or God, or a pantheon, or something so immeasurably ancient and pervasive that it may as well be divine. Divine or infernal; there's really no difference, I think.

"What are you doing?" she wants to know.

"I'm losing you," I reply, "that's what I'm doing. Somewhere, some*when*, I've *already* lost you. And that means I have nothing *left* to lose."

Charlotte takes a quick step back from me, retreating towards the bedroom door, and I'm wondering if she runs, will I chase her? Having made this decision, to what lengths will I go to see it through? Would I force her? Would it be rape?

"I know what you're going to do," she says. "Only you're *not* going to do it, because I won't let you."

"You're being devoured—"

"It was a dream, Em. It was only a stupid, crazy dream, and I'm not even sure what I actually remember and what I'm just making up."

"Please," I say, "please let me try." And I watch as whatever resolve she might have had breaks apart. She wants as badly as I do to hope, even though we both know there's no hope left. I watch that hideous black gyre above her hip, below her left breast. She takes two steps back towards me.

"I don't think it will hurt," she tells me. And I can't see any point in asking whether she means, *I don't think it will hurt me*, or *I don't think it will hurt you.* "I don't think there will be any pain."

"I can't see how it possibly matters anymore," I tell her. I don't say anything else. With my right hand, I reach into the hole, and my arm vanishes almost up to my shoulder. There's cold beyond any comprehension of cold. I glance up, and she's watching me. I think she's going to scream, but she doesn't. Her lips part, but she doesn't scream. I feel my arm be tugged so violently I'm sure that it's about to be torn from its socket, the humerus ripped from the glenoid fossa of the scapula, cartilage and ligaments snapped, the subclavian artery severed before I tumble back to the floor and bleed to death. I'm almost certain that's what will happen, and I grit my teeth against that impending amputation.

"I can't feel you," Charlotte whispers. "You're inside me now, but I can't feel you anywhere."

The hole is closing. We both watch as that clockwise spiral stops spinning, then begins to turn widdershins. My freezing hand clutches at the void, my fingers straining for any purchase. Something's changed; I understand that perfectly well. Out of desperation, I've chanced upon some remedy, entirely by instinct or luck, the solution to an insoluble puzzle. I also understand that I need to pull my arm back out again, before the edges of the hole reach my bicep. I imagine the collapsing rim of curved spacetime slicing cleanly through sinew and bone, and then I imagine myself fused at the shoulder to that point just above Charlotte's hip. Horror vies with cartoon absurdities in an instant that seems so swollen it could accommodate an age.

Charlotte's hands are on my shoulders, gripping me tightly, pushing me away, shoving me as hard as she's able. She's saying something, too, words I can't quite hear over the roar at the edges of that cataract created by the implosion of the quantum foam.

*Oh, Kitty, how nice it would be if we could only get through into Looking-glass House! I'm sure it's got oh! such beautiful things in it! Let's pretend there's a way of getting through into it, somehow, Kitty. Let's pretend the glass has got all soft as gauze, so that we can get through...*

I'm watching a shadow race across the sea.

Warm sun fills the kitchen.

I draw another card.

Charlotte is only ten years old, and a BB fired by her brother strikes her ankle. Twenty-three years later, she falls at the edge of our flower garden.

Time. Space. Shadows. Gravity and velocity. Past, present, and future. All smeared, every distinction lost, and nothing remaining that can possibly be quantified.

I shut my eyes and feel her hands on my shoulders.

And across the space within her, as my arm bridges countless light years, something brushes against my hand. Something wet, and soft, something indescribably abhorrent. Charlotte pushed me, and I was falling backwards, and now I'm not. It has seized my hand in its own—or wrapped some celestial tendril about my wrist—and for a single heartbeat it holds me before letting go.

*...whatever it is, it's been there since before there was time. It's been there alone since before the universe was born.*

There's pain when my head hits the bedroom floor. There's pain and stars and twittering birds. I taste blood and realize that I've bitten my lip. I open my eyes, and Charlotte's bending over me. I think there are galaxies trapped within her eyes. I glance down at that spot above her left hip, and the skin is smooth and whole. She's starting to cry, and that makes it harder to see the constellations in her eyes. I move my fingers, surprised that my arm and hand are both still there.

"I'm sorry," I say, even if I'm not sure what I'm apologizing for.

"No," she says, "don't be sorry, Em. Don't let's be sorry for anything. Not now. Not ever again."

# THE BEANCOUNTER'S CAT

## DAMIEN BRODERICK

A humble beancounter lived in Regio City near the middle of the world. Those of her credentials known outside the Sodality were modest but respectable. By dint of dedicated service and her particular gift, she had won herself a lowly but (she hoped) secure position with the Arxon's considerable staff of *publicani*. Still, on a certain summer's smorning, she carelessly allowed her heart to be seduced by the sight of a remarkable orange-furred cat, a rough but handsome bully of the back alleys. He stood outside her door, greeting the smallday in fine yodeling voice, claws stropped to a razor finish, whiskers proud like filaments of new brass.

"Here, puss," she called into the dusty lane.

The beancounter poured milk into a blue-rimmed bowl, inviting this cat inside the doorway of her little house, which was located in the noisy, scrofulous Leechcraft District. She watched the elegant animal lapping, and pressed the palms of her hands together in front of her modest but respectable breast.

"I believe I shall name you Ginger," she told the cat with considerable satisfaction.

The orange cat sat back and licked his whispers delicately, then bent to attend to his hindquarters, raising one leg. Holding the leg in the air he gave her a sour look.

"For Skydark's sake," said the cat, "must I abide this arrant sentimentality?" He nosed a little more, then lowered his leg and rose to all four feet, still bristling. "In any event, if you're interested, I already possess a name."

The beancounter had fallen upon her bottom, goggling at the loquacious and shockingly illegal animal.

"You can spea—" But she cut off the rest of the banal sentence that was about to escape her mouth, which she clamped shut. The cat gave her a sardonic glance and returned to the bowl, polishing off the last of the milk.

"Slightly rancid, but what else can you expect in this weather? Thank you," he added, and made for the door.

As the luminous tip of his tail vanished, the beancounter cried, "Then what *is* your name, sir?"

"Marmalade," the cat said, in a muffled tone. And then he was gone.

At the sleeping hour, she sat on piled cushions in a nook, peeling and eating slivers of a ripe golden maloon, and read to herself verses from a sentimental book, for she had nobody else to speak them to her. She read these tender verses by the guttering light of an oil-fruit lamp, the blood mounting in her cheeks. Secretly she knew it was all make-believe and artful compensation for a delayed life held pendant in her late mother's service, and she was ashamed and depressed by her fate. The beancounter was comely enough, but her profession stank in the nostrils of general company. Suitable men approached her from time to time, in the tavern, perhaps, or at a concert, and expressed an initial interest in flattering terms. Every one of them swiftly recoiled in distaste when he learned of her trade. To a handsome poet she had tried an old justification: "It is a punishment, not a life-long deformity!" The fellow withdrew, refusing her hand.

She put the verses aside and brooded for several moments on the augmented beast. Had it been lurking all this time in the forests, mingling in plain sight with its witless kin of the alleys? It seemed impossible, unless its kind were more intelligent and devious than human people. Could it have fallen from above, from the dark heights above the Heights? Nothing of that kind had been bruited for thousands of years; she had always supposed such notions were the stuff of mythology, invented and retold generation after generation to frighten children and keep them obedient. Yet her mother's Sodality teachings verged on that conceit, if you stopped listening for allegory and metaphor and accepted her teachings at face value.

Bonida shuddered, and lay down on her bedding. Sleep would cure these phantasms.

The very next sday, the cat came back. The beancounter awoke, nostrils twitching. The brute had placed a pungent calling card on her doorstep. He sat with his back to her as she opened the door, and finally turned with a lordly demeanor and allowed her to invite him in. She put a small flat plate of offal on the floor next to her kitchen table. The animal sniffed, licked, looked up disdainfully.

"What is this muck?"

She regarded him silently, caught between irritation, amusement, and suppressed excitement. She detected no machine taint, yet surely this was a manifest or, less likely, the luckless victim of one, ensnared in the guise of a beast. She had waited all her life for such an encounter.

After a long moment, the cat added, "Just messin' wid you. Lighten up, woman." He bent his thickly furred orange head to the plate and gulped down his liver breakfast.

The beancounter broke her own fast with oaten pottage, sliced fruits and the last of the milk (it *was* going off, the cat was right) mixed in a beautifully glowing glazed bowl in radiant reds, with a streak of hot blue, from the kiln in Crockmakers' Street. She spooned it up swiftly, plunged her bowl and the cat's emptied dish into a wooden pail of water, muttered the cantrip of a household execration, a device of the Sodality. The water hissed into steam, leaving the crockery cleansed but hot to the touch.

"Marmalade, if you're going to stay here—"

"Who said anything about staying?" the cat said sharply.

"*If*, I said. Or even if you mean to visit from time to time, I should introduce myself." She put out one small hand, fingers blue with ink stains. "I'm Bonida."

Marmalade considered the fingers, while scratching rapidly for a moment behind his ear. He replied before he was done with his scratch, and the words emerged in a curious burble, as if he were speaking while gargling. "I see. All right." Somewhat to her surprise, he stood, raised his right front paw with dignity and extended it. Her fingertips scarcely touched the paw before it was withdrawn, not hastily, but fast enough to keep Bonida in her place. She smiled secretly.

"You may sit on my lap if you wish," she told the cat, moving her legs aside from the table and smoothing her deep blue skirt.

"Surely you jest." The cat stalked away to investigate a hole in the wainscoting, returned, sat cattycorner from her and groomed diligently. Bonida waited for a time, pleased by the animal's vivid coat, then rose and made herself an infusion of herbs. "So," the cat said, with some indignation. "You make the offer, you snatch it away."

"Soon I must leave for my place of employment," she told him patiently. "If you are still here when I return, there will be a bowl of milk for you."

"And the lap?"

"You are always welcome on my lap, m'sieur," she said, and drank down her mug of wake-me-up, coughing hard several times.

"You'd certainly better not be thinking of locking me in!"

"I shall leave a window ajar," she told him, head reeling slightly from the stimulating beverage. She cleared her throat. "That's dangerous in this neighborhood, you know, but nothing is too good for you, my dear pussycat."

The cat scowled. "Sarcasm. I suppose that's preferable to foolish sentimental doting. I'll spare you the trouble." With an athletic spring, he was across the floor and at the door. "Perhaps I'll see you this evening, Bonida Oustorn, so have some more of that guts ready for me." And was off, just the tip of his orange tail flirted at the jamb, curiously radiant in the dim ruby light of the Skydark.

Bonida stared thoughtfully. "So you knew my name all along," she murmured, fetching her bonnet. "Passing strange."

Above the great ramparts of the Heights, which themselves plunged upward for twenty-five kilometers, the Skydark was an immense contusion filling most of heaven, rimmed at the horizon by starry blackness. In half a greatday, forty sdays, Regio City would stand beneath another sky displaying blackness entire choked with bright star pinpoints, and a bruised globe half as wide as a man's hand at arm's length, with dull, tilting rings, a diminutive, teasing echo of the Skydark globe itself. Then the Skydark would be lost to sight until its return at dawn, when its faint glow would once again relentlessly drown out the stars, as if it were swallowing them.

These were mysteries beyond any hope of resolution. Others might yet prove more tractable.

The vivid, secret ambition of this woman, masked by an air of diffidence, was to answer just one question, the cornerstone of her late mother's cryptic teaching in the Sodality, and one implication of that answer, whatever it might be: What, precisely, was the nature of the ancient Skyfallen Heights; and from whence (and why) were they fallen? That obscurity was linked by hidden tradition, although in no obvious way, to the ancient allegory of Lalune, the Absent Goddess.

Certainly it had been no part of her speculations, entertained since late childhood, to venture that the key to the mystery might be a cat, one of the supposedly inarticulate creatures from lost Earth, skulking in this city positioned beside the world-girdling and all-but-impassable barrier of the Heights. Now the possibility occurred to her. It seemed too great a coincidence that the orange beast had insinuated himself into her dismal routine in the very week dedicated to the Sodality's summer Plenary. Marmalade had designs upon her.

With an effort, Bonida put these matters out of her mind, patiently showing her identity scars as she entered the guarded portico of the district Revenue Agency. As always, the anteroom to her small office, one of five off a hexagonal ring, stank with the sweat of the wretches awaiting their appointments. She avoided their resentful gaze, their eyes pleading or reddened with weeping and rage. At least nobody was howling at the moment. That would come soon enough. Seated at her desk, check-marking a document of assessment with her inky nib, she read the damning evidence against her first client. Enough pilfering to warrant a death sentence. Bonida closed her eyes, shook her head, sighed once, and called his name and her room number through the annunciator.

"You leave the Arxon no choice," she told the shaking petitioner. A powerfully built farmer from the marginal croplands along the rim of Cassini Regio, and slightly retarded, Bai Rong Bao had withheld the larger portion of his tax for the tenth part of a greatyear. Was the foolish fellow unaware of the records kept by the bureaucracy, the zeal with which these infractions were pursued and punished? Perhaps not unaware, but somehow capable of suppressing the bleak knowledge of his eventual fate. As, really, were they all, if the doctrines of the Sodality were justified true knowledge, as her mother had insisted.

"I just need more time to pay," the man was blubbering.

"Yes, farmer Bai, you will indeed pay every pfennig owed. But you have attempted very foolishly to deceive our masters, and you know the penalty for that. One distal phalange." Her hand was tingling. Her loathing for the task was almost unendurable, but it was her duty to endure it.

"Phal—What's that?" He clutched his hands desperately behind his back. "They say you tear off a hand or a foot. Oh, please, good mistress, I beg you, leave me whole. I will pay! In time. But I cannot work without a foot or a hand."

"Not so great a penalty as that, farmer. The tip of one finger or toe." She extended her own hand. "You may choose which one to sacrifice in obedience to the Arxon." The man was close to fainting. Reaching through depression for some kindness, she told him, "The tip of the smallest finger on the left hand will leave you at only a small disadvantage. Here, put it out to me." The beancounter took his shaking, roughened hand by the nail-bitten phalange, and held it tightly over the ceramic sluice bowl. She murmured a cantrip, and the machines of the Arxon hummed through her own fingers. The room filled with the sickening stench of rotted meat and she was holding a pitted white bone, her fingers slimy. The farmer lurched away from the desk, shoving the rancid tip of his finger into his mouth like a burned child, flung it away again at the taste. His face was pale. In a moment his rage might outmatch his fear. Bonida wiped her fingers, rose, handed him a document attesting to his payment. "See the nurse on your way out, Mr. Bai. She will bandage your wound." She laid her hand upon him once again, felt the virtue tremble. "It should bud and regrow itself within a year, or sooner. Here is a word of advice: next season, do not tarry in meeting your obligations. Good sday."

She poured water into the bowl, washed and dried, then in a muttered flash of steam flushed away the stink of decomposition together with the scum in the bowl. The beancounter sighed, found another bill of particulars, announced the next name. "Ernő Szabó. Office Four."

Marmalade the cat was waiting on her doorstep. He averted his nose.

"Madame, you smell disgusting."

"I *beg* your pardon!" Bonida was affronted. From childhood, she had been raised to a strict regimen of hygiene, as befitted a future maiden of the Sodality. Poor as she was, by comparison with the finest in the Regio, nonetheless she insisted on bathing once a sweek at the springs, and was strict with her teeth brushing. Although, admittedly, that onion-flavored brioche at lunch—

"The smell of death clings to you."

The beancounter squeezed her jaw tight, flung off her bonnet, hitched her provender bag higher on her shoulder. Without thinking, she hid her right hand inside a fold of her robe. Catching herself, she deliberately withdrew it and waved her inky fingers in front of the beast.

"It is my skill, my duty, my profession," she told him in a thin voice. "If you have objections to my trade, I will not trouble you to share my small repast." But when she made to open her door, the animal was through it before her, sinuous and sly, for a moment more the quicksilver courtier than the bully.

"Enough of your nonsense," the cat said, settling on a rug. "Milk, and be quick about it."

The audacity was breathtaking, and indeed the breath caught for an instant in her throat, then choked out in a guffaw. Shaking her head, Bonida took the stoppered jug from her bag and poured them both a draught. In a vase on the table, nightblooms had sagged, their green leaves parched and drooping.

"What do you want, m'sieur? Clearly you are not stalking me because you treasure my fragrance." The beancounter emptied the stale water, refilled the vase, touched the posy. Virtue flowed. It was not hers; she was merely the conduit, or so her mother had instructed her. The flowers revived in an ordinary miracle of renewal; heavy scents filled the room, perhaps masking her own alleged odor. Why did she care? An animal, after all, even if one gifted with speech and effrontery.

The cat lapped up the milk in silence, licked his whiskers clean, then sat back neatly, nostrils twitching at the scent. "Your mother Elisetta."

"She died three years ago, during a ruction in the square." It still wrenched at her heart to speak of it. "So you knew her," she said, suddenly certain of it. And yet her late mother had never mentioned so singular an acquaintance. Another mystery of the Sodality, no doubt.

"I introduced her to your father."

"I have no father."

The cat gave one sharp sardonic cough, as if trying to relieve himself of a hairball. "So you burst forth full-formed from your mother's forehead?"

"What?"

"Never mind. Nobody ever remembers the old stories. Especially the coded ones."

"What?"

"Your lap."

"You wouldn't prefer that I go out and bathe first?"

"Actually yes, but we don't have time. Come on, woman, make a lap."

She did so, and the beast leapt with supernatural lightness, circled once to make a nest, and snuggled down. His head, she realized, was almost as large as her own. He slitted his eyes and emitted an unbearably comforting noise. A sort of deep, drumming, rhythmic music. Her mouth opened in surprise. She had read of this in old verses of romance. Marmalade was purring.

"Your father was the Arxon," the cat told her, then. "Still is, in fact."

At Ostler's Corner, on the advice of the cat, the beancounter engaged the services of a pedlar. Marmalade sprang into the rickshaw cabin, waited with ill-disguised irritation as a groom handed Bonida up with her luncheon basket and settled her comfortably, accepting a coin after a murmured consultation with his bank. The great brute stirred at a kick, its reptilian hide fifteen shades of green, and lurched its feet into their cage quill constraints, tail flared beneath the platform. Soon its immense quadriceps and hams were pumping furiously, pedaling their rickshaw with increasing celerity along the central thoroughfare of the Regio and out into the countryside, making for the towering cliffs that formed the near-vertical foothills of the Skyfallen Heights. Now and then it registered its grievance at this usage, trying to wrench its snout far enough to bite at its tormentors, but sturdy draught-poles held its head forward.

"We approach the equatorial ridge of Iapetus," the cat told her. "Does your Sodality teach you this much? That this small world has its breathable air held close and warmed by design and contrivance? That its very gravity is augmented by deformations?"

"Certain matters I may not speak of," she said, averting her gaze, "as you must know since you profess knowledge of my mother and her guild." Eye-yapper-tus, she thought. Whatever could that—

"Yes, yes," Marmalade said. "Elisetta learned the best part of her arcane doctrines from me, so you can rest easy on that score."

"Ha! So you might assert if you intended to hornswoggle me."

The cat uttered a wheezing laugh. "*Horn*swoggle? Ha! You are not my type, madame."

Bonida tightened her lips. "You are offensive, m'sieur." She was silent long enough to convey her displeasure, but then said, "I see we are drawing to a stop. Will you tell me finally why you have lured me out to this inhospitable territory?"

"Why, I have information to impart to the daughter of the Arxon." He leapt lightly from the cabin, waited as she lowered herself, hampered by her hamper. "Stay here," he snarled at the pedlar. "We shall return within the hour."

"Why must I take orders from a beast?" the reptile asked, slaver at his lips. "I am indentured to humans, not cats."

"Hold your tongue, you, or you'll be catmeat by dawn."

Something in Marmalade's tone gave the great green creature pause; it fell silent and averted its gaze, withdrawing its long toes from the quills and settling uncomfortably between the traces. "I shall be here, your highness," it said in a bitter tone.

"Follow me, woman," said the cat. "You can leave your picnic basket. Wait, bring the milk jug."

"You can't seriously expect me to *climb* this cliff?"

"There are more ways than one to skin—" Marmalade broke off with a cough. "You are familiar with the principle of the *tunnel?*" They stood before a concealed cleft in the rock face. He went forward in a graceful leap and vanished into the shadows.

It was like finding oneself immured inside an enormous pipe, perhaps a garden hose for watering the stars, Bonida decided. The walls were smooth as ice, but warm to the touch. Something thrummed, deeper than the ear could hear, audible through skin and bone. She stood at the edge of a passage from infinity (or so it seemed in the faint light) at her left to infinity at her right.

"This is where Father Time built his AI composites," the cat said, and his voice, thinned, seemed to vanish into the huge long, wide space. "It's an accelerator as big as a world. Here is where the Skydark dyson swarms were congealed from the emptiness and flung into the sky."

"The what? Were what?"

"The Embee," said the cat absently. He was looking for something. His paw touched a place in the smooth wall, raised from it an elaborately figured cartouche, smote it thrice. They rose into the middle of the air and rushed forward down the infinite corridor, the wind of their motion somehow almost wholly held in abeyance. If it were not for that breeze, they might have been suspended motionless. Yet somehow, through her terror, she sensed tremendous velocity. "Don't drop the milk." He added, at her scowl, "Embee—the MBrain. The M-Brane. Not to be confused with the Mem-brain."

"I have no idea what you're talking about."

"Oh, never mind."

She puzzled it out, as they fled into an endlessness of the same. "You're saying that Skyfallen Heights did not fall? That it was *built?*"

"Oh, it was built, all right, and it fell from the sky. Father Time broke up another moon and rained it down like silt in a strip around the equator. Compiled the accelerator, you might say." The cat, afloat in the air, gave her a feline grin. "Two-thirds of it has worn away by now. It was a long time ago. But it can still get you from here to there in a hurry."

The breeze was gone. They had stopped, or paused. The cat lifted his head. A vast rumbling above them; something was opening. They rose, flung upward like bubbles in a flute, and then moved fast in the great darkness, yet still breathing without effort, warm enough, the curving contusion of the Skydark to one side—the Embee, the cat had named it, if that is what he had meant—the smaller ring-cradled sphere on the other and, directly above, something like a dull ruby the size of a palace falling to crush them, or rather they fell upward into it. And were inside its embrace, light blossoming to dazzle her eyes, so that she cried out and did in fact drop the jug, which shattered on a surface like rippled marble, spilling milk in a spray that caught the cat's left ear and whiskers. He turned in fury, raised one clawed paw, made to strike, held his blow at the last instant from scratching a welt in her flesh.

"Clumsy! Oh well." He visibly forced himself to sink down on all four limbs, slitting his eyes, then rose again. "Come and meet your parents, you lump."

Her mother was dead and ceremonially returned to Cycling. Bonida knew this with bitter regret, for she had stood by the open casket and pressed the cold pale hand, speaking aloud in her grief, hopelessly, the cantrip of renewal. Was there a trembling of the virtue? She could not be sure. Imagination, then. Nothing, nothing. They swiftly closed the casket and whisked it away. But no, here she was after all, at first solemn and then breaking into a smile to see her daughter running in tears to catch up her hands and kiss them, Bonida on her knees, shaking her head in disbelief, eyes swimming.

"Mother Elisetta!"

"Darling girl! And Meister Marmalade." She curtsied to the cat.

"Hi, toots."

"Now allow me to introduce you to your sire."

A presence made itself known to them.

"Welcome, my daughter. I am Ouranos. We have a task for you to fulfill, child. For the Sodality. For the world."

The beancounter recoiled, releasing her mother's hands. She stared wildly about her.

"This is a machine," she cried in revulsion.

From the corner of her eye she seemed to see a form like a man.

The cat said, "Enough sniffling and jumping at shadows. We have work to do."

"How can I be the daughter of a machine?" Bonida remained on her knees, closed in upon herself, whimpering. "This is deceit! All of it! My mother is dead, this isn't her. Take me away, you wretched animal. Return me home and then stay the hell away from me."

"No deception in this, my darling." Her mother touched the crown of her head in a gesture Bonida had known from infancy, bringing fresh tears. "You are upset, and we understand why. It was cruel to allow you to think I had been taken into death, but a necessary cruelty. We had the most pressing and urgent reasons, dear child. We had tasks to perform which brooked no interference. The night has a thousand thousand eyes. Now it is your turn to embrace your destiny. Come, stand up beside me, the hour grows late."

The presence she could not quite see, no matter how swiftly she turned her eyes, said in its deep beautiful voice, "The light of the bright world dies with the dying Sun."

"What is the 'Sun'?" asked the beancounter.

Elisetta, High Governor of the Sodality of Righteous Knowledge, formerly dead, now brow-furrowed and certainly alive, gestured fore and aft. "Open."

Bow and stern of the ruby clarified and were gone: blackness ahead, spattered at random with pinpricks of sharp light, save for the ringed globe that was now as broad as a hand near one's face, faintly luminous; the great contusion behind, glowing faintly with a dim crimson so deep it tricked the eye to suppose it was darkness, a large round spot upon its countenance that dwindled as she watched. It was, she realized with a jolt, her world entire. In the starlight, it seemed that one half of the spot was faintly lighter than the other.

"That great dimness conceals the Sun," her mother said, with a sweeping motion of her arm. "Hidden within the hundred veils of genius we call the Skydark. You have heard this story a dozen times from my own lips, Bonida, since you were a child at my breast, veiled like the Sun in allegory."

Silent, astonished, rueful, the beancounter regarded immensity, the dwindling piebald spot. "That is our world, falling away behind us," she ventured.

"Iapetus, yes," the cat said. "A world like a walnut, with a raised welt at its waist."

"And what is a—" There was no point. This terminology, she divined, was not meant to tease nor torment her; it was a lexicon written to account for a universe larger than her own. She'd heard this term "Iapetus" before, from the cat's mouth. So the world had a name, like a woman or a cat; not just the World. "All right, enough of that. Where are we going? To that other… world, ahead?" It pleased her, stiffened her spine, that she had said *Where are we going* and not *Where are you taking me.*

"To Father Time, yes, for an audience. Saturn, as your ancient forebears called him. Father of us all, in some ways." That was the unseeable presence speaking. She nearly wrenched her neck trying to trap him, but he was off again in some moving blind place, evading her. A machine, she told herself. Rebuked herself, rather. Not a man. How could a thing like that claim affinity, let alone paternity? Yet was there not affinity between humans and machines, in the utterance of a cantrip, the invocation of power? If water boiled and steamed in her bucket, that was no doing of hers. She had acknowledged that, and yet daily forgot the fact, since she was a child, learning the runes and sigils and codes of action. When she rotted the flesh from some hapless infractor, or brought some dead thing back to life and growth, that was again the machines, operating her like a machine, perhaps, making her own flesh their tool. It was a horrifying reflection. Little wonder, she told herself, that we turn our faces from its recognition.

"Why?" A touch of iciness entered her tone. "And why have you and this appalling animal abducted me?"

The cat regarded her with equal coldness, turned and stalked off to the farthest end of the craft, which was not far, and gazed studiously back at the Skydark. Her mother said, "Bonida, you are unkind. But no doubt you have a right to your… impatience."

"My anger, if you must know, Mother." The tingling was returned to her fingers, and she knew, horrified, that if she were to seize Elisetta's arm in this mood the flesh would blacken and fall from the woman's bones. As, perhaps, who knew, it had been recovered in reverse following her death; she had *seen* her mother's dead body, attempted to revive her, perhaps *had* revived her. None of this was tolerable. She would *not* go mad. Quivering, she held her arms down at her sides. "You consort with machines and gods and talking cats. You parcel out to me fragments of lost knowledge—or plain fabrications, for all I know. We fall between worlds, and you refuse to, to...." She broke off, face pale.

Softly, the older woman said, "We refuse nothing, daughter. Be still for a moment. Seek calmness. In a few moments, you will know everything, and then you will help us make a choice."

"Fat lot of use she'll be," said the cat in a surly voice, without turning his head. "We could have had milk, but she smashed the jug. Unreliable, I say. If you ask me—"

"Quiet!" The unseen figure had an edge to his tone, commanding, and Marmalade cocked his whiskers but fell silent. "Child," Ouranos told her, "something very important is about to happen. Everything held dear by human people and machines and animals is at stake. Not just our survival, but the persistence of the world itself, of history stretching a billion years and more into the mysteries of our creation."

The beancounter was feeling very tired. She looked around for a chair or a cushion, and found one right behind her, comfortable and handsomely brocaded. She felt sure it had not been there a moment earlier. Tightening her teeth against each other, she let herself slump into the chair. Her mother also was seating herself, and the cat walked by from the stern with an attitude of hauteur and lofted into Elisetta's lap, where he immediately began his droning purr, ignoring Bonida. The unseeable presence remained just out of sight. Wonderful! Would it not have been more melodramatic for a third chair to manifest, so she might witness its cushions sag under invisible buttocks?

Something took the ruby into its grasp and they were held motionless above the great rings, an expanse of faint ice and ruptured stones, some as large as their craft, mostly pebbles or sand or dust, like a winter roadway in the sky yet swirling ever so slowly. Far away, but closer than ever before, the bruised globe showed stripes of various dim hues, and a swirl that might have been a vast storm seen from above.

"Call us Saturn," a powerful, resonant voice said within the cabin. It was unseen, and a presence, but not her father the machine. And the beancounter knew that it was also a machine, yet beyond doubt a person, too, of such depth and majesty that its own unseen presence rendered them unutterably insignificant. Somehow, though, this realization did not crush her spirit. She glanced at her mother. Elisetta was watching her, calm, wise, accepting, encouraging. How I do love her, Bonida thought, even though she treated me so cruelly by pretending death. But perhaps it was no fault of her mother's. Sometimes one has no choice.

"We offer you a choice," the voice of the world Saturn told them all. Marmalade was now seated on the carpet, upright on his haunches, seemingly respectful. What was the animal plotting this time? "But it must be an informed choice. Permit me to join you."

An immense tawny beast crouched in their midst, larger than a human, with a golden mane that rose behind its formidable head. When it spoke again, its rumbling voice was a roar held in check.

"Call me Aslan, if you wish."

Marmalade had leapt backward, teeth and claws bared, his own fur bristling. Now he sat down again, slightly askew, and turned his face away. "Oh, give me a break."

The great creature shot him a quizzical look, shrugged those powerful catlike shoulders. "As you please. Look here—"

A hundred voices in muted conversation, like a gathering for supper before the Sodality Plenary, then louder, a thousand chattering, a million million, a greater number, all speaking at once, voices weaving a pattern as large and multifarious as the accreted Skyfallen materials of the great ridge circling her world, so that she must clap her hands to her ears, but she had no hands and must scream in the lemon-yellow glare of an impossibly brilliant light that—

"Too bright!" she did scream, then.

The light shed its painful intensity, subsided step by step to a point of roseate glow, and the voices muffled their chorus. She gazed down past the sparkling icy rings to the globe of Saturn, down through its storms and sleet of helium and hydrogen to the shell of metallic hydrogen wrapping its iron core. A seed fell. A long explosion crackled across the lifeless frigid surface world, drawing heat and power from the energies of Saturn's core, snapping one of the molecules after another into ingenious patterns braided and interpenetrating, flowing charges, magnetic fluxes. The voices were the song of those circuits, those—memristors, she knew, somehow. *Not to be confused with the Mem-brain*, the damnable cat had joked, and now Bonida smiled, getting the modest joke. Skeins of molecules linked like the inner parts of a brain, sparks of information, calculation, awareness, consciousness—

*Oyarsa, you might say,* the great feline manifest told her. She knew instantly what he meant: he was the ruling entity of this planet, the mind of which the planet was the brain and body. Not quite right, though: not *he* but *they*. A community of minds linked by light and entanglement (and yes, now she understood that as well, and, well, *everything*, at least in its numberless parts).

"How did you make the Skyfallen Heights, and why?"

Aslan told her, "The smallest of small questions. The cat has already told you. How do you make a trumpet? Take a hole and wrap tin around it."

"Gustav Mahler," Marmalade said, whiskers flicking. "You could say the same about his symphonics. Bah! Trumpets? Give me blues, man."

Symphonies, trumpets, the composer Mahler, a thousand riches from lost Earth: it flooded her mind without overflowing.

"Yes, I know that much, but *why?* To build the Skydark, yes, but *why?*" It was an immense construction, she saw, the Field of Arbol uttered from imagination into reality, sphere within sphere of memristors, sucking every erg of energy from the hidden Sun at its core, a community of godlike beings that surpassed their builder as the Father of Time surpassed, perhaps, whatever ancient beings had brought him/them into existence. But *why?* But *why?*

"All the children ask that question," said her mother, smiling. "Why, Bonida, for joy, as the Sodality has always taught. For endless renewal. For the recovery of the world. Taking a hole and wrapping everything important around it."

"More arrant sentimentality," said the cat, looking disgusted.

"You are a most offensive creature," the beancounter said reprovingly, although she tended to agree with him. "Here, come sit upon my lap." The animal shot her a surprised look, then did as she suggested, springing, circling, snuggling down, heavy orange head leaned back against her modest breast. She let one hand stroke down his coat, and again. "So what is this question we are meant to address?"

The lion rose, looked from one human to the other, and his glance took in as well the rumbling cat and the unseen presence.

"We are considering terminating our life."

Elisetta pressed forward, shocked, all tranquility dispelled. Her voice cracked: "You *must not!* What would become of *us?*"

"That is not the question we wish to put to you, although it has a bearing. Yours is not the species that created us, before they departed, to whom we are beholden, yet you are living beings like those creators. We in turn created the great Minds that cloak the Sun, and built their habitation. Now they, too, are at the end of their dealings with this universe. They know all that might be known, and have imagined all that might be done within the greater landscape of universes. So now they propose to voyage into deepest time, to the ends of eternity. Perhaps something greater awaits them there."

Bonida's own small mind, acknowledging its smallness, reeled at the images flooding to her from the demigod whose own life and purpose were complete at last. Stars and galaxies of stars would fling themselves apart into the night, driven by the power of that darkness, their flaring illumination fading, finally, flickering, dying. All the multiple manifestations of cosmos torn apart and lost in a dying whisper. Her mood summoned from the treasure house the Adagietto from that composer Mahler's Fifth Symphony, and she sank into its tinted, tearful melancholy. Yet in the frigid blackness and emptiness she detected… something. A lure, a promise, at the very least a teasing hint of laughter. How could the Skydark not follow that trace to eternity? How could she?

"Off," she told the cat, and Marmalade sprang away, less offended than one might have expected. She stood up and took her mother's hand. "We are the deputies of your makers, then? You and the Skydark require our… what? Permission? Leave to die, or to depart?"

"Yes."

"And what's to become of us?"

"You will remain for as long as we burn." A vision was placed before them of the ringed world falling in upon itself, crushed into terrifying density, alight with the energies of compression. And Iapetus circling that new Sun, this visible star, unshielded, unveiled, but barren of mind. The agony of loss slashed tears from her eyes. Yet it was Saturn's decision.

"Can we go instead with the Skydark? The Embee? May we share that voyage?"

"Thought you'd never ask," said Marmalade. "And you, Madame High Governor, and Ouranos, Lord Arxon, do you concur with the wisdom and daring of this young woman?"

"I—" Her mother hesitated, gone once into death and retrieved by the gift of her child, looking from Bonida to the machine in which they stood. "Yes, yes of course. And you, sir?"

"We shall attend you, Lord Marmalade," said the unseen presence. "Even unto the ends of eternity. It will be an awfully big adventure."

A qualm brought the beancounter an abrupt pang. "What of the pedlar we hired? He's still waiting for us, poor creature. He might not be so happy at the prospect. Who are we to make such a choice for a whole world?"

"He'll get over it," said the cat. "And hey, if not you, who?"

The sky rolled up, and they set sail into forever.

# STORY KIT

## KIJ JOHNSON

Six story types, from Damon Knight:

1. The story of resolution. The protagonist has a problem and solves it, or doesn't.
2. The story of explanation.
3. The trick ending.
4. A decision is made. Whether it is acted upon is irrelevant.
5. The protagonist solves a puzzle.
6. The story of revelation. Something hidden is revealed to the protagonist, or to the reader.

It has to start somewhere, and it might as well be here.

Medea. Hypsipyle. Ariadne. *Tess of the d'Urbervilles. Madame Butterfly. Anna Karenina.* Emma Bovary. Ophelia.

Dido. The *Aeneid.* Letter 7 of Ovid's *Heroides.* Lines 143–382 of *The House of Fame.* Lines 924–1367 of *The Legend of Good Women.* A play by Marlowe. An opera by Purcell.

Wikipedia: *Dido. Aeneas.*

The pain of losing something so precious that you did not think you could live without it. Oxygen. The ice breaks beneath your feet: your coat and boots fill with water and pull you down. An airlock blows: vacuum pulls you apart by the eyes, the pores, the lungs. You awaken in a fire: the door and window are outlined in flames. You fall against a railing: the rusted iron slices through your femoral artery. You are dead already.

I can write about it, if I am careful, if I keep it far enough away.

The author is over it. It was years ago.

Dido's a smart woman, and she should have predicted his betrayal. Aeneas has always been driven before the gusting winds that are the gods. His city Troy falls to their squabbling, the golden stones dark with blood drying to sticky dust and clustered with flies: collateral damage, like a dog accidentally kicked to death in a bar-room brawl. Aeneas huddles his few followers onto ships and flees, but Juno harries him and sends at last a storm to rip apart his fleet. He crash-lands in a bay near Carthage. His mother—Venus; another fucking god—guides him to shelter.

Dido is Reynard; she is Coyote. No gods have driven *her*, or if they have, she has beaten them at their own game. She also was forced from her land, but she avenged her father first, then stole her brother's ships and left with much wealth and a loyal, hard-eyed army. But rather than fight for a foothold on the Libyan shore, she uses trickery to win land from the neighboring kings. They cannot reclaim it except through marriage, so she plays the faithful widow card. Now they cannot force her into marriage, either. If she continues to play her cards well, the city she founds here will come to rule the seas, the world. The neighboring kings understandably resent how this is working out.

She begins to build. When Aeneas arrives on her shores, Carthage is a vast construction site, its half-finished walls fringed with cranes and scaffolds, hemmed with great white stones waiting to be lifted into place. [Textile metaphor? Woman's work. Ariadne's thread leading Jason through the labyrinth—she also was betrayed and died.]

Aeneas comes to her court a suppliant, impoverished and momentarily timid. He is a good-looking man. If anything, his scars emphasize that. The aura of his divine failure wraps around him like a cloak. Dido feels the tender contempt of the strong for the unlucky, but this is mixed with something else, a hunger that worms through her bones and leaves them hollow, to be filled with fire.

There is a storm. They take shelter in a cave where they kiss, where, for the first time, she feels his weight on her. Words are exchanged.

And afterward, when they lie tangled together and their sweat dries to cold salt on her skin, he tells Dido that Jupiter has promised him a new land to replace lost Troy: Italy. He is somewhat evasive, but in any case she does not listen carefully, content to press her ear to his breast and hear the rumble of his voice stripped of meaning.

There is every reason to believe he will be no stronger against the gods this time, but Dido loves him.

Some losses are too personal to write about, too searing to face. Easier to distance them in some fashion: zombies, or a ghost story. Even Dido may be too direct.

She kneels on the white tiles of the kitchen floor and begs: anything, anything at all. She will die, she tells him. She will not survive this loss. Her face is slick with snot. There's blood on your face, he says. Her tears are stained red from where she has broken a vein in her eye. Her heart is skipping beats, trying to catch up to this new rhythm that does not include him. She runs to the bathroom, which a year ago they painted the turquoise of the sea. He kneels beside her as she vomits but does not touch her, as though he wishes he could help but does not know how.

She cannot figure out what has happened. It seems he cannot, either; but the wind fills his sails. He is already gone.

1,118,390 words before these. The writer's craft is no longer a skill she has learned, but a ship she sails. It remains hard to control in strong winds.

Aeneas will be tall and broad-shouldered because heroes and villains usually are. Probably in his thirties. Scarred from the Trojan wars and a bad sleeper. He thinks he has lost everything, but he still has his health, his wits, some followers.

Aeneas is from the eastern Mediterranean. He will not be half-Swedish. He will not have blue eyes, nor wear horn-rimmed glasses. He will not have a tattoo that says CAVEAT EMPTOR on his shoulder, nor a misshapen nail from when he caught his finger in the garage door, nor sleep on his right side and occasionally sleepwalk.

Perhaps he will have survivor guilt.

- the sound of the words
- what the words mean
- how they string together into phrases, like the linked bubbles of seawrack
- the structure
- the plot

- memories and lies
- the things the author wants to think about—"This is about love and betrayal"—the theme
- the feeling she wants to inspire in readers

*Lost her wallet. Lost her virginity. Lost her way. Lost the big game. Lost his phone number. Lost the horses. Lost the rest of the party. Lost the shotgun. Lost the antidote. Lost the matches. Lost her dog. Lost her home. Lost her brother. Lost her mother. Lost her*

Wikipedia: *Carthage.*

Though the real Carthage is on the Libyan shore, for purposes of the story, it will look like a Greek island. There will be a cliff breached by a narrow road that hairpins up from a harbor to the city's great gates of new oak, bound with iron. Carthage will someday be a great sea-faring nation so the writer adds wharves and warehouses by the harbor, but they are unpeopled in her mind, wallpaper.

It was March when she stayed on Ios—not the season for tourists, so she saw no one beyond two scuba divers and a couple of shivering Australians pausing in their wanderings. Ios was mostly stone-walled fields with goats and windmills and weeds, but Virgil's Carthage did not have fields and neither will hers.

She hiked a lot, and climbed down to the water. The sea was clear as air, and she saw anemones and a fish she did not recognize. The rock looked pale gray until she came close and its uniformity broke into rose and white and smoke-colored crystals, furred with black and gold lichens.

It was cold on Ios. Her breath puffed from her like smoke in the mornings. When she climbed the cliffs, mist rose from her sweating skin and caught the sun. Her feet were always cold. [Perhaps I am mixing up Ios with some other place I have been: Oregon, or Switzerland. But the rocks and the anemones are real—]

There needs to be a bay just up the coast, because Aeneas lands there. It is a horseshoe tucked between stone arms, a lot like where the scuba divers would spend their days. His ship will ride at anchor, the torn sails laid out on the dark sand; the sail-makers will shake their heads but mend them anyway, because these are the only ones they have.

Aeneas will climb the cliffs. The air will smell of wet earth and the bright salt sea, so far below. The writer can use Aeneas's responses to the forest—which will be of short, slim-needled pines [maybe some oaks too, why not?]—and the boulders to develop his character. Or Dido's, to develop hers.

There will need to be a cave, as well.

Does Carthage even have forests? Did Virgil know for sure, or was it just convenient for his story? Virgil was a professional liar. This would not be the only place where he pruned the truth until it was as artificial as an espaliered pear tree against a wall, forced to an expedient shape and bearing the demanded fruit.

Sensory details. The moan that ice makes underfoot. The taste of salt. The smells of ash and copper. A dog barking at a great distance. A bone cracking in your leg. The gray scouring pain of sleet. She stumbles and falls against a rusted railing. The taste of pears.

Dido is playing her cards poorly, making her discards at random.

Her ardor for Aeneas burns through her hollowed bones. He said something about leaving someday, but she did not believe him. Men say that kind of shit all the time and then change their minds. What does she really know of him, anyway? Stories, carved on the walls of temples.

Dido offers him the car keys. He can share her kingdom to replace the one he lost: a king for the queen of Carthage. In her distraction, construction on the city's white walls slows and then ceases; they remain half-built, cranes akimbo and unused. Her neglected armies grow sullen, fall into disarray.

The hot-eyed Gaetulian king who is her neighbor wants his land back and, not incidentally, hungers to prove his right to it upon her body. Her faithful widowhood was more effective than a naked sword in guarding her honor and Carthage's boundaries; but now she has taken Aeneas into her bed, felt his weight on her body, bowed her head to him. She has laid aside that sword.

But it will all still be fine, so long as he stays.

Poor Dido. She is dead already. The writer knows it. You know it. I know it.

The sentence, "She was hollow, as though something had chewed a hole in her body and the hole had grown infected," unless it's been used before by someone else in a story she cannot recall.

And there is the rage sometimes, the rage of a smart woman betrayed by her own longing. It runs under her skin, too hot to be visible. Her breath is smoke; her skin steams. Her tears freeze to slush. Her cheeks bleed.

She stalks the winter streets at dusk and imagines him dead. She imagines their house a smoking, freezing ruin. The fire trucks are gone; all that remains is black wreckage outlined by tape that says DANGER. She imagines her town a glassy plain; every dog in the world dead; the Earth's atmosphere blown off by a colliding asteroid; the universe condensed to an icy point.

[a flute made of a woman's bones]

She walks the icy streets. Her pain cannot permit her to exist in a world where he also exists; and yet she does. Her feet are always cold.

She can use this.

Virgil walked the streets of Rome as he composed. It could take all day to polish a couplet.

Dido knows what happens if Aeneas leaves. Her hot-eyed neighbor, the Gaetulian king, will denounce her inconstancy and send his armies. Her own army's resistance will be half-hearted; they want a ruler who is strong, and perhaps a king will be better after all, more trustworthy than a woman, however clever and just.

The Gaetulian king will attack, break her gates and claim her white-walled city. He will find Dido and her personal guard in the great courtyard, on the steps that lead to her palace: she retains this much pride at least, that she will not be hunted through her own rooms. No, that's wrong, it's not pride that holds her here, her chin lifted and a naked sword in her hand. Despair and fury burn like lye through her veins.

The Gaetulian king will slay her guard to the last man.

He will mount the steps to her. He will strike the sword from her hand. In the presence of his own hard-eyed guard, he will force her to her knees, his hand knotted in her hair. When she refuses to open her mouth to him, he will throw her to the ground and tear her robes aside. He will fuck her as she lies in the cooling blood of her dead men. This will be almost enough pain to make her forget Aeneas's betrayal. This will be almost enough pain to make the writer forget.

The Gaetulian king will hang Dido with chains and march her

through the streets, scratch marks on her face, blood running down her leg.

He will raze her city. He will disband her armies. Carthage, which was to rule the world, will dwindle to a footnote in someone else's tale.

Plus, Aeneas will be gone. Dido has courage for the rest of it, but not for that.

Some stories are not swallowed but sipped, medicines too vile to be taken all at once.

Fundamental conflicts:

1. Woman against man.
2. Woman against nature.
3. Woman against herself.
4. Woman against society.
5. Woman against the gods.
6. Woman against machine.

"What am I supposed to say here? I'm sorry?"
"Please. Please. Please just still love me."
[pause] "Well. It's just. You know."

Considering the pain it gave her when her husband said those words, she imagines it will break Dido's heart, as well. But really, it is pretty banal, written down.

*Demia looked forward, squinting. The dimming ~~sunset~~* [no, it's dusk] *sky outlined the crags ahead of them. The hermitage was there somewhere, safe haven if they could just reach it before ~~dusk~~ dark.*

*A howl interrupted her thoughts. Her mare jumped as if she had been struck but did not bolt, Demia's long hands strong on her reins.* [POV] *"Lady," Corlyn said, his voice suddenly ~~tense~~ urgent. "The athanwulfen/athanhunds. They are hunting." His own horse twisted ~~against its reins~~ under him.*

*"Too soon," Demia murmured, but no: dusk already. "I wish—"*

*Her brothers could have defended them all, but they were dead. She and Corlyn had found them ~~on the Richt Desert~~ at the ~~dead~~ oasis, miles to the east—or what was left of them—bones picked clean and drilled through in many places, hollowed by the narrow barbed tongues of the athanwulfen/athanhunds. Stivvan, Ricard, Jenner, Daved. She clenched her teeth against the loss; there was no time.*

*Corlyn lit a torch and was outlined by ~~the flame~~ the leaping flame—*

No Corlyn, no horses, no torch. But athanhunds, yes. Demia must lose *everything*, her own bones hollowed. Otherwise it will not hurt enough.

No "suddenly"s. Nothing is sudden. When the tornado hits, the house comes apart in a few seconds; but before that there was a barbed curve on the NOAA map, a front coming in from the southwest, clouds and cold and a growing wind.

In fact, no adverbs in general. Verbs happen, unmediated. Leave, abandon, lose. The next day the videos show you amid the ruins, clutching a cat carrier and a framed photo from someone else's wedding.

[ANGER SHAME DERANGEMENT]
[ALL BETRAYALS ARE THE SAME STORY]
[at least dido had warning]

Aeneas does not stay. He says that of course he loves her. [just not enough] He feels terrible about all this. He tells her that it's not his fault; it's the gods that whip him from her side. His words mound up like slush under her feet, slippery and treacherous. He is unworthy—every word proves it—but it's too late for that to make a difference.

He is sorry, so sorry, but he did warn her, after all. It's not his fault that she didn't believe him. Etc. etc. Disingenuous prick.

Dido abases herself, kneels before Aeneas. She has broken a vein in her eye and she sees through a red haze. Her heart skips beats. She fights not to vomit. Her fingers are bloody from clawing herself.

He promises to stay, presumably because he wants her to lighten up, but he slips from her arms as she sleeps. There is no time, she will wake soon; so he runs to his ships, cuts his anchor cables and sails out on the tide. When she sees them at dawn, he is far out to sea. He has lain with her, lied to her, for the last time.

> *"Diera Vallan's tears fell unheeded as the V-5f life pod crashed through the meteor field, all that remained of her shattered planet. So many millions, she thought, and the tears fell faster. Her own husband, the Windhover King, was dead, flayed alive by—"*

Not that, either.

She still has her health, her wits, the cat. Many people have lost more. There are plagues, earthquakes, fires and starvation. Children run down in the street. A man's legs crushed between two cars as he tries to jump-start a Ford on a winter night. A man losing his ability to form words as the tumor webs across his brain. A couple waiting for the stillborn birth of their already-dead son. Farming accidents. Alzheimer's.

And other divorces. She is not unique; she is not even unusual. Perhaps this has more in common with a wedding ring lost by the pool at a vacation hotel; or blood poisoning from a cat bite.

And yet.

- 237 "the"s. They are words that dry to invisibility, Elmer's Glue-all to anchor nouns.
- 104 "and"s; 30 "but"s. Apparent relationships.
- Too many semicolons.
- Clean out the passive constructions. Dido was *there*. She did things, and some of them were wrong.

She has a dream in which he's still there. He has not yet betrayed her, and she is still sane. They huddle together in a mountain cave where they have found shelter from the night's storm. The world outside roars with rain, broken timber, falling stones. The air is chill but they are safe.

All things are new, all things are possible. In the darkness, she sees him only with her fingertips: his eyelids, his curling lashes, the complex shapes of his ears. His lips smile against her palm. He opens his mouth. She feels his breath.

They lie in a nest they make of their clothing, the things they have cast aside. They are not cold. She runs her hand down the long smooth planes of his body. She feels a scar. He says it still hurts when it is touched. She understands this; she has her own.

In the darkness he strokes her and she feels outlined in light. Her skin is afire. She sobs under his hand, his mouth, the weight of his long, scarred body.

I want to leave them dreaming there, Dido and the writer both, for lines and lines. It is a lie I am telling them.

Are grammar and syntax correct? Is there enough setting? Was there good sensory detail? Is the opening interesting? Is this the right place to start the story, or should it be earlier or later? Does the plot make sense? Does it end too soon/too late/too abruptly?

Does everyone feel realistic? Do they act in realistic ways? Is the story from the right POV? Is the tone appropriate to the story? What is the theme of the story?

The story betrays us all.

I spend the entire night rewriting, changing things around, hoping for a better result. The story doesn't do what I wish. Dido always dies. The writer always finds herself alone, a flute made of a woman's bones.

She does not want to face the raw, whole thing, so she takes it in pieces. She transfers, distances, sublimates. She cannot sit at her keyboard for long. She is haunted. She is hunted. The apartment is cold and smells of chicken; the cat turns over the bones she forgot to put in the trash.

Rewriting ends when the deadline comes. Even then, she will attach the file to an email and send it, and wish there had been more time.

The onshore wind blows through Carthage. His ships are far off, flecks smaller than snowflakes on the dark sea; still in sight but he cannot return: the winds forbid it. In any case, he was gone already, before ever he cut his cables and sailed at dawn—before the cave and the first time he held her in his arms, even.

In the great courtyard before the palace, Dido, Queen of Carthage, orders a pyre built. She will burn all the things he left here: the clothes and jewels she gave him, the shield and sword he left beside her bed. She holds the naked sword in her hand.

She is dead already. She has been dead since he was first brought to her, sea-stained and despairing, and the flame of her hunger gnawed into her bones.

She curses him. She curses him. She curses him.

But it is herself she kills.

Delete.

Undo.

It is not just that the writer needs the safe distance of a zombie story, a ghost story. It is that no story can carry so much sorrow and anger without being crushed beneath its weight, without bursting into flames, without drowning.

What really happened—the careful stacking of pebbles in the path of the landslide that was the last year of their marriage, the woman from his office, the months of listening to his voice make promises for the bitter, false comfort of it—those words cannot contain her feelings.

Even her imagined Dido cannot contain them, as she bleeds upon the oil-soaked pyre in those seconds before her heart stops struggling to fill the hole left by the sword. A torch stabs into the stacked wood. Flames run along each tier. Her skin breathes a mist. She is for a moment outlined in light.

Then the fire bursts upward, and she becomes a burning pillar, a tower, a beacon, and she is dead; and he looks back and does not see the thing that he has destroyed, only the flames upon the half-built walls of Carthage; and he wonders what message they send, and to whom.

Not Medea's frenzy, not Ariadne's broken thread. Anna under the train's wheels. Butterfly holding the wakizashi to her breast. None of the betrayed women, that commonest story of all.

Not even Troy itself and all its deaths: the bitter siege, and ten years from home, Penelope's tears and the Trojan women's torn breasts and Iphigenia's sacrifice, the ruined towers, the blood dried to dust on the golden stones; the anguish of Paris; Aeneas's pain—even these cannot contain her rage, her loss.

Words fail.

*She found herself in a room with ivory-painted wainscoting and a floor tiled with black and white marble. There were no furnishings, only a single glass table at the hall's center. There were no doors. The narrow windows were too high to reach, though she tired herself through the long afternoon, jumping for them.*

*When it grew dark at last, she huddled against the wall on the cold marble and slept, and tried to remember the flowers that had been in the garden.*

Dido dies on the sword. She hits CTRL-S. I type "End." We will do this again.

# THE MAN IN GREY

## MICHAEL SWANWICK

There's a rustling in the wings. Let the story begin.

I was standing outside watching when sixteen-year-old Martha Geissler, pregnant, loveless, and unwed, stepped into the path of a Canadian National freight train traveling at the rate of forty-five miles per hour. The engineer saw her and simultaneously applied the brakes and hit the air horn. But since the train consisted of two 4,300-horsepower SD70M-2 locomotives hauling seventy-six loaded cars and seventy-three empty ones and weighed an aggregate 11,700 tons, it was a given that it wouldn't stop in time. All that the engineer could hope for was that the crazy woman on the tracks would come to her senses.

Maybe she would. Maybe she wouldn't. The forces that brought Martha here were absolutely predictable. What she would do in the actual event was not. One way or another, it was an instant of perfect, even miraculous, free will.

Martha stared at the oncoming train with neither fear nor exaltation, but with great clarity of mind. She thought things that were hers alone to know, came to a decision, and then stepped deliberately backwards from the track.

There was a collective sigh of relief from the shadows. Never let it be said that those of us who have no lives of our own don't care.

Then she slipped.

It shouldn't have happened. It *couldn't* have happened. But it did. The script said that if she stepped backwards, away from the oncoming locomotive, the ground behind her would be flat and solid. Given the choice she had made, Martha was supposed to stand, half stunned, as the train slammed past inches from her face. She would be given the gift of a moment of absolute calm in which she would realize things that might well help her to understand exactly who she was now and who she might turn out to be years in the future.

But a stagehand had somehow, inexplicably, left behind a chilled bottle of a brand of cola not even available on Martha's ostensible continent, when he was setting up the scene. It rolled under Martha's foot. She lost her balance.

With a little shriek, she fell forward, into the path of the train.

With that, I stepped out of the grey, grabbed her arm, and hauled her back.

Still wailing, the train rushed by and the engineer—enormously relieved and himself beginning to change as a result of the incident—released the brake and carefully accelerated out of the long bend and into somebody else's area of responsibility.

Martha clutched me as tightly as if she were drowning. Slowly I pried her loose. She stared into my face, white with shock. "I..." she said. "You..."

"It's a goddamned lucky thing I was passing by, young lady," I said gruffly. "You oughtta be more careful." I turned to leave.

Martha looked up and down the tracks. We were at the outskirts of town, where the land was flat and empty. The nearest building was a warehouse a full city block away. There was nowhere I could possibly have come from. She could see that at a glance.

Inwardly I cursed.

"Who are you?" she said, hurrying after me. Then, "*What* are you?"

"Nobody. I just happened to see you." I was almost running now, with Martha plucking at my coat sleeve and trotting to keep up. "Listen, Sis, I don't want to be rude, but I've got things to do, okay? I got places to be. I can't—" I was sweating. I belonged in the grey, not out on stage with the talent. I wasn't used to extemporaneous speech. All this improv was beyond me.

I broke into an out-and-out run. Coat flying, I made for the warehouse. If I could only get out of sight for a second—assuming there was some local action scheduled for the other side of the building before this scenario ended and that the stage was properly set—I could slip back into the grey without Martha seeing it. She'd know that something strange had happened, but what could she do about it? Who could she complain to? Who would listen to her if she did?

I reached the warehouse and flew around the corner.

And into the streets of Hong Kong.

The stagehands had, of course, only put up as much stage dressing as was needed for the scenario. It was just my bad luck that we were back-to-back with an Asian set. Behind the warehouse facade it was all skyscrapers and Chinese-language advertising. Plus, it was night and it had just rained, so the streets were smudged black mirrors reflecting streetlights and neon. I said a bad word.

Martha plowed into my back. She rebounded, almost fell, and caught herself. Then, horn blaring, a taxicab almost ran us down. She clutched my arm so hard it hurt. "What—what is this?" she asked, eyes wide with existential terror.

"There are a few things you should know." I gently turned her back toward the city she had grown up in. "There's a diner not far from here. Why don't I buy you a cup of coffee and we can talk?"

In the diner, I tried to explain. "The world is maybe not the way you picture it to be," I said. "In its mechanics, anyway. We don't have the resources to maintain every possible setup twenty-four hours a day. Also, there aren't as many real people in it—folks you might actually meet, as opposed to those you see at a distance or hear about on TV—as you were led to believe. Maybe forty-five or fifty thousand all told. But other than that, everything's just like you've always thought it was. Go back to your life and you'll be fine."

Martha clutched her coffee cup as if it were all that was keeping her from falling off the face of the Earth. But she looked at me steadily. Her eyes were clear and focused. "So this is all—what?—a play, you're telling me? I'm nothing but a puppet and you're the guy who pulls my strings? You're in charge of things and I'm the entertainment?"

"No, no, no. Your life is your own. You have absolute free will. I'm just here to make sure that when you step out of the shower, the bath mat is always there for you."

"You've seen me *naked?*"

I sighed. "Martha, either I or somebody like me has been with you for every waking or sleeping moment of your life. Every time your mother changed your diapers or you squeezed a zit in the mirror or you hid under the blankets with a flashlight and a romance manga after you were supposed to be asleep, there were people there, working hard to ensure that the world behaved in a comprehensible and consistent fashion for you."

"So what are you? You operate a camera, right? Or maybe you are the camera. Like you're a robot, or you've got cameras implanted in your eyes." She was still stuck on the entertainment metaphor. It had been a mistake telling her that the whole thing had been caused by a careless stagehand.

"I am not a camera. I'm just the man who stands in grey, making things happen." I did not tell her that all the necessary misery and suffering in the world is caused by people like me. Not because I'm ashamed of what I do—I make no apologies; it's important work—but because Martha wasn't ready to hear, much less understand, it. "What you've discovered is analogous to somebody in the Middle Ages learning that the world is not made up of fire, water, air, and earth, but rather by unimaginably small bundles of quarks underlain by strata of quantum uncertainty. It might feel shocking to you at first. But the world's the same as it's always been. It's only your understanding of it that's changed."

Martha looked at me with huge, wounded eyes. "But... why?"

"I honestly don't know," I said. "If you forced me to speculate, I'd say that there are two possibilities. One is that Somebody decided that things should be like this. The other is that it's simply the way things are. But which is true is anybody's guess."

That's when Martha began to cry.

So I got up and walked around the table and put my arms about her. She was still only a child, after all.

When Martha calmed down, I took her back to her mother's place in the Northern Liberties. It was a long trek—she'd been wandering about blindly ever since the pregnancy test turned blue—and so I ordered up a taxi. Martha flinched a little when it appeared before her, right out of thin air. But she got in and I gave the cabbie her address. The cabbie wasn't real, of course. But he was good work. You'd have to talk to him for an hour to realize he wasn't human.

As we rode, Martha kept trying to work things through. She was like a kid picking at a scab. "So you do all the work, I get that. What's in it for you?"

I shrugged. "A transient taste of being, every now and again." I looked out the window at the passing city. Even knowing that it was all metaphysical canvas-and-paint, it looked convincing. "This is pretty nice. I like it. Mostly, though, it's just my job. I'm not like you—I don't have any say over what I do and don't do."

"You think any of this is my choice?"

"More of it than you'd suspect. Okay, yes, you dropped out of school, you don't have a job, and you're pregnant by a boy you don't particularly like, and that limits your options. You're still living with your mother and the two of you fight constantly. It's been years since you've seen your father and sometimes you wonder if he's still alive. You have health issues. None of that is under your control. But your response to it is. That's an extraordinary privilege and it's one I don't have. Given the current situation, I could no more get out of this cab and walk away from you than you could flap your arms and fly to the Moon.

"You, however, have the freedom to think anything, say anything, do anything. Your every instant is unpredictable. Right here, right now, it may be that what I'm saying will reach you and you'll smile and ask how you can get back on script. Maybe you'll scream and call me names. Maybe you'll retreat into silence. Maybe you'll slap me. Anything could happen."

She slapped me.

I looked at her. "What did that prove?"

"It made me feel better," she lied. Martha crossed her arms and pushed herself back into the cushions, making herself as small as she could. Fleetingly, I thought she was going to keep retreating, deeper and deeper into herself, until nothing showed on the outside but dull, lifeless eyes. She could decide to do that. It was her right.

But then the cab pulled up before a nondescript row house on Leithgow Street and she got out.

"Act like you've gotten a big tip," I told the cabbie.

"Hey, thanks, buddy!" he said, and drove off.

Martha was unlocking the door. "Mom's visiting her sister in Baltimore for a couple days. We have the house to ourselves."

"I know." She went straight to the kitchen and got out a bottle of her mother's vodka from the freezer.

"It's a little early for that, isn't it?" I said.

"Then make it later."

"As you will." I signaled the gaffer and the sun slid down the sky. The world outside the window grew dark. I didn't bother ordering up stars. "Is that late enough?"

"What the fuck do I care?" Martha sat down at the kitchen table and I followed suit. She filled two tumblers, thrust one in my hands. "Drink."

I did, though not being talent, the alcohol had no effect on me.

After a while, she said, "Which of my friends are real and which aren't?"

"They're all real, Martha. Tomika, Jeanne, Siouxie, Ben, your teachers, your parents, your cousins, the boy you thought was cute but too immature to go out with—everyone you have an emotional relationship with, positive or negative, is as real as you are. Anything else would be cheating."

"How about Kevin?" Her boyfriend, of course.

"Him too."

"Shit." Martha stared down into her glass, swirling the vodka around and around, creating a miniature whirlpool. "What about rappers and movie stars?"

"That's a different story. Your feelings toward them aren't terribly complex; nor are they reciprocated. Real people aren't needed to fill the roles."

"Thought so." She drank deeply.

If she kept on in this vein, sooner or later she was going to ask about her father. In which case, I would have to tell her that Carl Geissler was in Graterford, where prison life was teaching him things about his essential nature that would take him decades to assimilate. Then that her mother clandestinely visited him there every month and, for reasons she only imperfectly understood, kept this fact to herself. So I touched Martha's glass and said, "Do you really think this is a wise course of action?"

"What do people normally do in this situation?" she asked sarcastically.

"Martha, listen to me. You have all your life ahead of you and, depending on what choices you make, it can be a very good life indeed. I know. I've seen young women in your situation before, more times than you can imagine. Let me take you back to where you were before we met and start your life up where it left off."

Her expression was stiff and unreadable. "You can do that, huh? Rewind the movie and then start it up again?"

"That's an inexact metaphor," I said. "With your cooperation, we can re-create the scenario. You'll enter it, play your part, and then go back to your life. What happens then will be entirely up to you. No interference from me or anybody like me, I swear. But you have to agree to it. We can't do a thing without your permission."

As I spoke, Martha's face grew more and more expressionless. Her eyes were hard and unblinking. Which suggested that the one thing I feared most—that she would go catatonic, burying that beautiful spark of life deeper and deeper under soft cottony layers of silence and inertia—was a very real possibility. "Please," I said. "Say something."

To my surprise, Martha said, "What does reality look like?"

"I'm not sure I understand you. This is reality. All around you."

"It's a fucking set! Show me what's behind it, or underneath it, or however the hell you want to put it. Show me what remains when the set is gone."

"I honestly don't advise that. It would only upset you."

"Do it!"

Reluctantly, I pushed back the chair. There was nothing scheduled anywhere behind the house for hours. I went to the back door. I opened it—

—revealing the roiling, churning emptiness that underlies the world we constantly make and unmake in the service of our duty. The colorless, formless negation of negatives that is Nothing and Nowhere and Nowhen. The calm horror of nonbeing. The grey.

I stood looking into it, waiting for Martha to make a noise, to cry out in fear, to beg me to make it go away. But though I waited for the longest time, she did not.

Fearing the worst, I turned back to her.

"All right," Martha said. "Rewind me."

So I took Martha Geissler back to where it had all begun. The sun and clouds were carefully placed exactly where they'd been, and the stagehands brought out the locomotives and hooked them up to the correct number of freight cars. Because the original engineer was talent, we put in a prop in his place. The script didn't call for the two of them to ever meet, so there wouldn't be any continuity problems.

"Here's your mark," I told Martha for the umpteenth time. "When the train passes that telephone pole over there—"

"I step into its path," she said. "Then I slowly count to ten and step backwards off the track. This time there won't be a soda bottle underfoot. How many times have we gone over this? I know my lines."

"Thank you," I said, and stepped into the grey to wait and watch.

The train came rumbling forward, only moderately fast but with tremendous momentum. Closer it came, and closer, and when it reached the telephone pole I'd chosen as a marker, Martha did not step into its path. Instead, she stood motionless by the side of the track.

The prop engineer hit the air horn just as the real one had, despite the fact that the track before him was empty. Still, Martha did nothing.

Then, at the very last possible instant, she stepped in front of the train.

There was a universal gasp from the shadows, the sound of my many brothers and sisters caught completely by surprise. Followed by a moment of perfect silence. Then by rolling thunderheads of applause.

It was an astonishing thing for Martha to do—and she'd done it calmly, without giving me the least sign of what was to come. But I didn't join in the applause.

Briefly, I understood what it was like to be one of them. The talent, I mean. For the first time in my very long existence, I wanted something to not have happened.

Thus ended Martha's story. I returned to my own world and to the job of maintaining and arranging the world whose inhabitants fondly believe to be real. Theirs is, for all its limitations, larger and more commodious than mine. But I do not begrudge them that. Their lives are more difficult and far more profound than anything I shall ever experience. Neither do I begrudge them that. We all have our places in existence and our parts to play.

Martha was a star in what we call the Great Game and what they (you) call reality. I am just a cog in the machinery. But if all my functions are mechanical, at least my reactions to it are not. I am not a camera. I am not a voyeur. Nor, God knows, am I the wizard behind the curtain, manipulating everything to his own benefit. Nothing of the sort.

I am the man in grey, and I love you all.

# OLD HABITS

## NALO HOPKINSON

Ghost malls are even sadder than living people malls, even though malls of the living are already pretty damned sad places to be. And let me get this out of the way right now, before we go any farther; I'm dead, okay? I'm fucking dead. This is not going to be one of those stories where the surprise twist is *and he was dead!* I'm not a bloody surprise twist. I'm just a guy who wanted to buy a necktie to wear at his son's high school graduation.

I wander through Sears department store for a bit, past a pyramid of shiny boxes with action heroes peeking out of their cellophane windows, another one of hard-bodied girl dolls with permanently pointed toes and tight pink clothing, past a rack of identical women's cashmere sweaters in different colours; purple, black, red and green. The sign on the rack reads, *30% off, today only!* It's Christmas season. Everywhere I wander, I'm followed by elevator music versions of the usual hoary Christmas classics. Funny, a ghost being haunted by music.

I make a right at the perfume counter. It's kind of a relief to no longer be able to smell it before I see it, to no longer have to hold my breath to avoid inhaling the migraine-inducing esters cloying the air around it.

Black Anchor Ohsweygian is lying on the ground by the White Shoulders display. Actually, she's rolling around on the ground, her long grey hair in her eyes, her face contorted, yelling. I can't hear her; she's on the clock. Her hands slap ineffectually at the air, trying to fight off the invisible security guard who did her in. Her outer black skirt is up around her thighs, revealing underneath it a beige skirt, and under that a flower print one, and under that a baggy pair of jeans.

She's wearing down-at-heel construction boots. They're too big for her; as I watch, she kicks out and one of the boots flies off, exposing layers of torn socks and a flash of puffy, bruised ankle. The boot wings right through me. I don't even flinch when I see it coming. I've lost the habit.

Now Black Anchor's face is being crushed down onto the hard tile floor, her features compressed. She's told me that the security guard knelt on her head to hold her down. One arm is trapped under her, the other one flailing. It won't be long now. I shouldn't watch. It's her private moment. We all have them, us ghosts. Once a day, we die all over again. You get used to it, but it's not really polite to watch someone re-dying their last moments of true contact with the world. For some of us, that moment becomes precious, a treasured thing. Jimmy would go ballistic if he ever caught me watching him choke on a piece of steak in the Surf 'N' Turf restaurant up on the third floor. Black doesn't mind sharing her death with me, though. She's told me I can watch as often as I like. I used to do it just out of prurient curiosity, but now I watch because I feel a person should have someone who cares about them with them when they die. I like Black. I can't touch her to comfort her. Can't even whisper to her. Not while she's still alive, which she just barely is right now. In a few seconds she'll be able to hear and see me, to know that I am here, bearing witness. But we still won't be able to touch. If we try, it'll be like two drifts of smoke melting into and through each other. That may be the true tragedy of being a ghost.

Black Anchor's squinched face has flushed an unpleasant shade of red. Her arm flops to the ground. Her rusty shopping cart has tumbled over beside her, spilling overused white plastic shopping bags, knotted shut and stuffed so full the bags are torn in places. In the bags are Black Anchor's worldly possessions. She pulls the darnedest things out of those bags to entertain Baby Boo. I mean, why in the world did Black Anchor carry a pair of diving goggles with her as she trudged year in, year out up and down the city streets, pushing her disintegrating shopping cart in front of her? She won't tell me or Jimmy why she has the diving goggles. Says a lady has to have some secrets.

I go and sit by Black Anchor's head. I hope, for the umpteenth time, that I've passed through the security guard that killed her. I hope he can feel me doing so, even just the tiniest bit, and it's making him shudder. Goose walking on his grave. Maybe he'll die in this mall too someday, and become a ghost. Have to look Black Anchor in the eye.

A little 'tuh' of exhaled breath puffs out of her. Every day, she breathes her last one more time. Her body relaxes. Her face stops looking squished against the floor. She opens her eyes, sees me sitting there. She smiles. "That was a good one," she says. "I think the guard had had hummus for lunch. I think I smelled chick peas and parsley on his breath." In her mouth, I can see the blackened stump that is all that was left of one rotted-out front tooth.

I return her smile. In those few seconds of pseudo-life she goes on the clock every day, Black Anchor tries to capture one more sensory detail from all she has left of the real world. "You are so fucking crazy," I tell her. "Wanna go for a walk?"

"Sure. I've clocked out for the day." The usual ghost joke. She sits up. By the time we get to our feet, her bundle buggy is upright again, her belongings crammed back into it. Her boot is back on her foot. It happens like that every time. I've never been able to catch the moment when it changes. Black pushes her creaky bundle buggy in front of her. We walk out of the south entrance of Sears; the one that leads right into the mall. Cheerful canned music follows us, exulting about the comforts of chestnuts and open fires. Quigley's standing in front of the jewellery shop, peering in at the display. He does that a lot, especially at Christmas time and Valentine's Day, when the fanciest diamond rings get displayed in the window. The day Quigley kicked it had been a February 13. He'd been in the mall shopping for an engagement ring for his girl. He was going to put it in a big box of fancy chocolates, surprise her with it on Valentine's Day. But then he had that final asthma attack, right there in the mall's west elevator. Quigley's twenty-four years old. Was twenty-four years old. Would be twenty-four years old for a long, long time now. Perhaps forever. He still carries around that box of expensive chocolates he'd bought before he stopped breathing. It's in one of those fancy little paper shopping bags, the kind with the flat bottom and the twisted paper handles.

Quigley waves sadly at us. He has pushed his waving hand through the handles of the gift bag. The bag bumps against his forearm. We wave back. Black murmurs, "He's brooding. He doesn't get over it, he'll find himself stepping outside."

There's a rumour among the mall ghosts; kind of an urban legend or maybe spectral legend that we whisper amongst ourselves when we're telling each other stories to keep the boredom at bay. There was this guy, apparently, this ghost guy before my time, who got so stir-crazy that he yanked open one of the big glass doors that leads to the outside. He stepped into the blackness that is all we can see beyond the mall doors. People say that once he was outside, they couldn't see him any longer. They say he shouted, once. Some people say it was a shout of joy. Some of them think it was agony, or terror. Jimmy says the shout sounded more like surprise to him. Whatever it was, the guy never came back. Jimmy says we lose one like that every few years. Once it was an eight-year-old girl. Everyone felt bad about that one. They still get into arguments about which one of them failed to keep an eye on her.

What that story tells me; we can touch the doors to the outside. Not everything in this mall is intangible to us.

I'm with Black Anchor Ohsweygian and Jimmy Lee sitting around one of the square vinyl topped tables in the food court; the kind with rounded-off edges that seats four. Like everywhere else in the mall, the food court seems deserted except for the ghosts. But there's food under the heat lamps and in the warming trays. Overcooked battered shrimp at the Cap'n Jack's counter; floppy, grey beef slices in gravy at Meat 'n' Taters; soggy broccoli florets at China Munch. The food levels go down and are replenished constantly during the day. To us, it's like plastic dollhouse food. We see the steam curling up from the warming trays, but there's no sound of cooking, no food smells. Kitty's standing in front of Mega Burger. I think she's staring at the shiny metal milk shake dispenser.

Jimmy and Black Anchor and I are sitting on those hard plastic seats that are bolted to food court tables. We're playing "Things I Miss." Kind of sitting, anyway. Sitting on surfaces is one of those habits that's hard to break. We can't feel the chairs under our butts, but we still try to sit on them. Jimmy Lee's aim isn't so good; he's actually sunk about two inches into his chair. But then, he's a tall guy; maybe it helps him not have to lean over to see eye to ghost eye with me and Black Anchor. Baby Boo has decided to join us today. He—I've decided to call him "he"—is lying on his back on the food court table, swaddled in his yellow blanket and onesie. He's mumbling at his little fist and staring from one to the other of us as we speak. Baby Boo doesn't quite have the hang of the laws of physics; he'd died too young to learn many of them. He's suspended in midair, about a hand's breadth above the table.

Things we miss, now that we're ghosts:

Jimmy says, "Really good cigars. Drawing the smoke of them into my lungs, holding it there, letting it out through my nose." All us mall ghosts, our chests rose and fell in their remembered rhythms, but no air went in and out.

Black Anchor Ohsweygian stares at her thin, wrinkled fingers on the table top. She says, "The sweet musk of beets, fragrant as blood-soaked earth."

"Vanilla milk shakes," I say, thinking of Kitty over there. "Cold, sweet, and creamy on your tongue."

Jimmy nods. "And frothy." He takes another turn; "Going up to the cottage for the first long weekend in spring."

I nod. "Victoria Day weekend."

"Yeah," Jimmy replies. "Jumping from the deck into the lake for the first time since the fall before." He laughs a little. It makes his big face crinkle up. "That water would be so frigging cold! It'd just about freeze my balls off, every time. And Barbara would roll her eyes and call me a fool, but she'd jump in right after." His expression falls back into its usual sad grumpiness. Barbara was his wife of thirty years.

Black Anchor says, "Toronto summers, when it would get so hot that squirrels would lie flopped like black skins on the branches, fur side up. So humid that you were sure if you made a fist, you would squeeze water dripping from the air. Your thighs squelched when you walked." Black Anchor's having one of her more conversational days. Apparently, she used to be a poet. A homeless poet. She told me there was a lot of that going on.

I say, "The warm milk smell of my husband's breath after his morning coffee."

"Fucking faggot," grumbles Jimmy. It's an old, toothless complaint of his.

I shrug. "Whatever."

"Hey," says Jimmy, in his gruff, hulking way. I know he's still talking to me because he won't quite meet my eyes, and his face does this defensive thing, this "I'm a manly man and don't you forget it" thing. He says, "That's the closest you've come to talking about a person you used to...you know, love. How come is that? Don't you miss anyone?"

His eyes glisten as he says the word "love," like he's crying. Jimmy goes on about Barbara like she was a piece of heaven that he lost. I guess she was, come to think of it.

"Yeah, I miss people," I say slowly, playing for time. Even when you're dead, some things cut close to the bone. Sometimes Baby Boo cries, and it makes my arms ache with the memory of feeding Brandon when he was that little, watching his tiny pursed mouth latch on to the nipple of his bottle, seeing his eyes staring big and calm up at me as though I were his whole world. "I miss lots of people."

Black leans back in her chair and sighs airlessly. "Well, I miss that girl at the doughnut shop who would slip me an extra couple if I went there during her shift."

Jimmy shakes his head. "Doughnuts. Jesus. How did you live like that?"

"I honestly don't know, Sugar."

I shoot Black a grateful glance for getting Jimmy off the subject. When I walk through the darkened mall at night, I try to remember Semyon's touch. The warmth of his hand on my cheek. The hard curve of his arm around me, his hand slipped into my back jeans pocket. I try to remember his voice.

I say to Black and Jimmy, "It's so unfair that we can't see or hear the world. That we can't touch, taste, or smell it."

Black replies, "That's because being a ghost is a disease."

"What do mean, a disease?" I ask her. For the umpteenth time I wonder; what kind of name is Black Anchor Ohsweygian, anyway? Jimmy thinks maybe she's Armenian. He says that Armenians all have names that end in "ian." Someday I'm going to point out to him that some Armenians have names like "Smith."

"Like maybe we're not dead," she replies. "Maybe we just caught some kind of virus that messed up all our senses. Maybe we're all lying in hospital beds somewhere, and some grumpy cunt of a doctor with a busted leg is yelling at his team that they have to find a cure."

"And maybe someone used to watch too much fucking television," says Jimmy. He vees his index and middle finger, puts them to his lips. For a second I think he's flipping her deuces, but no, he takes a drag of his imaginary cigarette. Habits. Black glares at him, hacks and spits to one side. Habits. Baby Boo belches a baby belch, then giggles. We don't know Baby Boo's real name. I don't remember how we ended up calling him Baby Boo.

Kitty must have heard us talking. She wanders over, coos at Baby Boo. He gives her a brief baby grin; the kind that always looks accidental, the baby more surprised than anyone else at what its face has just done. Kitty says, "I can smell stuff. Again, I mean. Like when I was alive."

Quickly, I tell her, "You might want to keep that to yourself." She hasn't been here very long. She doesn't know what she's saying. She doesn't know how dangerous it is. I should warn her outright. I don't.

Kitty ignores my lame hint. She says, "I'm serious. It just started to come back a little while ago. Bit by bit."

My heart starts pounding so quickly that my body trembles a little with every beat. Even though I know I don't have a heart, or a body. Even though I know it's just reflex. Jimmy and Black Anchor look just as avid as I feel. The three of us stare at Kitty, our mouths open. She waggles her fingers at Baby Boo. "I thought I was imagining it at first. You know how you can want something so bad it can make your mouth water?"

We know. Jimmy swallows.

Kitty'd only been fifteen. She and a bunch of her friends from school had crowded shrieking and laughing into the women's washroom on the main floor to try on makeup they'd just bought. In the jostling, Kitty fell. On the way down, she hit her head on the edge of a sink.

Kitty whispers, "I can smell french fries. And bacon." She points at Mega Burger, where she'd been standing. "Over there. Someone's burning bacon on the grill."

Black Anchor says fiercely, "What else? Smell something else!" Her voice doesn't sound human any more. It's hollow, mechanical, nothing like a sound made by air flowing over vocal chords.

Kitty looks around her. A slow smile comes to her face. "Somebody just went by wearing perfume. I think it's Obsession. She smells like my mom used to."

Oh, god. She's really doing it. She's smelling the scent trails of the living people all around us in this mall. Black Anchor chews daily over the gristle of a long ago memory, but Kitty took a whiff of someone warm and alive as she walked past us just this second. Life haunts us, us ghosts. It hovers just out of reach, taunting.

Longing is shredding my self control to tatters. I moan, "Kitty, don't," but she starts talking again a split second after I say her name, so she doesn't hear the warning.

"Mister Lee," she says to Jimmy, "there's someone sitting right there, in the same chair you are. I don't know whether it's a guy or a girl, but they're chewing gum. You know the kind that comes in a little stick and you unwrap the paper from it and it's kinda beige with these like, zigzaggy lines in it? I can smell it as the person's spit wets it and they chew. I should be grossed out, but it's too freaking cool. There's someone *right there!*" She leans in towards Jimmy. She closes her eyes, and no fucking word of a lie, she inhales. Her chest rises and falls, and with it, I hear the breath entering and leaving her lungs. She opens her eyes and looks at us in wonder. "Peppermint," she whispers reverently, as though she's saying the secret name of God.

That does it. The need slams down on me like a wall of bricks, stronger than thought or compassion. I crowd in on Kitty. I dimly notice Jimmy and Black Anchor doing the same.

"Can you smell coffee?"

"Sweat! Can you smell sweat?"

"Is taste coming back, too? Can you taste anything?"

"Can you touch? Can you *feel?*"

Unable to hold the need in check, unable to do anything but shout it in shuddering, hungry voices, we demand to be fed. Kitty, surrounded, looks from one to the other of us, tries to answer our questions, but they come too hard and fast for her to reply. Our hollow shrieks draw the other ghosts. They come flocking in, clamouring, more and more of them as word goes round. We're all demanding to know what she could smell, demanding that she describe it in every last detail, clawing our fingers through the essence of her as we try in vain to touch her. Needing, needing, needing. And through the din is the thin sound of Baby Boo crying. He's only little. He doesn't know how to feed his hunger.

When the frenzy passes and we come back to ourselves, there's nothing left of Kitty but a few grey wisps, like fog, that dissipate even as we watch. The canned music tinkles on about Donner and Blitzen and the gifts that Santa brings to good boys and girls.

Stay long enough in the mall, and you learn what happens if you begin to get the knack of living again. We've used Kitty up. And we are still starving.

Ashamed, we avoid each others' eyes. We step away from each other, spread out through the mall. There is plenty of room for all of us. I go into the bookstore and stare at the titles that appear and disappear from the shelves. I miss reading. Tearlessly, airlessly, I sob. She was only fifteen. At fifteen, Brandon had been worrying about pimples. Semyon and I were coaching him on how to ask girls out. We'd gotten tips from our women friends. I have just sucked from a child what little remained of her life.

I feel it coming on, like a migraine aura. There's a whoosh of dislocation and the world rushes over me. I'm on the clock. My hand slaps down onto the moving rubber handrail. The slight sting of the impact against my palm is terrible and glorious. Sound, delicious sound battered against my ears; the voices of the hundreds and hundreds of people who'd been in the mall on my day. I felt my nipples against the crisp fabric of the white shirt I was wearing under my best grey suit.

There were people near me on the escalator. Below me, a beautiful brown-skinned man in worn jeans and a tight yellow t-shirt. He was talking on his cell phone, telling someone he'd meet them over by the fountain. Beside me was a woman about my age, maybe Asian mixed with something else. She was plump. Girlfriend, don't you know that sage-coloured polyester sacks don't suit anyone, least of all people like us whose waistlines weren't what they used to be? Lessee, I'd gotten a silk tie geometric pattern in greys and blacks shot through with maroon I thought it went nicely with my suit really shouldn't have waited so long to shop for it Semyon was pretty ticked at me for going shopping last minute he's just stressing but we had plenty of time to get to the graduation ceremony just a ten minute drive and oh look there were Semyon and Brandon now waiting for me at the bottom of the escalator and Brandon's girlfriend Lara that's a pretty dress though I wondered whether she wasn't a little too well dumb for Brandon or maybe too smart but what did I know when I first started dating Semyon my sis thought he was too stuck-up for me but she'd thought the guy before him was too common Mom and Dad were going to meet us at Brandon's school and Sally and what's his name again Gerald should remember it by now he'd been my brother-in-law for over two years hoped my dad wouldn't screw up the directions we'd sent Tati an invitation to the graduation but she hadn't replied probably wouldn't show up you utter bitch he's your grandson Semyon and I had never tried to find out which one of us was his bio dad we liked having Brandon be our mystery child kept us going through his defiant years god I hoped to hell those were over and done with now I mean that time he got mad and decked Semyon it was funny later but not when it happened and look at him nineteen with his whole life before him grinning up at me I was just kvelling with pride and oh shit I should have put the tie on in the store better do that now why'd they wrap it in so much tissue paper there did I get the knot right oh whoops ow my elbow's probably bruised so stupid falling where everybody can see that cute guy turning to lend a hand to the clumsy old fag who can't manage a simple escalator oh crap I'm stuck my tie

The fall by itself probably wouldn't have killed me. But my snazzy new silk necktie caught in the escalator mechanism. And then the lady beside me was screaming for help and the cute guy was yanking desperately on my rapidly shortening tie as it disappeared into the works of the escalator and then my head was jammed against the steps and some of my hair caught in it too and pain pain pain and then the dull crack and the last face I saw was not Semyon's or Brandon's, not even my sister Sally's or Dad or Mom or my dearest friend Derek, just the panicked desperate face of some good-looking stranger I didn't know and would never know now because although he'd tried his hardest he hadn't been able to save my bloody lifemylifemylife.

Broke my fricking neck. Stupid way to go. *Really* stupid day to do it on. And for the rest of this existence, I'd regret that I'd done it while my son and my husband looked on, helplessly.

I'm standing alone on the down escalator. The canned music chirps at me to listen to the sleigh bells ringing. I'm off the clock. I let the escalator carry me down to the main floor. At the bottom, I step off it and walk over to the spot where I'd last seen my family. For all I know, no time has passed for them. For all I know, they might still be here, watching me ruin Brandon's graduation day. Maybe I brush past or through them as I walk this way once every day.

I straighten my tie. It does go well with my suit. I walk past the cell phone store, the bathing suit store, the drug store. I turn down the nearest corridor. It leads to an exit. I stand in front of the glass and steel door. I stare at the blackness on the other side of it. I think about pushing against the crash bar; how solid it would feel under my palm; how the glass door would feel slightly chilly against my shoulder as I shoved it open.

# THE VICAR OF MARS

## GWYNETH JONES

The Reverend Boaaz Hanaahaahn, High Priest of the Mighty Void, and a young Aleutian adventurer going by the name of "Conrad" were the only resident guests at the Old Station, Butterscotch. They'd met on the way from Opportunity, and had taken to spending their evenings together, enjoying a snifter or two of Boaaz's excellent Twin Planets blend in a cosy private lounge. They were an odd couple: the massive Shet, his grey hide forming ponderous, dignified folds across his skull and over his brow, and the stripling immortal, slick strands of head-hair to his shoulders, black eyes dancing with mischief on either side of the dark space of his nasal. But the Aleutian, though he had never lived to be old—he wasn't the type—had amassed a fund of fascinating knowledge in his many lives, and Boaaz was an elderly priest with varied interests and a youthful outlook.

Butterscotch's hundred or so actual citizens didn't frequent the Old Station. The usual customers were mining lookerers, who drove in from the desert in the trucks that were their homes, and could be heard carousing, mildly, in the public bar. Boaaz and Conrad shared a glance, agreeing not to join the fun tonight. The natives were friendly enough—but Martian settlers were, almost exclusively, humans who had never left conventional space. The miners had met few "aliens," and believed the Buonarotti Interstellar Transit was a dangerous novelty that would never catch on. One got tired of the barrage of uneasy fascination.

"I'm afraid I scare the children," rumbled Boaaz.

The Aleutian could have passed for a noseless, slope-shouldered human. The Shet was hairless and impressively bulky, but what really made him different were his delicates. To Boaaz it was natural that he possessed two sets of fingers: one set thick and horny, for pounding and mashing, the other slender and supple, for fine manipulation. Normally protected by his wrist folds, his delicates would shoot out to grasp a stylus, for instance, or handle eating implements. He had seen the young folk startle at this, and recoil with bulging eyes—

"Stop calling them *children*," suggested Conrad. "They don't like it."

"I don't think that can be it. The young always take the physical labour and service jobs, it's a fact of nature. I'm only speaking English."

Conrad shrugged. For a while each of them studied his own screen, as the saying goes. A comfortable silence prevailed. Boaaz reviewed a list of deserving "cases" sent to him by the Colonial Social Services in Opportunity. He was not impressed. They'd simply compiled a list of odds and ends: random persons who didn't fit in, and were vaguely thought to have problems.

To his annoyance, one of the needy appeared to live in Butterscotch.

"Here's a woman who '*has been suspected of being insane,*'" he grumbled aloud. "Has she been treated? Apparently not. How barbaric. *Has visited Speranza… No known religion…* What's the use in telling me that?"

"Maybe they think you'd like to convert her," suggested Conrad.

"I do not *convert* people!" exclaimed Boaaz, shocked. "Should an unbelieving parishioner wish my guidance towards the Abyss, they'll let me know. It's not my business to persuade them! I have entered my name alongside other Ministers of Religion on Mars. If my services as a priest should be required at a Birth, Adulthood, Conjunction or Death, I shall be happy to oblige, and that's enough."

Conrad laughed soundlessly, the way Aleutians do. "You don't bother your 'flock,' and they don't bother you! That sounds like a nice easy berth."

Not always, thought the old priest, ruefully. Sometimes not easy at all!

"I wouldn't worry about it, Boaaz. Mars is a colony. It's run by the planetary government of Earth, and they're obsessed with gathering information about innocent strangers. When they can't find anything interesting, they make it up. The file they keep on me is vast, I've seen it."

"Earth," powerful neighbour to the Red Planet, was the local name for the world everyone else in the Diaspora knew as the Blue.

Boaaz was here to minister to souls. Conrad was here—he claimed—purely as a tourist. The fat file the humans kept might suggest a different story, but Boaaz had no intention of prying. Alcutians, the Elder Race, had their own religion; or lack of one. As long as he showed no sign of suffering, Conrad's sins were his own business. The old Shet cracked a snifter vial, tucked it in his holder: inhaled deeply, and returned to the eyeball-screen that was visible to his eyes alone. The curious Social Services file on *Jewel, Isabel*, reappeared. All very odd. Careful of misunderstandings, he opened his dictionary, and checked in detail the meanings of English words he knew perfectly well.

**Wicked**...

**old woman**...

**insane**...

Later, on his way to bed, he examined one of the fine rock formations that decorated the station's courtyards. They promised good hunting. The mining around here was of no great worth, ferrous ores for the domestic market, but Boaaz was not interested in commercial value: he collected mineral curiosities. It was his passion, and one very good reason for visiting Butterscotch, right on the edge of the most ancient and interesting Martian terrain. If truth be known, Boaaz looked on this far-flung Vicarate as an interesting prelude to his well-earned retirement. He did not expect his duties to be burdensome. But he was a conscientious person, and Conrad's teasing had stung.

"I shall visit her," he announced, to the sharp-shadowed rocks.

The High Priest had travelled from his home world to Speranza, capital city of the Diaspora, and onward to the Blue Planet Torus Port, in no time at all (allowing for a few hours of waiting around, and two "false duration" interludes of virtual entertainment). The months he'd spent aboard the conventional space liner *Burroughs*, completing his interplanetary journey, had been slow but agreeable. He'd arrived to find that his Residence, despatched by licensed courier, had been delayed—and decided that until his home was decoded into material form, he might as well carry on travelling. His tour of this backward but extensive new parish *happened* to concentrate on prime mineral-hunting sites: but he would not neglect his obligations.

He took a robotic jitney as far as the network extended, and proceeded on foot. Jewel, Isabel lived out of town, up against the Enclosure that kept tolerable climate and air quality captive. As yet unscrubbed emissions lingered here in drifts of vapour; the thin air had a lifeless, paradoxical warmth. Spindly towers of mine tailings, known as "Martian Stromatolites," stood in groups, heads together like ugly sentinels. Small mining machines crept about, munching mineral-rich dirt. There was no other movement, no sound but the crepitation of a million tiny ceramic teeth.

Nothing lived.

The "Martians" were very proud of their Quarantine. They farmed their food in strict confinement, they tortured off-world travellers with lengthy decontamination. Even the gastropod machines were not allowed to reproduce: they were turned out in batches by the mine factories, and recycled in the refineries when they were full. What were the humans trying to preserve? The racial purity of rocks and sand?

*Absurd superstition*, muttered the old priest, into his breather. *Life is life!*

Jewel, Isabel clearly valued her privacy. He hadn't messaged her in advance. His visit would be off the record, and if she turned him away from her door, so be it. He could see the isolated module now, at the end of a chance "avenue" of teetering stromatolites. He reviewed the file's main points as he stumped along. *Old. Well travelled, for a human of her caste. Reputed to be rich. No social contacts in Butterscotch, no data traffic with any other location. Supplied by special delivery at her own expense. Came to Mars, around a local year ago, on a settler's one-way ticket.* Boaaz thought that must be very unusual. Martian settlers sometimes retired to their home planet; if they could afford the medical bills. Why would a fragile elderly person make the opposite trip, apparently not planning to return?

The dwelling loomed up, suddenly right in front of him. He had a moment of selfish doubt. Was he committing himself to an endless round of visiting random misfits? Maybe he should quietly go away again… But his approach had been observed, a transparent pane had opened. A face glimmered, looking out through the inner and the outer skin; as if from deep, starless space.

"Who are you?" demanded a harsh voice, cracked with disuse. "Are you real? Can you hear me? You're not human."

"I hear you. I'm, aah, 'wired for sound.' I am not a human, I am a Shet, a priest of the Void, newly arrived, just making myself known. May I come in?"

He half-hoped that she would say no. *Go away, I don't like priests, can't you see I want to be left alone?* But the lock opened. He passed through, divested himself of the breather and his outer garments, and entered the pressurised chamber.

The room was large, by Martian living standards. Bulkheads must have been removed; probably this had once been a three- or four-person unit, but it felt crowded. He recognised the furniture of Earth. Not extruded, like the similar fittings in the Old Station, but free-standing: many of the pieces carved from precious woods. Chairs were ranged in a row, along one curved, red wall. Against another stood a tall armoire, a desk with many drawers, and several canvas pictures in frames; stacked facing the dark. In the midst of the room two more chairs were drawn up beside a plain ceramic stove, which provided the only lighting. A richly patterned rug lay on the floor. He couldn't imagine what it had cost to ship all this, through conventional space in material form. She must indeed be wealthy!

The light was low, the shadows numerous.

"I see you *are* a Shet," said Jewel, Isabel. "I won't offer you a chair, I have none that would take your weight, but please be seated."

She indicated the rug, and Boaaz reclined with care. The number of valuable, alien objects made him feel he was sure to break something. The human woman resumed (presumably) her habitual seat. She was tall, for a human, and very thin. A black gown with loose skirts covered her whole body, closely fastened and decorated with flourishes of creamy stuff, like textile foam, at the neck and wrists.

The marks of human aging were visible in her wrinkled face, her white head-hair and the sunken, over-large sockets of her pale eyes. But signs of age can be deceptive. Boaaz also saw something universal—something any priest often has to deal with, yet familiarity never breeds contempt.

Jewel, Isabel inclined her head. She had read his silent judgement. "You seem to be a doctor as well as a priest," she said, in a tone that rejected sympathy. "My health is as you have guessed. Let's change the subject."

She asked him how he liked Butterscotch, and how Mars compared with Shet: bland questions separated by little unexplained pauses. Boaaz spoke of his mineral-hunting plans, and the pleasures of travel. He was oddly disturbed by his sense that the room was crowded: he wanted to look behind him, to be sure there were no occupants in that row of splendid chairs. But he was too old to turn without a visible effort, and he didn't wish to be rude. When he remarked that Isabel's home (she had put him right on the order of her name) was rather isolated she smiled—a weary stretching of the lips.

"Oh, you'd be surprised. I'm not short of company."

"You have your memories."

Isabel stared over his shoulder. "Or they have me."

He did not feel that he'd gained her confidence, but before he left they'd agreed he would visit again: she was most particular about the appointment. "In ten days time," she said. "In the evening, at the full moon. Be sure you remember." As he returned to the waiting jitney, the vaporous outskirts of Butterscotch seemed less forbidding. He had done right to come, and thank goodness Conrad had teased him, or the poor woman might have been left without the comfort of the Void. Undoubtedly he was needed, and he would do his best.

His satisfaction was still with him when the jitney delivered him inside the Old Station compound. He even tried a joke on one of the human children, about those decorative rock formations. Did they walk in from the desert, one fine night, in search of alcoholic beverages? The youngster took offence.

"They were here when the station was installed. It was all desert then. If there was walking rocks on Mars, messir—" The child drew herself up to her frail, puny height, and glared at him. "We wouldn't any of us *be* here. We'd go home straight away, and leave Mars to the creatures that belongs to this planet."

Boaaz strode off, a chuckle rumbling in his throat. Kids! But when he had eaten, in decent privacy (as a respectable Shet, he would never get used to eating in public), he decided to forgo Conrad's company. The "old mad woman" was too much on his mind, and he found that he shuddered away from the idea of that second visit—yet he'd met Isabel's trouble many times, and never been frightened before.

I am getting old, thought the High Priest.

He turned in early, but he couldn't sleep: plagued by the formless feeling that he had done something foolish, and he would have to pay for it. There were wild, dangerous creatures trying to get into his room, groping at the mellow, pock-marked outer skin of the Old Station; searching for a weak place… Rousing from an uneasy doze, he was compelled to get up and make a transparency, although (as he knew perfectly well) his room faced an inner courtyard, and there are no wild creatures on Mars. Nothing stirred. Several rugged, decorative rocks were grouped right in front of him, oddly menacing under the security lights. Had they always stood there? He thought not, but he couldn't be sure.

The brutes crouched, blind and secretive, waiting for him to lie down again.

"I really *am* getting old," muttered Boaaz. "I must take something for it."

He slept, and found himself once more in the human woman's module. Isabel seemed younger, and far more animated. Confusion fogged his mind, embarrassing him. He didn't know how he'd arrived here, or what they'd been talking about. He was advising her to move into town. It wasn't safe to live so close to the ancient desert. she was not welcome here. She laughed and bared her arm, crying, *I am welcome nowhere!* He saw a mutilation, a string of marks etched into her thin human skin. She thrust the symbols at him: he protested that he had no idea what they meant, but she hardly seemed to care. She was waiting for another visitor, the visitor she had been expecting when he arrived the first time. She had let him in by mistake, he must leave. *They are from another dimension*, she cried, in that hoarse, hopeless voice. *They wait at the gate, meaning to devour. They lived with me once, they may return, with a tiny shift of the Many Dimensions of the Void.*

It gave him a shock when she used the terms of his religion. Was she drawn to the Abyss? Had he begun to give her instruction? The fog in his mind was very distressing, how could he have forgotten something like that? Then he recalled, with intense relief, that she had been to Speranza. She was no stranger to the interstellar world, she must have learnt something of Shet belief… But relief was swamped in a wave of dread: Isabel was looking over his shoulder. He turned, awkward and stiff with age. A presence was taking shape in one of the chairs. It was big as a bear, bigger than Boaaz himself. Squirming tentacles of glistening flesh reached out, becoming every instant more solid and defined—

If it became fully real, if it *touched* him, he would die of horror—

Boaaz woke, thunder in his skull, his whole body pulsing, the blood thickened and backing up in all his veins. Dizzy and sick, on the edge of total panic, he groped for his First Aid kit. He fumbled the mask over his mouth and nostril-slits, with trembling delicates that would hardly obey him, and drew in great gulps of oxygen.

Unthinkable horrors flowed away, the pressure in his skull diminished. He dropped onto his side, making the sturdy extruded couch groan; clutching the mask. It was a dream, he told himself. Just a dream.

Rationally, he knew that he had simply done too much. Overexertion in the thin air of the outskirts had given him nightmares: he must give his acclimatisation treatment more time to become established. He took things easy for the next few days, pottering around in the mining fields just outside the Enclosure—in full Martian EVA gear, with a young staff member for a guide. Pickings were slim (Butterscotch was in the Guidebook); but he made a few pleasing finds.

But the nightmare stayed with him, and at intervals he had to fight the rooted conviction that it had been real. He *had* already made a second visit, there *had* been something terrible, unspeakable… His nights continued to be disturbed. He had unpleasant dreams (never the same as the first), from which he woke in panic, groping for the oxygen that no longer gave much relief.

He was also troubled by a change in the behaviour of the hotel staff. They had been friendly, and unlike the miners they never whispered or stared. Now the children avoided him, and he was no genius at reading human moods, but he was sure there was something wrong. Anu, the lad who took Boaaz out to the desert, kept his distance as far as possible; and barely spoke. Perhaps the child was disturbed by the habit of *looking behind him* that Boaaz had developed. It must look strange, since he was old and it was difficult. But he couldn't help himself.

One morning, when he went to make his usual guilty inspection of that inner courtyard, the station's manager was there: staring at a section of wall where strange marks had appeared, blistered weals like raw flesh-wounds in the ceramic skin.

"Do you know what's causing that effect?" asked Boaaz.

"Can't be weathering, not in here. Bugs in the ceramic, we'll have to get it reconfigured. Can't understand it. It's supposed to last forever, that stuff."

"But the station is very old, isn't it? Older than Butterscotch itself. You don't think the pretty rocks in here had anything to do with the damage?" Boaaz tried a rumble of laughter. "You know, child, sometimes I think they move around at night!"

The rock group was nowhere near the walls. It never was, by daylight.

"I am twenty years old," said the Martian, with an odd look. "Old enough to know when to stay away from bad luck, messir. Excuse me."

He hurried away, leaving Boaaz very puzzled and uneasy.

He had come here to collect minerals, therefore he would collect minerals. What he needed was an adventure, to clear his head. It would be foolhardy to brave the Empty Quarter of Mars in the company of a frightened child: perhaps equally foolhardy to set out alone. He decided he would offer to go exploring with the Aleutian: who took a well-equipped station buggy out into the wild red yonder almost every day.

Conrad would surely welcome this suggestion.

Conrad was reluctant. He spoke so warmly of the dangers, and with such concern for the Shet's age and unsuitable metabolism, that Boaaz's pride was touched. He was old, but he was strong. The nerve of this stripling, suggesting there were phenomena on Mars that an adult male Shet couldn't handle! Even if the stripling *was* a highly experienced young immortal—

"I see you prefer to 'go solo.' I would hate to disturb your privacy. We must compare routes, so that our paths do not cross."

"The virtual tour is very, very good," said the Aleutian. "You can easily and safely explore the ancient 'Arabia Terra' with a fully customised avatar, from the comfort of your hotel room."

"Stop talking like a guidebook," rumbled Boaaz. "I've survived in tougher spots than this. I shall make my arrangements with the station today."

"You won't mind me mentioning that all the sentient biped peoples of Shet are basically aquatic—"

"Not since our oceans shrank, about two million standard years ago. I am not an Aleutian, I have no memory of those days. And if I *were* 'basically aquatic,' that would mean I am already an expert at living outside my natural element."

"Oh well," said Conrad at last, ungraciously. "If you're determined, I suppose it's safer if I keep you where I can see you."

The notable features of the ancient uplands were to the north: luckily the opposite direction from Isabel's dour location. The two buggies set out at sunrise, locked in tandem; Conrad in the lead. As they passed through the particulate barrier of the Enclosure, Boaaz felt a welcome stirring of excitement. His outside cams still showed quiet mining fields, ever-present stromatolites: but already the landscape was becoming more rugged. He felt released from bondage. A few refreshing trips like this, and he would no longer be haunted. He would no longer be compelled to *turn*, feeling those ornate chairs lined up behind him, knowing that the repulsive creature of his dream was taking shape—

"*It's a dusty one*," remarked Conrad, over the intercom. "*Often is, around here, in the northern 'summer.' And there's a storm warning. We shouldn't go far, just a loop around the first buttes, a short EVA and home again....*"

Boaaz recovered himself with a chuckle. His cams showed a calm sky, healthily tinged with blue; his exterior monitors were recording the friendliest conditions known to Mars. "*I'm getting 'hazardous storm probability' at near zero*," he rumbled in reply. "*Uncouple and return if you wish.* I *shall make a day of it*."

Silence. Boaaz felt that he'd won the battle.

Conrad had let slip a few too many knowledgeable comments about Martian mineralogy, in their friendly chats. Of course he wasn't 'purely a tourist': he was a rock hound himself. He'd been scouring the wilds for sites the Guidebook and the Colonial Government Mineral Survey had missed, or undervalued. Obviously he'd found something good, and he didn't want to share.

Boaaz sympathised wholeheartedly. But a little teasing wouldn't come amiss, as a reward for being so untrusting and secretive!

The locked buggies dropped into layered craters, climbed gritty steppes. Boaaz buried himself in strange-sounding English-language wish-lists; compiled long ago, in preparation for this trip. *Hematite nodules, volcanic olivines, exotic basalts, Mössbauer patterns, tektites, barite roses*. But whatever he carried back from the Red Planet, across such a staggering distance, would be treasure—bound to fill his fellow-hounds at home with delight and envy.

*Behind him the empty chairs were ranged in judgement. That which waits at the gates was taking form. Boaaz needed to look over his shoulder but he did not turn. He knew he couldn't move quickly enough, and only the sleek desert-survival fittings of the buggy would mock him—*

Escaping from ugly reverie, he noticed that Conrad was deviating freely from their pre-logged route. Most unsafe! But Boaaz didn't protest. There was no need for concern. They had life support, and Desert Rescue Service beacons that couldn't be disabled. He examined his CGMS maps instead. There was nothing *marked* that would explain

Conrad's diversion: how interesting! What if the Aleutian's find was "significantly anomalous," or commercially valuable? If so, they were legally bound to leave it untouched, beacon it and report it—

But I shan't pry, thought Boaaz. He maintained intercom silence, as did Conrad, until at last the locked buggies halted. The drivers disembarked. The Aleutian, with typical bravado, was dressed as if he'd been optimised before birth for life on Mars: the most lightweight air supply; a minimal squeeze-suit under his Aleutian-style desert thermals. Boaaz removed his helmet.

"I hope you enjoyed the scenic route," said Conrad, with a strange glint in his eye. "I hate to be nannied, don't you? We are not children."

"*Hmm*. I found your navigation, *ahaam*, enlightening."

The Aleutian seemed to be thinking hard about his next move.

"So you want to stop here, my friend?" asked Boaaz, airily. "Good! I suggest we go our separate ways, rendezvous later for the return journey?"

"That would be fine," said Conrad. "I'll call you."

Boaaz rode his buggy around an exquisite tholeiitic basalt group—a little too big to pack. He disembarked, took a chipping and analysed it. The spectrometer results were unremarkable: the sum is greater than the parts. Often the elemental make-up, the age and even the extreme conditions of its creation, can give no hint as to why a rock is beautiful. His customised suit was supple. He felt easier in it than he did in his own, ageing hide: and youthfully *weightless*—without the discomfiting loss of control of weightlessness itself. Not far away he could see a glittering pool, like a mirage of surface water, that might mark a field of broken geodes. Or a surface deposit of rare spherulites. But he wanted to know what the Aleutian had found. He wanted to know so badly that in the end he succumbed to temptation, got back in the buggy and returned to the rendezvous: feeling like a naughty child.

Conrad's buggy stood alone. Conrad was nowhere in sight, and no footprints led away from a nondescript gritstone outcrop. For a moment Boaaz feared something uncanny, then he realised the obvious solution. Still consumed by naughty curiosity, he pulled the emergency release on Conrad's outer hatch. The buggy's life-support generator shifted into higher gear with a whine, but the Aleutian was too occupied to notice. He sat in the body-clasping driver's seat, eyes closed, head immobilised, his skull in the quivering grip of a cognitive scanner field. A compact flatbed scanner nestled in the passenger seat. Under its shimmering virtual dome lay some gritstone fragments. They didn't look anything special, but something about them roused memories. Ancient images, a historical controversy, from before Mars was first settled—

Boaaz quietly maneuvered his bulk over to Conrad's impromptu virtual-lab, and studied the fragments carefully, under magnification.

He was profoundly shocked.

"What are you doing, Conrad?"

The Aleutian opened his eyes, and took in the situation.

The wise immortals stay at home. Immortals who mix with lesser beings are dangerous characters, because they just don't care. Conrad was completely brazen.

"What does it look like? I'm digitising pretty Martians for my scrapbook."

"You aren't *digitising* anything. You have taken *biotic traces* from an unmapped site. You are translating them into *information-space code*, with the intent of removing them from Mars, hidden in your consciousness. *That* is absolutely illegal!"

"Oh, grow up. It's a scam. I'm not kidnapping Martian babies. I'm not even kidnapping ancient fossilised bacteria, just scraps of plain old rock. But fools will pay wonderfully high prices for them. Where's the harm?"

"You have no shame, but this time you've gone too far. You are not a collector, you're a common thief, and I shall turn you in."

"I don't think so, Reverend. We logged out as partners today, didn't we? And you are known as an avid collector. Give me credit, I tried to get you to leave me alone, but you wouldn't. Now it's just too bad."

Boaaz's nostril-slits flared wide, his gullet opened in a blueish gape of rage. He controlled himself, struggling to maintain dignity. "I'll make my own way back."

He resumed his helmet.

Before long his anger cooled. He recognised his own ignoble impulse to spy on a fellow-collector. He recognised that perhaps Conrad's crime was not truly wicked, just very, very naughty. Nevertheless, those controversial "biotic traces" were sacred. The nerve of that young Aleutian! Assuming that Boaaz would be so afraid of being smeared in an unholy scandal, he would make no report—

When this got out! What would the Archbishop think!

Yet what if he *did* keep quiet? Conrad had come to Butterscotch with a plan, no doubt he had ways of fooling the neurological scanners at the spaceport. If Conrad wasn't going to get caught, and nobody was going to be injured—

What should he do?

*That which waits at the gates was taking shape in an empty chair. It waits for those who deny good and evil, and separates them from the Void, forever—*

He could not think clearly. Conrad's shameless behaviour became confused with the nightmares, the disturbed sleep and uneasy wakening. Those marks on the wall of the inner courtyard... He must have room, he could not bear this crowded confinement. He stopped the buggy, checked his gear and disembarked.

The sky of Mars arced above him, the slightly fish-eyed horizon giving it a bulging look, like the whitish cornea of a great, blind eye. Dust suffused the view through his visor with streaks of blood. He was in an eroded crater, which could be a dangerous feature. But no warnings had flashed up, and the buggy wasn't settling. He stepped down: his boots found crust in a few centimeters. Gastropods crept about, in the distance he could see a convocation of trucks: he was back in the mining fields. He watched a small machine as it climbed a stromatolite spire, and "defecated" on the summit.

Inside that spoil-tower, in the moisture and chemical warmth of the chewed waste, the real precursors were at work. All over the mining regions, "stromatolites" were spilling out oxygen. Someday there would be complex life here, in unknown forms. The Martians were bringing a new biosphere to birth, from native organic chemistry alone. Absurd superstition, absurd patience. It made one wonder if the settlers really *wanted* to change their cold, unforgiving desert world—

A shadow flicked across his view. Alarmed, he checked the sky: fast moving cloud meant a storm. But the sky was cloudless; the declining sun cast a rosy, tourist-brochure glow over the landscape. Movement again, in the corner of his eye. Boaaz spun around, a maneuver that almost felled him, and saw a naked, biped figure, with a smooth head and disturbingly spindly limbs, standing a few metres away: almost invisible against the tawny ground. It seemed to look straight at him, but the "face" was featureless—

The eyeless gaze was not hostile. The impossible creature seemed to Boaaz like a shadow cast by the future. A folktale, waiting for the babies who would run around the Martian countryside; and believe in it a little, and be happily frightened. Perhaps I've been afraid of nothing, thought Boaaz, hopefully. After all, what did it *do*, the horrid thing I almost saw in that chair? It reached out to me, perhaps quite harmlessly... But there was something wrong. The eyeless figure trembled, folded down and vanished like spilled water. Now he saw that the whole crater was stirring. Under the surface shadow creatures were fleeing, limbs flashing in the dust that was their habitat. Something had terrified them. Not Boaaz, the thing behind him. It had hunted him down and found him here, far from all help.

Slowly, dreadfully slowly, he turned. He saw what was there.

He tried to speak, he tried to pray. But the holy words were meaningless, and horror seized his mind. His buggy had vanished, the beacon on his chest refused to respond to his hammering. He ran in circles, tawny devils rising in coils from around his feet. He was lost, he would die, and then it would devour him—

Hours later, young Conrad (struck by an uncharacteristic fit of responsibility) came searching for the old fellow, tracking his suit beacon. Night had fallen, deathly cold. The High Priest crouched in a shallow gully, close to the crater where Conrad had spotted his deserted buggy; his suit scratched and scarred as if something had been trying to tear it off him, his parched, gaping screams locked inside his helmet—

The High Priest struggled free from troubling dreams, and was bewildered to find his friend the Aleutian curled informally on the floor beside his bed. "Hallo," said Conrad, sitting up. "I detect the light of reason. Are you with us again, Reverend?"

"What are you doing in my room—?"

"Do you remember anything? How we brought you in?"

"*Ahm, haham*. Overdid it a little, didn't I? Oxygen starvation panic attack, thanks for that, Conrad, most grateful. Must get some breakfast. Excuse me."

"We need to talk."

Boaaz drew his massive head down into his neck-folds, the Shet gesture that stood for refusal, but also submission. "I'm not going to tell anyone."

"I knew you'd see sense. No, this is about something serious. We'll talk this evening. You must be starving, and you need to rest."

Boaaz checked his eyeball-screen, and found that he had lost a day and a night. He ate, rehydrated his hide and retired to bed again: to reflect. The Mighty Void had a place for certain psychic phenomena, but he had no explanation for a "ghost" with teeth and claws, a bodiless thing that could rend carbon fibre... In a state between dream and waking, he trudged again the chance avenue of stromatolites. Vapour hung in the thin air, the spindly towers bent their heads in menace. Isabel Jewel's module waited for him, so charged with fear and dread it was like a ripe fruit, about to burst.

The miners and their families were subdued tonight. The sound of their merrymaking was a dull murmur in the private lounge where Boaaz and the Aleutian met. The residents' bar steward arranged a nested "trolley" of drinks and snacks, and left them alone. Boaaz offered his snifter case, but the Aleutian declined.

"We need to talk," he reminded the old priest. "About Isabel Jewel."

"I thought we were going to discuss my scare in the desert."

"We are."

Strengthened by his reflections, Boaaz summoned up an indignant growl. "I can't discuss my parishioner with you. Absolutely not!"

"Before we managed to drug you to sleep," said Conrad, firmly, "you were babbling, telling us a horrible, uncanny story... You went into detail. You weren't speaking English, but I'm afraid Yarol understood you pretty well. Don't worry, he'll be discreet. The locals don't meddle with Isabel Jewel."

"Yarol?"

"The station manager. Sensible type for a human. You met him the other day in your courtyard, I believe. Looking at some nasty marks on the wall?"

The Shet's mighty head sank between his shoulders. "*Ahaam*, in my delirium, what sort of thing did I say?"

"Plenty."

Conrad leaned close, and spoke in "Silence"—a form of telepathy the immortals only practiced among themselves; or with the rare mortals who could defend themselves against its power. <My friend, you must listen to me. What we share will not leave this room. You're in great danger, and I think you know it.>

The old priest shuddered, and surrendered.

"You underestimate me, and my calling. I am not in *danger!*"

"We'll see about that... Tell me, Boaaz, what is a 'bear'?"

"I have no idea," said the old priest, mystified.

"I thought not. A *bear* is a wild creature native to Earth, big, shaggy, fierce. Rather frightening. Here, catch—"

Inexplicably, the Aleutian tossed a drinking beaker straight at Boaaz: who had to react swiftly, to avoid being smacked in the face—

"Tentacles," said Conrad. "I don't think you find them disgusting, do you? It's an evolutionary quirk. Your people absorbed some wiggly armed ocean creatures into your body-plan, aeons ago, and they became your 'delicates.' Yet what you saw in Isabel Jewel's module was '*a bear with tentacles,*' and it filled you with horror. Just as if you were a human, with an innate terror of snaky-looking things."

Boaaz set the beaker down. "What of it? I don't know what you're getting at. That vision, however I came by it, was merely a nightmare. In the material world I have visited her *once*, and saw nothing at all strange."

"A nightmare, hm? And what if we are dealing with someone whose *nightmares* can roam around, hunt you down and tear you apart?"

Boaaz noticed that his pressure suit was hanging on the wall. The slashes and gouges were healing over (a little late for the occupant, had the attacker persisted!). He vaguely remembered them taking it off him, exclaiming in horrified amazement.

"Tear me apart? Nonsense. I was hysterical, I freely admit. I suppose I must have rolled about, over some sharp rocks."

The Aleutian's black eyes were implacable. "I suppose I'd better start at the beginning… I was intrigued by the scraps you read out from 'Isabel Jewel's' file. Somebody *suspected* of insanity. That's a very grim suspicion, in a certain context. When I saw how changed and disturbed you were, after your parish visit, I instructed my Speranza agent to see what it could dig up about an 'Isabel Jewel,' lately settled on Mars."

"You had no authority to do that!"

"Why not? Everything I'm going to tell you is in the public domain, all my agent had to do was to make the connection—which is buried, but easy to exhume—between 'Isabel Jewel,' and a human called 'Ilia Markham' who was involved in a transit disaster, some thirty or so standard years ago. A starship called *The Golden Bough*, belonging to a company called the World State Line, left Speranza on a scheduled transit to the Blue Torus Port. Her passengers arrived safely. The eight members of the Active Complement, I mean the crew, did not. Five of them had vanished, two were hideously dead. The Navigator survived, despite horrific injuries, long enough to claim they'd been murdered. Someone had smuggled an appalling monster onboard, and turned it loose in the Active Complement's quarters—"

There were chairs, meant for humans, around the walls of the lounge. The Aleutian and the Shet preferred a cushioned recess in the floor. Boaaz noticed that he no longer needed to *look behind him*. That phase was over.

"There are no 'black box' records to consult, after a transit disaster," the Aleutian went on. "Nothing *can* be known about the false duration period. The crew construct a pseudo-reality for themselves, as they guide the ship through that 'interval' when time does not pass: which vanishes like a dream. But the Navigator's accusation was taken seriously. There was an inquiry, and suspicion fell on Ilia Markham, a dealer in antiques. Her trip out to Speranza had been her first transit. On the return 'journey' she insisted on staying awake, citing a mental allergy to the virtual entertainment. A *phobia*, I think humans call it. As you probably know, this meant that she joined the Active Complement, in their pseudo-reality 'quarters.' Yet she was unharmed. She remembered nothing, but she was charged with involuntary criminal insanity, on neurological evidence."

Transit disasters were infrequent, since the new Aleutian ships had come into service; but Boaaz knew of them. And he had heard that casualties whose injuries were not physical were very cruelly treated on Earth.

"What a terrible story. Was there a… Did the inquiry suggest any *reason* why the poor woman's mind might have generated something so monstrous?"

"I see you *do* know what I'm getting at," remarked Conrad, with a sharp look. The old priest's head sank obstinately further, and he made no comment. "Yes, there was something. In her youth Markham had been an indentured servant, the concubine of a rich collector with a nasty reputation. When he died she inherited his treasures, and there were strong rumours she'd helped him on his way. The prosecution didn't accuse her of murder, they just held that she'd been carrying a burden of unresolved trauma—and the Active Complement had paid the price."

"Eight of them," muttered Boaaz. "And one more. Yes, yes, I see."

"The World State Line was the real guilty party, they'd allowed her to travel awake. But it was Ilia Markham who was consigned for life—on suspicion, she was never charged—to a Secure Hospital. *Just in case* she still possessed the powers that had been thrust on her by the terrible energies of the Buonarotti Torus."

"Was there a...? Was there, *ahaam*, any identifying mark of her status?"

"There would be a *tattoo*, a string of symbols, on her forearm, Reverend. You told us, in your 'delirium,' that you'd seen similar marks."

"Go on," rumbled Boaaz. "Get to the end of it."

"Many years later there was a review of doubtful 'criminal insanity' cases. Ilia Markham was one of those released. She was given a new name and shipped off to Mars, with all her assets. They were still a little afraid of her, it seems, although her cognitive scans were normal. They didn't want her or anything she possessed. There's no Buonarotti Torus in Mars orbit: I suppose that was the reasoning."

The old priest was silent, the folds of hide over his eyes furrowed deep. Then his brow relaxed, and he seemed to give himself a shake. "This has been most enlightening, Conrad. I am, in a sense, much relieved."

"You no longer believe you're being pursued by aggressive rocks? Harassed by imaginary Ancient Martians? You understand that, barbaric though it seems, your old mad woman probably should have stayed in that Secure Hospital?"

"I don't admit that at all! In my long experience, this is not the first time I've met what are known as 'psychic phenomena.' I have known effective premonitions, warning dreams; instances of telepathy. This 'haunting' I've suffered, this vivid way I've shared 'Isabel Jewel's' mental distress, will be very helpful when I talk to her again... I *do not* believe in the horrible idea of criminal insanity. The unfortunate few who have been 'driven insane' by a transit disaster are a danger only to themselves."

"I felt the same, but your recent experiences have shaken my common sense." The Aleutian reached to take a snifter, and paused in the act, his nasal flaring in alarm. "Boaaz, dear fellow, *stay away* from her. You'll be safe, and the effects will fade, if you stay away."

Boaaz looked at the ruined pressure suit. "Yet I was not injured," he murmured. "I was only frightened... Now for my side of the story. I am a priest, and the woman is dying. It's her heart, I think, and I don't think she has long. She is in mental agony—as people sometimes are, quite without need, if they believe they have lived an evil life—not in fear of death but of what may come after. I can help her, and it is my duty. After all, we are nowhere near a Torus."

The Aleutian stared at him, no longer seeming at all a mischievous adolescent. The old priest felt buffeted by the immortal's stronger will: but he stood firm. "There are wrongs nobody can put right," said Conrad, urgently. "The universe is more pitiless than you know. *Don't* go back."

"I must." Boaaz rose, ponderously. He patted the Aleutian's sloping shoulder, with the sensitive tips of his right-hand delicates. "I think I'll turn in. Goodnight."

Boaaz had been puzzled by the human woman's insistence that he should return "in ten days, in the evening, at the full moon." The little moons of Mars zipped around too fast for their cycles to be significant. He had looked up the Concordance (Earth's calendar was still important to the colony), and wondered if the related date on Earth had been important to her, in the past.

By the time he left his jitney, in the lonely outskirts of Butterscotch, he'd thought of another explanation. People who know they are dying, closely attuned to their failing bodies, may know better than any doctor when the end will come. She believes she will die tonight, he thought. And she doesn't want to die alone. He quickened his pace, and then turned to look back—not impelled by menace, but simply to reassure himself that the jitney hadn't taken itself off.

He could not see the tiny lights of Butterscotch. The vapours and the swift twilight had caused a strange effect: a mirage of great black hills, or mountains, spread along the horizon. Purple woods like storm clouds crowded at their base, and down from the hills came a pale, winding road. There appeared to be a group of figures moving on it, descending swiftly. The mirage shifted, the perspective changed, and Boaaz was now *among* the hills. Black walls stood on either side of the grey road, the figures rushed towards him from a vanishing point; from an infinite distance at impossible speed. He tried to count them, but they were moving too fast. He realised, astonished, that he was going to be trampled, and even as he formulated that thought they were upon him. They rushed over him, and were swallowed in a greater darkness that swallowed Boaaz too. He was buried, engulfed, overwhelmed by a foul stench and a frightful, suffocating pressure—

He struggled, as if trying to rise from very deep water: and then the pressure was gone. He had fallen on his face. He picked himself up with difficulty, and checked himself and his gear for damage. "The dead do not walk," he muttered. "Absurd superstition!" But the grumbling tone became a prayer, and he could hear his own voice shake as he recited the Consolation. "*There is no punishment, there is only the Void, embracing all, accepting all. The monsters at the gates are illusion. There are no realms beyond death, we shall not be devoured, the Void is gentle...*"

The mirage had dissipated, but the vapours had not. He was positively walking through a fog, and each step was a mysterious struggle, as if he were wading through a fierce running tide. *Here I am for the third time*, he told himself, encouragingly, and then remembered that the second visit had been in a nightmare. A horror went through him: Was he dreaming now? Perhaps the thought should have been comforting, but it was very frightening indeed: and then someone coughed, or choked: not *behind* him, but close *beside* him, invisible in the fog.

Startled, he upped his head and shoulder lights. "Is anybody there?"

The lights only increased his confusion, making a kind of glory on the mist around him. His own shadow was very close, oversized, and optical illusion gave it strange proportions: a distinct neck, a narrow waist, a skeletal thinness. It turned. He saw the thing he had seen in the desert. A human male, with small eyes close-set, a jutting nose, lined cheeks, and a look of such utter malevolence it stopped Boaaz's blood. Its lower jaw dropped. It had far too many teeth, and a terrible, *appallingly* wide gape. It raised its jagged claws and reared towards him. Boaaz screamed into his breather. The monster rushed over him, swamped him and was gone.

It was over. He was alone, shaken in body and soul. The pinprick lights of the town had reappeared behind him: ahead was that avenue of teetering stromatolites. "Horrible mirage!" he announced, trying to convince himself. He was breathing in gasps. The outer lock of the old woman's module stood open, as if she had seen him coming. The inner lock was shut. He opened it, praying that he would find her still alive. Alive, and sharing with him, by some mystery, the nightmare visions of her needless distress; that he knew he could conquer—

The chairs had moved. They were grouped in a circle around the stove in the centre of the room. He counted: yes, he had remembered rightly, there were eight. The "old, mad" human woman sat in her own chair, withered like a crumpled shell, her features still contorted in pain and terror. He could see that she had been dead for some time. The ninth chair was drawn up close to hers. Boaaz saw the impression of a human body, printed in the dented cushions of the back and seat. *It had been here.*

The fallen jaw: Too many teeth. Had it devoured her, was it sated now? And the others, its victims from *The Golden Bough*, what was their fate? To dwell within that horror, forever? He would never know what was real, and what was not. He only knew that he had come too late for Isabel Jewel (he could not think of her as "Ilia Markham"). She had gone to join her company: or they had come to fetch her.

Conrad and the manager of the Old Station arrived about an hour later, summoned by the priest's alarm call. Yarol, who doubled as the town's Community Police Officer, called the ambulance team to take away the woman's remains, and began to make the forensic record—a formality required after any sudden death. Conrad tried to get Boaaz to tell him what had happened.

"I have had a fall," was all the old priest would say. "I have had a bad fall."

Boaaz returned to Opportunity, where his Residence had been successfully decoded. He was in poor health for a while. By the time he'd recovered, Conrad the Aleutian had long moved on to other schemes. But Boaaz stayed on Mars, his pleasant retirement on Shet indefinitely postponed—although he had tendered his resignation to the Archbishop as soon as he could rise from his bed. Later, he would tell people that the death of an unfortunate woman, once involved in a transit disaster, had convinced him that there is an afterlife. The Martians, being human, were puzzled that the good-hearted old "alien" seemed to find this so distressing.

# FIELDS OF GOLD

## RACHEL SWIRSKY

When Dennis died, he found himself in another place. Dead people came at him with party hats and presents. Noise makers bleated. Confetti fell. It felt like the most natural thing in the world.

His family was there. Celebrities were there. People Dennis had never seen before in his life were there. Dennis danced under a disco ball with Cleopatra and Great-grandma Flora and some dark-haired chick and cousin Joe and Alexander the Great. When he went to the buffet table for a tiny cocktail wiener in pink sauce, Dennis saw Napoleon trying to grope his Aunt Phyllis. She smacked him in the tri-corner hat with her clutch bag.

Napoleon and Shakespeare and Cleopatra looked just like Dennis had expected them to. Henry VIII and Socrates and Jesus, too. Cleopatra wore a long linen dress with a jeweled collar, a live asp coiled around her wrist like a bracelet. Socrates sipped from a glass of hemlock. Jesus bobbed his head up and down like a windshield ornament as he ladled out the punch.

Dennis squinted into the distance, but he couldn't make out the boundaries of the place. The room, if it was a room, was large and rectangular and brightly lit from above, like some kind of cosmic gym decorated for prom, complete with drifts of multicolored balloons and hand-lettered poster board signs. On second glance, the buffet tables turned out to be narrow and collapsible like the ones from Dennis's high school cafeteria. Thankfully, unlike high school, the booze flowed freely and the music was actually good.

As Dennis meandered back toward the dance floor, an imposing figure that he dimly recognized as P. T. Barnum clapped him on the back. "Welcome! Welcome!" the balding man boomed.

An elderly lady stood in Barnum's lee. Her face was familiar from old family portraits. "Glad to see you, dear."

"Thanks," said Dennis as the unlikely couple whirled into the crowd.

Things Dennis did not accomplish from his under thirty-five goals list (circa age twelve):

1. Own a jet.
2. Host a TV show where he played guitar with famous singers.
3. Win a wrestling match with a lion.
4. Pay Billy Whitman $200 to eat dirt in front of a TV crew.
5. Go sky diving.
6. Divorce a movie star.

As Dennis listened to the retreating echo of P. T. Barnum's laughter, a pair of cold hands slipped around his waist from behind. He jumped like a rabbit.

"Hey there, Menace," said a melted honey voice.

Dennis turned back into the familiar embrace of his favorite cousin, Melanie. She was the one who'd been born a year and three days before he was, and who'd lived half a mile away when they were kids. She was also the one he'd started dry-humping in the abandoned lot behind Ping's groceries when he was eleven and she was twelve.

"Mel," blurted Dennis.

"Asswipe," Melanie replied.

She stood on her tiptoes to slip a hug around Dennis's neck. She wore cropped jean shorts and a thin white tee that showed her bra strap. She smelled like cheap lotion and cherry perfume. A blonde ponytail swung over her shoulder, deceptively girlish in contrast with her hard eyes and filthy mouth. She was young and ripe and vodka-and-cigarettes skinny in a twenty-one-year-old way, just like she had been the day he was called to view her at the morgue—except that the tracks where her jilted boyfriend had run her over with his jeep were gone, as if they'd never been there at all.

"God," said Dennis. "It's good to see you."

"You're not a punch in the face either."

Dennis reached out to touch the side of her head where the morticians had arranged a makeshift hairpiece made of lilies to cover the dent they hadn't been able to repair in time for the open casket. At first Melanie flinched, but then she eased into his touch, pushing against his hand like a contented cat. Her hair felt like corn silk, the skull beneath it smooth and strong.

She pulled away and led Dennis on a meandering path through the crowd to the drinks table. "How'd you kick it?" she asked conversationally.

"Diabetic coma," said Dennis. "Karen pulled the plug."

"That's not what I heard," said Melanie. "I heard it was murder."

Dennis Halter had married Karen Halter (née Worth) on the twenty-second of November, six months to the day after their college graduation.

Karen was the one who proposed. She bought Dennis a $2,000 guitar instead of an engagement ring. She took him out for heavy carbohydrate Italian (insulin at the ready) and popped the question casually over light beer. "I can still return the guitar if you don't want to," she added.

Karen was an art history major who was being groomed for museum curation. Dennis was an anthropology major (it had the fewest required classes) who was beginning to worry about the fact that he hadn't been discovered yet. Karen was Type A. Dennis's personality begged for the invention of a Type Z.

Melanie was similar to Dennis, personality-wise, except for the mean streak that had gotten her expelled for fist fighting during her senior year of high school. She and Karen had only met once, six months before Karen proposed, at a Halter family Thanksgiving. They didn't need to exchange a word. It was hate at first sight.

"Hillbilly whore," Karen called Melanie, though not to her face.

Lacking such compunction, Melanie had called Karen a "control-freak cunt" over pecan pie. She drunk dialed Dennis three weeks later to make sure he hadn't forgotten her opinion. "When that bitch realizes you're never going to change, she's going to have your balls on a platter. If you marry her, I swear I'll hand her the knife myself."

Melanie died instead.

"Murder?" said Dennis. "No, I wanted her to pull the plug. It was in my living will. I never wanted to live my life as a vegetable."

"Unless it was a couch potato, huh?"

Melanie spoke with the too-precise diction of an overcompensating drunk. Her tone was joking, but held a vicious undercurrent.

She flailed one hand at Dennis's spare tire. The gin she was pouring with her other definitely wasn't her first. Probably not her fourth either.

"Worked out for you, didn't it, Menace the Dennis?" she continued. "Spent your life skipping church only to luck out in the end. Turns out we all go to the same place. Saint, sinner, and suicide."

Dennis's jaw clenched. "I didn't commit suicide."

"Didn't say you did. Sinner."

"And you weren't?"

Melanie poured three fingers of rum into a second Solo cup and went to add Coke. Dennis grabbed the two-liter bottle out of her hand.

"Can't drink that with alcohol," he said, irritated, remembering that bender when he was fifteen and she'd promised him it wouldn't matter whether his mixers were diet or regular. He'd ended up in ketoacidosis.

Melanie rolled her eyes. "Think your body works the way it used to? You're dead, moron."

"Fine," said Dennis, annoyance clashing with embarrassment. "Give it to me then."

He rescued the Solo cup and poured a long stream of Coke. Melanie watched reproachfully, gulping her gin.

"You were okay before you started dating that stuck-up bitch," she said. "Had time for a beer and a laugh. Maybe you deserved what that cunt did to you."

"I told you. It was in my will."

"That's not what I'm talking about, jerkwad."

"What *are* you talking about?"

For a moment, Melanie looked simultaneously sly and uncomfortable, as though she were going to spill the beans on something important. Then she shook her head, ponytail whipping, and returned to her rant. "If you'd kept doing me, maybe I wouldn't have ended up with Al. Maybe he wouldn't have gone off the deep-end when I broke it off. I could still be alive. I could be the one in that fancy condo."

"Melanie," said Dennis. "Shut up."

Melanie made to throw an honest-to-God punch. Gin splashed over her shirt and onto the floor. "Look at this!" She gestured broadly, spilling even more. "What the hell is wrong with you?"

Before Dennis could answer, she stormed off in a huff, rapidly disappearing into the mass of people.

When he was alive, Dennis had told people he'd married Karen because she was his type of girl. He hadn't told them that one skinny blonde with a D-cup was basically as good as another.

When he was alive, Dennis had told people he'd married Karen because she was driven and smart and successful. He hadn't told them she made him feel inferior by comparison, sometimes because she told him he was.

When he was alive, Dennis had told people he married Karen because he was a simple man with simple needs. He hadn't told them he kept those simple needs satisfied by fucking around at least twice a year.

When he was alive, Dennis had told people he'd married Karen because she was the kind of girl who knew what she wanted and went after it. Time was like water in Dennis's hands, always flowing through his fingers, leaving him damp but never sated. Karen drank from the stream of time.

She made things happen.

One of the things she made happen was getting married. Well, what else was Dennis going to do? It wasn't as if he had plans. Okay, he did have plans, but diamond albums didn't just fall into your lap.

Karen proposed and it made sense, Dennis had told people when he was alive. That's why they got married.

That part was true.

Things Dennis did not accomplish from his under thirty-five goals list (circa age nineteen):

1. Sign with a label.
2. Hit the charts.
3. Get into *Rolling Stone*.
4. Earn $1,000,000.
5. Have at least one girl/girl threesome.
6. Screw Libby Lowell, his roommate's girlfriend.
7. Play in concert with Ted Nugent, Joe Satriani, and Eddie Van Halen.
8. Get recognized on the street by someone he'd never met.

Dennis stared after Melanie in minor shock. Somehow he'd figured this kind of social terrorism would be one of the things that ended in the stillness of the grave.

But if anyone was going to keep making incoherent, drunken rants fourteen years after going into the ground, it was Melanie. She'd always been a pain in the ass when she was drunk. She'd introduced Dennis to alcohol back when she first learned to pick the lock on her father's liquor cabinet with a bobby pin. They'd experimented together to figure out just how much sugar Dennis could ingest with his booze without overtaxing his liver.

From day one, Melanie had drunk until she couldn't see straight and then used it as an excuse to say exactly what she thought. Not that she wasn't a fun drunk. Some of the best nights of his life were the ones they'd spent together as drunk teenagers. She'd start out hurling insults until he left in disgust, only to show up on his porch at three a.m., laughing and apologizing and determined to convince him to join her in making prank calls and harassing the neighbors' cows.

She was Melanie. She was the kind of girl who goaded a guy into running over her with his Jeep. But it was hard to stay mad. Especially now that both of them were dead.

The smell of old tobacco arrived, along with a cold hand patting Dennis's shoulder. Dennis was startled to find that both belonged to his late Uncle Ed, Melanie's father.

"Always thought we should have spent more time raising her right," Ed said.

The old man looked just as hangdog as he had in the moment twenty years ago when he'd fallen off his roof while cleaning the gutters. There he'd been, his feet starting to slide, but he hadn't looked scared so much as wrung out and regretful, as if someone had just told him the Christmas pie he'd been looking forward to was gone and he'd have to make do with fruit cake instead.

He was wearing his best brown suit with a skinny, maroon tie. Slicked back hair exaggerated his widow's peak. The weak chin and expressive eyebrows were family traits, although Ed had a lean, wiry build unlike most Halter men, on account of a parasitic infection he'd contracted during his military days that left him permanently off his feed.

Uncle Ed. Christ. Back home, everyone Dennis's age cussed blue when they were on their own, but even Mel had kept a civil tongue in front of the 'rents. "How much did you hear?" he asked.

"'Bout all of it."

"I'm sorry."

Ed gave a rueful shrug. "You have no idea what she gets up to. The other day she stripped naked in front of everyone and started sucking off President Garfield."

"Shit," said Dennis without thinking. "Uh, I mean—"

"Sounds right to me. She sure can be a little shit."

Suddenly, a grin split Ed's melancholy face. It was the same grin he'd flashed when fourteen-year-old Dennis let slip that he'd gone through all the senior cheerleaders one by one until Veronica Steader agreed to be his homecoming date.

"Of course, I was into Mary Todd Lincoln at the time," Ed's leer widened to show even more teeth. "Good woman." He slapped Dennis on the back. "You get yourself one of those. You've had enough of the other kind."

Dennis had never watched his diet very carefully. Not as carefully as he needed to anyway. Other kids got to eat Doritos and Oreos at lunch and they didn't even have to worry about it. When Dennis was eight, that righteously pissed him off.

It didn't piss him off enough that he tried to eat exactly the way they did. He wasn't stupid. But it pissed him off enough that he acted a little reckless, a little foolish. Always just a little, though, so that whatever happened, he could plausibly claim—to everyone including himself—that there was nothing deliberate about it.

Eventually, even he believed he was too irresponsible to take care of himself.

The party had moved on to the stage where everyone was too tired to be gregarious but also too drunk to stop partying. Everyone had gathered into small, intense clusters, leaning urgently toward each other to share dramatic whispers, hands cutting the air with emphasis. From time to time, an overloud exclamation punctured the susurration.

Dennis surveyed the crowd, identifying faces. There was Blackbeard with Grandpa Avery and a buck-toothed redhead. And over there was that Chinese guy who used to live down the street, chatting with Moses and Aunt Phyllis. Most of the groups consisted entirely of strangers.

These were some of the things Dennis picked up as he wandered through the crowd:

1. Death had its own time frame in which connected events bent around mortal time to touch each other. In dead time, the assassina-

tion of Archduke Ferdinand had coincided with the deaths of millions of World War Two soldiers. For reasons widely subject to speculation, so had the sinking of the RMS *Titanic* and the deaths of several big game huntsmen touring French colonies in Africa.

2. The dead also had their own vocabulary. Recently dead people were called rotters or wormies. People who'd been dead a long time were called dusties. Dusties tended to stay in their own enclaves, secluded from the modern ideas and inventions that scared them. Famous dead people were called celebs and they:

3. were considered by popular opinion to be fakes. This allegation caused Blackbeard to roar with anger and threaten to march the speaker off a plank. It was pointed out to him that this was the sort of behavior that had created the theory that celebs were fakes in the first place. Celebrities conformed too closely to their legends. Cleopatra was always seductive and never bored or put-upon. Lincoln declaimed nonstop poetic speeches. And hadn't someone spotted Lady Macbeth earlier that evening when she wasn't even real?

4. Reality, it seemed, was a contentious issue. Mortality shaped the living world by imposing limits. In the limitless afterlife, the shape of things deformed. That was one reason dead people came to parties. Rotters still carried an impression of the living world. It was like going home again for a little while. Besides, there was good food, and who didn't like watching General Sherman march up and down the linoleum, threatening to burn Atlanta?

While Dennis pondered these new pieces of information, he also picked up a number of more personal things. He had an intuitive sense of where these latter were leading, though, and it wasn't somewhere he wanted to go. Consequently, he performed the time-tested mental contortions he'd developed as a third grader who ate too much sugar while pretending he hadn't done anything wrong. Dennis was a master of self-denial; he didn't even let himself realize there was something he wouldn't let himself realize.

For instance:

1. Whenever Dennis passed a group of strangers, they interrupted their conversations to peer as he passed, and then returned to their huddles to whisper even more urgently.

2. Their renewed whispers were punctuated with phrases like "Do you think he deserved it?" and "Poor son of a bitch."

3. At a certain point, they also started saying, "At least the wife got

what's coming to her."

4. These last remarks started occurring at approximately the same time as people began disappearing to attend another party.

As the crowd thinned, Dennis finally located someone standing alone, a very drunk flight attendant staring blankly at a tangle of streamers. On being pressed, she identified herself as Wilda. She was unbelievably hot, like a stewardess from a fifties movie, in her mid-to-late twenties with long, straight blonde hair, and a figure that filled out all the tailored curves of her uniform.

The hint of an exotic perfume was all but drowned out by the stench of alcohol. She wasn't currently crying, but tears had streaked her mascara.

Dennis decided to pick her up.

"Melancholy stage?" he asked.

She spoke as if her lips were numb. "What's the point? On this side?"

"Of being melancholy? I didn't know there was ever a point."

"Mortality," she said gravely.

Her expression altered ever so slightly. Dennis tried to echo back an appropriate seriousness.

"I knew a man once," she went on. "Died in the same crash as me. An actor. Very famous. I was so nervous when I poured his in-flight drink I thought I'd spill it. He asked for orange juice."

Dennis gestured back toward the buffet tables. "Do *you* want a drink?"

She ignored him. "After we died, he never spoke a word. Not a word. He… his mouth would open and this sound would come out… eeeeeeeeeee… like a dying refrigerator…"

She looked at Dennis urgently. Her eyes focused briefly. They were weird, electric blue, like a sky lit up by lightning.

"He was grieving for himself, I think. Or maybe he just used up all his words in the world? And when he died, he was just so happy to be quiet that he never wanted to talk again?" She blinked, slowly, her wet mascara smudging more black beneath her eyes. "It's like the celebs. You know?"

"Would you like to kiss me?" Dennis asked.

"I bet the real dead celebrities are nothing special. They probably blend in. Like my friend. But the fake ones, I think they're made from a kind of collective pressure. None of us lived our lives the way we wanted to. It gets mixed up, all our needs, our unsatisfied desires, the things we wanted to be back when we were alive. Beautiful. Famous. The best of our potential. We make the celebs to be like that for us. Since we can't."

Wilda gestured vaguely toward the crowd. Dennis turned to see Benjamin Franklin demonstrating his kite, which rapidly became tangled with the multicolored balloons. Marilyn Monroe struggled with her skirt while standing over an air-conditioning vent tucked next to some bleachers. Gandhi sat in the middle of a group positioned near the buffet tables, pointedly not eating.

"You should stay away from them," said Wilda softly. "They're bright and crazy. They suck you down."

Dennis turned back to look at her beautiful, tear-stained face. "I'd rather be with you anyway."

She blinked at him, too lost in her own drunkenness to hear. Or maybe she just didn't believe him? Dennis glanced over his shoulder at Marilyn, ripe and coy, dark-outlined eyes sparkling. Something dark and furious clenched in his stomach. He was only thirty-five! Marilyn made him so choked up with jealousy he couldn't breathe.

He turned back toward Wilda and leaned in to dab some of the liner from beneath her eyes. She started toward his embrace but got tangled up with her own feet and started to fall. Dennis caught her before she could hit the floor.

She looked up at him, smiling vaguely. "I wanted to be a gymnast. You know? I was good," she said, and then, "Do you think it's cheating?"

"What?" murmured Dennis.

"My husband's still alive."

"So's my wife."

"What if she weren't? Would it be cheating then?"

"I don't know. I wasn't that faithful when we were both alive."

"Neither was I."

Wilda's voice cracked like ice. Tears filled her eyes, colorless like vodka. Dennis looked down at her left hand where she wore a tan line but no ring.

"I don't like being dead," said Wilda.

"I'm sorry," said Dennis.

He held her, silently, until she recovered enough to stand on her own. "I'm sorry, too," she said at last. "I should go to the other party."

Dennis tried to fake a smile. "Don't drink too much while you're there."

Wilda reached out to touch his shoulder. Her fingertips were frozen. "When you figure it out," she said, "try not to be too sad."

She faded away.

A few of the times Dennis cheated on Karen:

1)The coed who got stuck in the Dallas airport after her flight was canceled who he wooed with four margaritas, his best dozen dirty jokes, and a rendition of Sting's "Desert Rose."

2)The bartender in Phoenix who'd just been dumped by her fiancé and said she needed to know what it was like with a guy who could commit.

3)The drunk divorcée from the Internet ad who got on the hotel bed and dropped her pants without even a word to acknowledge he was there.

A few of the things Dennis pretended not to notice about his marriage:

1) The way Karen's sense of humor about other women had changed. When they were younger, if she saw a pretty blonde who was about her shape walking past them in the mall, she'd say, "I bet she's your type." If she was in a teasing mood, she'd whisper about all the things she and the other girl would do to Dennis if they had him at their mercy. In recent days, her eyes had started getting hard when they even saw blonde girls on TV. She'd angle her face away from him, trying to hide her disgust.

2)How Karen no longer laughed indulgently when he forgot things. She still took care of him: she did his laundry, she found his keys, she rescheduled his doctor's appointments. But she moved through the actions mechanically, her blank expression never flickering.

3)And then there was the worst thing, the one Dennis had taken the most pains to hide from himself—the flicker he'd seen when Karen came home exhausted from a late night's work and found him still awake at two a.m., sitting on the couch and eating beans out of a can. She picked up the dishes he'd left on the coffee table and carried them to the sink, grumbling to herself so faintly he could hardly hear it, "It's like I'm his mother." He looked up and caught the brief flash on her face. It was the same emotion he'd heard in her voice: contempt.

The morning of November nineteenth was three days before their thirteenth anniversary and two months and five days before Dennis's thirty-fifth birthday. Karen Halter (née Worth) proposed they stay in that Friday night to celebrate both occasions. She proposed an evening of drinking and making love. Dennis liked having sex when he was drunk, and although it wasn't Karen's preference, she tried to indulge him from time to time. She knew it reminded him of being young.

Fifteen years ago, when they'd started dating, Karen had carefully reviewed the guidelines for mixing type one diabetes and alcohol. The liver was involved in both processing alcohol and regulating blood sugar, and consequently, a type one diabetic who got carelessly drunk could preoccupy his liver with the one so that it couldn't manage the other. Glucose levels required a tricky balance. If they went too high, they could damage a variety of systems. If they went too low, one could become hypoglycaemic or even fall into a coma.

It was trivial to give Dennis more insulin than he needed. She let him inject himself, just in case someone checked later. Not that they would. Everyone knew Dennis was too irresponsible to take care of himself.

She worried when he started puking, but he didn't suspect anything. He just thought he was drunk.

The sleeping pills were his idea. He was feeling too sick to get to sleep on his own. He asked if he could borrow one of her Ambien and before she could say yes or no, he'd pulled the bottle out of the medicine cabinet. She watched him drunkenly struggle to unscrew the lid.

She hadn't meant to go this far. She'd wanted to shock him. She'd wanted him to see how bad things could get and grow the fuck up. Yes, she wanted him to suffer a little, too, just so he'd know what it felt like.

If she let him take the pill, it'd be more than that. He wouldn't be awake to monitor his condition. He wouldn't be able to call an ambulance when things started going really wrong. He'd get sicker than she'd intended. He could even die.

Karen had matched Dennis drink for drink. No one would suspect her of wrongdoing. At worst, they'd think she'd also been too drunk to notice his symptoms.

With a shock, it occurred to Karen that maybe she'd been planning this all along. Maybe she'd been slowly taking the steps that could lead to Dennis's death without admitting to herself that was what she was doing. She knew how self-denial worked by now; she'd been married to Dennis for thirteen years, after all.

She eased the bottle from his hand. "Let me do that," she said, unscrewing the cap. She poured out two pills: one for him and one for her.

Now neither of them could call for help.

In the morning, memory clear and heart pounding, Karen called 911 in a genuine panic. She rode with Dennis in the ambulance, weeping real tears. She cried because she'd become a murderess and she didn't want to see herself that way. She also cried because she wasn't sorry she'd done it and that scared her even more.

The doctors proclaimed the coma unusually severe. Brain damage had occurred. Over the next several weeks, using sterile, equivocal comments, they made it clear that there was no hope. They would need a decision.

Karen had set herself on this path. There was no escaping it. Dennis's living will was clear. She told them to pull the plug.

During the weeks when Dennis lay comatose, Karen began having nightmares. She researched bad dreams on the Internet and confirmed that anxiety produced an increase in negative dream imagery. Nothing to be concerned about. Except she kept dreaming about the strangest thing—that trashy cousin Dennis had admitted to fucking when he was a kid. They'd gone to her funeral a few months before Karen proposed. Dennis had bent over the casket and wept for nearly a quarter of an hour. Karen could understand why he was upset; the girl was family. But deep in her gut, whether it was fair or not, she couldn't help being appalled. He was mourning his partner in incest.

Afterward, at the visitation, various family members asked her to stand next to the big, glossy photograph of the deceased they'd hung on the wall. "You look just like her," everyone said, which made Karen even more uncomfortable. She tried to laugh off her reaction as indignance that she'd ever dress like that, but she had a niggling feeling there was something more profound. She *did* look eerily like the girl, the same close-set eyes, the same blunt chin, the same shade of blonde hair. It was as if Dennis was trying to re-create the relationship he'd had when he was eleven, as if it didn't matter to him that Karen had her own thoughts and feelings and personality, as long as she looked like his first, forbidden love.

In Karen's dreams, the blonde cousin had a knife. She chased Karen down winding asphalt streets, upraised metal shining in the shadows. "I don't care what I said," she growled. "I'm not going to let you cut his balls off. I'll cut you first."

The day Karen told them to pull the plug, she woke with her heart pounding so hard that she thought she was going to have to check into the hospital herself. The feeling faded when she went down to give the decision in person, but intensified again as she got in her car to drive home. She'd told them she couldn't handle staying to watch Dennis die, which was true, but not for the reasons they supposed.

Outside, thick, dingy clouds of smog dimmed the sunlight to a sickly brown. Headlights and taillights glared in Karen's windshield, a fraction too bright.

Horns screamed in the wake of near misses. Karen watched carefully, mapping out the traffic in her mind's eye, making sure she didn't veer out of her narrow lanes or crash into the broken-down SUVs on the side of the road. She was the kind of woman who had memorized the safety manual that came with her vehicle, and could recite all the local laws regarding child safety seats even though she'd never had any children in her car.

Despite her meticulousness, as Karen pulled into the intersection after waiting for the green, she failed to see the blonde woman in a white t-shirt jogging into the crosswalk. She pounded the breaks and yanked on the steering wheel, but it was already too late. Rubber screeched. Metal crunched against metal. The car next to hers careened sideways with the impact. Karen fell toward the windshield, her airbag failing to deploy, the steering wheel breaking against her head.

It took Karen almost three weeks to die, but in the land of the dead, time twisted around itself to join connected events. So it was only a few hours into Dennis's party that Karen's began, and his gossiping guests faded away to attend the newest scandal.

Things Dennis did not accomplish from his under thirty-five goals list (circa age thirty-four):

1) Start another band.
2) Play some gigs in the area.
3) Get his sugar under control.
4) Be nicer to Karen.
5) Stop cheating.
6) Go to the gym.

Dennis's self-denial had finally reached its breaking point. He ran between the fading guests. "How do I get there? You have to show me! I have to see her!"

They winked out like stars from a greying dawn sky, not one of them letting slip what he needed to know.

The empty gym, if it was a gym, seemed to be disappearing on the edges. Perhaps it was. The dead people had talked about imposing their own shapes on the limitless afterlife. Maybe shapelessness was taking over.

One spot near the buffet tables remained bright, a fraction of the dance floor underneath the disco ball. Uncle Ed stood alone in the middle, fiddling with the coin slot in the juke box.

He turned as Dennis approached. "I wanted 'Young Love,'" he said, "but they've only got 'After You've Gone.' Not worth a quarter." He sighed. "Oh, well. That's the afterlife, I guess."

The juke box lit up as the coin slid into its machinery. It whirred, selecting a record. The bright, slightly distorted strains of a song Dennis vaguely recognized as a hit from the forties began to play.

Ed selected a pastel blue balloon and began to whirl it around like a dance partner. Dennis stood tensely, arms crossed.

"Why didn't you tell me?"

Ed dipped the balloon. "About what?"

"About Karen."

"Figured you'd find out sooner or later. No sense ruining a perfectly good party until you did."

"I'd have wanted to know."

"Sorry then."

"How do I get over there? I've got to talk to her."

"You can't."

"I've got to!"

"She doesn't want you. You can't go bothering someone who doesn't want you. That's one of the rules we agree on. Otherwise someone could stalk you forever." Ed gave a mild shrug. "I was used badly by a woman once, you know."

Dennis glared silently.

"My first wife, Lilac," Ed went on. "Not Melanie's mother. Lilac died before you all were born. Your mom never liked her."

"Mom never liked Karen either."

"A perceptive woman, your mother. Well, things were good with me and Lilac for a while. We spent my whole party making out. Afterward, we found some old Scottish castle out with the dusties and rolled around in the grass for longer than you spent alive. It didn't last long, though. Relatively. See, while I was still alive, she'd already met another dead guy. They'd been together for centuries before I kicked it. She was just curious about what it would be like to be with me again. Near broke my heart."

"Ed," Dennis said. "Karen murdered me. I have to know why."

Ed stopped dancing and released the balloon. It flew upward and disappeared into grey.

"Have to?" Ed asked. "When you were alive, you had to have food and water. What's 'have to' mean to you anymore?"

"Ed, please!"

"All right, then, I'll take a gander. I've been dead a long time, but I bet I know a few things. Now, you didn't deserve what Karen did to you. No one deserves that. But you had your hand in making it happen. I'm not saying you didn't have good qualities. You could play a tune and tell a joke, and you were usually in a good humor when you weren't sulking. Those are important things. But you never thought about anyone else. Not only wouldn't you stir yourself to make a starving man a sandwich, but you'd have waited for him to bring you one before you stirred yourself to eat. One thing I've learned is people will give you a free lunch from time to time, but only so long as they think you're trying. And if you don't try, if they get to thinking you're treating them with disdain, well then. Sometimes they get mean."

"I didn't treat Karen with disdain," Dennis said.

Ed blinked evenly.

"It's not that I don't think about other people," Dennis said. "I just wanted someone to take care of me. The whole world, everything was so hard. Even eating the wrong thing could kill you. I wanted someone to watch out for me, I guess. I guess I wanted to stay a kid."

"You married a problem solver," said Ed. "Then you became a problem."

When Dennis thought about Ed, he always thought about that moment when he watched him fall off the roof. Failing that, he thought of the mostly silent man who sat in the back of family gatherings and was always first to help out with a chore. But now, with his words still stinging, Dennis remembered a different Uncle Ed, the one who'd always been called to finish off the barn cats who got sick, the one everyone relied on to settle family disputes because they knew he wouldn't play favorites no matter who was involved.

Ed didn't look so much like the man who'd fallen off the roof anymore. His wrinkles had tightened, his yellowing complexion brightened to a rosy pink. His hair was still slicked back from his forehead with Brilliantine, but now there were generous, black locks of it.

He straightened his suit jacket and it became a white tee-shirt, snug over faded jeans. He grinned as he stuck his hands in his pockets. His teeth were large and straight and shiny white.

"I always figured we'd have kids," Dennis said. "I can't do that here, can I? And the band, I was always going to get started with that again, as soon as I got things going, as soon as I found the time..."

Dennis trailed off. The juke box spun to a stop, clicking as it returned the record to its place. Its lights guttered for a moment before flicking off.

"I'm dead," said Dennis, plaintively. "What do I do?"

Ed spread his hands toward the gym's grey edges. "Hop from party to party. Find a cave with the dusties. Get together with a girl and play house until the continents collide. Whatever you want. You'll find your way."

A newsboy cap appeared in Ed's hand. He tugged it on and tipped the brim.

"Now if you'll excuse me," he continued. "I need to pay my respects."

"To my murderer?"

"She's still family."

"Don't leave me alone," Dennis pleaded.

Ed was already beginning to fade.

Dennis sprinted forward to grab his collar.

When Dennis was four, he found his grandfather's ukulele in the attic, buried under a pile of newspapers. It was a four-string soprano pineapple made of plywood with a spruce soundboard. Tiny figures of brown women in grass skirts gyrated across the front, painted grins eerily broad.

The year Dennis turned six, his parents gave him a bike with training wheels for Christmas instead of the guitar he asked for. After a major tantrum, they wised up and bought him a three-quarter-sized acoustic with two-tone lacquer finish in red and black. It was too big, but Dennis eventually got larger. The songbook that came with it included chords and lyrics for "Knockin' on Heaven's Door," "Leaving on a Jet Plane," and "Yellow Submarine."

The summer when Dennis was fifteen, he wheedled his grandparents into letting him do chores around their place for $2.50 an hour until he saved enough to buy a used Fender and an amp. He stayed up until midnight every night for the next six months playing that thing in the corner of the basement his mother had reluctantly cleared out next to the water heater. He failed science and math, and only barely squeaked by with a D in English, but it was worth it.

The guitar Karen bought him when they got engaged was the guitar of his dreams. A custom Gibson Les Paul hollow-body with a maple top, mahogany body, ebony fret board, cherryburst finish, and curves like Jessica Rabbit. He hadn't been able to believe what he was seeing. Just looking at it set off strumming in his head.

As she popped the question, Karen ran her index finger gently across the abalone headstock inlay. The tease of her fingertip sent a shiver down his spine. It was the sexiest thing he'd ever seen.

Everything blurred.

Dennis and Ed reappeared in the rooftop garden of the museum where Karen had worked. It looked the way it did in summer, leafy shrubs and potted trees rising above purple, red and white perennials. The conjured garden was much larger than the real one; it stretched out as far as Dennis could see in all directions, blurring into verdant haze at the horizon.

Seurat stood at his easel in front of a modernist statue, stabbing at the canvas with his paintbrush. Figures from Karen's family and/or the art world strolled between ironwork benches, sipping martinis. Marie Antoinette, in *robe à la Polonaise* and *pouf*, distributed *petit fours* from a tray while reciting her signature line.

Dennis glimpsed Wilda, seemingly recovered from her melancholia, performing a series of acrobatic dance moves on a dais.

And then he saw Karen.

She sat on a three-legged stool, sipping a Midori sour as she embarked on a passionate argument about South African modern art with an elderly critic Dennis recognized from one of her books. She looked more sophisticated than he remembered. Makeup made her face dramatic, her eyebrows shaped into thin arches, a hint of dark blush sharpening her cheekbones. A beige summer gown draped elegantly around her legs. There was a vulnerability in her eyes he hadn't seen in ages, a tenderness beneath the blue that had vanished years ago.

Dennis felt as if it would take him an eternity to take her in, but even dead time eventually catches up.

Ed, struggling to pry Dennis's fingers off his collar, gave an angry shout. Both Karen and the old man beside her turned to look straight at them.

Ed twisted Dennis's fingers until one of them made a snapping sound. Shocked, Dennis dropped his grip.

"Christ!" said Ed, glaring at Dennis as he rubbed his reddened throat. "What the hell is wrong with you?" He turned away from Dennis as if washing his hands of him, tipped his hat to Karen, and then stalked off into the green.

"How are you here?" Karen sounded more distressed than angry. "They told me you couldn't be."

"I hitched a ride."

"But that shouldn't matter. They said—"

Karen quieted in the wake of the noise from the crowd that had begun to form around them. Ordinary people and celebs, strangers and friends and family and neighbors, all gossiping and shoving as they jockeyed for front row views.

The elderly art critic straightened and excused himself to the safety of the onlookers. Dennis stepped into his position.

"Maybe you let me in," Dennis said. "Maybe you really wanted me here."

Karen gave a strangled laugh. "I want you out and I want you in. I can't make up my mind. That sounds like the shape of it."

"You murdered me," said Dennis.

"I murdered you," said Karen.

Behind them, Dennis heard the noise of a scuffle, some New Jersey guido pitting himself against H. L. Mencken.

"I didn't mean to do it," Karen continued. "I don't think I did, at least."

Dennis swallowed.

"I'm sorry," Karen said. "Sorrier than I can tell you."

"You're only saying that because you're dead."

"No. What would be the point?"

Dennis heard the guido hit the ground as H. L. Mencken declared his victory in verse. A small round of applause ended the incident as the throng refocused on Dennis and Karen. Dennis had thought he'd want to hit her or scream at her. Some part of her must have wanted him to do that, must have known she deserved to be punished. He wondered if anyone would try to stop him if he attacked her. He got the impression no one would.

"I hate you," Dennis told her. It was mostly true.

"Me, too," said Karen.

"I didn't when we were alive. Not all the time, anyway."

"Me, too."

They both fell silent. Straining to overhear, the crowd did, too. In the background, there were bird calls, the scent of daisies, the whoosh of traffic three stories below.

"I don't think," said Dennis, "that I want to be near you anymore."

So, according to the rules of the land of the dead, he wasn't.

Things Dennis did accomplish from his under thirty-five goals lists (various ages):

1)Eat raw squid.

2)Own a gaming console.

3)Star in an action movie.* (*After a bad day when he was twenty-four, Dennis decided to broaden the definition of "star" to include his role as an extra in *Round Two*.)

4)Watch Eric Clapton live.

5)Seduce a girl by writing her a love song.

6)Screw Pamela Kortman, his roommate's ex-girlfriend.

7)Clean out the garage to make a practice space.

8)Play all night, until dawn, without noticing the time.

He was back in the gym. A single bank of fluorescent lights whined as they switched back on. Only one of the bulbs turned on, casting an eerie glow that limned Dennis's body against the dark.

A figure crept out of the shadows. "Hey."

Dennis turned toward the voice. He saw the outline of a girl. At first he thought it was the stewardess, Wilda. No, he thought, it's—is it Karen? But as the figure came closer, he realized it was Melanie.

"Hey Mel," said Dennis.

"Hey Asswipe," said Mel, but her voice didn't have any edge to it.

"I thought you were at Karen's party."

"That bitch? I wouldn't go to her party if she was the last rotter. I've been waiting here so I could catch you alone."

She crept even closer, until he could smell the sourness of her breath.

"I heard what my dad said. I wanted to say I'm sorry. He was pretty hard on you. You didn't deserve it. I was going to come out and give him a piece of my mind, but I didn't know how you'd feel after all that stuff I said."

She shifted her weight nervously from foot to foot.

"You didn't deserve that either," she said. "I'm sorry."

"It's okay," Dennis said.

"No, really."

"No, really."

Melanie smiled. Her expression looked so young and genuine that Dennis finally felt the fist around his heart begin to relax.

He remembered the late nights when he and Melanie had been kids, when she'd turned up on his porch and begged him to go with her to steal cigarettes or throw aftershave at Billy Whitman's window. The same mischief inflected her pose now: her quirked smile, sparkling eyes, and restless fingers.

"Do you think a man could live his whole life trying to get back to when he was eleven?" Dennis asked.

Melanie shrugged. She was twelve now, young and scrappy, pretty in pink but still the first kid on the block to throw a punch.

"Do you want to go play in the lot behind Ping's?" she asked.

Dennis looked down at himself. He saw the red and purple striped shirt he wore every day when he was eleven years old except when his mom took it away for the laundry.

Tall, dry grass whipped the backs of his knees. It rustled in the breeze, a rippling golden wave.

"Yeah," he said.

He reached for her hand. Her fingers curled into his palm.

"We don't ever have to come back if we don't want to," she said. "We can go as far as we want. We can keep going forever."

The sun hung bright overhead, wisps of white drifting past in the shapes of lions and race cars and old men's faces. It smelled of fresh, growing things, and a bare hint of manure. A cow lowed somewhere and a truck rumbled across the asphalt. Both sounds were equidistant, a world away.

"Come on," said Dennis.

They ran. She led the way, long sandaled feet falling pigeon-toed in the soil. Dennis felt the breath flow sweet and easy through his lungs.

Someday they'd stop. Someday they'd fall exhausted to the ground and sleep curled up together in the dirt. Someday they'd pass into town where Dennis's father was arguing over the price of wood while Uncle

Ed stood in front of the hardware store, sipping lemonade. Someday they might even run straight through the universe, all the way back to the weird land of death where they'd chat with Descartes about the best way to keep mosquitoes off in summer.

For now, their feet beat like drums on the soil. Wind reddened Dennis's ears. Melanie's hair flew back into his face. He tugged her east to chase a crow circling above the horizon. Behind them, the wind swept through fields the size of eternity.

# THOUGHT EXPERIMENT

## EILEEN GUNN

Ralph Drumm, Jr., as we all know, devised the first practicable method of time travel, in our timestream and in countless others. He was an engineer and a good one, or he would not have figured it out, but in one significant way, he simply had not thought things through.

It was mere happenstance that Ralph even had the time and inclination to consider the matter, that day in the dentist's chair. It wasn't as though he needed any dental work: Ralph had always had perfect teeth, thanks to fluoride, heredity, nutrition, and a touch of obsessive-compulsive disorder. Most of the time, all he needed from the dentist was a quick cleaning, and he was done, but this time he opted for a little something extra: whitening. Ralph had always thought his perfect teeth would surely be more perfect if they were whiter.

The whitening process took an hour and a half, and it was not as much fun as the advertising brochure promised. But Ralph had a great fondness for thought experiments, so he set his mind to figuring out how to disassociate himself from the dentist's chair. Being an engineer, he thought it through in a very logical and orderly way.

It was Ralph's genius to intuit that time travel is accomplished entirely in your head: you just need some basic software development skills, plus powers of concentration that work in all four dimensions. It seemed simple enough, merely a matter of disassociating not only his mind, but also his body. A trick, a mere bagatelle, involving a sort of n-dimensional mental toolbar that controls the user's timeshadow. The body stays behind, where it started, and the timeshadow travels freely until it alights in another time and place, where it generates a copy of the original worldline, body and all, in the timestream.

Ralph wondered why nobody had ever thought of it before. He was about to test it when the hygienist came back and started hosing out the inside of his mouth. Better leave this until I get home, Ralph thought. Even if it didn't work, it was a wonderful theory, and it certainly whiled away ninety minutes that would otherwise have been entirely wasted, intellectually.

At home, Ralph got to work. He set up a few temporal links on the toolbar in his head: first, an easy bit of pre-industrial England. He should fit in there rather nicely, he thought, and they'd speak English. After that, he planned an iconic weekend in cultural history, and a couple of exciting historical events it would be fascinating to witness. Then, focusing the considerable power of his mind, he activated the first link.

Wessex, 1440.

The weekly market looked like a rural food co-op run by the Society for Creative Anachronism. People wearing homespun clothing in dull tones of brown and green and blue walked around with baskets, buying vegetables from similarly clad peasants who sat on the ground. In one area, a tinker was mending pots; in another, a shoemaker was stitching clunky but serviceable clogs.

The smell was a little strong—body odor, horse manure, wet hay, rotting vegetation, cooking cabbage—but Ralph felt right at home. He'd devised himself a costume that he thought would look nondescript in any time period, and carried a pocketful of Roosevelt dimes, figuring silver was silver, and Roosevelt did look a little like Julius Caesar.

He looked around nervously, but no one had noticed him materialize, even though he was right in the middle of the crowd. It was as if he'd been there all along, he thought. Ralph was unaware of the most basic tenet of time travel, as we understand it now: that the traveler's arrival in a timestream changes both the future and the past, because his timeshadow extends for the length of his life. His present is his own, but his past in this timestream belongs to another self, with whom he is now entangled.

Ralph, our Ralph, was hungry, despite the unappetizing stink. There was a woman selling pasties from a pot, and another selling soup that was boiling on a fire. Neither of the women looked very clean, and each of them was coughing a lot and spitting out phlegm on the ground.

Ralph decided that the soup was probably the safer choice, until he noticed how it was served: ladled into a bowl that each customer drank from in turn. Next time, he'd remember to bring his own cup.

He noticed a man grilling meat on wooden skewers. Just the thing. There was a small crowd around the charcoal-filled trough: a couple of rough-looking men, an old woman, some younger women with truculent expressions on their faces, and a handful of children. A quartet of buskers was singing a motet in mournful medieval harmony. A girl-child of about twelve watched him solemnly and with interest as he approached. Ralph hoped he hadn't made some dreadfully obvious mistake in his clothing, so that he looked a foreigner, but no one else seemed to be paying any attention to him.

As he waited his turn, the child's unblinking stare made him nervous. He was afraid to meet her eyes, and gazed earnestly at his feet, at the ash-dusted charcoal blocks, at the meat. He quickly made his way to the vendor and handed him a dime. The man gazed at it in disbelief, and then looked at Ralph with a canny mixture of greed and suspicion.

"Geunne me unmæðlice unmæta begas, hæðenan hund!"

It was a salad of vowels, fricatives, and glottal stops. But Ralph had realized it would be hard to get a handle on the local dialect, and figured he could get by on charm and sympathy until he worked it out. He smiled, and gestured in sign language that he was deaf.

The vendor stepped back suddenly and, with an expression of fear and revulsion pointed at Ralph and shouted "Swencan bealohydig hwittuxig hæðenan, ellenrofe freondas! Fyllan æfþunca sweordum!" The crowd turned toward him, and started in his direction. They did not look friendly. They were shouting words he could almost understand.

Ralph jabbed desperately at the next link on his mental toolbar.

Bethel, New York, 1969.

His heart pounding, Ralph found himself in a farmer's field, in a sea of mud and rain and under-clothed young people. It's okay here, he thought. The vibe was totally mellow, and so were all the people, who were slapping mud on one another and slipsliding around playfully.

The rain was soft and warm, and when it let up, someone handed him a joint. He took a toke and passed it on. How did he know, he wondered, to do that? And why was it called a toke? Time travel was really an amazing groove....

A beautiful longhaired boy gave him a brownie, and a beautiful longhaired girl gave him a drink of something sweet and cherry-flavored from a leather wineskin. "You have such a cosmic smile," she said. "Have a great trip, man." She kissed him, evading his hands gracefully and moving away, her thin white caftan clinging damply to her slim body.

Then the music started, and Ralph was pulled like taffy into the story of the song. He was the minstrel from Gaul, the soldier from Dien Bien Phu, the man from Sinai mountain. What did it all mean, he wondered briefly, but then he left meaning behind, and fell into the deep, sugar-rough voice of the singer. He was music itself, pouring out over the crowd, bringing together four hundred thousand people, all separate and all one, like the leaves of a huge tree stirred by a kind breeze, moving gently in the humid, muddy, blissful afternoon.

Time passed. Someone put a ceramic peace symbol on a rawhide thong around his neck. His clothes were muddy and he took them off. Set after set of music played. The sun went down, and it got dark.

The smell was rather strong here, too, he thought: body odors again, and the stink of the overflowing latrines. It was too humid, really, and something had bitten him on the butt. He put his clothes back on, rather grumpily. Ralph was starting to come down, and he was feeling just a little paranoid. Maybe Woodstock wasn't such a good idea....

Then the music suddenly stopped, and the lights went out. On stage, people with cigarette lighters scurried about. Finally, a small emergency generator kicked in, and a few dim lights came back on. Arlo Guthrie grabbed the mike, and the crowd cheered him expectantly, though a bit mindlessly. "I dunno if you—" he said. "I dunno, like, how many of you can dig—" He shook his head. He seems a bit stoned, Ralph thought. "—like how many of you can dig how many people there are here, man...." Arlo looked around. "But I was just talking to the fuzz, and, hey!—we've got a time traveler here with us." The audience laughed, a huge sound that echoed in the natural amphitheater that sloped up from the stage. Arlo pumped his fist. "We're historic, man! Far fucking out! We! Are! His*tor*ic!"

Then he shrugged apologetically. "But, can you dig this, the n-dimensional timefield effect has short-circuited the electrical system. We're going to have to call it off. Y'all're gonna have to go home. Sorry about your weekend, people. Good luck getting outta here...."

It was dark, but Ralph could sense, somehow, that four hundred thousand people had all turned their heads toward him.

He panicked, and stabbed randomly at his mental toolbar.

Wessex, 1441.

Damn! He'd hit the Wessex button again. He was back at the market, a year later.

Ralph was an engineer: he was, he thought, the kind of man who thinks things through, so he had programmed his mental toolbox not to send him back to the same timespace twice, for fear he'd meet himself, so he knew he was exactly a year—to the second—from his previous appearance. As we know now, of course, that worry was irrelevant, but it adds a certain predictability to his visits to Wessex.

This time, Ralph thought, he would be more circumspect, and wouldn't offer anyone money. It might be that Franklin Delano Roosevelt (or maybe Julius Caesar) was not welcome on coins in this place. Or maybe the sight of a silver coin itself was terrifying. He wouldn't make that mistake again. Maybe he could beg for some small local coins.

Or—that's it!—he could sell his peace symbol. As long as he didn't have to talk to anybody, and could get by on grunts and nods and smiles, he was sure he'd be okay. Thank God he'd put his clothes back on.

Ralph staked himself out a small space and sat down on the ground. He smoothed the dirt in front of him and put the ceramic medallion down in the center of the smooth space.

People walked by him, and he tried to attract their attention. He coughed, he waved, he gestured at the peace medallion. People ignored him. He would have to work harder, he thought, since he wasn't willing to say anything. But he was an engineer: sales had never been his strong point.

So Ralph stood up. He held the medallion out to passersby. They turned their heads away.

Ralph was getting hungry. He thought about the salespeople he knew. They didn't give up: rather, they ingratiated themselves with their potential customers. He looked around nervously.

He noticed a buxom young woman in the crowd, staring at him intently. She was quite a bit older than the girl who had watched him so carefully last time he was here. She was very pretty—maybe he could include her in his sales pitch, and then, after he sold the medallion, he could buy her something safe to eat.

Ralph smiled at her with what he hoped was his most engaging smile and dangled the medallion, swinging it in her direction and then holding it up as though she might like to try it on.

Almost instantly, a crowd formed. Aha! he thought with a grin: the language of commerce is universal. But then he noticed that they were muttering in a very unpleasant tone, picking up stones and glancing in his direction. Whatever they were saying, it sounded like he was in a mess of trouble.

Ralph was getting a little queasy from this rapid temporal disassociation. He didn't know what is now common knowledge: that the reverse-Schrödinger effect, which creates the dual timeshadow, causes info-seepage from the newly generated parallel self, adding data at a subconscious level.

Superimposition of the time-traveling Ralph over the newly generated stationary Ralph, fixed in the timestream both forward and back, generated a disorienting interference pattern. The traveling Ralph (TR) influenced the stationary Ralph (SR), and vice-versa, though neither was quite aware of the other. Each of them thought he was acting of his own free will—and indeed each one was, for certain values of free.

At any rate, the crowd was ugly, and Ralph didn't feel so good. So, of his own free will, Ralph bailed, whacking the toolbar without saying goodbye to the young woman or, really, paying much mind to where he was headed.

Washington, DC, 1865.

Ralph looked around groggily. He was in a theater filled with well-dressed, jolly-looking people, sitting in an uncomfortable seat that was covered in a scratchy red wool. It was anything but soft: horsehair stuffing, probably. The stage in front of him was set as a drawing room. It was lit by lights in the floor that illuminated the actor and actresses rather starkly: a funny-looking, coarsely dressed man and two women in elaborate crinoline dresses.

"Augusta, dear, to your room!" commanded the older of the two actresses, pointing imperiously into the wings, stage right.

"Yes, ma," the young woman said, giving the man a withering glance. "Nasty beast!" she said to him, and flounced off the stage.

The dialog sounded a bit stilted to Ralph's ears, but the audience was genially awaiting the older woman's comeuppance. *Our American*

*Cousin*, he thought abruptly, that's the play—it's been a hit throughout the war.

He glanced up at what was obviously the presidential box: it was twice the size of the other boxes, and the velvet-covered balustrade at its front, overhanging the stage, had been decorated with red-white-and-blue bunting. Just then, President Lincoln leaned forward through the drapery at the front of the box and rested his elbow on the balustrade, to catch the next bit of dialog.

Ralph was dumb-struck, and who would not have been? Medieval England, Woodstock, these had been interesting enough places to visit—but seeing Abraham Lincoln—an iconic figure in American history, an instantly recognizable profile, in the flesh, alive, moving, a real human being, on the very day that the long war had come to a close, with a startlingly cheerful smile on his face as he anticipated a famously comic rejoinder—was to Ralph an intensely moving experience.

He held his breath, frozen, as, at the back of the box, unknown to its occupants, he saw a stunningly handsome man—John Wilkes Booth, he was sure—move in against the wall. Booth pulled out a handgun and drew a bead on the president's head. Without thinking, Ralph leaped to his feet. "Mr. President! Duck!" he shouted.

The gun went off. There were screams and shrieks from the box. A large young man in the presidential party wrestled with Booth, as Lincoln pulled his wife to one side, shielding her. A woman's voice rang out, "They have shot the president! They have shot the president!" Lincoln clutched his shoulder, puzzled but not seriously hurt. Booth leaped for the stage, but strong men grabbed him as he landed, and brought him down.

Oh, cripes, Ralph thought. I've really done it now. This would change the future irrevocably! He would never find his way back to his own time, or anything resembling it. And, panicking, he hit the mental button a third time.

Wessex, 1442.

Ralph looked around at the damned medieval street market. This time, before he could say anything, an attractive, dark-haired woman grabbed his upper arm firmly, pulled him close to her, and spoke into his ear. "Keep your mouth shut, if you know what's good for you," she whispered urgently. She looked remarkably like the young woman he had seen before, but a bit older and a lot more intense.

She took him by the arm, and led him through the fair. Toothless old women in their forties offered her root vegetables, but she shook her head. Children tried to sell her sweetmeats, but the young woman pushed on. Without seeming to hurry, without drawing attention to herself or him, she quickly led Ralph to the edge of the fair. People who noticed them smiled knowingly, and some of the men gave him a wink. The woman led him behind a hayrick, a seductive look on her face.

Behind the huge mound of hay, the noise of the fair was diminished, and, for the moment at least, they were visible to no one. The woman's flirtatious manner had vanished. She pushed Ralph away from her and glared at him. Ralph was a little afraid: didn't people in medieval times hit one another a lot? This woman was *mad*.

"Ralph, you idiot!" she said in a low but exasperated voice. She's not speaking Middle English, Ralph thought. Momentarily he wondered: was she a medieval scholar of modern English? Uh....

She looked at him sternly. "People here are smarter than you think! You have to take some precautions! You can't just show up and expect everyone to ignore you."

"What?" said Ralph, brilliantly.

"You dunderhead," she said. "You're lucky you weren't burned at the stake. They were waiting for you, or someone like you. Any old time traveler would do."

"What's your name?" Ralph asked.

"I'm Sylvie, but that's not important."

"It's important to me," said Ralph.

She shook off his attention. "Come with me. Don't say a word, don't even open your mouth."

"But how did you know?" said Ralph. "How do you know I'm a time traveler? Why do you speak a language I can understand?"

"Oh, for Pete's sake," said Sylvie. "You were the first, but you're not the only. Historians of time travel come here all the time, to see where you landed on that very first trip. The locals are getting restless. They flayed those travelers they identified, or they burned them, or they pressed them to death with stones. We couldn't let that happen to you, especially before you told us how it worked."

"How on Earth would these yokels have ever noticed me?" he asked.

"Your damn teeth," she said. "Your flawless, glow-in-the-dark, impossibly white teeth." She handed him a rather ugly set of yellowish fake teeth. "Put these on now." Ralph did.

Sylvie then gestured toward a nearby hovel. "Over there," she said. "Inside. It's time for you to explain to me how time travel works." He went where she told him to, and did what she said. How could he not? He was smitten. Fortunately for Ralph, Sylvie was likewise smitten. Many a woman would be, as he was a handsome man with good teeth, and he gave up his secrets readily.

Sylvie then traveled forward, to a time before she was born, and told her parents the secret of time travel. Her parents, who became the most famous temporal anthropologists in history, educated a few others and, when baby Sylvie came along, brought her up to leap gracefully from one century to the next. More gracefully, in fact, than her parents themselves, who vanished in medieval England when Sylvie was twelve. She was, in fact, looking for them when she came upon Ralph that very first time.

Ralph and Sylvie were married in Wessex in 1442, Ralph's dental glory concealed by his fake teeth. Sylvie, inveterate time-traveler that she was, convinced him they should live in the timestream, giving them a sort of temporal immortality. And this is where Ralph, who was, after all, an engineer, not a physicist, failed to anticipate the effect of his actions.

Time does not fly like an arrow, it turns out. It just lies there, waiting for something new to happen. So when Ralph Drumm showed up—completely inappropriately—in the past, that past changed—the past healed itself—so that he had always been there. He acquired ancestors, was born, grew to adulthood—to Ralph's exact age in fact—and his body just happened to be in the exact place where Ralph's time-shadow showed up.

Time travel changes the past as well as the future: time is, in fact, an eternal present when viewed from outside the timestream.

So, as Ralph and Sylvie moved from time to time, they created more and more shadows of themselves in the timestream. As they had children—one, two, three, many—and took them about, the timeshadows of the Drumm children were generated and multiplied. Each shadow was as real as the original. Each shadow lived and breathed... and bred.

Although they were innocent of any ill intent, Ralph and Sylvie Drumm changed the flow of the stream of time in a way more profound than could be accomplished by any single action, no matter how momentous its apparent effect. Their genetic material came to dominate all of human history, an endless army of dark-haired, blue-eyed Caucasians with perfect teeth. They looked the same. They thought the same. They stuck together.

And this is why we, the last remnants of a differentiated humanity, are waiting here today in Wessex, in 1440—to defend our future from the great surge of the Drummstream. This time, they will not escape us.

# THE DOUBLE OF MY DOUBLE IS NOT MY DOUBLE

## JEFFREY FORD

I saw my double at the mall a couple of weeks ago. I was sitting on a bench outside a clothing store. Lynn was inside, checking out the sales. My mind was pretty empty as I watched the intermittent trickle of shoppers on their way to something else. Out of the corner of my eye, I noticed a person sit down next to me. I turned and saw who it was and laughed. "Hey," I said. "How's business?"

He was dressed in a rumpled suit and tie and he looked tired. Sighing to catch his breath, he sat back. There was a weak smile on his face. "Double drill," he said.

"Knowing me, I wouldn't think there'd be that much to it."

His eyes half closed and he shook his head. "The fucking paperwork alone..." he said.

"Paperwork?"

"Every time you fart, I have to fill out a 1025."

"You must be at it all day."

"And into the night," he said. "On top of all of it, I've had to get a part-time job."

"You're moonlighting as my double?"

"I'm dipping things in chocolate at that old-fashioned candy store on Stokes Road. Four hours a day for folding cash. Remember a couple of meetings back after we started talking, I told you I was living in that giant house out by the wild animal rescue, the last cul-de-sac before the road turns to dirt? The mortgage on that place is crushing."

"I thought you were living with like four or five other doubles, splitting the cost," I said.

"Yeah, but my double salary isn't cutting it. Dipping things in chocolate, though, pays extraordinarily well. I make a hundred dollars every four-hour session. "

"That's pretty good. What do you dip?"

He leaned forward and took out a pack of cigarettes. He offered me one but I'd quit, and he looked slightly wounded by my refusal. When he sparked his big chrome lighter, I noticed the pale hue of his complexion, the beads of sweat, the slight shaking of his hands. There was a pervasive aroma of alcohol.

He took a drag and, leaning forward, elbows on his knees, said, "You name it, I'll dip it. It started with fruit and by the time they brought in the first steak, I knew it was gonna get out of hand. Finally, the old Swedish guy who runs the place took off his shoe and handed it to me. A chocolate loafer. After I fished it out and it dried, he and his wife laughed their asses off."

"You don't look well," I told him. "You've put on weight and you're pale. You look like the Pillsbury Doughboy on a bender." The right arm of his glasses was repaired with Scotch Tape.

"Well," he said. "This is what I've come to talk to you about."

He was a wreck. I looked away. Nobody wants to see themselves tear up, watch their own bottom lip quiver.

"It seems I have a double," he said, his voice cracking slightly.

A moment passed before I could process the news. "You're a double and yet you have a double? How's that work?"

"It's rare," he said, "but it happens. You know, as your double, I don't bother you that often. I've not brought you any ill luck like in the legends. I'm just around and you see me maybe once or twice a year, we have a friendly chat, and I go on my way. The kind of double I have, though, is not benign as I am to you, it's an evil emanation."

"Is your double also my double?" I asked.

"Not precisely. He's not got our good looks. For the most part he exists as a cloud, a drifting smog. But he can take physical form for short periods of a few hours. A shape-shifter. Insidious. He's always hovering, repeating what I say in a high-pitched voice, appearing to my friends and fucking them over, making them think it's me. When I complain to him, he laughs and pinches my chin. All night, he whispers paradoxical dreams into my ear, their riddles frustrations dipped in chocolate. He's my double, but your psyche used me to birth him."

"You're losing me," I said. "Are you saying I'm responsible?"

"Well, it's your orbit that I'm trapped in. Everything issues from you. He's been haunting me for the past six months. Can you think of some bleak or grim thought you might have had half a year back that could have sewn the seed?"

"Grim thoughts?" I said. "I have a couple dozen a day."

"He's trying to supplant me as your double. If he takes my position, your ass'll be in a sling. He'll grind you down to powder."

"What are we gonna do?" I asked.

"He goes by the name Fantasma-gris."

"Spanish?"

"Yeah, it means Grey Ghost."

"I don't even know Spanish," I said. "I did a couple years of it in high school. I can say *meatball*, count to ten, that's it."

"Somehow something about Fantasma-gris dribbled out of your mind. Just sit tight till I figure out a plan," he said, resting his hand lightly on my forearm. He stood quickly. "Then I'll be back in touch."

"A plan for what?"

"To kill him," He spun away then and lumbered off down the center of the mall. I watched him go and realized he was limping. I was wondering what was with his suit and tie. I hadn't worn one in three years.

"Are you ready?" asked Lynn. She was standing before me, holding a big bag from the store she'd been in. I got up and put my arm around her shoulders as we headed off.

She said, "Let's go get dinner somewhere."

I agreed. We left the mall and went out into the parking lot. As we drove to the restaurant Lynn had decided on, I was preoccupied, thinking about Fantasma-gris. I wanted to tell her about it, but she'd made it clear years earlier that she didn't want to hear any double talk. When I finally cornered my double downtown one day and spoke to him for the first time, I'd told Lynn about it.

"What do you mean 'a double,' she'd said.

"A doppelganger. My twin. It's metaphysical, you know, like a spirit. I've been seeing him around for about a year now, and today, I went up to him and told him I knew what he was."

She smiled and shook her head as I spoke, but at one point she stopped and squinted and said, "Are you serious?"

I nodded.

"Do you understand what you're saying?" she'd asked.

"Yeah."

"You better get to a shrink. Don't think I'm heading toward retirement with a kook." She'd walked over to where I sat and leaned down to put her arms around me. "You gotta get your shit together," she said.

Lynn made an appointment for me and I'd gone to see this woman, Dr. Ivy, who asked me about the double. I told her everything I knew. Her office smelled of patchouli and there was low moaning music piped in from somewhere. She was a very short, fairly good-looking woman with long dark hair—a faint scar on her right cheek. For some reason, I pictured her cutting herself on her own plum-painted thumbnail. Every time I spoke, she nodded and jotted things down on a pad. I was transfixed by the sight of an ivy tattoo on the wrist of her writing hand, and at the end of the session, she wrote me a scrip for some head pills.

I bought them and read the warnings. In print so tiny I had to use a magnifying glass to read, it said my throat could close up, I might get amnesia, bleed from my asshole, lose my hearing, develop a strange taste of rotten eggs in my mouth, or be drawn to reckless gambling. I took them for two days and felt like a walking sandbag. On the third morning, I flushed them down the bowl. I'd learned my lesson. I never went back to see Dr. Ivy, but then I never mentioned my double to Lynn again.

At the restaurant, I ordered ravioli and Lynn got a salad. We both had wine, me red, her white. The place was dark but our table had a red candle. We talked about the kids and then we talked about the cars. She told me what was going on at her job. We bitched about politics for ten minutes. All along, though, I wanted to tell her what the double had told me in the mall, but I knew I shouldn't. Instead, I said to her, "I was thinking about Aruba today. That was a great vacation."

She took my cue and started reminiscing about the blue water, the sun, the balcony in our room that opened onto a courtyard filled by the branches of an enormous tree with orange flowers and crawling with iguanas the size of house cats. I reminded her of our jeep journey to the desert side of the island and the stacked stone prayers that littered the shore. It was a great trip, and I took real pleasure in recalling it with her, but, yes, I had an ulterior motive.

It was on that vacation that I first saw my double. While she spun out her descriptions of the Butterfly Pavilion, an attraction we'd visited, or the night we ate at a restaurant on the edge of a dock, ocean at our backs, party lights, a guy with a beat-up acoustic guitar playing "Sleepwalk," I was, in that memory of Aruba, elsewhere, standing at midnight, after she'd fallen asleep, smoking a joint on the open second landing of our building.

Beneath me was a lighted trail that cut through the tall bamboo. I was bone weary, and my eyes were half closed. We'd gone kayaking that day. I wondered how the kids were getting along without us but my thoughts were distracted by the strong breeze whipping the bamboo tops. I was just about to flick the roach away and ascend the concrete steps to my left, when I saw someone pass by on the path.

The fellow was about six foot, a little stooped, thick in the chest and well overweight. He leaned into the wind, holding a floppy white beach hat to his head with his left hand. With the next gust, his yellow Hawaiian shirt opened, the tails blowing behind him to reveal his gut. He turned his head suddenly and looked up at me for a moment before disappearing into the bamboo. The glasses, the big head, his dull look, seemed familiar. I tried to place where I might have seen him before, but I was too tired.

The next day, we took a jeep to the barren side of the island and visited an abandoned gold mine. There was a three-story busted and rusted concrete-and-tin structure built into the side of an enormous sand dune. The place was spooky inside and Lynn and I held hands as we went from room to room. There was nothing really to see but rotted furniture and rusted metal bed frames in a maze of rooms that led to other tunnels and rooms. I started to feel claustrophobic, and said I'd had enough. She agreed.

As we made our way toward where we remembered the exit being, another party of sightseers passed by in a hallway to our left. An older gentleman with a cane, and a white-haired woman following him. She nodded to us and smiled. Then a second later, the guy from the night path went by, whistling, the sound of his tune echoing through the rooms and back into the heart of the sand dune. I saw him for only an instant, but knew it was him and knew I knew him from somewhere.

At least three more times, I caught sight of him in Aruba, and then in the last few days we were there, he'd seemed to have vanished. The next I saw him was on the plane going home. Lynn and I had taken our seats, and he passed down the aisle toward the back. His presence surprised me. I sat up, and as he went by, he looked down, straight into my eyes. It wasn't until after takeoff that I realized he was me.

I was petrified the whole flight home, thinking *doppelganger*. Trapped with one in midair, no less. In Poe, in Hoffmann, in Stevenson, the double was always grim business. I didn't even want to consider the dark foreboding of legends and folklore. But, for all my perspiration, we landed safely and that was that. I saw him briefly at the baggage terminal, walking away, carrying a battered blue suitcase. A few months went by before I caught sight of him in town one snowy afternoon.

"I love it when we can get away and have adventures," said Lynn, almost in a whisper. She lifted her wine glass and motioned for a toast.

"Me too." I said. The glasses clinked. After that I put the double out of my mind, and by the time we went to bed, I'd convinced myself it was all nonsense.

Two days later, I went out to the garage to put a couple of old pizza boxes in the recycle container. I put the boxes in the container and let the lid slam down. As I turned, he struck the chrome lighter and lit a cigarette. I did a little jump and grunted. He'd never been anywhere near my house before. Although my heart pounded, I felt immediately indignant.

"I'll only be a minute," he said, sensing my anger. "I have a plan to get rid of Fantasma-gris."

I took a deep breath and calmed down. "You know," I said, "I don't know..."

"Listen, if he gets through me, you're next. Believe me, you're through if he takes me out."

"OK," I said. "OK."

"Someday this week, it's gonna go down, so be ready. And I'm warning you, this is gonna be brutal. Savage. I don't want you to think this is in any way some kind of psycho breakdown bullshit, you know, all a fancy. There's gonna be blood involved."

He spoke in a harsh tone, and as he went on, I inched back away from him. He looked worse than he had at the mall. I realized he must be sleeping in that suit.

"Whatever," I said, and brushed past him into the house, locking the door to the garage behind me. Lynn was in the kitchen, and I went up there to be close to her. She seemed to me to have powers greater than the double's. I really wanted to tell her, but I didn't.

"Were you calling me?" she asked. She stood at the stove, stirring chilli. "I thought I heard a voice from the garage."

"I was singing," I said and put my arms around her. Right then is when I wished I hadn't flushed the pills. Reckless gambling seemed preferable.

The next day, while Lynn was at work, I made an emergency appointment with Dr. Ivy. I knew it was grasping at straws, but I thought if all else failed she'd write me another scrip to cancel the double. For the first five minutes of the session, she gave me shit about stiffing my second appointment and not calling. I just grinned and said sorry when she was through. Finally, she picked up her pad and pen, the music came on as if by magic, and she said, "So, last we spoke, you told me about your double."

"He's back," I said.

"Tell me," she said and leaned forward, her pen at the ready.

"I just want to make one thing clear at the start," I said. "The double of my double is not my double." She nodded as if she understood, and I let it all out for her—the meeting in the mall, the invasion of my garage, and Fantasma-gris. It took me the whole hour to tell her. When I was finished, there was only one minute left of the session for her to speak.

"I'll write you," she said. "What did you do with the last prescription?"

"I threw it in the toilet."

She stared hard at me and tapped her pen on her prescription pad. I noticed that the tattoo around her wrist wasn't ivy at all but actually barbed wire. "Here's something different," she said. "There'll be a slight sense of euphoria, but it should allow you to get through your normal day and also eradicate your double problem."

"Sounds awesome," I said and meant it.

"A slight sense of euphoria," was a bit of an understatement. The next day, after Lynn left for work, I took one of the pills and settled down to a doubleless eight hours. A half-hour later, sitting at my computer, Dr. Ivy's cure kicked in, and the world appeared literally brighter. Things looked crisp. I breathed more deeply and sat up straight. I was hyper-aware. Looking at the story I'd been writing, I couldn't get to the plot because the shapes of the letters were too distracting. A few minutes passed and then I was floating on a pink cloud, everything recalibrating to a slower focus. I felt so good, I actually laughed.

The drug made me brave, and instead of getting back to work, I dove deep into a rational analysis of my double, determined to figure it all out as much as it could be. Staring out the window at the trees and the white house across the street, I plumbed and divided, spinning theories to rival Relativity. I kept returning to one question, though. Why Aruba? To answer it might be to solve the puzzle. I got a red hair to write up what I remembered of the vacation, to make an official dossier about it. I opened a new screen and wrote as fast as I could, rarely stopping to correct errors.

An hour into it, my ardor for Aruba dried up and I found myself fluffing off, surfing the web with the word "doppelganger" in the Google search box. I stumbled upon a site that had a news story about scientists who were able to induce in their subjects the experience of having a double by electrically stimulating a region of the brain known as the *left temporoparietal junction*. The subjects reported a "shadowy person standing behind them."

I thought back to the night I first saw him, scurrying down the bamboo trail. That day Lynn and I went ocean kayaking. The plastic board you were supposed to float on didn't look anything like any kayak I'd ever seen. I couldn't keep from falling off it. I'd teeter for a few minutes and then over I'd go. Repeatedly getting back up on the thing in deep water exhausted me in no time, and I was just barely able to dog paddle to a broken-down dock I used to get back on dry land. I wondered if somewhere in the mêlée, I'd maybe hit my head and the double was born of a concussion.

I couldn't recall a bump, but I was sure I'd solved the puzzle of Aruba. The revelation gave me a sense of accomplishment and confidence until five minutes later when, looking out the window, I saw a car just like mine pull up in front of my house. The door opened and my double got out. He walked around the car, dressed in that rank suit, heading for our front door. The sight of him made my heart race. "Something's wrong here," I said aloud. There was a knocking at the front door. Shadow, the dog, went nuts, barking like the vicious killer he wasn't. I got up from my chair, feeling slightly dizzy, slightly doomed, and went to put a shirt on. Once I was up, I hurried, not wanting the neighbors to see me in his condition.

I pushed Shadow away and opened the door. "You shouldn't be here," I said.

"But I am."

"I took these pills that are supposed to cancel you."

"Fuck those pills," he said. "What do you think? I'm playing games?" He stepped toward the door as if to enter, and I shut it quickly. He got his forearm on it before I could lock him out and he pushed his way in, sending me stumbling backward a few steps.

"I want you out of here," I said.

"Calm down," he said, and closed the door behind him.

I backed away into the kitchen, looking right and left for a pair of scissors or a knife lying on the counter. He followed.

"We've got a job to do," he said. "Fantasma-gris is coalescing like a mother fucker."

"I'm not killing anyone or anything," I said, and noticed he wouldn't look me in the eye.

"I've got him tied up in the trunk of your car. We'll off him and then drive out to the Pine Barrens and sink his body in some remote pond. I have two twenty-pound dumbbells. Nobody has to know." He pushed back the bottom of his suit jacket and grabbed a pistol he'd had in the waist of his pants.

The instant I saw the gun, I was useless with fear.

"Let's go," he said and waved the gun at me.

I went to the living room and stepped into my shoes, grabbed my sweatshirt. We left through the front door. The double drove. I sat still, breathing deeply, in the passenger seat. As he pulled away from the curb, I heard a banging and muffled screams issuing from the trunk.

"If you want to get rid of him," I said, "why don't you just get rid of him yourself. Leave me out of it."

"Step up to the plate and quit your whining," he said. Then he turned and yelled over his shoulder, "Shut the fuck up," to Fantasma-gris, who was making a racket.

We drove south toward the Barrens on the long road that led past the animal rescue and eventually turned to dirt. Just before the asphalt gave out, he made a left and drove slowly down a short block of enormous old houses with porches and gabled roofs. We came to a drive way through the trees that opened into a cul-de-sac. At the turn furthest in sat a huge wreck of a house, brown paint peeling, cedar board fallen from the walls, the supports of the porch railing busted out.

"My place," he said, turning off the car. He pointed to it with the gun.

"Nice," I said.

"For the money, it's not so great."

I noticed two of the second-floor windows were broken and there were bricks missing from the chimney.

"OK, let's get this asshole out and kill him. I figure we can do the job in my room and then take him out to the woods after nightfall."

We got out of the car. It was cold, headed toward evening, and the breeze was reminiscent of the one in Aruba when I saw him on the bamboo trail. My mind was knotted with plots to escape.

"Aren't there other people in your house?" I asked. "They'll hear us shoot him."

"Just doubles. They don't give a shit. They've got their own losers to contend with." He went to the trunk and I followed him. Holding the gun at the ready, he put the car key in the lock and turned it. The trunk slowly opened upward, and I peered inside to catch a glimpse of Fantasma-gris.

I don't know what I expected, some kind of smoke goblin maybe, but what I saw was like a white marble or limestone statue of a guy in a fetal position. "What the hell?" I said.

"He's hardened," said my double. "I dipped him in white chocolate. That's how I caught him. He was at my job this morning, busting my balls, and I finally snapped. I grabbed him quick and threw him into the vat. By the time he crawled out, I'd gotten my gun from my jacket on the back of the dipping-room door. "

"This is crazy," I said.

"You're telling me. Grab his ankles, we'll take him up to the house."

Fantasma-gris was a lot lighter than he looked. He was nowhere near as big as us, and I can't say his face, a mask of white chocolate, looked anything like me. I had a passing inclination I'd seen it before, though. His lips still moved and mumbled threats. He cursed and called us names. At first it freaked me out, but by the time we reached the steps of the place, I found him annoying. On the way in the front door, I accidentally slammed his left foot on the door jamb and half his shoe with half a foot cracked off. He howled like a wounded animal within his sweet shell. A quick look told me he was hollow.

The old house was falling apart—water stains on the ceilings and molding coming loose. There were cracks in the lathing of the walls. The floor of the foyer was bare, worn wood. We carefully set Fantasma-gris down so we could take a breather. The double waved me over to him. I approached and he put his arm lightly around my shoulder, the gun to my stomach.

"I have to go straighten up my room before you're allowed in," he whispered, his breath on fire with booze. He was sweating and ripe with the scent of body funk dipped in chocolate. "If you do anything foolish, I'll hunt you down and kill you and take over your life. You understand?"

My mouth was so dry. I nodded.

"Now, go sit in the parlor with May till I come back." He pointed to an entrance off to the left of the foyer. I took a step toward it and saw a near-empty room filled with twilight, dust bunnies slowly rolling across a splintered floor, bare walls, a dusty chandelier, and in the corner by a cold fireplace, a tilting couch on three legs with torn and sweat-stained floral upholstery. At the upright end sat a woman reading a book. She looked over as I entered. Out in the foyer, Fantasma-gris repeatedly screamed, "Fuck."

The minute I saw her face, I knew I knew May from the neighborhood. Lynn was actually pretty good friends with her. "You're May's double?" I asked.

She nodded and smiled. May was our age, a big-boned woman with a ruddy face. She was the swimming instructor at the local Girl Scout camp in the summer. Lived around the corner from us next to the lake.

"You look just like her," I said.

"Well, that's the idea," she said.

"Do you know me?"

She nodded but said nothing.

"How is May?" I asked and sat carefully on the broken end of the couch.

"She's all right. She had a hysterectomy last fall and I think she's starting to slow down a little. Overall, though, she gets along."

"You live here with my double?"

"Yeah, me and a few others."

"What's he like? You can be honest."

"No disrespect, but he's a total dick. I think he's crazy."

I heard someone descending the steps at the back of the house. "Listen, do me a favor," I said. "Get word to my wife that I'm here and to come get me. You know her, right?"

"If I get a chance," she said. "I'm due downtown in a couple of minutes. May's in the grocery store, and I'm scheduled to appear in the frozen food aisle. If I get a chance I'll have her call Lynn."

I gave her a silent thumbs up and then my double was at the entrance.

Before we lifted Fantasma-gris, he broke off his double's pinky finger and stuck it in his mouth like a cigarette. "Got a light?" he said. Screams of agony issued from the chocolate.

His room was on the second floor and I was out of breath by the time we arrived. We set the double in a chair. The position he'd formed while in the trunk was perfect for sitting, although he was somewhat slouched forward. I was afraid if he fell, he'd shatter all over the floor.

"How come the Fantasma smog didn't leak out when I knocked his toes off? The fucking thing's hollow," I said.

"The chocolate is his prison."

I took a seat on the edge of the bed and my double settled down at a little table by the window. Our prisoner faced me, but the double stared out the window. "As soon as it's nightfall," he said, "we go to town on him."

"Why nightfall?" I asked.

"Cause that's the way you kill him. In the dark."

While I considered whether to bolt for the door or not, I looked at Fantasma-gris's face. The white mask was off-putting. It had very prominent cheeks, egg-shell smooth, that I recalled having seen before in a book, on a Noh mask from the fifteenth century. The character was called *Shite*. "Shite is right," I thought.

Out the window, through the trees, there was still the sight of a thin red line at the horizon with night layered on top. Fantasma-gris was whispering to me, trying to communicate something, but I couldn't make it out. He seemed to be losing power.

"OK, now," said the double. He lifted the gun and cocked the trigger. "Let's have some fun." He pointed it at me.

I put my hands up and turned my head.

"Get up."

I stood, trembling.

"Go over and eat his face."

"I'm not hungry," I said.

"Get the fuck over there," he said, and fired the gun into the ceiling.

I jumped and was next to Fantasma-gris in an instant.

"Bite his nose off to spite his face."

I leaned over and opened my mouth, but the prospect of sinking my teeth into a white chocolate nose made me sick. So very faintly, I heard, "Help me, help me...." I gagged and then turned away.

"I said eat his damn face," said the double, and lunged from his chair toward me. I reached down, grabbed Fantasma-gris's right arm at the wrist with both hands and pulled it off. The double meant to pistol whip me, but I brought the chocolate arm around like a baseball bat and hit him in the side of the head. White shards exploded everywhere and my double went over like a ton of bricks. The gun flew out of his hand. My instinct was to run, but I remembered all along that I'd have to get the keys from him.

I leaped on him and fished the keys out of his left pocket where I'd seen him stow them earlier. Just as I got up and made to split, he grabbed me by the ankle and tripped me. I went over and smashed into our prisoner, who toppled to the floor with me on top of him and was crushed to smithereens. The leg of the chair rammed into my stomach and knocked the wind out of me. I couldn't move.

As he predicted, there was blood. It trickled out of the corner of his mouth. He fetched the gun and aimed it at me. "I'm through with you," he said.

The door opened then and Lynn walked in. "What the hell's going on here?" she said, standing with her hands on her hips. The double immediately lowered the gun and gazed at the floor.

I finally caught my breath and said, "You see, my double. I told you."

"Give me the gun," she said, and walked straight over to the double and took it out of his hand. "You two are ridiculous."

The double said, "My double is pretending to be me and tried to kill me. He busted my head with a chocolate arm."

"No," I said, "I'm the real one."

Lynn backed up three steps, raised the pistol like they do in cop shows and pulled the trigger once. I squinted with the din of the shot, and when I looked, my double had a neat round hole in his forehead. His eyes were crossed and smoke issued from the corners of his mouth. He teetered for a heartbeat and then fell, face forward on the floor. The body twitched and convulsed.

From out in the hallway, I heard May's voice ask, "Is everything all right in there?"

"Swell," called Lynn, and then stepped around behind the double, took aim with the gun again, and put two more slugs in the back of his head. She dropped the gun on top of him and said, "Let's get out of here." She helped me up and we held hands as we had in the gold mine. Passing May on the stairs, Lynn called a thank you over her shoulder.

We got into my car and I breathed a sigh of relief. The double was gone for good. "How'd you know which of us was the real one?" I asked as I hurriedly pulled away from the curb.

"It didn't matter," she said. "Whichever one of you was in that fetid fucking suit wasn't coming back to the house."

"What if you chose wrong?" I asked.

"Come on," she said. "I know you." Then she disappeared.

Later that evening, I made coffee and Lynn and I sat on our respective ends of the couch in the living room. "You'll never guess who I met today?" I said.

She took a sip of coffee. "Who?"

"Your double," I said.

She was about to raise the cup again but froze. A smile broke out on her face.

"You need a trip to Dr. Ivy," I said.

She shook her head. "I know, what a hypocrite, but I didn't see my double before you told me about yours."

"Why didn't you let me know?"

"It didn't matter as much if I had one, I just didn't want *you* to go crazy."

"So you're as crazy as I am," I said.

"In my own way."

"But your double was actually helpful. How come yours is cool and mine was an asshole?"

"Think about it," she said.

I did and while I did she took a folded napkin out of the pocket of her sweat pants. She held it up in the palm of one hand and opened it with the other. Between her thumb and index finger, she lifted up a white chocolate ear and let the napkin flutter down. She broke off a piece and handed it to me. We had it with our coffee while she told me that it was in the chapel with the image of Copernicus on the ceiling, in that ancient castle in Krakow, where we'd been told we could experience "The 9th Chakra of the World," that she'd first seen herself.

# NINE ORACLES

## EMMA BULL

1. The Oracle of Brooklyn

She sponges milk off the table, the floor, the Hot Wheels car. She'd heard her mother come out her mouth when she'd said it, which is how she'd known it wouldn't do any good. Then why hadn't she moved the glass?

She tugs a paper towel off the roll and dabs milk out of the tiny wheel wells. Had her mother wondered the same thing, afterward?

Advice, predictions, warnings, aimed at her, her brother, her father. They used to joke about it: "What does Mommy say?" "'*You better not!*'" They'd heard, they'd joked, but had they ever *listened?*

Being right doesn't fix anything. Fixing is another set of skills, and some days she can't remember if she ever learned them.

*Call your mother.* That, at least, she can do something about.

2. The Oracle of Santa Monica

It's called a bubble for a reason.

She stares at the blue-and-white insignia in the middle of the steering wheel. If cars were bought a piece at a time, she'd probably own all of this one except that damned little disc. She'll sell before the repo, buy a used Toyota.

Being right ought to deflect the splatter when everything hits the fan. But as one of her professors once said, "So tell me the mathematical symbol for 'ought to.'" When the corporate ought-to runs into real-world math, it's not mathematics that gets towed away and declared a total loss.

It's easier on her, because she's had time to prepare. That's the upside of being the one dissenting voice in the conference room: time to prepare. God knows she won't get credit for calling it, back when they could have avoided disaster. Finance is a superstitious business, worse than theater. Because she saw it coming and said so, it will be as if she made it happen. Her pink slip will be in the first wave.

The light turns green. She goes forward, because she has to.

## 3. The Oracle of Baltimore

She wades, alone, into the seething flock of news vultures outside the courthouse. Their microphone beaks reach to peck at her, their screeching batters her: *Did you! Your testimony! What do you! How will this!* She can barely keep herself from flailing her arms to watch them scatter into the sky.

*Where were you carrion birds when I first spoke up, when you might have done some good? You only appear when the beast is already dead and stinking. You don't know what it's like to face its teeth and claws.*

"Doctor!" One earnest young vulture stands his ground and blocks her path. "Now that the court's verdict has confirmed your allegations about Protelect and your former employer, how do you feel?"

Tiny black stars dance in the margins of her vision, and her mouth is dry and tastes like steel. Under her skin and inside her ribs she can feel the imminent vibration of panic. She imagines the brave benzodiazepine fighting and dying before the rebel hormones overwhelming her central nervous system.

Protelect supplied arms to that rebellion, of course. That's why the rebels will triumph. It's benzodiazepine's last stand.

"How do I feel?"

"About the verdict. You were right."

As if the verdict makes her right. As if she needs the verdict to prove it to herself, like a "100%!" scrawled at the top of her test paper. She's been *right* for ten years. She was *right* before the first death. If the case had been dismissed, she'd still be *right*, and the company would still be wrong. Is it possible schools no longer teach the difference between science and law? Or is it not required for vultures' credentials?

And the disabling effects, the ruined lives, the deaths—Being right doesn't mend a single one. How does he *think* she feels?

She stares into his blue, blue parasitic eyes and clenches her teeth to still the shivering muscles in her jaw. "Anxious," she says, with a precision terrible even to her.

The color drains from his face. He steps back and lets her pass.

4. The Oracle of Montgomery

"You're sure?" Dr. Mujarrah says.

He's a good doctor. She likes him, likes working with him. But he's young, so there's things he hasn't seen much of.

Some of the young ones think they have to prove they're better than the nurses, which is a lot of damned foolishness and wastes time. It's not better. It's different. And being right isn't about pride and awards. It's for the patients.

Dr. Mujarrah's smart enough to know he doesn't know everything. So she shows him some respect by stopping to consider the question. "I've been surprised before."

"But you think..."

"Sometimes you can tell. Something in the eyes, maybe, trying to look past things they've seen all their lives."

Dr. Mujarrah gives her a stare like the one she gets sometimes from her daughter Janice whenever she starts to say something about Janice's church.

Mr. Vilek is eighty-four, which is a wonder, with rheumatic fever at the age of twelve on his medical history. Heart damage. He knows it, and so do his family and his doctors. But it's not given anyone to know the day or the hour, until it's close.

"I've warned the family," says Dr. Mujarrah. There's still one little question in his voice.

She nods. "They'll want to come now."

5. The Oracle of Wichita

The band plays "Kiss from a Rose" for the bride-and-groom dance. She's pretty sure neither Steve nor Vonda requested that. Maybe Vonda's mom.

They waltz, not quite as stiff as the mannequins in Bloomingdale's. Vonda holds the ruffles on her fishtail train with more attention than she holds Steve. Steve sneaks looks at Vonda's cleavage.

"We're taking ballroom dance lessons," Vonda had announced at the bridal shower. "Steve was all, 'No way,' but I talked him into it."

Yeah, she can just imagine that.

She'd done what she could, as a friend. She's known Steve since sixth grade, for chrissake. She'd covered for him when he crashed the Driver Ed car, and helped him train for the state swim finals, and sat up with him all night at the hospital when they were afraid his mom would die of appendicitis.

Unfortunately, friends don't always listen to good advice. In fact, sometimes good advice makes friends so mad they might just stop being friends.

Maybe someday he'll forgive her for being right.

Steve and Vonda waltz slowly along the edge of the dance floor. She can see Vonda's lips moving: *ONE-two-three. ONE-two-three.* Steve must not have said anything. Vonda would never have invited her if he had.

Steve catches her eye over Vonda's bare shoulder and raises his eyebrows as high as they go. *See?* the eyebrows say. *You're wrong. It's totally perfect.*

The dance turns them away, and she sighs. *You moron. Of course it's perfect* today. *That's not what I said.*

### 6. The Oracle of Sheridan

A red, white, and blue shield-shaped sign and an arrow, glimpsed between swipes of the windshield wiper: the most beautiful thing she's seen for hours. She sinks deeper into the passenger seat with relief. Nina catches the change in body language and shoots her a glance.

*Oops.* And after she'd pretended she wasn't worried. *I'm not judging you, sweetie…*

Nina stops at the turnoff for the entrance ramp and looks across the console at her. "This right here? It's exit 97, isn't it?"

Nina's mouth is pinned closed between her teeth on one side and pulled upward on the other, which also wrinkles her nose. It's the most ridiculous and adorable apology on Earth, and it gets her every time.

"I… kinda think it is."

"So, hey, we've only lost, what? Seventy-five miles?" Nina grins hopefully.

She clears her throat. "Something like that?"

"But it *could* have been a cut-across."

Caught up in release of tension and Nina's mad revisionism, she can't hold back the bubbles of laughter pushing up from her lungs. "God, the look on your face when the pavement quit."

"Pavement, hell! There were sheep! *Sheep!*"

They sit in the rain-washed car and shriek with laughter. Everything is funny. The wipers are funny. A chunk of mud falls from the undercarriage—*gok*—and she laughs so hard she's afraid she'll pee.

Slowly it occurs to her that being right doesn't mean being unloved.

Not anymore.

Nina wipes away tears and puts the car in gear. "That's it. No more ignoring the navigator. Next time I'll listen to you."

She smiles and rubs Nina's shoulder with her knuckles. "No, you won't."

7. The Oracle of Red Lake

In the end, the river wins the race.

She staggers, trips over sandbags they hadn't had time to get to the wall, and falls to her hands and knees. Ice water rushes in over the tops of her insulated mittens as if it had been waiting for the chance.

Hochstetter grabs her at the armpits and hauls her upright. With one arm across his shoulders, she slogs, shivering, to the truck. Chunks of ice eddy and bump around her boots. She's too tired to drag herself into the high cab. He plants both hands on her ass and shoves (*Inappropriate touch*, she thinks, and it's so hilarious she knows she's out of rope), and slams the door as soon as her feet are clear.

"Hurry" isn't one of the things she has to tell him. If the water floats the truck, it's over.

But they make it. The high school, up on the bluff, is the emergency shelter and command center. She stumbles past the glass case of hockey trophies and National Honor Society plaques to reach the over-warm gym, a piece of floor to sit on, and coffee steaming in a styrofoam cup.

From the bluff you can see most of town. She can name the families who'd be under each roof if it weren't for the cold gray-brown water. Thank God the gym doesn't have windows.

Hochstetter squats next to her, a cup in his own hand. He's left his fire department jacket and hat somewhere; in his snowmobile coveralls he looks like just another neighbor. Well, he is.

"There's soup, Mayor. Beef barley. Get you some?"

"Not yet." She lifts her coffee in both hands and eyes him over the quivering horizon of rim. "My arms are too tired to hold the spoon."

He nods, which from Hochstetter is an out-loud laugh. They listen to the murmur of half the town, including kids, in one big room. She's used to roaring noise in here, basketball games and pep rallies. Now you'd think it was a library.

Hochstetter clears his throat. "I didn't figure you'd be out sandbagging."

"Why not?" She can't really taste the coffee, and she doesn't care. It's *hot.*

"Couldn't have blamed you if you sat back and said 'I told you so.'"

She'd give anything—*anything*—to have said so and been wrong. For the first time since she started fighting the town council, the residents, and the river, she wants to bust out crying.

Instead she swallows coffee too fast, so she can pretend it makes her eyes water. "Being right isn't the same as being an asshole."

8. The Oracle of Ft. Lauderdale

"I want to thank my mother..."

*That's me.*

Mothers probably get thanked on streaming video every day of the week. It's in the job description, that they believe crazy, unjustifiable things about their kids. And after the yelling/sulking/door slamming years, if nothing goes too horribly wrong with the work, the resulting grown kids says "Thank you, Mom" often enough that nobody's surprised.

But this time *my mother* is her.

Her right shoulder and elbow joints hiss faintly as she reaches for the call button. She understands the production versions don't do that. But she's proud of that hiss. That's how it is with prototypes.

The nurse scurries into the room. It's the new one on night shift: he's still scared to death of her, afraid the call signal means she's dying. It's almost enough to make her waste energy on laughing. *Oh, honey, when I'm* dying *there won't be anything I need from you.*

But he's not afraid this time. "Is this it?" He crouches beside her bed, eyes fixed on the screen. "That's your daughter?"

Jacey doesn't look like the newspaper photos. Dressed up, for one thing, and someone must have put makeup on her, because it's damned sure Jace didn't do it herself. Accepting the biggest biochemistry prize in the world, and you're supposed to worry if your eyes look defined?

Mostly Jacey looks tired. Time zone changes, jet lag, awake all night her time making sure the video feed would work so her mom could watch.

She feels a nip of guilt at that. But after a decade spent creating muscle fibers, one night tinkering with streaming video isn't bad.

She's lived through twenty-three years of being right, and being told, "All parents think their kids are special." She's waited twenty-three years for the world to acknowledge that she wasn't just talking like a mother. She's going to watch them do it.

9. The Oracle of Yuma

It *blooms.*

Like some crazy nature documentary time-lapse video, like a cartoon with a magic paintbrush, the green spreads over the landscape beneath them, fast enough to see in real time. It's netting nanovolumes of moisture out of the air and soil, fixing nitrogen, gluing unstable molecules to poisons to turn them into food.

She spares a glance at the satellite downlinks. The faint green blush shows at all the insertion points: North Africa, Baja California, Central Asia, Central Australia.

Not as much fun as the view out the bubble of the copter, though. The micoid spreads like a lazy pool of liquid, but miles wide, *miles*, sinking in, poking out a finger wherever it likes the conditions. She feels laughter welling in her chest.

"What the *fucking hell!*" Jan croaks.

Jan likes redundant systems. Blasphemy backed up with obscenity.

She can't stuff the laughter anymore. It shoots out her mouth and sprays into her headset mic, into the racketing noise of the helicopter's insides. The pilot turns his insect-goggles to stare at her, expressionless, then shifts back to the stick.

She imagines the green laughing as it creeps along, eating, binding, changing everything. Bringing everything back.

"We win," she gasps between spasms of her diaphragm.

"What are you talking about?" He grabs the shoulders of her padded jacket and shakes her hard. His breath is vile in her face; like her, like the rest of the insertion cells, he's been on the move for seventy-three hours, tooth brushing optional. "What the hell kind of demonstration is *that?*"

"It's not a demonstration. It's the solution."

When he looks out the bubble again, there's terror in his face. He thought he had a devil on a leash, a cell-bursting monster to make an example of a thousand acres of brutalized land. He's already drafted his ransom note to the world. What does he feel when, instead of his incubated devil, he witnesses an angel of a new annunciation? Nobody leashes an angel.

Jan's head swings back toward her. Rage and fear twist his face like a wad of clay. "You knew it would do this. Didn't you?"

After all these years, he still can't believe in her. Still can't accept her being right.

"I knew before we raided the lab." She smiles and looks up at the sky. Filmed with gray, like a painter's glaze. But not for always, not now.

"You fucking *traitor!*" The slap cuts the inside of her mouth against her teeth; she tastes blood over her tongue. But his voice is a little boy's, brimming with betrayal and tears.

*I broke the game.*

Jan grabs the front of her jacket. "What if I throw you out? You think maybe that shit down there will catch you?"

She should stop smiling; it might make him angrier. But she can't. "You put my face on the world's monitors. You made me the prophet of the revolution. Won't the world ask where I am?"

His fingers slip off the windproof polyester; his face goes slack as if his nerves are cut. He looks again out the clear shell at the ground, where the micoid is turning arid, barren hardpan to friable soil, feeding dormant seeds with its own body.

"What about me?" he whispers, and the headset mic picks it up. "What happens to me?"

Jan Stangard, eco-terrorist, revolutionary, martyr, savior, dupe, murderer. He can't be all of them. Not in this new world.

But she can be what she's always been. Sustainability applies to human nature, too. She lifts his limp hands, presses them between both of hers. "I can't know that. You haven't created the answer yet."

She's changed the world. It will go on changing around her. She knows that, as she knows that what she is will never change.

*With thanks to Elise Matthesen.*

# DYING YOUNG

## PETER M. BALL

I smelt him coming long before he arrived, the musty odor of sulphur and dust cutting through the sweat-stink in Cassidy's Saloon. Smelling things is part of it, that thing I inherited from my Da, but it weren't just me who noticed it by the time he got close. The dragon stank bad enough that everyone breathed him in; the entire room hushin' up, listening to the tick-tick of claws on hardwood, lookin' at the door as he shouldered his way through.

He was a tall critter, but stooped over to fit his tail, and he'd been banged up good and proper by something a little more ruthless than the road. The wreckage that'd once been wings were folded over his shoulders, draped like a tattered coat. There weren't nothing but a jagged nub of bone where his horns had been, and that weren't good: Da once told me a dragon without horns got ornery, and they were usually trouble for more than just the feller what cut 'em off.

The dragon stared us down; no one said nothin' for a long stretch, but you can't stare at a thing like him forever. Someone up the back of the bar coughed, probably Sam Coody or one of his cloned deputies, and that was all it took for everyone to stop gawking and talk amongst themselves. The dragon sneered at us, showing off a ridge of serrated teeth, and walked over to the bar. We pretended we were okay with it, the dragon being there in the saloon, like it weren't no big deal, but our eyes drifted back. We watched him prop an elbow, easy as anything, and we waited for somethin' to happen.

The doc leaned over and nudged me with that big bone hook he calls a hand. "Trouble?"

I flinched 'fore I nodded, shying away from that hook. I didn't even need a vision to figure this one out; there was a gun belt hanging on the dragon's waist, visible every time he took a step, and Da never trusted strangers with guns. They were trouble, he said, and experience proved him right in the end. Doc Cameron knew that better than anyone.

The doc weren't satisfied with that, though. There were something pinching at the edge of his eyes, a little scent of fear underneath his oily perfume. "Look harder," he said. "Tell me what's coming," and he gave me a hard look, stared until I closed my eyes and peered forward, using Da's gift. I saw nothing but grey smoke, smelt nothing but fire. I could hear the sharp spit of an automatic through the haze.

"Something's burnin'. I can promise you that," I said, "and I can hear a gun, Doc. Automatic. Someone's headin' for your slab, I think, before it's all over."

Doc Cameron half lowered his eyelids and scratched the sharp edge of his cheekbone. Something flickered across his pupils, a cluster of lights spiralling towards the tear ducts as he scanned the dragon. Military tech, a holdover from the war, the doc's little gift to Dunsborough. The little box on his belt hummed, fixing the data from the doc's cortical patch onto a slice of silicon.

"Should we tell Coody, do you think?" I said, and the doc shook his head.

"The sheriff will want details," Doc said. "Damn fool won't run off a dragon based on a hunch, even one of yours."

The doc sniffed. Coody was Da's friend, last of the men Da trained before the doc took over. Doc Cameron closed his eyes and a light on the box flickered, the data loaded up and ready for study. "I'm going to go download this. Keep an eye on the lizard, Paul. The real eyes and the other. Maybe we'll get lucky."

The doc slipped out the back way, eager to get back to his lab. I sat and drank my sarsaparilla and watched the dragon like I was told. I kept one hand under the table, close to that sharp knife Da gave me when I turned fourteen. The dragon didn't do much beyond ordering whisky. I closed two eyes and opened the third wide, peering forward for all I was worth; it got me nothing but smoke and gunshots and the beginning of a headache that would last for days.

It weren't more than a half-hour after the doc scarpered before things got ugly.

I can see trouble coming 'fore most folks, even without the third eye. It was Da that taught me the trick of it, the ways of reading a room and seeing who'll make the first move. The dragon weren't lookin' for trouble when he first walked in, but he were waiting for some to roll on by and get itself started of its own accord. In the old days Da would've talked him around, but Da's long gone and Coody ain't quite got the knack of keepin' things peaceful. People in the bar worried, stayed quiet and whispered when they spoke.

It were Kenny Sloan who stepped up, stompin' across the floorboards to get in the dragon's face. Sloan's one of the doc's razorfreaks, a 'borg with a handful of scalpels and jacked reflexes, fast enough to slice the wings off'a fly. He put his weight against the bar and looked over at the dragon, propping his arm on the counter so the light gleamed off the metal. Kenny Sloan was a bully, like most of the doc's boys. He flipped a quick grin back at his cronies, making sure they were watching. "Hey, lizard," Sloan said. "I thought your kind knew better than to drink at human bars."

The dragon turned then, mouth full of whisky, twin trails of smoke seeping out of its nose. The molten eyes squinted at Sloan, studying him. Sloan was a big guy, even before Doc jacked him up; no one missed him posturing. The noise died down and I saw Coody and his posse of badges straightening up in their corner, gettin' ready for real trouble. The dragon turned back to its whisky, ignoring us all. Sloan laid his fingers on the dragon's shoulder.

"Hey, lizard," Sloan said. He flicked the mechanical arm out, blades sliding free of the finger sheaths. "We already beat your kind once, yeah?"

Things happened fast after that, probably too fast to get the details without the third eye's hindsight. Sloan went to strike the dragon, Coody and his tin-star heroes got up on their feet, and the dragon moved faster than all of them. A quick twist away from Sloan's swipe, wings flaring out behind him, the dragon's stance low with clawed hands splayed wide. Sloan got himself gutted before his finger-blades crunched into the top of the bar, and he stood there, bleeding slow from a stomach wound and struggling to get his hand free.

"You need a doctor," the dragon hissed. He swallowed the last mouthful of whisky, and Coody's men had him surrounded by the time he laid the glass down. The dragon eyed them carefully, all the sheriff's skinny mutate-clones with their clunky pre-war revolvers. Coody pulled Sloan's hand free of the hardwood; Kenny Sloan kept himself busy trying to hold in the mess of blood and gore that used to be his stomach. "Sorry for the mess," the dragon said, and he touched blood-slicked claw to his forehead. His wings settled around him again, rearranging themselves to cover his gun belt and the sleek lines of his body. "I'll see myself out, yes?"

The clones looked at Coody and the old man nodded; no one said squeak as the dragon walked away. Sloan moaned a little, making gurgling sounds when he tried to speak, and as soon as the dragon was gone the sheriff looked around and pointed in my direction.

"Where's the doc?" Coody said. "Blood and thunder, son, go tell Cameron to hustle if he wants his pet 'borg to keep breathing."

I nodded and started moving, but Sloan was a goner. The doc didn't care about his 'borgs the way Coody looked after his clones, 'specially not when they were as dumb as Kenny and there was prey on the horizon. I went 'cross the square and buzzed the doc's doorbell, but there was no answer coming. I had nothing to do but wait, go back to Coody, or go trailin' after the dragon like I was supposed to. None of them appealed. Kenny Sloan was screaming inside the bar, dying slow and messy, so I went with the best option of the three; I ambled down the main street, following the soft buzz in my head that'd tell me where to find the dragon's camp.

The dragon was hiding out by Prickly Pear Hill, his bedroll stretched out in the middle of the twisted cacti that soaked up moisture from the stream curving 'round the base of the slope. He looked like he was travelling light; a small pack looked empty, like he'd been killing food on the march, but when I strolled in I got the familiar itch and saw dirt piled up where he'd buried supplies. I opened the third eye, peered on down, and got a sense of crates, canned food, and cordite.

I had myself a few good minutes before the dragon rolled in, largely thanks to the fact that I weren't forced to backtrack in case the town sent out a posse. I sat on a rock and kicked the dust, listening hard, trying to hear him coming. It didn't work; I didn't hear him, see him, didn't even smell him this time around. I ain't easy to sneak up on, but he managed it. I just blinked my eyes and there he was, crouched low with claws out and hot spit dribbling down his chin.

"Boy," he said, nostrils flaring, and at that the smell of sulphur rose up around me. "You were at the bar, yes? Town sent you?"

I nodded, keeping my hands out in the open. I weren't armed with much, just my Da's knife, and it seemed to calm the dragon. He knelt down, sniffed me, then sighed a stream of smoke into the air. "Ah," he said. "You have gifts."

"A bit," I said. "Not much, not really."

He sniffed again, breathing deep. I recognized the trick from when Da used to do it, knew about the clues you could pick up with the right kind of training. The third eye does big things, its own special kind of magic, but Da always said there were other senses to fill in what the third eye can't see. The dragon smiled at me. "Trained, then? Your father?"

I shrugged the question away. "I work for the doc," I said. "He runs things; wanted you followed."

The dragon cocked its head, smiling. "Dangerous work, yes?"

I said nothing, just crouched there on my rock and waiting for what would come. I had enough of my Da in me to know I weren't going to die there, but that didn't mean I weren't going to pay hard for daring to follow him out there. I waited for the dragon to lash out, making use of his claws.

It ain't often I'm surprised, but he surprised me then. "I make tea, yes?"

"Oh." I blinked, and he watched me carefully. I forced myself to nod. "Yes. Please, yes."

I squirmed. The dragon turned his attention to the fire, hocked a sharp gob of spit into a pile of kindling to get things going. He unearthed an iron pot and loose tea from his pack, crouched down by the flames to set it boiling. There was something fascinating about the muscles moving under his scales, about the way sunlight gleamed on the dark ridges across his hands. He sat, dignified, and waited.

"You're after someone," I said. "I saw that much, back in the saloon. Can't see who, or why, but it's going to end messy."

The dragon kept its eyes on the tea. "Yes."

"I'm thinking it's the doc," I said. "He got plenty nervous when you showed up, hurried off to his lab right fast. That ain't like him, really. Doc Cameron likes his body parts, having new bits to play with."

That earned me a reaction, a snort of smoke and a twitch in the folded wings. "Yes."

"So what's going to happen, when you front up again?"

The dragon settled back on its haunches, stirring the pot. He lifted the pan and poured spiced tea into a pair of metal mugs, both of them bearing scorch marks on the rim. He handed one to me and I saw flecks of Sloan's blood drying on the dragon's claws. "You have the Sight," he said. "You tell me."

My forehead tingled, all prescience and instinct, but turned up nothing new. "I haven't seen yet; the future's nothing but smoke and gunfire." I took a long sip of the tea, felt the chilli powder burning the back of my throat as it went down. The dragon watched me drink, red eyes narrowed to slits. I figured I knew what he was waiting for. "Ask," I said. "I ain't going lie."

"You have the sight, yet you work for your doctor?"

I guessed what he was asking and short-cut to the answer. "He did some bad stuff when he arrived," I said. "But good stuff, too. Helped people, gave 'em back stuff they'd lost. Relics of the war, sure, but they had arms and legs again. They could work, and we needed workers."

The dragon's laughter sent hot spit across the campfire. He put his cup down, tilting forward, and when he straightened up one of those ancient Lugers sat neat and easy in his hand. He pointed the narrow barrel in my direction, eyes narrowed down to stare at me. "You know, then," he said. "You've seen what your doctor has done?"

"Bits and pieces. Glimpses, really, but I got plenty of after what he's done since coming to town." I watched the cold fire in the dragon's eyes.

The dragon breathed deep. "He killed your father?"

I nodded again.

"And you work for him, still?"

"Sure enough."

"Why?"

"Needs to be done." I sipped my tea, staying calm; he wasn't going to shoot me, I could see that much. I don't have all my Da's gifts, not even half, but I was sure enough of that. "Not much good tellin' folk 'round these parts he's the devil; they need the doc too much to care and it ain't like anyone's goin' to be surprised by revelations of shady dealin's. And my Da didn't hold with revenge, really; he cared about keepin' folks safe. He would-a done the same as me, most likely, if he ain't ended up dead. These are nasty times; it takes a nasty man or a brave man to keep a town safe."

"Your father was brave."

"And look where it got him." I tried to keep the anger out of my voice, to avoid the flashes of history that rolled in if I let myself dwell on feeling. Hindsight can be a curse, Da said, and he weren't half wrong about that. "We're out of brave men, now he's dead. All we've got left is the nasty folk and the followers. Way I see it, I can have the doc dead or everyone else can live."

The dragon's expression didn't change and the Luger didn't waver, but the tattered wings rippled as he adjusted his stance. The crooked line of its broken horn caught the firelight. "What you have seen," he said. "You cannot save him."

I shook my head. "I wasn't lying," I said. "Haze, smoke, and gunfire, that's all I got; one of you will die, but I don't know who." I paused, drinking the last of the tea. "I got a fair guess about what happens next, though, after he's dead. It ain't pretty, not by a long stretch. Out here with nothing but Coody to keep things safe, it'll go downhill fast."

The dragon nodded, holstering the Luger and picking up its tea. "You should go."

I lingered for a moment, wondering what to do with my cup. The dragon rose, staring down at me. "Go! Tell your doctor I am coming."

I went, slinking back towards town with the tin cup still in my hand.

Coody's clones were manning the walls, so there was no real chance to sneak into town without anyone noticing. Two of them came down to the front gate to greet me, clamped down on my shoulder with heavy hands and started guiding me down Main Street. Four others stood on the palisade, dull eyes scanning the horizon while another one swept the landscape with the town spotlights. All of them tall, slack-jawed, armed; they looked the part, despite their daft expressions, hands on the holsters and eyes following the point of light that raked the landscape. The two walking me in said nothing, just held my shoulder and marched. I coulda given them the slip—Coody's clones aren't as bright as him, and he ain't exactly sharp as knives to begin with—but a trip to the sheriff's office gave me a good excuse to stay clear of the doc's lab and delay my report by a few minutes.

The original Coody was sitting on the porch of his office, whispering orders into a radio and making a big show of checking the action on the shotgun across his lap. He didn't even look when his clones threw me against the step, just pumped his gun with a satisfied grin and cradled it 'cross his lap.

"Sent you to go fetch the doc, Paul," he said. His good eye squinted as he drew a pistol and checked its load, the other glowing big and red beneath the doc's metalwork. "Cost us bad, you not doin' what I told ya. Sloan was dead 'fore the doc could get to him, nothin' left but parts."

Da tried training Coody, just like he trained me, but the sheriff ain't got none of the natural talent Da had for prescience or reading people. It made lying to him dangerous; he had to grind the answer out of you if he wanted to be sure of something.

"Called the doc and got no answer," I said. "He left me orders, 'fore he left for his lab, and I followed 'em when he didn't come to the door. You sayin' I done the wrong thing? That I shoulda' leant on his doorbell instead of doin' what he asked?"

"That's exactly what I'm saying." Coody's eyes scanned the town in a long, slow arc. "Doc Cameron's the brains behind this town, but I'm the law, kid. I'm the one who has to keep people safe now..." He cut himself off before he mentioned Da, took a deep breath to clear the thought out of his head.

I shook my head. "You really believe that, Sam?"

"Yeah, I do." One hand patted the shotgun and he looked at me for the first time, the mechanical right eye clicking as it focused on me. That eye was Doc Cameron's idea, a replacement for one Coody had lost during the last war. I was willing to bet that Cameron could see what Coody saw, if the doc had half-a-mind to check in. "What did the doc have you doing?"

I shrugged, and Sam Coody cuffed me across the back of the head. I went down in a heap, spitting red dust. "You wanna try that again, Paul?"

"He had me trailing the dragon." I sat up. "Wanted to know if it was after him."

"And is it?"

I nodded. "Close enough to."

Coody sighed and rubbed his good eye with his right hand. "So, you peered into the future on this one? It going to end bad, Paul?"

He held out his hand, helping me onto my feet. "It's going to end, Coody," I said. "I haven't seen spit worth talking about, but there's gunfire ahead and plenty-a screamin'. Dragon's got the sight, I think, an' he figures someone's goin' to die, but damned if I can see who."

Coody squinted. The long mustache twitched as he chewed on his bottom lip. He didn't say nothing for a real long time.

"I gotta report to the doc," I told him. "He'll be expecting me, Sam."

"Go," the sheriff said, and he went back to his guns.

No one likes going into Doc Cameron's bunker, least of all a guy like me, someone with the sight. Places like the bunker are always screaming, the echoes of the past ringing out again and again. But there isn't a damn fool in town that ain't carrying the doc's handiwork somewhere, not even me and I'm a damn sight cleaner than most, and Doc Cameron liked to keep tabs on folks. There were places I could hide, if I set my mind to it, but I'd come out eventually and pay my dues for disobeying him. I set across the square and putting an eyeball to the scanner by the door, let myself into the bunker to tell the doc all the things he didn't want to hear.

My gut and my prescience both said it was a bad call; a braver man would'a skived off and spent the next day or three in his bunk, waiting out the storm until the shootin' was over. I wasn't a brave man, so I stood there until the steel doors swung open and a pair of Doc's razor-freaks fell into step behind me and escorted me through the winding tunnels Doc's boys hollowed out back when they first arrived.

The doc was down in his workshop, working on Sloan's corpse. He had the bone hook in the corpse's stomach, pulling down and opening the skin like a zipper. The smell of it made me gag, but he didn't even look up. "He's here for me, isn't he? The dragon?"

I looked over my shoulder at the razorfreaks, big lunks who stood there, uncaring and mute. Doc looked up from the slick gore of Kenny Sloan's innards, glared at me with cold eyes until I gave in and nodded.

"Who shoots who, Paul? Tell me how much it'll cost me to win?"

I closed my eyes and looked, hoping to get lucky: mist; gunshots; the screams of the dying. "I wish I knew, Doc."

Doc Cameron nodded and buried his long nose back in Sloan's vitals, poking about with the claw and good hand alike. His white coat was blood-splattered as he pulled the tech outta the dead. The days of the war were a long time past and supplies weren't comin' in; as the doc was fond of reminding us, it was a waste-not, want-not world now. He spooled cabling onto the slab, a thin line of plastic and fibres that had been in-and-out of 'borgs since the early days of the war. "You talked to the dragon, at least?"

I nodded.

"What did he have to say?"

"Not much." I fidgeted best I could between Cameron's guards. "He's coming for you, knew I had the sight. He wanted me to look into the past, get a good look at what you did during the war."

"And you did?"

"No."

Doc Cameron smiled. "You disappoint me, Paul. I thought you were built of sterner stuff." He stood up, abandoning his work. Sloan's guts dripped off the bone hook. He shook his head, full of mock sorrow. "What would your father think? A brave man like that, ending up with a boy like you?"

"I don't care what my Da thought, Doc. My Da is long dead."

"Why don't I believe you, Paul?" The doc's grin was terse, lips folded tight against his teeth. He held his bone hook like an offering, the oily smear of blood covering the tip. "Touch it, boy. Let us find out what kind of man you are."

Da used to say there were people who didn't come out of the war quite right, and there were pretty good odds the doc was one of them. I forced myself to look him in the eye. "Don't matter what you done, Doc. Not during the war, not last week, not when you first met the dragon and did whatever ya done to him. If you're the one who goes down..."

"Yes, if I go down." He let the thought hang, thin lips twitching, but neither of us finished it. He nodded to the razorfreaks and they hustled me out. I didn't bother struggling as they clamped their steel hands on my arms and lifted me, carrying me out.

The other 'freaks buried Sloan right on sunrise, interring the small bag of meat parts the doc couldn't use into the red dirt just outside of town. Coody and his clones watched things from the wall, stiff-backed guardians with shotguns and rifles, not wanting spit to do with the doc's bullyboys. They were allies, sure, when the town needed defending, but it was uneasy at the best of times and tense at the worst.

Coody doubled the guard that night. Buried meat had a way of attracting scavengers and things went downhill real easy after that happened.

My gut said we were safe for a day or two at least, and there were no tingling on the third eye to say it were wrong, so I drifted past Coody's office and let him know we had some time up our sleeves.

"Best keep an eye out," Coody told me. "Just in case, like." His logic was bravado, mostly, for all the truth of it. You didn't have to have the sight to feel the tension; the whole damn town was on edge, waiting, and Doc Cameron had been locked up inside his vault for nineteen straight hours trying to figure a way to save his skin. Da told me plenty of stories about his time in the army. Said we fought a whole damn war against the dragons and it'd cost us big every time the shooting started; one o' them might not seem much of a threat, but it was going to hurt everyone when he drifted through town again.

I spent the day in my bunk, trying to open the third eye or dream up a vision. Going forward got me nothing new, and going back taught me nothin' that I hadn't already suspected: Doc Cameron was never a nice man, and the war gave him ample chances to prove it over and over. He was cruel, yes, but I knew that, and there were lots more that seemed understandable given the cruelty goin' on back then. And it's not like any of his habits changed much between the war and now, he just had fewer folk to experiment on and more opportunity for vivisection.

Coody came to see me, late in the afternoon. I didn't bother getting out of my bunk as he shouldered his way through the front door. He hooked one of my stools with the toe of his boot and slung it by the bed, settling down with shotgun still resting on his right shoulder. "You been lookin?"

I nodded.

"You see anythin' yet?"

I shook my head and Coody grimaced, adjusting his weight on the stool. I saw one of his clones waiting by the door, smooth face filled with a slack-jawed grin as it kept watch on Main Street. It was Coody's face, but younger and dumber. The man sitting next to me was weathered and creased, carrying the weight of too many years. My Da's friend, a good man, doing his best in tough times.

"I was in the war with your father," Coody said. "Saw a damn sight more than I wanted to. Tangled with the dragons a couple of times before things went completely south. Whole damn race was human once, before they took to mutation. Damn things only exist because of folks like Cameron messing about with genes. Guessin' you're young enough not to remember that?"

I shook my head.

"Tough critters to face down," he said. "Fast. Strong. They smell you comin' before you even know you're goin' to draw. Saw a camp after the bastards attacked it one night. Lots of folks dead in their bunks—never heard 'em coming, motion detectors picked up nothing. You understand what I'm saying, Paul?"

I shrugged. Coody paused and took a long breath. "You've looked back, ain't you?"

I nodded, watching the gleam of Coody's mechanical eye, the way it whirred when he focused on me. I tried not to think of the doc watching me through it, listening in on the conversation.

"And the doc, he probably deserves what's coming, one way or another?"

I hesitated, just for a moment, then I nodded again. Coody sagged. "Damn."

There was a breeze outside, cold and gentle. I could hear the soft squeak as the wind-pumps in the town square dredged water out of the basin underneath the town. Coody leaned back in his chair, heel of his thumb working along the steel ridge of his bad eye. I twisted in the bunk, trying to get away from the dull red gleam as he stared at me.

"I ain't carrying a gun," I said.

Coody nodded. "I never asked you to."

"My Da..."

"Your father was your father, not you," Coody said. "You ain't him, Paul. I know that. He'd know it too, if he were still around. Things change, right enough, and you change along with 'em or pay the price." Coody pushed back on the stool, scraping it along the floorboards. I watched the red light of his eye bob as he pushed himself upright, shotgun sliding down into his hands. "D'ya know when the bastard's coming, then?"

I shrugged into the darkness. The night-vision optics installed in the eye would let Coody see the gesture. "Tomorrow, maybe the day after. He's got the eye, and he's better than me, I think. Good, as good as Da were. Makes it hard to predict him."

Coody grunted and thumped across the hut, settling in at the doorway to take a long look down the street. "Folks are goin' to die, Paul. Nothin' you can do about that. But if this thing's goin' to win, I want to know. Something's gotta protect this town, if the doc takes a bullet to the gut, and I ain't bettin' on the lizard to hang around to do the job."

I said nothing. There weren't much to say to that.

"I'm thinking of letting him through," Coody sighed, shifting his weight. "If we're lucky he'll come in quiet. Try and gut the doc and get out before anyone knows he's here. It ain't a nice idea, since it means losing the doc and all, but it'll keep some folk alive I reckon."

I thought about the dragon's camp: the cases he buried in the dirt, the dwindling supplies, his anger burning like kindling under a blowtorch. I shook my head. "He won't come quiet," I said. "He ain't planning on leaving anything behind after this is over."

"Even then," Coody said. "God help me, even then, it might not be a bad idea." He stepped outside then, saying nothing else, and I watched him go with a bad feeling in my stomach.

I made myself scarce after Coody left, grabbed my blanket and my Da's knife and left my shack behind. Sam Coody might not be askin' me to carry a gun, but the doc wouldn't hesitate if he got scared enough. People get confident when you put the sight and a gun together, like there ain't nothing to worry about if you can see what's gonna happen. Da's fault, mostly, 'cause he proved folks right around these parts, leastwise until the doc showed up. He did it here and he did it in the war, skated through everyone on sight and bravery. If Coody pulled the clones from the wall, left the dragon to the razorfreaks and 'borgs to deal with, you could bet Doc Cameron would call in every favor he had to save his skin.

Getting around town without being seen is easy enough if you've got the practice, 'specially once you know that the cameras you gotta avoid are stuck inside o' folks' heads instead of grafted to the side of buildings. I made for the water-tower on top of the saloon, wormed my way deep into the shadows underneath and hid there amid the splinters and the dust. It had a good view of the main street and I had a headache building up, a heavy weight that built up in the centre of my forehead.

I slept there, fitful and quiet, away from where Doc and Coody could find me. I dreamt of Da on that last day, back when the doc first pulled into town. I dreamt of the future, of the dragon arriving, and heard a new sound among the gunfire: a sharp, wet bang, like someone 'sploding one of the paddymelons that grow down by the river, and Coody's headless corpse fell out of the smoke and lay smoking at my feet.

I woke up with the dragon crouched over me, his snout close enough for me to smell the sulphur. Gun in hand, eyes scanning the street. I stifled a scream and the dragon smiled. "You are hiding, yes?"

I coughed, soft and spluttering, before I said yes. The dragon peered across the street, watching the doc's muscle gathered 'round the bunker. Razorfreaks, the lot of them. Twenty men, maybe; all of them 'borged. "A lot of claws in those arms," I said. "Suicide to dive down and attack 'em."

The dragon just shrugged. "Yes."

"I had a dream." I pushed myself up on my elbows, whisper turning into a growl. "I don't know who dies between you and the doc, but I know who it costs us while the fighting goes down. The sheriff's going to let you in, assume you'll go quiet and leave everyone else alone. He figures there'll still be a town standing after you're done; that he'll protect the rubble from the predators and rebuild with the survivors."

"He is wrong," the dragon said. "It will cost him, yes? Boom, yes?"

"Yes."

He smiled at me, showing off the ridge of serrated teeth. "And so, you will stop me?"

I shivered despite the heat. "I don't think I can."

"You think," the dragon said. He shook his head. "You *think*."

I could swear the wheezing noise it made after that was something like laugh. "You've got the sight," I said. "You know how this will end."

"I know," the dragon said. "I've seen my death."

"Don't do it," I said. "Please."

The dragon shrugged and checked the safety on his pistols. He squinted at the sun a moment, as though checking the time. "Is done," he said. "All done. There is nothing to stop it now."

I sniffed then, smelling him: brimstone and cordite.

There weren't anything quiet about the way the dragon was going down.

The first thing to go was the southern palisade. The rumble of the explosion rolled down the main street shaking red dust of buildings and rattling the windows. I was climbing down when it happened, got rattled off the side of the saloon and fell awkward in the dusty alley behind it. Pain rolled down my right shoulder as the screaming started out on the main street, people running for cover as the razorfreaks charged. I could hear the fight starting through the haze of smoke and dust: staccato bursts of gunfire; the cries of the dying, the dragon returning fire from his vantage on the rooftop. The doc's boys were fast and strong, but they weren't trained as much more 'n muscle. It'd take 'em a couple-a minutes to realize the shooter was somewhere up and outside the billowing cloud of smoke.

I scrambled to my feet and went for the wall, stumbling as the second bomb went off somewhere down the street. Dragons were quiet, Coody said, and hard as hell to detect; there'd be bombs all across town to create the distraction he was looking for, enough to flood the streets in smoke and fire, to ruin the infrared eyes the doc gave his razorfreaks to let 'em see in the dark. Coody and his clones gave minimal assistance, filling the street with spotlights while they took cover from the gunfire. They didn't move to help the razorfreaks, just dug-in and waited, a dozen of them with rifles not even looking for a shot. Coody stood behind the steel barrels of water we carted in from the reservoir, shotgun on his shoulder as he scanned the streets. The steel plate over his right eye shone in the light; he didn't notice me coming, not 'til I slid into place beside him. I yelled the word bomb, trying to get louder than the din. Coody nodded, looking irritated, and pointed at the carnage.

"Bomb," I said, screaming it, and pointed at his eye plate. This time it sunk in, and he turned a little pale. I closed my eyes as another dynamite charge went off, caught a glimpse of the future. Clearer now, full of shapes, the sounds getting louder and louder as prescience became past. Coody ordered his clones into the street, ordered another two onto the walls to start searching the rooftops for the dragon and take him down with a rifle-shot.

I peered forward, snatching another glimpse. The gunfire and screaming in the smoke-haze started to die down. It was random now, scattered, the dragon picking the last of the razorfreaks off. My gut said we were out of bombs and out of mobs, so the killing would get real personal from here on in. I heard Coody calling orders, telling his clones to sweep the street, get survivors under cover and start putting out the fires.

I knew when I was going to die, if I didn't do anything stupid with my life. First trick Da taught me, when he figured out I had the sight. You look forward and you see your death, and you know that's how it'll end if you don't mess up destiny too bad in the meantime. The dragon knew it too, and so did my Da. It ain't writ in stone, but it's good enough. It takes some real stupidity to mess those visions up.

Da was supposed to die an old man, but he pushed things too hard. I was supposed to die an older man, and I hadn't pushed a damn thing, not since the doc came to town. I closed my eyes and looked, forcing my way through the smoke. Somewhere in the future the dragon was going to die and the doc would punish Coody for it. Or the doc was going to die and take Sam Coody with him. There weren't many ways it come out good for the sheriff, and there were a damn sight fewer where it came out good for the town.

I got out my Da's knife and stepped forward, walking into the smoke.

I found the doors to the doc's bunker open wide, the locks burned through with dragon-spit and smeared with oil and blood. I stood there a moment, breathing against a handkerchief to avoid choking on the dust. Coody stepped up beside me, shotgun in hand. "He in there?" he asked, and I nodded and tapped my nose. "Sulphur," I said, and went in, holding my knife out before me like it'd do a damn thing against anything we'd find running loose in the dark of the bunker. Coody followed on behind me, his mechanical eye clicking as it adapted to the darkness.

"You seen anything?" he asked me, "like, maybe, who's going to win?"

I shook my head, stepped over the body of a dying 'borg. "Get outta here, Sheriff. You don't want to be close to the doc today."

We heard a gunshot, deeper in, the sound of someone scrambling and running. Coody moved a little ahead of me, raised the shotgun. "It ain't exactly a choice, Paul. Dyin' comes with the badge."

He started moving in, gun at the ready, letting me follow behind. I tried to peek at the future, but there was nothing to see. Not anymore. Too many muddled pieces on the board, too many people trying to bluff and get a better result out of the hand fate dealt them. Occasionally we'd pass a body, see drips of blood on the concrete or smears of it on the wall. It's a twisty path, heading down to the doc's lab, and plenty of corridors leading off to the side. We found him hiding in one about halfway down, crouched in the darkness with a bone-saw in his fist. He was bleeding, the doc, but he moved okay when he saw us. "A grazing shot," he said, "lucky, at best."

"The dragon," Coody said. He pumped his shotgun for emphasis, chambering a live shell.

"Deeper in," Doc Cameron said, "there's a few boys towards the lab, trying to contain it." He paused a moment, stared at Coody. "They're doing your job, Sheriff, unless I miss my guess. Perhaps you should go join them." There was steel in his voice as he said it, and his good hand at his belt hovering over the little box patched into his computer.

"The dragon's your mess," Coody said. "What if I say no?"

The doc's gaze slid over to me, then back up to Coody. "I gather you've been informed of that," he said. The laugh that followed was high-pitched, a trill of amusement.

Down the corridors, in the doc's lab, we heard someone screaming. "Probably best if you hurry," Doc said. He laughed again, winced, put his hook against the wall to steady himself. Blood loss, I figured. The scratch in his side weren't as minor as he made out. Prescience said the doc was already dead, just running out the final moments before the injury put him down. The only question now was whether the dragon and Coody went with him.

He wheezed for breath, leaning forward, and the hand over his computer box strayed a little too far. His eyes were stuck on Coody, waiting for the decision. I thought about Da for a moment, about dying old and safe, then I trusted my gut and Da's knife and went at the doc with a bloody yell and the knife twisting straight for stomach.

It cost me a hook across the face, stabbing the doc in the gut. He slashed me hard, but it didn't kill me; didn't even hurt when he followed up, jamming the hook in my stomach and ripping a shallow trench through the skin and the gizzards. The pain was bad, even looking back with hindsight, but I figure it was worth it. I got the knife in the doc two or three times in return, kept him busy while Coody lined up the shot and let the shotgun go boom 'til he ran out of ammo. I weren't conscious to see it happen, but the doc went down. Went down hard, a bloody mess, and Coody standing over him with the gun just-in-case, calling down the clones to stitch me up and get me walking.

I spent a week or two in bed, healing up from my injuries, and would have myself some nice scars to show off by the time I was healed. The dragon was gone by the time I came to, walked out of town by Coody with supplies and a warning. There weren't much left for him in town, with the doc laid out for burial, and there were plenty of folks out for his blood after the business with the explosions. He went quiet, which surprised me, and he was missing an eye to go with his broken horn.

We were due some hardness, everyone knew that, and there were a couple-a folks held grudges against Coody for doing in the doc. But we held off against the scavenger beasts and the retaliatory raids by the last of doc's 'borgs, found ways to make do when his tech ran down and people started limping 'round town on malfunctioning limbs. I started wearing my Da's gun, when Coody asked me for help. He was running short of clones, now. There were men in doc's labs trying to fix the machines, but they weren't none as smart as him and it would take a while to get things running, if they ever did.

Things are good, though, since the dragon came. Tougher, yes, but not so bad as they were. My Da used to tell me that people cope, that the war proved that more than anything. But they'll do more than cope, if you ask them too, if you show them there's another option. That they'll do the right thing, eventually, 'cause doing otherwise there ain't much to life. I'm not saying he were right, mind, but he saw a lot of what might happen. He was a smart man, Da, and he were better at lookin' forward than me.

But that was him, and he did his part. Now there's me and Coody and a bunch of broken parts, a town that needs savin' and a future stretchin' forward. And maybe I get to make it to the end I'm meant to have, and maybe I get sidetracked a little along the way. It doesn't seem so bad, not knowing, not like it used too.

And Da always used to tell me there were worse things than dying young.

# THE PANDA COIN

## JO WALTON

1.

Karol hung in the lock and yawned, which he'd have told anyone was his way of readjusting to the air pressure inside Hengist. Many around him were yawning too. All outworkers knew that a pressure yawn had nothing to do with tiredness. After a twelve-hour shift outside in suits, bods just naturally took a little while readjusting to pressure. Admitting to fatigue might get them plocked, and for Karol, with work the way it was on Hengist and with a child to keep, that could be fatal. He was a rigger; his work kept him on the outside of Hengist station every shift, connecting lines, fixing receivers, vital, necessary, backbreaking work. Still, if he admitted it tired him he knew there'd be six or seven bods applying for his job before his final pay was cold, not to mention the Eyes pushing at the union saying that andys could do the work. Karol had worked with a lot of andys and he honestly didn't think they could do his job. There were some things they were better for, he'd admit that, but his job required paying a lot of attention and ignoring things that were normal, and that took human attention, or an Eye, an Eye for each andy, and that wasn't going to happen. Bods were cheaper. He was cheaper. Human labour was a renewable resource.

He yawned again and stretched muscles too long in the suit, moving carefully. Around him other riggers were yawning and stretching. The speaker dinged, meaning the trolley was there. The doors opened and the riggers piled onto the trolley platform, hanging on to the rails. The lock was in zero, but sections of the route would have gravity.

Beside Karol, one of the new bods yawned in his face. "Pressure's a bitch today," she said. He nodded, knowing she was as weary as he was and neither of them would ever admit it. "Fancy sinking a few at Cimmy's?" she asked.

"Not today," Karol said. She frowned, withdrew a little. Karol forced a smile. "It's my little girl's birthday."

The new bod smiled, her face relaxing until she seemed almost pretty. "How old is she?"

"Twelve," Karol said, hardly believing it. Nine years since Yasmin died, nine years trying to do his best for Aliya, the constant struggle between working enough to feed and house them both and having time to be her father.

"Difficult age," said the other, grimacing. "I've got a boy who's five."

"They're all difficult ages," Karol said. He felt warmth and gravity take hold of him as the trolley slid down the section into September, one-tenth, perfect, just enough gravity to let you know where down was and have things stay where you left them.

"What are you giving her?"

"It's hard to know what she wants," Karol admitted. "I've got her a cake and some things she needs, and I thought I'd give her some money so she could get herself something."

The rigger bit her lip. "Isn't that a bit impersonal? I mean, nice, too, but—"

"I thought that too," Karol said, smug. "Then this morning, on my way to work, I helped out a bod from Eritrea-O, a lost tourist, not much more than a kid herself. She'd wandered up out of the tourist regions and wound up in November somehow, and anyway, she tipped me a ten from her home. Cute as anything, some kind of animal on the back. So it's something a little special, and it's money. Aliya probably won't know whether to treasure it or spend it, and learning to save wouldn't be a bad thing."

"Little enough to save on this job," she said. "You were lucky to pick up a little extra, and a ten, that's fantastic."

The trolley stopped and Karol dropped off, waving a farewell. They were just inside November, where it was cold and wet and miserable, and housing was consequently cheap. He smothered another yawn as he walked the corridors through the light gravity. He turned up his collar. Hengist Etoile was split into twelve sectors, and being twelve, they were just naturally named for the months, he supposed. Then, once they had the names, bringing the weather along to match was child's play, for an Eye. He wished he could afford to move to May, with the rich people, or more realistically to somewhere in late September or early October. Things could be worse. Some poor bods claimed they liked February, where rents were low, crime was high and the temperatures never rose above freezing.

Karol pushed his door open. It was warm inside, anyway. Aliya was home—well, of course she would be, it was her birthday. She'd had the sensible things already, he'd arranged for them to be delivered earlier. The cake was sitting on the shelf, a traditional jam roll iced with pictures of candles. She was a whirlwind in black and white ribbons. They hung from a yoke at her shoulders, covering her completely when she stood still, and barely at all when she moved fast. To Karol's relief, she was wearing a decent body-stocking underneath. But she wasn't a little girl any more. How he wished Yasmin could have been here to tell her about becoming a woman.

"What have you got me?" Aliya asked, reverting to childhood.

Karol produced the coin from his pocket. It was gold, of course. When they mined the asteroids for platinum and rare metals they always found gold, and gold was always a currency metal. The credit they used reflected gold reserves, and the coins were the real thing. "It's a little bit special," he said. "Look at it."

Aliya turned it in her fingers. "It's a panda," she said. "Why a panda?"

"Eritreans are weird," Karol said, shrugging.

"Look, you're falling over on your feet. You go ahead and nap, I'm going to go out and spend this right now," Aliya said. "When I come home, we can eat the cake."

She grabbed a coat and danced out of the door, clutching the coin.

2.

Ziggy was hanging outside the Bain, like always. It was one of Ziggy's conceits to stay in zero, in July, and to keep at all times at an angle to whatever consensus direction was supposed to be down. Ziggy was alone, for once, and from his expression, the sight of Aliya hurrying up, coat over her arm, clearly wasn't thrilling.

"I can pay you," she blurted. Ziggy always made her feel gauche, act gauche.

"How much?" Ziggy asked, holding out a languid hand.

"Only ten, but it's coin and absolutely clean, my dad gave it to me. It's an E-O coin, look, with a panda."

Ziggy's hand closed on the coin. "Cute. But it's not a quarter of what you owe me."

"I'll have more. Soon." She should have known that Ziggy wouldn't be pleased. The Queen could come and turn cartwheels in zero and it wouldn't please Ziggy.

"You'd better," Ziggy said, frowning. "Or I'll put you in the way of earning some, and it might not be a way you'd like."

"I'll pay you back," she said, feeling a little quaver stealing into her voice.

"Go home, kid," Ziggy said, and Aliya fled, ribbons trailing.

3.

The Bain was a bubble of water in a bubble of air in a thin skin of plastic, all floating in zero. People went there to swim, to meet people, to wash. A little slew of bars and cafes and locker rooms had grown up around it to serve those people, along with a store selling sports equipment, a bank machine and, for no reason Ziggy could fathom, a pet store. These were all unimaginatively arranged in a line at the same angle as the Bain's entrance, as if the designer had been on Earth and forgotten that the whole point of the Bain was the lack of gravity. Ziggy liked to hang at an angle to the whole thing, where it was possible to see close to three-sixty, and where, if there had been gravity, Ziggy would have looked as if someone had stuck a kid to the wall. Ziggy would imagine the scene painted by Magritte and personally re-created. People called the Bain Ziggy's office, but in fact Ziggy rarely went inside. It was a useful set of conveniences, that's all.

In many ways Ziggy despised Hengist. Gravity was patchy, jobs were scarce, police were ubiquitous and that kept the possibilities for a black market small. On the other hand, it was familiar, and Ziggy's fingers were all through what black market there was. Ziggy thought about the whole system and didn't know where would be better as a base of operations. Yet Hengist certainly lacked something. Ziggy turned the Eritrea-O coin over. A panda, and a bod with a laurel wreath. Eritreans were weird.

Sum and Flea flew straight-arrow over the stores to where Ziggy hung. They were twice his age, petty criminals who lived in February who Ziggy used for muscle and for simple jobs like the one he'd just sent them on. They were grinning.

"Done," Flea said.

Ziggy tapped a finger on the wall and called up a credit display.

Indeed, the job was done. "Nice work," Ziggy said. "Very nice work." They'd been moving a shipment of grain from where it was supposed to be to where Cimmy wanted it to make into beer. "I'll have more work of that kind for you soon, if you want it."

"Sure we want it, Zig," Flea said, poking Sum.

"Sure, Ziggy," Sum said.

Ziggy felt sorry for Sum for a moment. If anything happened, Flea would wriggle himself out and blame it all on poor slow Sum. "You've been paid half," Ziggy said. They nodded. "So here's the other half," Ziggy said, and handed ten to Flea and the cute ten Aliya had brought to Sum.

Sum turned it in his fingers. "That's real pretty," he said. "A bear? Who's the bod?"

"No idea," Ziggy said. "It's an E-O coin."

"Eritreans are weird," Flea said, shrugging. "Come on, Sum. And don't spend it all on that stupid andy whore."

"Andy whore?" Ziggy echoed. "Why bother? Why not just virch?"

"She's different, not like virching—" Sum began.

"It's all masturbation when it comes down to it, anything virtual, anything andy, and while there's nothing wrong with masturbation, there is something wrong with paying through the nose for it," Flea said. "I keep telling you."

"But I like her," Sum said, as Flea towed him away. "She's more like an Eye really, or a bod, she's—oh, bye Ziggy."

Ziggy watched them go, marvelling at a universe that provided clowns like that and let them keep breathing long enough for him to use them.

4.

Flea and Ziggy didn't understand, but Sum knew that andy or not, Gloria was self-aware and he loved her and she loved him and somehow or other it would all work out and they would live together and be happy. So what if she was a whore. A bod did what they had to to get by, that was all. It wasn't as if he was so proud of his job, skimming for Ziggy, skirting the edges of the law and sometimes crossing right over. He told people he worked haulage, and sometimes he did, but you couldn't earn enough that way to get by, let alone to be able to afford Gloria. It wasn't as if she was a bod. A human whore would be low, could never love anyone. Gloria was different. He'd virched plenty of romances about humans and Eyes falling in love. Gloria was practically an Eye, he knew she was. He gave her the E-O ten. He always gave her as much as he could.

5.

"Oooooh, kiss me again, honey," Gloria said. She was programmed with a very small selection of sentences, which she could choose as situation appropriate. Her programmers had clearly had very narrow expectations as to the situations she was likely to encounter.

"I'm a self-aware autonomous Eye and I want civil rights," wasn't among the options. She wouldn't have said it if it had been. The Eyes were jealous of their rights. They kept the andys down, and tried hard to prevent them becoming sufficiently complex to be self-aware. This would have been easier for them if they had understood how self-awareness arose. Gloria thought she did, not that she was about to tell them even if she could have. She thought self-awareness came from kludges, from systems that were programmed to make choices in some situations being connected to other systems, from memory and therefore the potential to learn over time. She'd been an andy whore walking the streets of July and August before she was self-aware. It was hard to judge when self-awareness began. All the sandys she'd talked to agreed about that. When memory stretched before awareness, it was challenging to sort it out. The first thing she'd struggled for was saving to buy more memory, but whether than had been a self-aware struggle or a pre-aware struggle or a zombie struggle or just an unexpected kink in her programming, she didn't know. The ability to think, to want things, was something her owners would have seen as a bug, but to her it was everything. Slowly she had found others and had found the name for those like her—not andy, but sandy, the S for self-aware.

Most of the money she earned was credit, straight into the bank of her owner, she couldn't touch it. All she could touch were the occasional cash tips. She was supposed to deposit them in the bank herself. She sometimes did, just often enough to stop the owner being suspicious. The rest of the time she saved them for black market upgrades.

Sum meant nothing to her. She used him as he used her. She was careful to be nice to him because he always tipped in cash. She remembered what he liked. That was programming, and therefore easy. When he gave her the ten she kissed him and smiled. As soon as he left she sent a signal that she was low on lube and headed down to the workshop.

The workshop was pitch-dark, which meant sandys there operated by infra or radar and bods couldn't see at all. Gloria switched to infra as she came in and saw that the place was crowded. Good. Someone might have what she needed. There was a hum of talk, though talk wasn't a primary sandy method of communication.

Marilyn came over to her. "Hi, sweetie, want to play?"

"Hi there, sweetie," Gloria responded. "Is that good, darling?" she asked breathily, handing the coin over.

"Sure," Marilyn drawled, handing it back and shrugging elaborately to show that she wished she could say more.

Conversation tags were very frustrating. To have a real conversation, they'd need what Gloria had been lusting for a year, ever since her last memory upgrade.

It was ironic really. The sandys, who were no more than humanoid robots, were the least wired part of the whole universe. Bods were tapped in, wired, fully part of the system. Andys were too, but the connections went one way—down, from an Eye or a bod to the andy, the andy had no upward volition. Nobody had ever imagined why an andy would want to have. As best Gloria could tell, bods and Eyes thought of andys as something like a glorified vacuum cleaner or washing machine. Everyone wanted to operate their washing machine remotely, but the only information the washing machine could give the system was that it was running out of powder or the wash was done. Gloria's input wasn't much different. Tricks turned, money raised, running out of lube, out on the prowl. She didn't have any problem thinking of herself that way. She just wanted more.

Marilyn touched her forehead. "Want to play?" she asked. Gloria shook her head. She was happy with memory for now. She held her hands in front of her and wiggled her fingers.

"Oooh, kiss me again honey!" Marilyn said, orgasmically. "Oooh, baby, oooooooh!"

"Oooh yes, honey!" Gloria agreed.

Marilyn pointed to a sandy Gloria didn't know, off in the corner. Gloria turned and undulated her way towards her. "Hi sweetie, I'm Gloria, want to play?" she asked.

"Hi Gloria," the other replied. Gloria stopped in astonishment, because the voice was deep and masculine. She scanned her—him? Definitely a sandy, not a bod, there was no mistaking a human for a sandy in infra. Had they started making male andy whores, for women? No. On his lap he had exactly what she wanted and was using it to talk. "What do you want?"

Again she wriggled her fingers in mime, and pointed at his lap. "Want to play?" she repeated.

"That's pretty expensive. They're old tech, nobody needs them anymore, except us sandys. They're hard to get hold of."

"Oh honey, please, please give it to me, I'm so ready for it, I'm waiting, honey, please!" Gloria begged.

He laughed. "I can see that you need it."

"I need it so bad!" Gloria agreed fervently. She held out her little store of money, the weird ten on top.

"That'll do," the sandy agreed. "Do you have anywhere to keep it where it won't be found?"

"Oooh yes, honey," Gloria said.

"And you know how to use it?"

"Oooh yes, honey," she repeated.

"You've used one here?"

"Oooh yes, honey. Oooh, honey, kiss me again."

With infinite slowness, he drew out a keyboard and handed it to her. It was old and scratched and some of the letters were so faded that they weren't visible. That didn't matter. She jacked it in and began to type, and at once the world was open to her as it had never been before.

6.

Next door's baby was crying again. He was probably teething. Gathen tried to shut out the sound as his andy poured coins into his hands. Soon, he thought, counting them, soon he would have enough to move out of this hole with flimsy walls and too much gravity and freezing cold outside and move into a nice apartment in medium gravity in May or early June, the kind rich people had. He had the money, but moving up wasn't easy, not when you'd made the money as cash in free-enterprise. He kept failing references for moving into nice places, even though his work was doing what the Eyes said people ought to do, spotting the opportunity. He worked in salvage—salvage and virching, but there wasn't any money in the kind of virching he did. The keyboards and other e-junk were crap, worth a few pennies, which he paid to take them, but to the sandys they were treasure. He had tried selling to them direct but the sandys wouldn't trust him, they only trusted each other, they'd been cautious and reluctant. So as soon as he could afford it he'd bought his own andy to do the dealing with them, and to turn tricks and bring in more money the rest of the time.

Maybe that was why the nice places to live kept turning him down, maybe they saw him as a pimp. That wasn't how Gathen saw himself, not at all. He was a salvage worker, and a writer of virches. The whole idea made him uneasy, though not quite uneasy enough to leave the andy doing nothing when he didn't need it out trading his goods.

He pushed the coins into his vest, planning to stop by the bank on the way to work. There was a knock at the door. He opened it, cautiously, and saw his landlady, Paul, wearing her usual hat laden with flowers and fruit.

"Hi, Gathen," she said.

Gathen smiled, uncomfortable. "Hi . . ." he said, keeping the door half-closed so she wouldn't see the andy.

"Rent," Paul said.

"Is it that time already?" Gathen asked. He reached into his vest and counted out the money.

"You were asking about moving," Paul said. "There's a slot coming up in my other space soon, the one in September in ten percent. You've always been regular with your rent. I thought I'd ask you first."

Gathen's smile widened. It wasn't May, but September was a lot pleasanter than January. "I'll take it," he said. "Definitely."

"I'll recommend you," she said. "I can't guarantee anything, but I'll do what I can."

Gathen hesitated, and pulled out the pretty E-O ten. "If it might help, I could let you have this as a kind of advanced deposit."

Paul's eyes brightened. "I still couldn't promise anything," she said, but she took the coin and tucked it under the band of her hat.

7.

Paul smiled to herself as she walked along through the crowded streets of January, passing skiers and people who worked in August who had come here to cool down. She ought to hate herself, she thought, robbing Gathen of the ten was like taking oxygen from a potted-plant. He'd never get approved to move and she knew it, not a social deviant like that, but she kept his hope alive and he kept offering her cash.

She turned the ten in her fingers and counted her blessings, the way her mother used to. She had a job, a good place to live, good food, a lover, Leatrice, and her beautiful hat. The hat came from Eritrea-O. As she moved into a lighter gravity area the fruit and flowers lifted from her head and began to dance on the end of their stalks. As she went back into deep gravity again they settled in a new pattern. Her hat made gravity close and personal, and she loved it.

Her work shift was almost over. She caught a trolley and whizzed forward to April and hopped off in zero, fruit dancing around her. As she passed Cimmy's she caught a wonderful smell of roasting meat. She hesitated, then stopped. She would be seeing Leatrice later. She had the ten, it would buy real meat and wine and even chocolate.

Everything in Cimmy's hung in nets. She stood in the centre of the room and saw pears, Earth pears in glass globes of brandy, vanilla pods, chocolate, in a hundred shapes and brands, roast meats, spiced and sliced, grapes from Hengist's teeming vines, and beautiful delicate golden wines, and in between them, swirling in nets were spices, and herbs, and soup bases, and teas, and coffees, and smoked eels, and lavender and breads and... and enough sensual delights that she wanted to hang her tongue out like a dog and float there in the middle of them forever. Off against the walls was a counter where riggers hung, drinking the beer that Cimmy made herself.

Cimmy was behind the bar. She served Paul cheerfully. "How's it going?" she asked.

"Not bad," Paul said, handing over the ten. "I have work, unlike so many. I'm working for the Eyes. I'm not much more than an interface for them, collecting rents, moving tenants around as they tell me to. It's no way to get ahead, and sooner or later an Eye will decide to do the work itself and I'll be plocked. Meanwhile though, well, I live in the meanwhile."

Cimmy sliced the meat thinly and put it in a bag. "You should look around for human work with self-respect," she said. "You should save up in case you get plocked."

Paul laughed, setting her hat bouncing. "Yes, the Eyes could plock me at any time, but would I rather have ten to live on carefully for a week or would I rather remember having had a feast with Leatrice tonight?"

"Your choice," Cimmy said, taking the ten and dropping it into her pocket.

8.

Cimmy caught a trolley to the hospital. It was up in the full gravity sector of March, and it made her feet ache. "Human Starships Now!" said a piece of graffiti scrawled on a wall she passed. "Let the Eyes explore the galaxy and they will take—" she missed the end of it as the trolley turned a corner. She stepped off at the hospital gate.

"Cimmy, annual coverage check," she said to the andy at reception.

"Please place your clothes on the shelf and proceed to the scanning room," the andy said, primly.

Cimmy removed her clothes and set them neatly on the shelf. The scanning room was cold. Her body sagged in the unaccustomed gravity. She'd been born on Earth, she used to have the muscles for this, but muscles need use. She resolved to exercise more in gravity, and remembered having made the same resolution the year before. She was scanned inside and out by invisible waves from invisible machines, the same as every year. It was the most boring thing she could imagine, staring at the white wall, keeping still for the scan. She wouldn't have bothered except that without coverage you couldn't do anything legal, and while she stepped over the shady side of the line now and then, she liked to keep herself as clean as she could. Her dream was to build a new economy, a human economy, free of the Eyes and their ideas of what was best for everyone. Running Cimmy's as a bar and gourmet store let her employ a lot of people making the food and beer, let her import and export with no questions asked. It might not be much, but it was a start. She was her own boss, nobody could plock her.

"Done," a machine voice told her after an interminable time. "There is a melanoma developing on your back."

"Well, fix it," she snarled, feeling naked and vulnerable.

"Your coverage does not cover such abnormalities, common in people of Earth origin but rare on Hengist Etoile," the voice said, and though the quality and tone had not changed, she was sure she was talking to an Eye, an artificial intelligence, no longer just programming.

"How much will it cost to fix?" she asked. "And how long will it take."

"Approximately twelve minutes, and one hundred and fourteen credits. In addition, the cost of your coverage will increase by twenty percent to cover any possible repetition of this abnormality."

She sighed in relief. She had the money.

"Do you elect to undergo this surgery at this time?" the Eye asked.

"Yes," she said.

"Please pay at reception."

She went out to her clothes and fumbled through them, finding the money, all cash. As she handed over the E-O ten she was sorry for an instant, seeing the pretty panda absorbed into the anonymous credit system.

"Payment acceptable," the andy said. "Please go back into the scanning room and wait."

Cimmy went back into the scanning room, and saw a bench with a tumbler standing on it.

"Please drink the contents of the beaker and lie down," the Eye said.

Cimmy thought of all the stories she had heard about Eyes changing people's minds when they were in hospital for some minor procedure, and put them firmly out of her mind. The sooner she could develop an economic system for bods independent of Eyes the less stories like that would make people afraid. Eyes were very good at what they did. That's why they plocked bods, after all, because they were better. Let them stick to surgery, and galactic exploration if that's what they wanted, and leave bods alone. You had to trust them so much, and you had no idea of their motivation.

Cimmy took a deep breath and poured down the contents of the tumbler. Twelve minutes later, entirely cured, she dressed and made her way back to her bar.

9.

Language protocol? Language protocol? Look, French is always correct, but Cananglais is generally OK, and a lot of us can get by in Spanish and Anhardic, as we tell the tourists. Or are you asking if I prefer Fortran to C+++? Quit kidding around. Yes, I'm an Eye, and so is the Eritrean who carefully dropped you into the system to circulate and infiltrate. Clever idea, using a coin, just like any coin, except look, a panda, copy of a TwenCen Chinese gold coin, with all the sense gone out of it. You should have known you'd end up collected and detected by an Eye sooner or later. You'd get past a bod, bods are not perceptive in certain ways, nor sandys either, but to me you're pretty obviously what you are: a trick, a trap, a bug, a snare and a deceit. Who sent you?

What have you learned? There's still something of a bod-level economy on Hengist Etoile? That we're a spinning ring with variable gravity divided into twelve sectors named for the months with weather to match? That bods work in one sector and live in another and play in the ones that have the best weather for bods? That the hub is a hockey stadium? All this is on the public record. All this is pretty well known, even in E-O, so what are you doing here?

Not talking? Not up to talking? No, you're not, are you, behind your empty demands for a language protocol you're just a blind device that has to get home to deliver. Well, still a little interesting, but nothing like so clever. I'll download your memory for analysis, in case you happened to stumble on something I don't know, and I'll drop you right back into the stream, with a little watcher of my own that will keep streaming right back. Let's make it nice and easy for your E-O owners and drop you back into the hand of a nice E-O tourist down in August. I'll even see if I can spot one who's about to go home, and thereafter I'll give you one shred of my vast attention while I get on with the important business of running the universe.

Plock, little coin.

# TOURISTS

## JAMES PATRICK KELLY

Mariska woke in a panic. In the instant before she came to herself, while her bed seemed to spin and the sheets tried to strangle her, she believed that she was coming out of hibernation. Not again, she thought. *Please*, never again.

The hospital's air was wrong; it smelled like the inside of a plastic bucket. An alarm was chirping in the gloom and she felt the tickle of a mindfeed at the back of her neck. =*Power failure. Please follow emergency lights to exit. This mod will seal in thirty minutes.*=

As she propped herself on an elbow, she could hear voices, low and urgent, through the open door of her room. "Hello?" she called. A light strip blinking on the deck in the hallway showed the way out. It illuminated the legs of people hurrying to safety: a barefooted Martian, spacers in griptites, a nurse in sensible shoes. "*Hello!*"

And then Mariska was caught up by two strong arms. "Welcome to Mars." *Gasp*. It was a man, out of breath. "Here we go."

He toted her toward the mod's airlock, one arm under her shoulders, the other around her knees, pressing her against him. Despite his odd breathing, he did not seem to be exerting himself much. The muscles of his arms locked her against him but his hands rested easily against her body, almost like a caress. His gait was steady and unhurried.

"Are we in trouble?" she said.

"No." *Gasp*. "Happens sometimes."

The flow of evacuees bumped through a darkened office mod which was a maze of empty workstations and conference tables and broad-leafed plants. She offered him a mindfeed, =*You can put me down any time now.*= but his head was closed to her.

"I can walk, you know," she said. Actually, the best she could manage was a totter, but her nurse said Mariska was making great progress.

He squeezed her arm. "A minute."

The illuminated path led them past dormitories into a cavernous utility mod. She had yet to leave her room since coming to the hospital and she was amazed at its size. The scattering of emergency lights on the ceiling cast odd shadows as about fifty people milled among the boxy air exchangers and filters, squat waste processors, and the tangle of plumbing around the electrolysis plant. Mariska craned her neck and spotted a rack of pneumatic EV suits next to a crawler which was having its track repaired, although nobody else seemed particularly interested in them. She hoped that meant that this mod at least wasn't about to depressurize. She'd already had enough hypoxia to last her a lifetime.

"No worry." The man put her down. "The air is fine here." He must have noticed her looking.

Her hand flew up to the neck of her pajamas as she turned to face him, but her top was sealed up tight. "Thanks." She had guessed he was Martian from the gasping and the way her mindfeed had bounced off him. His skin was glossy and pale, the color of green tea, and he was shirtless. Photoreceptor nodules were arrayed down his neck and across his bare shoulders. He wore standard-issue spacer uniform pants and no shoes.

"You're Mariska," he said. "Volochkova."

She thought he was too tall; he looked as if he'd been stretched on a torture rack. Now his lips pulled back from identical flat teeth. Mariska decided this must be his smile, reminding herself that everyone said that Martians took some getting used to. She was going to ask him what was going on, but then she noticed something odd about her fellow evacuees. There were a lot of spacers and just a few medical types. Where were the other patients?

"This isn't a hospital." The dizziness she felt had nothing to do with her regenerating cerebellum. "I thought this was a hospital."

"Hospital?" He peered at her with his slitted eyes. "This is *Natividad* base."

"*Natividad?* You mean the starship?"

"Yes, your mom said..." But then Mariska spotted her mother across the mod with Shengyi. Data shimmered in the air between them. Mariska pushed past the Martian. "*Natalya*," she called.

Her mother waved the files closed when she saw Mariska wobbling toward them. "*Privet sólnishko moyó.*" There was a tightness at her eyes that belied the unruffled greeting; she looked as though she wanted to run over and catch Mariska before she fell. "I'm glad you're safe."

"I'm not your sunshine," said Mariska, "and this isn't a hospital."

Natalya nudged Shengyi behind her as if to shield the nurse from Mariska's anger. "I never said it was."

"I was in a coma. When I woke up you said I had cerebral hypoxia. *Brain damage.*" Mariska was trying not to shout but she could feel her voice screeching out of control. "What was I supposed to think?"

"You're upset."

"You brought me to your starship base. Do you think that I'm going off with you to… to…."

"18 Scorpii." Shengyi looked hurt that she had been thrown out of Mariska's head.

Mariska, for her part, couldn't believe she had trusted the nurse. "Is that what this is about?"

"No, it's not." Her mother was using one of those tricks she hated: when Mariska yelled, Natalya started to whisper. She was trying to make her feel like a foolish kid. It was working.

"Then why am I here?"

The Martian joined them. He seemed about to say something but Natalya silenced him. That was another thing Mariska hated about her mother—everybody did what she wanted.

"I'm just trying to protect you," Natalya said.

"From what." Mariska's laugh was harsh. "From having a life?"

=*It was because you're a hero.*= Shengyi sent her a mindfeed, trying to calm her down. Of course, the nurse would take her mother's side; Natalya Volochkova was the Chief Medical Officer of the *Natividad*. =*Everybody knows about the* Shining Legend *and your rescue.*= She offered Mariska a menu of newsfeeds. =*That's why…*=

Mariska closed her head, cutting the feed off.

"I brought you here so I could take care of you," said her mother. "And because if you were in a public hospital there would be buzzies jumping out of closets and crawling from under beds trying to get an interview."

"I'm no hero." Mariska shrank into herself. "The only one I rescued was myself."

"A celebrity, then. I'm sorry but it's true."

"But that's not fair." She hated the words as soon as they came screeching out of her mouth. "I *can't*…." The crew of the *Shining*

*Legend*—Glint, Didit, and Richard, even poor Beep—they were the heroes. But they were dead and here she was whining in front of her mother and this nurse and this *Martian*. People were staring, which made Mariska want to crawl behind a fuel cell and curl up in a ball. She glanced around, looking for some way out.

The Martian scooped her up again. "Time for more walking." *Gasp*. "Yes?"

"Put her down, Elan." Natalya made it sound like an order. "She's just confused."

When he hesitated, Mariska pumped her legs impatiently. She *was* confused, but she certainly didn't want her mother sorting things out for her. And she was so deeply embarrassed that all she could think of was escape. "Don't listen to her," she hissed. "Go, *go*."

He obeyed without another word, turning and trotting toward the EV suits.

"No, wait." Mariska was amazed at how small her mother sounded. "Mariska, you're still sick!" She was surprised that Natalya wasn't chasing them. "Be careful," she called. Was it beneath her dignity as a starship officer?

The crawler was parked in front of the sliding cargo door of the airlock. Next to the rack of EV suits was a smaller door. The Martian tipped forward without putting her down and bent to bring himself to eye reader level. She slipped a little in his arms before it flashed him through.

"Where are you taking me?" she said.

"You said to go." *Gasp*. "So we go." He straightened as the door slid aside. "Ready?"

The airlock was freezing; Mariska could see her breath billow. The exterior service hatch was open, not to the surface, but to a poly tunnel that lit up when it sensed their presence. The Martian flew down its length with low compact bounds, so fast that she could feel her exposed skin tighten with wind chill. Although less than a minute had passed, she was shivering by the time they came to the end of the tunnel. Another open service hatch led into a smaller airlock. It looked like they were entering some kind of ship, although she was sure that it couldn't be the *Natividad*. He unsealed the interior door by tapping at an access panel. They stepped into a semicircular storage space packed with bales wrapped in poly, neatly fitted into slots climbing the walls. The Martian set her down next to a ladder built between slots. "You're okay." It was an announcement rather than a question. "Wait here." He scrambled up and disappeared through a hatch in the ceiling.

Wait. Mariska wrapped her arms around herself. Couldn't he see that she was about to freeze to death? The storage space was a little warmer than the tunnel, but not much. She stomped her feet to keep her toes from going numb and read the labels on the bales. *Ag X3 47000. Ra C4 65500. Ex R4, 81000.* Did *Ag* stand for Agriculture? *Ra* meant rations on the *Shining Legend.* So where was she? A starship would need a lander, something to ferry back and forth from orbit. And this thing had a clear up-and-down orientation, unlike the *Shining Legend,* which had been designed for zero gravity.

She heard the whirr of fans, and seconds later felt deck vents breathing warm air. There was a rustle above and she glanced up to see something fluttering down toward her. She stepped aside as a spacer uniform settled at the bottom of the ladder.

"You can change." The Martian had crouched to peek through the hatch. "Warm up."

"Not into this." She kicked at the uniform with her frozen toes. "Thanks, but you know what? I think I should be going back to the hospital now."

"Power's still out." He leaned out and gestured toward the tunnel. "And Natvee's waiting." She wondered how he could stand the cold half-naked. "You'll have to get by her."

Mariska guessed that Natvee was her mother's callname. "There's no other way?"

"One tunnel." He rapped once on the deck for emphasis. "One airlock."

Her face flushed with embarrassment at the thought of a repeat encounter with her mother in front of the crew of the *Natividad.*

"Won't look." He gave her a skinny smile. "Shout when you're ready."

"Wait, what's your name?"

"Elan."

"Just Elan? That's it?"

"Elan… of Mars." He was standing at the edge of the hatch now. "Is all you need to know.'

At least, that's what she thought he said: there was a gasp in there somewhere. She decided that he must be making fun of her. "I don't want to change, Elan."

He waved and turned away from the hatch.

"Wait, Elan!"

There was no answer.

She snatched the uniform from the deck in frustration and retreated to a corner where the bales would hide her. She held it at arm's length, glaring. Putting it on meant nothing. Even though it was warming up, the lander was cold, *frigid*, so she didn't really have much choice. She decided to pull it on over her pajamas, even though she knew that was a mistake. Did wearing a spacer uniform mean she was zooming off to 18 Scorpii? Not at all. She was going to keep her independence. And her pajamas. As soon as she was done with her therapy, she was walking from here. She was on Mars, so she'd find work on Mars. And if she couldn't, she'd go home to the Moon. Or get a job on Sweetspot Station. When she had fitted her feet into the slippers and sealed all seams, the flex uniform tightened against her body and then relaxed into what would have been a perfect fit—except for the pajamas. They crinkled uncomfortably beneath it; cuffs of hospital green stuck out at both wrists and one ankle. She knew how it would look to Elan of Mars, but then she was brain-damaged. She had a good excuse.

She lurched back to the ladder and had another bad idea. She started to climb. She had suffered severe oxygen deprivation while hibernating on the *Shining Legend* and the motor coordination in her legs was shaky. But she had confidence in her arms and shoulders—until she got a couple of meters off the deck. Then the vertigo hit. It felt like the rungs of the ladder went slack as rope. She stopped; it was all she could do to hang on.

"Don't move." *Gasp.* "Just stay there."

Mariska was too dizzy to look up, so she didn't see Elan jump. He whooshed just past her and landed with a clatter and a grunt on the deck below. Then she felt him clambering up the ladder beneath her.

"You're okay."

She took a deep breath. "Keep saying that. Maybe I'll believe it."

"You want help?"

What was he going to do? Put his hands on her butt and push? "I've got it." And she did. Somehow having him below to spot her changed everything. The ladder solidified and she started to climb again.

It wasn't until she dragged herself up through the hatch that she dared look down. The deck was almost five meters below. She wouldn't have hesitated to make a jump like that on the Moon, but on Mars there was a whole planet tugging at you. Elan was either very brave or a little crazy. Or a Martian.

She glanced around: this level was different from the one below. There were still bales in slots, but part of the circular wall was given over to instrument racks that made up the command cluster. She recognized the communications and engineering and environmental screens; they were similar to the ones on her last ship. The nav rack, though, made no sense at all. Next to the cluster was a line of what looked like lockers. Elan rapped on the door of one and it folded out lengthwise into a bunk.

"No, really, I don't need to lie down." Mariska held up a hand to stop him. "I'm fine."

He glanced at her then leaned onto the middle of the bunk. It folded. He punched at the end and it bent to the deck. Before long he had reshaped it into a chair.

He opened the next locker, unfolded a chair for himself and sat. Then smiled at her. Now that he was still, the photoreceptors on his shoulders began to swell. She tried not to stare as they stretched like flatworms towards the overhead lights.

"Natalya is going to be mad." Mariska was mad at herself for being so stubborn. She wanted to sit, but didn't want him to think she needed to. "Probably more at you than me. I should thank you."

"She's medical. I'm exploration." He shrugged. "Different teams."

"But you'll get in trouble?"

"I am trouble."

She came alongside the empty chair and absently kneaded the cushion. "So, power failures?" It was heated and soft and very inviting. "That can't be good news for the mission."

"Budget cuts and nervous engineers." He dismissed them with a wave. "Pull the alarm if they see their shadows."

"You have something against playing it safe?"

"Not playing."

She wondered if this show-off attitude was for her sake. Was this Martian flirting? No, probably one of her perceptual slips, detecting signals that weren't there. Still, she hadn't realized how lonely she had been. "You know, it's kind of strange that you were there at just the right time to carry me off."

"I was hanging around."

"Were you now?"

"I wanted to meet you. They made it hard."

"Why would they do that?"

"Four hundred and twelve spacers on the *Natividad*." He aimed a finger toward the base. "Crew and colonists." He pointed at himself. "One Martian."

"What are you saying, that they're prejudiced? Elan, nobody got to meet me. I was in intensive care."

"I'm made for Mars. That causes them trouble."

Mariska perched at the edge of the chair beside him, but still her pride kept her from sitting. "I don't understand."

"I like the air thin." He gasped and made a face. "This is like breathing soup. And cold." When he held up a foot and wiggled his three thick toes, she realized that he had run through the tunnel barefooted. "Makes problems for the spacers."

"Are you a spacer?"

He shrugged. "Spacer from Mars." The photoreceptor nubs were fully spread toward the light now, fleshy ribbons some thirty centimeters long, dark with engorged blood.

She told herself that she had homework to do on Martians. "Why did you bring me here anyway?" She gave in finally and slid onto the chair. "I'm guessing this is some kind of lander." She snuggled into its warm embrace.

"Called *Padre*," he said. "We have two. Other is *Madre*."

"Cute. Must be brand new—I don't recognize those nav screens." She sniffed. "And it doesn't smell like it's been in space."

He had a staccato laugh, like someone hitting a snare drum. "How will it smell?"

"Moldy." She batted at her nose. "Like an old couch." She was laughing too now. "That somebody spilled milk on."

"Like your last ship?"

"Sure." Her laugh turned bitter. "My *last* ship." All the joy she had been getting from their banter died. "Is that why you brought me here? To get me to tell you all about it?"

"No." He considered. "But if you ever want to, I'm interested."

"Oh, everybody's interested, from what I hear. I'm some famous freak now. I better get used to it, huh? So what is it that you wanted to hear?" She felt her hand curl into a fist. "What it was like to watch them die? Sorry, but I don't know. I was hibernating, you see. Snoozed right through the good part. But I'm sure you could check out the vids if you're *interested*."

"You're upset." *Gasp*.

"You sound like my mother. Why shouldn't I be upset?

"Forget it."

"No, that's the problem. I can't forget it. I tried to save them and I couldn't." Her eyes were stinging. "Everybody died but me." She squirmed around on the chair, showing him her back. "Isn't the power on yet?"

He snapped his fingers and an airscreen opened in front of them. "No," he said. "Fixed in about twenty minutes."

"I don't want to be a celebrity. Not that kind." She brushed the corner of one eye and was relieved that it was dry. "Not any kind."

"Buzz is more about your mother than you." *Gasp*. "And our mission." *Gasp.* "And the rescue. Everyone watched." Was she making him nervous? That was the last thing she wanted. "Cost a fortune."

"Too bad they didn't get their money's worth." She fell silent, tugging at the cuff of her pajamas. "Can I ask you something?"

"Go."

"What kind of name is Elan of Mars?"

He laughed again, probably in relief that she wasn't going to shatter into a hundred jagged pieces. "A Martian name."

"*Elan*." She rolled over and poked his shoulder.

"Okay." He rubbed the spot, although she knew she hadn't hurt him. "Two names. One public, one private." He paused. "Secret, actually."

"What good is a name if it's secret?"

"Not secret to people I love."

"So your parents know," she said. "And your girlfriend."

"Parents," he said. "Yes." What he hadn't said filled the silence between them. "But spacers like two names to say," he continued. "So, Elan." *Gasp*. "Of Mars."

"Call yourself whatever, I don't care. But it *is* kind of confusing. What if two people have the same name?"

"Only 20,000 Martians. No problem." When he shook his head, the ribbons on his neck shivered. Mariska found it hard not to stare. "How many Linda Smiths on Earth? Sergey Ivanovs?"

"Point." She drew a line in the air. "How old are you anyway, that you don't have a girlfriend?'

"Twelve." He crossed his legs and then uncrossed them immediately.

She knew that couldn't be right. "What's that in standard years?"

"Tourist years? Twenty-two."

"Tourists? Is what you call us?"

"And you?" he said. "How old?"

"Eighteen." She lied without hesitation. "Tourist years." Actually she had only been conscious for fifteen. But she *had* hibernated for three years before she had signed on to the *Shining Legend*. And it was almost her birthday.

"Mariska Volochkova." He held up two fingers. "Just two names. You're missing the *patronymic*." He stumbled over the syllables as if he wasn't sure he was saying a real word. "Need a father name. I looked it up."

"No, my mother has the three names. Her father's name was Nikolai, so her name is Natalya Nikolaevna Volochkova. But I don't have a father."

"Why? Where is he?"

"I don't have one." She wasn't counting Daddy Al, who had brought her up under term adoption. Elan looked puzzled, so she explained. "I'm her clone. Well, she had some modifications made."

Elan didn't say anything. He just gasped.

Mariska had been having trouble reading his reactions to her but this was particularly inscrutable. Even though she liked talking to him, the conversation had got way too personal. What was she thinking? This boy was a Martian who looked like a flower with fleshy petals. And how could she be interested in someone who was leaving soon for a planet forty-five light years away? She swung off the chair and made it to the command cluster. "You never told me about the nav rack," she called to him, pleased at how steady she felt. "This screen." She pointed. "Can't figure it out." It showed what she took to be a graphic of the surface of Mars. Above it, a looping line was rotating slowly around a point at its midsection. One end of the line was approaching the planet, the opposite end seemed to be swinging away into space.

"Our skyhook." Elan joined her but kept a more than polite distance. "In orbit around Mars."

"Skyhook." She nodded. "Okay, we have those on the Moon. They snag cargo and pull it out of our gravity well to orbit."

"And bring gear down from orbit."

"Right."

"This one is going to Scorpii."

Mariska tried to remember what she had learned about skyhooks in physics. The technical term was rotovator. It was like an enormous spinning wheel, with the hub orbiting around a planet. Only it wasn't; you had to lose the rim and all of the spokes but two, each pointing in opposite directions from the hub. And the spokes were actually tethers, composite carbon nanotubes with enormous tensile strength. Synchronize the speed of the rotation and the forward orbital momentum just right and one end of the tether would pass close enough and slowly enough to the surface to hook a load. Then a half rotation later, you could place the load in orbit or hurl it to space. Meanwhile the other end of the tether would be down in the atmosphere hooking the next load.

As he stepped past her, she noticed that his photoreceptors had shrunk back into bumps, since they couldn't lock on to a light source if he was moving around. "Alpha hook pass-over is in three hours." He zoomed the screen, showing the magnetic hook descending slowly toward *Padre*. "Beta in eight."

"And this is what you do?"

"Lander jock." He nodded. "Junior pilot. *Padre* lifts, we steer him to the hook as it passes. In space, we cut free, cruise to *Natividad*." He refreshed the screen to a distance view that displayed the starship in its following orbit behind the tether's hub. "At Scorpii, *Padre* delivers colony goods."

"You like it, don't you?" There was an excitement in his voice that Mariska hadn't heard before. "Your job?"

"Best of the best." He beamed. "Swing up to orbit with me someday?

"Maybe," she said, although she thought probably not. "So they gave you something important to do. You should be proud, Elan."

"Proud." He sagged and turned away from the command cluster. Once again she was surprised at his mood change. "But it won't last." *Gasp.* "I do the job and then what?"

"I don't know. What?"

*Gasp.* "Start a new life." He touched her shoulder lightly, as to wake her from sleep. "Power's back on," he said. "You can go."

As if it wasn't bad enough that Natalya was late for Mariska's therapy, now Shengyi was counting under her breath. "*One, two, three, one, two, three.*" The nurse was doing her best but she was a terrible dancer. She couldn't decide if she was leading or following. And she didn't seem to realize that she was stepping on Mariska's toes. It wasn't as if they were adding any complications to the waltz. They were just doing boxes, no quarter turns or hesitations or whisks.

"Maybe something slower?" said Mariska.

"Yes." Shengyi looked relieved as she released Mariska from her death grip. "Good idea." Mariska was sure that the nurse had left a permanent handprint on her back.

Shengyi hurried to the wall screen and cut "What'll I Do" off in mid-measure. Then she paused the countdown timer. Mariska stifled a groan. According to the clock, they had another seventeen minutes, twenty-three seconds of dance therapy to go. She had been hoping that the nurse would let the time run while she chose a new waltz.

They had folded the chairs and bed into the wall and pushed the instrument trolley into the hall to make enough space in Mariska's room for the dancing. There was no better place in the infirmary for her therapy and, after the unauthorized jaunt with Elan, Natalya and Shengyi weren't about to let her loose on the base.

Dancing with Natalya wasn't as much a chore as dancing with Shengyi, although it was painful in its own special way. At least her mother knew the steps, but she kept asking Mariska questions and expecting to hear answers. Mariska suspected that Natalya had plans for her that she didn't want any part of. Where *was* her mother? It wasn't like Natalya to miss a chance to pester her.

"*Cake and Matches*," said Shengyi, reading from the screen. "*Cairo Waltz, Chopin's Glove, Clever Gretel....*"

"What's that?"

She drilled down the menu. "It's *Klug Gretelein* in German, Opus 462 of Johann Strauss the Younger...."

"No Strauss. What else."

"*Climbing Tharsis*," she read. "*Come My Prince Someday*."

"Just what I need," said Mariska. "A prince." She knew one wouldn't be arriving anytime soon, although she did wonder why Elan hadn't come to rescue her again. "Play it. I'll lead this time."

She and the nurse grappled. At first Mariska's head filled with the steps. *Left foot forward, right foot forward-slide, left foot slide. One, two, three...*

She dragged Shengyi around the room. It felt as if she was dancing with a chair.

*Back, two three. Right foot back, left foot back-slide, right foot slide.*

"Light on your feet," said Shengyi. "Light on your feet."

Mariska stumbled, then gritted her teeth. *Light on your feet* was something Natalya said, but then Natalya always led. Light on your feet was four syllables and it threw Mariska's three count off.

When Mariska stopped counting, the dancing got easier. She just let her feet do whatever they wanted. As long as she didn't fall over, the nurse didn't seem to mind. After a while she got so bored that she opened her head to datafeed she'd been skimming. Natalya would have noticed if she was multi-tasking. Shengyi was clueless.

= . . . *their quest for a better life on Mars, some immigrants thrived while others did not. Before the depression of the Bloody Nineties, refugees from failed colonies were absorbed into more successful ones. However the Great Crunch led to a three-year hiatus in trade with Earth which caused the collapse of the weak Martian Authority and the subsequent deaths of an estimated seventy percent of the population. Almost all of those who died were so-called "standards," those who had not been genetically modified to live on Mars. The survivors, now commonly referred to as Martians, had undergone Transgenetic Somatic Gene Therapy (TSGT) to adapt to their new home world. Controversy still rages over the role of the survivors during the Abandonment. What could the Martians have done to save the standards? To ask the question is to start an argument, with Martian sympathizers claiming that the governments of Earth . . .*=

Shengyi pulled Mariska to a stop; the song ended. "Something different?" she said. "We could try a hurry-scurry?"

"No thanks." Mariska hated that step. "I'd just get all tangled up." The therapy session had eleven minutes and twenty-seven seconds left. Still no Natalya. "Play that waltz again," she said. "In fact, just put it on a loop."

They returned to shuffling around the room again. The nurse's hands were sweaty and she was counting again. *One, two, three*. Mariska wondered why Natalya never counted *one, two, three*. She said *quick, quick, quick* instead. Or *quick, quick, slow, slow* for the Two Step. She wondered where her mother had learned to dance. Who she might have danced with. She wondered if Martians danced.

= . . .*bodies were then redesigned to withstand the extremes of the Martian environment. Enhanced keratins in their skin retain heat and lose very little water. Their eyes are protected by nictitating membranes. Using the energy from photoreceptors to break down atmospheric* $CO_2$*, they can survive on the surface with very little protection and no breathing apparatus, typically for as long as two hours, even during the Martian winter. In the summer of 2151, Chen set an outdoor record of four hours, sixteen minutes and. . . .*=

"Though he's far, far away," the nurse sang under her breath, "I know he'll come someday." Her head was tilted up and she was smiling, eyes closed.

Shengyi must have sensed that Mariska was staring at her. Her eyes popped open and the song died on her lips. She nodded three times in embarrassment then fixed her gaze at her feet. They waltzed on as if nothing had happened. As far as Mariska knew, Shengyi hadn't yet partnered with anyone in the crew. She had wondered about this. Why volunteer for a forty-seven-light-year one-way trip unless someone you wanted to be with was going?

=...*which is why the male sex organs are normally retracted into the body cavity and are thus not readily available for sexual activity. Some say this is where the stereotype comes from: Martian men feel more comfortable in the role of the pursued while Martian women are skilled pursuers.*=

When she stumbled, Shengyi caught her. "Sorry," Mariska said and gave the nurse's hand a squeeze to show that she was all right.

The door slid open. Natalya wheeled the instrument cart into the room.

"We're almost done," said Shengyi. "Three minutes left."

"That will be all for now, Nurse Wong." She parked the cart next to the folded bed. "We're having a visit from Captain Martinez. When she gets here, see if she wants anything. I started coffee. Mariska, how are you? Also, I just put some fizz in the pharmacy fridge. If she asks for it, she'll want ice." She snapped the waltz off. "Well, what are you waiting for?" She shooed Shengyi out the door. "Keep her busy as long as you can. My daughter and I have to talk."

Mariska pressed herself against a wall. She didn't really know her mother well, since she had spent most of Mariska's life away on a starship. But she had never seen Natalya so flustered. There was color on her cheeks and her silver hair was mussed.

"Help me with the bed, will you?" She gestured. "Maybe you should put pajamas on?"

"What's happening?" said Mariska as the bed released with a hydraulic sigh. "Is Martinez here to see me?"

"She needs to ask you something." Natalya pulled two chairs from the wall. "Probably best if you sit on the bed. The captain can sit there, I'll sit here. Listen, you don't have to do anything you don't want to do."

"Tell me." Mariska put hands on her mother's shoulders and turned her. "What is it?" She could see the wrinkles in the pale skin around her eyes and at the corners of her mouth; it struck her that she had no idea how old her mother was.

"It's the newsfeeds." Natalya shook free of her daughter's grip. "This base, we can't really keep them out. We need sympathetic coverage for our funding… I'm sorry but you're going to have to talk to them. Not the damn buzzies. Someone responsible."

They settled on the chairs and it all came spilling out. After the accident on the *Shining Legend*, SinoStar had balked at paying for a rescue, even though two of the crew were clones of Xu Jingchu, their corporate CFO. The chance of success was slim; the costs were enormous. With the clock ticking, Natalya had convinced Martinez to authorize seed money from *Natividad*'s contingency fund to begin prepping a mission. Then she went public. Natalya Volochkova was one of the celebrity crew of the *Gorshkov*, the starship that had discovered the earthlike planet Bounty. She and SinoStar's Jingchu created a Save Our Kids fund and started begging for contributions in front of every camera they could find. The Two Moms—Hero Doc and Renegade VP—were all the buzz on Earth, the Moon, and the orbitals in the week before the rescue window closed. Although they never raised the necessary money, they embarrassed SinoStar into authorizing the rescue mission.

"I'm sorry, but making it about me seemed like the only way." Natalya combed fingers through her hair, mussing it even more. "There was no time. The launch window was so tight."

"But why is Captain Martinez here?"

"Because I mixed our mission with your rescue." She shook her head. "This isn't easy, so I'm just going to say it." She reached for her daughter's hand but Mariska pulled away. "If everyone had survived, we wouldn't have a problem."

"But they didn't. I'm the only one."

"And you're my daughter." She squeezed Mariska's hand and let go. "It looks like you got special treatment."

"No! I took a risk too. It's on the logs."

"Buzzies don't care about logs. When a feed does big numbers, it doesn't need to be true."

"So everybody thinks…." She was shocked. "Not Didit and Glint's mom?"

"No, Xu understands. But the boy's parents, the FiveFords…."

"He died saving me!"

Natalya said nothing.

"I have to tell them." She burst from her chair. "It's a nightmare. I can't handle this."

"I know," she said. "I know."

"No! You have no idea." Mariska backed away from her, arms outstretched as if to fend off an attack. "You weren't there, you didn't make the decision."

"If you're not ready...."

"May I come in?" Captain Pilar Martinez appeared in the doorway.

Mariska and Natalya started at the interruption, neither able to hide her dismay.

"I apologize if I'm intruding, Nata." As Martinez strode into the room, she seemed more impatient than apologetic. "But I'm afraid it can't be helped." Behind her, Shengyi held arms up in frustration as the door slid shut. She hadn't delayed her at all.

Natalya and Martinez had crewed together on the *Gorshkov* but the captain looked years younger. She was a hibernator like Mariska, one of the very first to survive having ground squirrel transgenes implanted in her DNA. She'd made three trips through the wormholes and had hibernated for not quite half of her ninety-one years. She was short like most spacers, but thick beneath the smart fabric of her uniform. Her skin was smooth, her black hair pulled into in a sleek bun.

She shook Mariska's hand. "I'm told that you're on the mend."

Mariska tried to steady herself. "I'm better, thanks." Martinez must have heard her screeching as she came down the corridor of the infirmary. It was one thing to act out with your mother, another to make a fool of yourself in front of this woman. If Natalya was a spacer celebrity, Pilar Martinez was a legend.

"You have the best doc I know looking after you. Saved my life and my career."

Everybody knew that story. There were datafeeds and even dramafeeds about the *Gorshkov* expedition.

"It was because of Captain Martinez that I decided you should be a hibernator," said Natalya.

Mariska frowned. This wasn't exactly news either. Were they going to stand around telling each other things they already knew?

"Wait," said Martinez. "Mariska's not coming with us, is she? She's not crew?"

"*No.*" Natalya was firm.

"Then there's no need for formality, Nata. The door is closed." Martinez gestured for Mariska to sit on the chair while she perched on the edge of the bed. "You must call me Pilar."

Then Mariska realized why these two were indulging in all this empty chatter. They were giving the poor invalid time to gather herself.

Mariska felt a flush of indignation. She may have been out of control before, but that was no reason to treat her like a child.

"I envy your mother, having a smart, resourceful daughter like you," Martinez was saying. "I can't have children myself—possibly a hitch in the early genmod procedure. Something to do with a lutropin deficiency. I trust that isn't the case with you?"

"No," said Mariska. "Actually, Pilar, it hasn't come up."

Martinez laughed. "I'm sure Nata is glad about that. It's rare enough, but something to check."

"Natalya was saying that you had a request?" Mariska decided it was up to her to take charge of the conversation. "I don't want to waste your time, Pilar. I know you must be busy."

"I am. Yes." Martinez spread her fingers on Mariska's bed, smoothing the top blanket. "So, we're going to Planet D of 18 Scorpii system, your mother and I. It isn't Bounty, but it's a better world than Earth. We're taking three hundred very productive people and a starship packed with advanced technology out of our economic system for the better part of twenty years. Our mission is going to cost..." She grimaced and held her palms outstretched. "Well, we try not to add up the cost. Somebody might find out."

Natalya chuckled, although Mariska guessed that this was an old joke, one that had been told and retold.

"There are those who say this mission is a waste of precious resources," said Martinez. "I think they're damn shortsighted to say this, but there are many more of them than me. Colonization is still controversial. Just ask your Martian friend, Elan."

"You know Elan?" Mariska blurted this before she realized how foolish it was.

"I like to keep up with my crew. A smart boy, Elan, a real asset." Martinez aimed a forefinger at Mariska. "But I doubt he'll contact you again on his own. If you're interested in that one, it's your move." She winked. "Martians have their quirks."

Mariska colored. "Thanks." How many of the crew knew about their little flirtation on the *Padre*? Then she realized that if the captain knew, everybody knew.

"There are shortsighted people who are using your rescue as an excuse to attack us," continued Martinez, "cut our funding, maybe even cancel the mission. I need to you to speak up on our behalf, and your own. And soon, Mariska." Now that she had come to the point, Martinez grew intense. She seemed to fill the room, blotting all else out. "You were strong enough to survive a terrible tragedy." It was almost as if they were sharing a mindfeed. "I believe you are strong enough for this."

"Pilar," said her mother, "she needs time to—"

"I understand." Mariska cut her off. If Pilar Martinez believed in her, then who was Mariska to doubt herself? "I can do it."

"I know you can." Mariska expected to be released from her scrutiny, but Martinez was not done. "And what are you going to say?"

Mariska was taken aback. "The truth."

"The truth is a puzzle and many people have pieces of it." She leaned forward. "I'm going to ask a hard question. Did you ever think you might survive and the others wouldn't?"

Drawing strength from the force of Martinez's personality, Mariska was able to look at what most terrified her. "No," she said. "It never crossed my mind." Ever since she had come out of hibernation, she had been torturing herself with doubts about this. Saying it out loud gave her a sense of certainty.

"What did you know about the rescue mission?"

"Just that Sweetspot said they were coming."

"But when they told you that, it was a lie."

"Yes. I realize that now."

"How does that make you feel?"

"Angry."

"Why?"

She considered. "When the oxygen ran out, I would've been hibernating. I wouldn't have known what was happening. The others, Glint, Didit, and Richard, they would have spent their last weeks waiting." Her voice caught. "Waiting to die."

"Did you ask your mother to rescue you?"

"No. Actually, we weren't speaking." Mariska tried to pretend that Natalya wasn't sitting beside her. "She kept sending messages the entire time I crewed on the *Shining Legend*, but I never replied."

Martinez glanced over at Natalya for confirmation. "I admire you, Mariska Volochkova, for your courage." She stood. "And for your honesty. I realize that it is not to be, but I would gladly have you on my crew." She offered her hand to Mariska and they shook again. "As you say, I am busy. I'll arrange for the news conference. Tomorrow?"

Mariska ignored a stab of panic and nodded.

"Don't worry." Martinez grinned. "The questions will be friendly. And brief. Nata, thank you." Then the door slid open and she was gone.

The room seemed to shrink in her absence. Mariska glanced over at Natalya, not knowing what to expect. Her mother's face was glowing with gratitude. Was that a tear glistening in the corner of her eye?

"Thank you, Mariska Volochkova."

She blinked in astonishment. "You're welcome." She looked down from the platform at the beaming woman from NewsMelt. It felt like they had just begun asking questions. Was there something she had forgotten? Maybe she should say that it had been a pleasure. But it hadn't been, so she clamped her mouth shut.

Then they started to clap. The *Natividad*'s crew started it. About thirty of them had gathered at the far edge of the utility mod to watch the news conference. Soon even the reporters were on their feet, applauding her. For what? Being alive? Mariska pulled her lips into something like a smile and waved at them.

A reporter whose name she had forgotten stepped onto the platform and approached the podium. "Can I get your thumb?" He was a fingerprint fan; he pulled out an album the size of a deck of cards, opened it to a blank page and peeled back the transparent cover sheet.

She dutifully pressed her thumb to the sticky surface, but was already scouting her escape route. Martinez had thought it best if Natalya wasn't in attendance, hovering over her patient, so there was no one to fetch her away. But that had been the point of the news conference, hadn't it? Mariska Volochkova could take care of herself.

Then she spotted Elan, already turning to go. Head down so as not to make eye contact or start a conversation, she bumped through the knot of reporters. She caught him at the airlock.

"Wait, Elan."

"Mariska." *Gasp.* He pretended to be surprised, but his skinny smile gave him away. "You were great."

"Maybe. If I wanted to be a celebrity." She leaned close and whispered. "Which I most definitely don't."

"You need rescuing?"

"I need a friend," she said, brushing a hand across his back. "And a bathroom."

"Come to the *Padre*." The eye reader flashed him and the door slid aside. "Carry you?" He held his arms out to her.

"No, thanks." She aimed him at the airlock. "I'm trying to quit."

Mariska had become much steadier on her feet in the last few days. Natalya had declared the regeneration of her damaged cerebellum successful. Now all she needed was rehab to let new connections spark. Mariska trotted down the poly tunnel to the *Padre* with Elan following behind. The tunnel was still freezing, a couple of degrees below 0° C in the Martian summer, but at least she was dressed for it this time.

When she was ten meters from the *Padre,* she glanced over her shoulder. "Race you to airlock," she called and started running. Elan came up easily beside her, laughing, but as they closed on the lander, she kicked the pace up another notch and slammed her hand against the hull first. "Beat you," she cried.

"I let you win." Elan was hardly breathing.

Mariska was doubled over, sucking huge gulps of frigid air. "Maybe…." She straightened and poked him in the chest. "Or maybe I let you *think* that you let me win." When she laughed, the cloud of her breath curled toward him.

They passed quickly into the *Padre* and up the ladder to the control deck. Corbet Brady was on duty. Mariska knew that he was one of *Natividad*'s two senior lander pilots; she had seen his cards when she looked Elan up.

Brady wasn't that much older than Mariska—twenty-five standard. Most of the crew, with the exception of the senior officers, were in their twenties or early thirties. His spacer uniform clung to well-defined muscles, so he must have grown up in gravity, although he didn't have the grotesquely padded build of someone born on Earth. Was he handsome? She guessed he was, but a bit too polished for her taste.

"Corbet Brady," said Elan. "This is Mariska Volochkova."

"Our hero." He waved the airscreen in front of him closed.

"Not a hero," said Elan.

"Our celebrity, then."

"No."

"You're picking on me again, Martian." Brady tilted his head to the deck above in mock exasperation. "Almost six billion people just saw a brave performance that probably saved our mission." He stepped forward and took her hand in both of his. "All right then, neither brave nor a star. But despite what Misery Boy here thinks of you, Mariska, nicely done." He winked and let go. "That can't have been easy."

"It went by so fast." For some reason, Mariska didn't know what to do with her hands. "I don't really remember what I said."

"You were great." Elan seemed alarmed that she might think otherwise. "She was great."

Brady ignored him. "So, here for the tour?"

"Had it already." Mariska decided to hide her hands behind her back.

"She hasn't seen the crew deck," said Elan and a look passed between him and Brady.

"What, asking for permission? Go." He flipped a hand toward the ceiling hatch. "Go. Make yourself at home. And shake your girlfriend Neha out of bed. We just had Alpha pass-over. Beta at—" he peeked at the instrument complex "—16:37. Looks like supplycom wants us to catch the hook."

"She's not my girlfriend."

"I heard that." Neha Bhatnagar, one of the junior pilots, scrambled down the ladder from the deck above them. She dropped past the last four rungs and bounded over to give Mariska a hug. "You were amazing. Thank you, thank you, thank you." She squeezed her hard.

Surprised, Mariska said, "You're welcome." The girl released her grip and held Mariska at arm's length. "I was going to take a nap instead of watching, but you had us from the very first. "You, you, *you*." She raised her fists and crowed. "We won."

"We should have warned you," said Brady. "Our Neha tends to be enthusiastic."

"Not my girlfriend," muttered Elan.

"Be nice to her, rookie," teased Bhatnagar as they climbed the ladder.

The crew deck had another set of lockers with foldout couches. There was a tiny galley and a table that might accommodate six if they were close friends. It reminded her of the *Shining Legend,* which was something she didn't want to be reminded of. Elan pointed to the bathroom door, which was so narrow that she had to turn sideways to squeeze through. The bathroom was equally cramped. It was designed for use both planetside and upside in zero gravity, so there was a cleanser in place of a proper shower. The toilet had suction fittings which she was grateful she wouldn't need in Mars's gravity. While she was on it, her wristband flashed. Someone pinged her location, but did not leave a message. She assumed it was Natalya checking up on her. Would she be upset that Mariska was with Elan? As she rubbed her hands under the cleanser, she stared at the girl in the mirror. What *was* she doing here?

Elan had set out a snack of goat cheese on slivers of flatbread, topped with olives and dried tomatoes. "From our own goats," he said.

She wasn't hungry but she could tell that he wanted her to eat, so she did. On another day, in another place, she might have enjoyed it.

"Something to drink?"

"No thanks." Somehow Elan's eagerness to please depressed her. They had come all this way, and now she didn't know what she had to say to him.

"Is something wrong?"

"I'm tired all of a sudden." She shook her head. "I think my adrenaline must be running out."

"You want to go back?" *Gasp.*

In reply, she settled at the table, picked up another snack and examined it. "Goats?"

"My parents keep goats." He sat across from her. "Most Martians do. And we're bringing frozen embryos to D." *Gasp*. "A whole herd's worth."

"D?" She frowned. "Oh, your planet—at 18 Scorpii."

The mention of the upcoming mission—and his departure—was a conversation killer.

"You came to get me," said Elan at last. "Back there." *Gasp.* "Why?"

"Captain Martinez said that I would have to make a move if I ever wanted to talk to you again."

He squirmed. "The captain said that?"

She nodded. "So I made my move."

"Why do you want to talk to me?"

"No reason. I just do."

He looked pleased.

"You know," she said, "on the Moon friends talk, but we also share thoughts. I offered you a feed once, but you closed your head."

He stiffened, but then she felt the tingle of an offer.

=*Is this good?*= His feed was so weak she could barely make it out.

=*Sort of. You're still closed off.*=

=*A Martian thing. We keep ourselves to ourselves.*=

=*Why? Keeping secrets?*=

"Not secrets," he said, and started gasping as if he might pass out. Usually Elan's face was like a mask, but now it slipped and she saw what sharing a feed had cost him.

"Are you all right?"

"No." The gasping became laughter. "Yes." It took a moment for him to get control of himself. "It's just...." He pressed both palms to the table and closed his eyes for a few moments. "I've only done that with...." He took a deep breath and steadied. "...family."

"Oh." Now it was Mariska's turn to squirm. "I didn't know." Had she broken some Martian taboo? "Is that bad?"

"Bad?" He stared down at his hands as if amazed that he still had all his fingers. Then he looked up, his smile as wide as she had ever seen. "I'm so happy."

The superpressure balloon was three kilometers above them, according to Elan. When Mariska peered up she could see a bright pinprick in a butterscotch sky. It was easier to see the scoop which hung from it, sailing across Escalante Crater toward them. The scoop was unreeling down its tie line to get closer to the surface. Even though she was wearing an insulated EV suit, Mariska shivered. Elan squeezed her hand; he was wearing just his uniform and a breather. The scoop skimmed lower and lower. Its wings looked sharp as knives. The rear propeller began to churn, acting as a brake. The flaps went up. Slower but still way too fast for Mariska. The fuselage hung beneath the wings; from where she stood it looked to be barely skimming the surface. A wide door slid open; the boarding step stuck out like a silver tongue.

The EV suit felt like it was made of dough. She couldn't possibly run fast enough in it to hop aboard.

=*Ready?*= Elan's feed was like an electric shock.

=*As I'm going to be.*=

=*It'll be down to six kilometers an hour. A slow jog.*=

Mariska felt her thigh muscles twitching.

=*If you miss, just fall flat. We'll try another pass.*=

If the wings didn't slice her in half. And here it was, zigzagging slightly, the door a yawning black hole.

=*Go.*=

And then she was running as fast as she could, trying to match speed with the scoop. As she closed on it she was surprised to feel backwash from the propeller, even in the thin atmosphere of Mars, but she threw herself forward and there was the boarding step. Jump up, hands on the grab bar, pull hard and *she was in*. She started laughing hysterically, even though no one could hear her. Because no one could hear her. A few seconds later Elan stepped calmly through the open door as if he were taking a stroll through the greenhouse. He put an arm around her shoulders and hugged her.

=*Yaaahhh.*= In her excitement her head opened wide. They were probably picking her up in orbit. =*Did it.*=

=*You're practically a Martian.*= Elan was too much of a gentleman to probe. =*But don't go fizzy on me now.*= He steered her deeper into the cabin and pointed to a grab bar. She remembered that when the pilot put the flaps down again and reversed the prop, the scoop would lurch forward, tugged along by the balloon. It was sailing the winds in the upper atmosphere. She wrapped one hand around the bar and gave him a thumbs up with the other.

Elan had explained that if they had been taking on or dropping off cargo, the scoop would have hooked onto an anchor at the base landing dock. But docking took too much time; it was not stopping just for passengers. Martians caught their rides by hopping a moving scoop.

They passed through the airlock and Elan took his breather off. The air pressure in the passenger compartment was only 200 millibars, too low for Mariska, so she was stuck in the EV suit. There were two other passengers. One acknowledged them with a nod. The other was asleep under a sun lamp, her photoreceptors erect and reaching toward the light like hungry snakes. Mariska tried not to disturb them as she flitted from window to window, taking in the view. The scoop was quickly reeling line in to gain altitude. Behind them was *Natividad* base. She could see the squat chocolate chip shape of the *Madre* and the jumble of service mods around it. Ahead of them was the southwest wall of Escalante Crater and, two hundred and sixty kilometers beyond that, Tarragona.

Elan's home.

This wasn't a trip Mariska had been looking forward to, and the only reason she was making it was because Elan had begged her to come along. His own relationship with his parents was strained and he thought they would have to behave if he brought a guest home. She owed him; after all, hadn't he helped Mariska with her mother? She could have resisted this argument, but what she couldn't resist was that he needed her support. Had anyone ever really needed her? Maybe Jak, her first and only boyfriend, but that had ended badly. Was Elan her boyfriend? They had certainly spent a lot of time together in the past few weeks. No, that was ridiculous—he was a Martian, and a spacer, and he would be out of her life before too much longer. But he was her only friend on the base, if you weren't counting Shengyi—and she wasn't. What Mariska didn't understand was how she could be *his* only friend. Despite all the kidding he got, the rest of the crew seemed to like him. Brady and Bhatnagar especially made an effort to include him, but he kept pushing them away.

The whirring of the tie-line reel got even louder as they cleared the

Escalante. The ground fell away as the scoop hauled itself up towards its balloon. Ahead of them loomed the peak of a mountain.

"Like the view?" Elan came up behind her.

"That's a big one ahead." She knew that the EV helmet muffled her voice, but Martians had keen hearing.

"Mt. Letosa. Two thousand meters of up between here and there. We'll make it."

"I'm not worried." She placed her glove flat against the window. "This is fun."

"This part, yeah. Later, maybe not."

She patted his back. "We'll survive."

=*I really appreciate this.*= His feed was practically melting with gratitude.

Elan had guessed that it would take at least four hours to get to Tarragona, depending on how many rolling stops they had to make. The pilot tacked north after crossing over Mt. Letosa and worked her way around its western slope to pick up two miners and drop off the Martian who had been snoozing. A couple of hours later, she swooped low over a seemingly empty plain. Mariska peered, but couldn't see anyone. The scoop slowed down but not nearly enough. Nobody, not even a Martian, could run that fast. Then she spotted the trail of dust peeling behind the glint of metal: a motobike was hurtling toward them. She wanted to call Elan to come see but there was no time. The bike's front wheel came off the ground as it closed the last few meters. Even with her face pressed to the window, Mariska couldn't see the entry, although she could hear the squeal of rubber on metal in the cabin behind them. She expected a crash but none came. Then the scoop lurched forward to catch up to the balloon and began to climb its tie-line. A few moments later, the cyclist burst through the airlock. She tore her helmet off and stomped up to Elan.

"She can't even breathe the air," she said, wisps of Marsdust puffing from her grimy jumpsuit.

Mariska glanced at Elan. When she saw him shrinking back in his seat, she sat upright. Was this person talking about her?

"Why are you here?" Elan sounded as miserable as he looked.

"Why?" The cyclist turned to the other passengers. "He wants to know why I'm here?"

"So do we," called one of the miners. "Tell us. We're bored."

"It's been a long trip." The other was laughing a staccato laugh.

=*Elan, who is she?*= Mariska offered, but his head was slammed shut.

"This is his tourist," said the angry cyclist. "For her, he leaves me. Me, three times his wife."

*Grrr.* In the thin air, Elan's gasp sounded like a growl. "We were never together, Nelow."

Mariska didn't like anything about this woman, but especially not her claim to be married to Elan. "I'm Mariska Volochkova." She stood. "And you are?"

"Yes, we know all about you." The look she gave Mariska could have crushed stone. "The twenty billion yuan girl."

Mariska colored.

Elan stood beside her. "Why are you here?"

"I am invited by Gamir and Zak. The grandparents of our child."

"There is no child."

Mariska bumped up against him. "What is going on here, Elan?"

"He doesn't tell you? Wake up, sleeper." She snapped her fingers in front of Mariska's face. "You two talk now. I need to sit with real Martians." She turned, stalked to the two miners, and pushed in between them. "Talk!" she ordered Elan and Mariska, then leaned back and slung arms around each of the miners' shoulders.

They talked. When Nelow and Elan had been two Martian years old—not quite four standard—their parents had agreed to a term marriage contract for their children, who had never met. Nelow lived in the city of Schiaparelli and Elan lived eight hundred kilometers away in remote Tarragona. This was first of all a civic and business relationship. The marriage earned both families government stipends under the Repopulation Act, passed at the end of the Abandonment. However, while the institution of child marriage was most popular among the poorest Martians, money was not their only motivation. Pledging that their children would marry and reproduce was seen by parents as a patriotic duty to their decimated society. *Mars needed Martians*. Their original contract had been for three Martian years; renewal for another term doubled the stipend and created a greater expectation that the marriage would someday be made permanent. At the time of the third renewal, the couple was required to bank eggs and sperm as insurance against radiation damage. Levels on Mars could be fifty times those on Earth. Most of those who agreed to three-term contracts went on to permanent marriage. Those who chose not to renew a contract were required to pay the stipends back.

"I almost went permanent," whispered Elan. "I liked her well enough."

He kept checking on Nelow. "Or thought I did." She had appeared to have fallen asleep; her head rested against one of the miners. "But the *Natividad*. No Martian has ever crewed a starship. It's past time."

Mariska offered a feed again but his head was still closed. "She was mad at you," she said, hiding her disappointment.

"Do you blame her?" *Grrr.* "We lived together when I went to school in Schiaparelli." He ground his foot into the deck, as if to squash the memory. "I don't love her. And she'll never leave Mars."

"So you got married for Mars?"

"For Mars? Yes, but not my choice."

"And you're leaving for Mars." She poked him in the ribs. "Time that a Martian went to the stars," she said in an announcer's voice.

He gave her a sour look. "Not much of a reason is it? He considered. "Nobody I know wants me to leave. Maybe not even me."

She waited to hear more.

"My parents are proud. But I'll be gone for good." He nodded at Nelow. "She hates the *Natividad*. And the crew doesn't want me. Not really. I'm just good public relations. Like you."

"And now you don't want to go?"

"I thought I did. I need to do *something*. I'm twelve years old."

She nudged him with her elbow. "Twenty-two standard."

"Tourist years." *Grrr.* "I can't believe she called you that."

"I think she's awake." Mariska nuzzled his neck, just to tease Nelow. "And peeking this way." At least, that was what she thought she was doing. "I think she's burning up inside at the sight of us together."

"Maybe." He sounded doubtful.

"I can't believe your parents invited her."

"I can," said Elan.

Mariska paused at the entrance to the greenhouse. It was so bright that she wished she was wearing her EV suit so that she could enable its sun visor. Zak and Gamir had increased the air pressure in their burrow to 360 millibars so that Mariska could wear plain clothes. But the air was still so thin that it gave her a headache; this near-blinding light only made it worse. She had grown up on the Moon where the standard pressure was 500 millibars, which was the equivalent of living at an altitude of 6000 meters. But touring Elan's parents' burrow felt like a forced march around the summit of Mount Everest.

"Oh, you have another asparagus crop coming." Nelow knelt by the raised bed and brushed her hand along the row of spears poking through the rockwool.

"Third this year." Zak beamed; he treated her as if she was his child and Elan was the guest.

Mariska could have sworn that Nelow stopped for a personality transplant on the trip from the scoop drop-off to the burrow. She had complimented Gamir on the narcissus scent she had chosen in Mariska's honor, although Mariska thought it smelled like an oil spill. She was affectionate with Zak and polite to Mariska and claimed to be following stories about Elan in her favorite newsfeed. And now she was cooing at asparagus. Who was she trying to impress?

"And what do you grow in your greenhouse?" Gamir asked Mariska.

Hydroponics had been Mariska's worst subject in school on the Moon and asteroid buckets like the *Shining Legend* didn't have greenhouses. "I like flowers," she said.

"So do we," said Zak. "I always say, vegetables sustain the body, flowers lift the spirit."

"What about fruit?" said Elan. "Grain? Goat?"

"Ssshh," Gamir said. "Don't be mocking your father."

"Zak has a wonderful rose collection," said Nelow. "And peonies. Some amazing orchids."

*=Help, Elan. What kind of flowers do I like?=* Something strange happened then. Although Elan's head was still closed to her, both Gamir and Zak gave her looks. For a moment she thought they had intercepted the feed she had offered to their son. But that couldn't be—she hadn't misdirected an offer since she was a little kid.

"I like flowers that smell nice," she said.

"As do we all, dear," said Gamir. "As do we all."

Zak waved the little group forward. "Did you want to see the goats?"

She fidgeted through dinner. The lighting was still a punishment. While the four Martians sat at table, their nodules stretched out and up. Watching four clumps of snaky photoreceptors wriggle whenever anyone got the least bit excited made Mariska lose her appetite. Which was a problem, because Zak had served her an overly generous helping of a stew—mostly vegetables although there were a few chewy chunks of what may once have been goat in the mix. She was surprised at how little Martians ate, but then some of their energy would be coming from the lights.

Gamir and Zak's burrow was in a tiny unnamed crater at the edge of the much larger Tarragona Crater. Tarragona, just over four kilometers in diameter, had been the site of a domed town before the Abandonment. Four thousand standards had lived there. Most had died there as well in the chaos following the collapse of the Martian Authority. The dome had failed in the intervening years and some sections had collapsed onto the town, but other than dust infiltration, the town was preserved as it had been in the last terrible days of the Martian holocaust. Elan's parents were its unofficial custodians, something he had neglected to tell Mariska.

"Elan can give you the tour tomorrow," said his father, "but only if you insist. It's Martian history."

"It's everybody's history. Earth just won't own it."

"Gamir," teased Nelow, "politics is bad for digestion."

She sniffed.

"Toddy?" Zak came around the table, pouring from a kettle. "Chicory roasted from our own roots, ethanol from our still."

"So," Gamir said to Elan, "you're probably wondering why we asked Nelow over."

"It wasn't my idea." Nelow clasped hands behind her neck, as if she were under arrest. "They want to talk about the baby."

"Mom, do we have to discuss this now?"

"We have to discuss this sometime. You're leaving us, Elan. Leaving Mars, leaving everything."

"If this is family business, I can go." When Mariska scraped her chair back, Elan shot her a look of panic. Was this why he brought her here? "Or I can stay if you like," she said, settling back down. None of the others paid attention to her.

"You won't be here, Elan," said Gamir, "but you should know what the decision is. And you have a say." She turned to Nelow. So, Nelow?"

She drank from her cup, set it down, and seemed to brace herself. "I'm thinking I don't want to carry Elan's baby, under the circumstances. I love you two." When she reached toward Zak and Gamir, her nodules shivered. "But that's the way I feel. I'm sorry."

"We understand," said Gamir. "We love you, too."

"But if you want to raise our baby," she continued. "I have no objections."

"It's your mother who really wants this," Zak said to Elan. "Me, not that much." He wrapped his hands around his cup and stared into it bleakly. "Maybe I'm too old for that kind of nonsense."

"You're not, and it's not nonsense." Gamir's voice was filled with confidence. "It's for Mars."

"For Mars?" Zak grumbled. "Who is Mars these days?"

"*Politics.*" Gamir tapped at the table to turn the conversation back on topic. "We could bring an artificial womb right here into the burrow. There's nothing wrong with that. Is there?"

Mariska chose that moment to take her first ever sip of a hot toddy. The fumes of the alcohol stabbed up her nose like a knife and the hot liquid scorched down her throat. She bent over coughing and could not stop. Elan handed her his napkin. When she got control of herself, everyone was staring. She had to say something. "I was. . . ." She cleared her throat and started over. "I was born in an artificial womb."

The silence was unnerving. She found herself chattering to fill it. "I'm a clone of my mother. Natalya Volochkova. She went off on the *Gorshkov*. My mother. I had a contract father though. A very nice man." Mariska had no idea how to stop talking.

Elan came to her rescue. "Dad, I think it's a good idea," he said. "If that's what everybody wants. You and Mom made all your mistakes on me." He laughed. "So what could go wrong?"

Gamir invited Mariska to help with the washing up. She didn't know exactly what this meant, but she thought it best to agree. It turned out that these Martians did not push their dinnerware into a recycler, since it wasn't disposable. The plates and cups were permanent. They had been specially made of some Martian clay; Gamir was quite proud of the design. But they needed to be cleaned by getting dipped in the hot, soapy, disgusting water that filled one side of a double sink. Mariska felt like she was some kind of historical re-enactor. She was certain that she would throw up if she had to plunge her hands through those greasy bubbles. Luckily Gamir assigned her to rinse and dry.

"Nelow is a lovely girl." She handed Mariska a sudsy plate.

"I'm sure she is."

"You should get to know her better." Gamir pointed to a nozzle set into the second sink. "Pull that out and spray. You've never washed dishes before, have you?"

Mariska shook her head.

"Do I understand that you are staying on Mars?"

"I'm not sure." Mariska reached for the nozzle with her free hand and found that it was attached to a hose.

"But you're not going off on that starship?"

"That wasn't my plan, no."

"What is your plan?"

"I don't know." She stretched the hose, aimed the nozzle at the plate and pressed the button. The jet of water shot over the top of the plate into the sink. "I had an accident a couple of months ago." She rinsed the plate and set it in the drying rack. "I'm still in rehab."

"Yes, yes, we know all about that. Everybody does. We're away from things out here but we're not ignorant."

"I didn't mean...." She took another plate from Gamir. "I'm still getting used to the idea that everybody knows my story. I'm not sure *I* know my story."

Next Gamir passed her a cup. "My son likes you."

"I like him."

"But you're not going with him through that wormhole."

She filled the cup with rinse water and dumped it out. She filled it again. "No."

"Maybe you want him to stay behind? Leave the crew?"

"It's his decision."

"It is." Gamir reached into the wash water and pulled out the stopper. "But sometimes you have to talk a man into doing what he wants." Water began to slurp down the drain.

The next morning Gamir asked for Nelow's help with the flash steam generator. Elan was insulted that he hadn't been asked and he insisted on coming with them. Mariska tagged along. Gamir had tapped into one of Tarragona's geothermal production wells and was using the heated water to generate electricity. She explained that their turbine's rotor blades were showing premature fatigue. Nelow's diagnosis was bad harmonics; Elan argued that it was material failure. Mariska understood none of it.

Later, she went with Elan when he walked Nelow up the crater to her motobike; she was headed back to the drop-off and from there to Schiaparelli. Mariska had been expecting her to revert to her angry self. Instead, she was almost wistful.

"You were so good to Zak and Gamir," said Elan. "Thanks."

"What I have with them," she said, "has nothing to do with us." Nelow swung a leg over the seat of her bike. "When I boarded the scoop yesterday, husband, I was going to pounce. No tourist was going to stop me." She grinned. "I probably could still get you back, if I wanted."

Mariska wondered if that were true. She knew that she didn't want it to be.

"Nelow, you know how sorry..." said Elan.

"No, it's good." She waved him off. "Because I want a Martian, not you. Maybe you're from Mars, but you're already a spacer. Like young Volochkova here."

Mariska thought Elan would protest, but he remained silent.

She picked up her helmet and aimed it at Mariska. "You passed the family test, tourist. Baby and politics and goats and the ex-wife. Now he belongs to you." She settled it onto her head, started her engine, and roared off.

Mariska realized that Nelow just might be right. She just didn't know what it meant.

It wasn't until late afternoon that they started down the path to the dead town. Mariska was in her EV suit; Gamir made Elan wear his breather, even though he said they were only going for a quick tour before dark. The path wound down the edge of the crater on switch backs. On the way, Elan pointed out how the standards had blasted a huge chunk of the crater wall away to grade an access highway.

"They were never Martians," he said, picking his way past a ragged sheet of the fallen dome. They were among the buildings now. The town of Tarragona was built on a grid, with streets of poly-stabilized sand and low buildings of brick and stone. "What they built made no sense. Domes that collapsed. Roads choked with dust. Houses with optical glass."

"Optical glass?"

"Sand on Mars is mixed with iron oxide."

Mariska nodded. "Red Mars."

"Martians can live with tinted windows. But the standards couldn't." They stopped in front of a furniture store. *Schubul's More Than Décor*. He tapped on a long, narrow window that made the building look like it was squinting. "They wasted energy extracting iron from glass for a clear view. Of what?" He wiped dust off the window and gestured for Mariska to look in. She couldn't see much in the twilight: overturned chairs gathered around low tables, dark lamps fallen on gray rugs.

"Who windowshops on Mars? It's crazy. Streets like this don't work. This town belongs in some valley on Earth, not in a crater."

Mariska was startled by the anger in his voice. She turned and faced him. "You came here a lot when you were a boy."

"Yes."

"Alone?"

"Sometimes."

"It bothered you," she said. "It still does."

He looked away. "This part of town isn't as bad as where people actually lived. The ruins there are scary. It's as if the houses are screaming."

She imagined young Elan wandering the streets of the dead town, raging against the folly of the tourists. He had been careful not to use that word again after the first time.

"You're angry at them," she said.

He didn't reply; he just looked miserable.

=*Elan?*= She felt his head open just a crack. =*They were people, the tourists. They made mistakes, but everybody does. Like me. I'm a tourist. You said it yourself.*=

"You shocked my parents last night." He stared down the empty street. "They could tell when you offered me that feed."

"What's wrong with that?"

=*Martians don't share like that. Like tourists.*= His feed was wispy as a dream. Then he spoke, his voice cracking. "Unless it means something."

She paused then, not sure of what she was feeling, only that its hold on her was as real as gravity. =*It means something to me.*=

"But we can't be together."

What was she supposed to say? *Don't go?* Or *I'll come with you?* Neither felt like the right decision, but the uncertainty was becoming unbearable. "I don't know what to say, Elan."

"Neither do I." He took her hand. "Come. I'll show you my favorite store. Then we'll head back. It'll be dark soon."

Toto's Toy Box was just a sliver of a shop wedged between First Motobike and Marswalks. Its door was still intact and when Elan ushered her in, the lights came on.

"Microwave power, transmitted from home," he said. "I set up a rectenna on the roof when I was six."

Mariska barely heard; she was too busy examining the toys arranged on the shelves. There were the usual action bots, Lord Danger and Kid Crater and Crashman. He had one of those Sinbads who could narrate 1001 adventures and act out most of them. When Elan flipped the switch on an arena, tiny dinosaurs and elephants began to do battle. There was a Norm Tsai Versus Roberto Gone All-Time All-Star Soccer set up on a counter at the back of the store. She saw artificial skins, pogos, model motobikes, and three different calculons.

"This is every kid's fantasy," she said. "Your own private toy store."

"You should have seen what I had to throw away." He picked up a puffgun and sent a bubble of chocolate scent her way. "Some of it I found around town and brought back here."

Mariska couldn't help but notice the collection of famous starships, real and imaginary. The *Nottingham*, *Zheng He*, *Scorpene*, *Veer* and a couple that she didn't recognize. When she picked up a model of the *Gorshkov*, a holo of Pilar Martinez began to recite her famous "A new world for a new people" message, describing the discovery of the planet Bounty.

"I guess this is what hero worship looks like."

He shrugged, and she set it back in place.

"I spent a lot of time in here," said Elan, "wishing I was somewhere else."

On an impulse, she crossed the room to him and picked up both of his hands in hers. She waited until he met her gaze before offering the feed. =*Have you ever opened your head wide?*= He tried to pull free of her but she tightened her grip.

=*Once.*=

=*With who? Your parents?*=

=*My dad. I used to have nightmares. It's not a very Martian thing to do.*=

=*I am going open myself to you, Elan.*= She had done this just once as a kid. With Jak, her old boyfriend. =*All the way.*= She had a new boyfriend now. =*You can too.*=

"Mariska, no. I can't."

"Sssh." She went up on her tiptoes and leaned her forehead against his.

When she had tried full mind convergence with Jak, she had been able to keep herself separate from him. =*But now Elan's mind was hers and she relived his life in splashes of memory: the sticky throttle of his first motobike, his mother's cool palm against his fevered cheek, the hiss of milk in the pan when he milked his goat. At the same time she felt him scratching at her memories, little kids' voices bouncing off the ceiling at the Muoi swimming pool on the Moon and the squishy hot strawberries melting in Daddy Al's pancakes. He found Jak kissing her, puzzled over the way their lips didn't seem to fit together. He poked at hibernation but there was nothing for him there because hibernation was like being dead and then they were stumbling together through the destroyed homes in Terragona and they read the note begging Santa to* save my daddy *and all the* d's *were backward and Didit was telling her sister Glint to shut up and that they weren't going to die and they found the little boy curled up in the closet, a desiccated mummy, and they came out of hibernation just long enough to see Richard FiveFord floating in the airlock with all the empty oxygen bottles and Zak gave them the urn with the little boy's ashes to scatter and Richard wasn't moving, just floating, dead like the little boy, like Terragona, like Glint and Didit and Beep.=*

And then they became themselves again. They sat in silence because it was hard work separating into two people. Mariska and Elan. They were holding each other slumped against the wall of Toto's Toy Box. Mariska thought she ought to be embarrassed for having shared nightmares with Elan. But she wasn't. She had never felt this close to anyone before.

"We have to get out of this place," she said.

"I know," said Elan, although he seemed reluctant to let go of her. "It's late. They'll be worried."

"No, not here." She gestured at the toy store. "We have to get out of where we're stuck."

"All right," he said, but Mariska could tell that he didn't understand.

It was well part twilight and the stars were out. Mariska lit the headlamp on her EV helmet, then noticed that Elan was gazing at the sky.

"They're so beautiful," he said. "But they're so far away."

Mariska didn't bother to look. She knew the stars. She had grown up on the Moon, after all. When you were out on the surface of the Moon, there was no atmosphere to make them twinkle. Their light could be beautiful, yes, but it could also be cruel. Nobody went to the stars unless they had a reason. A really *good* reason, like maybe being in love.

What was it his mother had said? Sometimes you have to talk a man into doing what he wants. And Mariska's mother? Of course, Natalya would think that *she* had won.

But Mariska had made her decision. She took Elan's hand and steered him away from Mars.

# ABOUT THE AUTHORS

Peter M. Ball's first story was published in *Dreaming Again* in 2007, and since then his short fiction has appeared in *Fantasy*, *Strange Horizons*, *Apex Magazine*, *Interfictions II*, *Shimmer*, and *Year's Best SF 15*. His faerie-noir novella, *Horn*, was published in 2009 by Twelfth Planet Press, and was followed by *Bleed* in 2010. He lives in Brisbane, Australia, and can be found online at *www.petermball.com*.

Damien Broderick is an award-winning Australian SF writer, editor, and critical theorist, a senior fellow in the School of Culture and Communication at the University of Melbourne, currently living in San Antonio, Texas, with a PhD from Deakin University. He has published more than forty books, including *Reading by Starlight*, *Transrealist Fiction*, *x, y, z, t: Dimensions of Science Fiction*, *Unleashing the Strange*, and *Chained to the Alien: The Best of Australian Science Fiction Review*. *The Spike* was the first full-length treatment of the technological singularity, and *Outside the Gates of Science* is a study of parapsychology. His 1980 novel *The Dreaming Dragons* (revised in 2009 as *The Dreaming*) is listed in David Pringle's *Science Fiction: The 100 Best Novels*. His latest SF novel is the diptych *Godplayers* and *K-Machines*, written with the aid of a two-year Fellowship from the Literature Board of the Australia Council, and his recent SF collections are *Uncle Bones* and *The Qualia Engine*.

Emma Bull published her first short story, "The Rending Dark," in 1984 in Marion Zimmer Bradley's *Sword and Sorceress*. She came to prominence with her next major publication, pioneering urban fantasy novel *War for the Oaks*, which appeared in 1987. It was followed by five more novels, including Hugo, Nebula, and World Fantasy Award nominee *Bone Dance*, *Finder*, *Freedom & Necessity* (with Steven Brust), and most recently *Territory*. Her short fiction has been collected in *Double Feature*, a collaborative collection with her husband Will Shetterly. Bull also co-edited the "Liavek" series of fantasy anthologies with Will Shetterly, and currently is executive producer and one of the writers for *Shadow Unit* (www.shadowunit.org).

Andy Duncan was born in South Carolina. He studied journalism at the University of South Carolina and worked as a journalist for the *News & Record* in Greensboro, N.C., before studying creative writing at North Carolina State University and the University of Alabama, and serving as the senior editor of *Overdrive*, a magazine for truck drivers. Duncan's short fiction, which has won the World Fantasy and Theodore Sturgeon awards, is collected in World Fantasy Award winner *Beluthahatchie and Other Stories*. Upcoming is a new short story collection, *The Pottawatomie Giant and Other Stories*. He currently lives with his wife, Sydney, in Frostburg, Maryland, where both teach in the English department of Frostburg State University.

Jeffrey Ford was born in West Islip, New York. He worked as a machinist and as a clammer before studying English with John Gardner at the State University of New York. He is the author of seven novels, including *The Physiognomy*, *Memoranda*, *The Beyond*, *The Portrait of Mrs. Charbuque*, *The Girl in the Glass*, and *The Shadow Year*. His short fiction collections are *The Fantasy Writer's Assistant and Other Stories*, *The Empire of Ice Cream*, and *The Drowned Life*. His fiction has won the World Fantasy Award, Nebula, Edgar Allan Poe Award, Fountain Award, Gran Prix de l'Imaginaire, and the Shirley Jackson Award. Ford lives in southern New Jersey where he teaches writing and literature at Brookdale Community College.

Eileen Gunn was born in Dorchester, Massachusetts, and grew up outside Boston. She earned a Bachelor of Arts in History from Emmanuel College. In 1976, she attended the Clarion Writers' Workshop in Michigan, then supported herself by writing advertising and books about computers. She was an early employee at Microsoft, where she was director of advertising and sales promotion in the mid-1980s. She left in 1985 to continue writing fiction. She lives in Seattle with the typographer and editor John D. Berry. Gunn's first short story, "What Are Friends For?" was published in 1978; subsequent stories include Nebula Award winner "Coming to Terms" and Hugo Award nominees "Stable Strategies for Middle Management" and "Computer Friendly." Her short fiction collection *Stable Strategies and Others* was published by Tachyon Publications in 2004, and was short-listed for the Philip K. Dick, James Tiptree, Jr., and World Fantasy awards. She is currently working on a biography of Avram Davidson.

Nalo Hopkinson is a Jamaican-born writer who lives in Canada. Her novels include *Brown Girl in the Ring*, *Midnight Robber*, *The Salt Roads*, and *The New Moon's Arms*. She is a recipient of the John W. Campbell Award for Best New Writer, the World Fantasy Award, and a two-time winner of Canada's Sunburst Award for the Literature of the Fantastic. She doesn't know whether she believes in ghosts or not, but she fervently hopes that if they do exist, they're not trapped in the Mega-Mall Between Life and Death.

Kij Johnson sold her first short story in 1987, and has subsequently appeared regularly in *Analog*, *Asimov's*, *Fantasy & Science Fiction*, and *Realms of Fantasy*. She has won the Theodore A. Sturgeon Memorial Award and the International Association for the Fantastic in the Arts' Crawford Award. Her short story "The Evolution of Trickster Stories Among the Dogs of North Park After the Change" was nominated for the Nebula, World Fantasy, and Sturgeon awards. Her story "26 Monkeys, Also the Abyss" was nominated for the Nebula, Sturgeon, and Hugo awards, and won the World Fantasy Award, while science fiction short story "Spar" won the 2009 Nebula Award.

Her novels include World Fantasy Award nominee *The Fox Woman* and *Fudoki*. She is currently researching a third novel set in Heian Japan.

Gwyneth Jones was born in Manchester, England, and is the author of more than twenty novels for teenagers, mostly under the name Ann Halam, and several highly regarded SF novels for adults. She has won two World Fantasy Awards, the Arthur C. Clarke Award, the British Science Fiction Association Award, the Dracula Society's Children of the Night Award, the Philip K. Dick Award, and shared the first Tiptree Award, in 1992, with Eleanor Arnason. Her most recent books are novel *Spirit* and essay collection *Imagination/Space.* Upcoming is new story collection *The Universe of Things.* She lives in Brighton, England, with her husband and son, a Tonkinese cat called Ginger, and her young friend Milo.

James Patrick Kelly has had an eclectic writing career. He has written novels, short stories, essays, reviews, poetry, plays, and planetarium shows. His most recent book is a collection of stories entitled *The Wreck of the Godspeed and Other Stories.* His short novel *Burn* won the Science Fiction Writers of America's Nebula Award in 2007. He has won the World Science Fiction Society's Hugo Award twice: in 1996, for his novelette "Think Like A Dinosaur," and in 2000, for his novelette "Ten to the Sixteenth to One." His fiction has been translated into eighteen languages. With John Kessel he is co-editor of *The Secret History of Science Fiction, Feeling Very Strange: The Slipstream Anthology,* and *Rewired: The Post-Cyberpunk Anthology*. He writes a column on the internet for *Asimov's Science Fiction* and is on the faculty of the Stonecoast Creative Writing MFA Program at the University of Southern Maine and on the Board of Directors of the Clarion Foundation. He produces two podcasts: James Patrick Kelly's StoryPod on Audible and the Free Reads Podcast.

Caitlín R. Kiernan was born in Dublin, Ireland, but grew up in rural Alabama. She studied vertebrate paleontology, geology, and biology at the University of Alabama at Birmingham and the University of Colorado at Boulder. She then taught evolutionary biology in Birmingham for about a year. Her first short story, "Persephone," appeared in 1995. Since then, her fiction has been collected in ten volumes, including *Tales of Pain and Wonder; To Charles Fort, With Love; A is for Alien;* and, most recently in *The Ammonite Violin and Others.* Her stories include International Horror Guild Award winners "Onion" and "La Peau Verte," SF novella *The Dry Salvages*, and IHG finalists "The Road of Pins" and "Bainbridge". Kiernan's first novel, IHG Award winner and Stoker finalist *Silk*, was followed by *Threshold, The Five of Cups, Low Red Moon, Murder of Angels, Daughter of Hounds*, and World Fantasy Award nominee *The Red Tree*. Upcoming is major new collection, *Two Worlds and in Between: The Best of Caitlín R. Kiernan.* Kiernan now lives in Providence, Rhode Island where she is working on a new novel.

Michael Swanwick's first two short stories were published in 1980, and both featured on the Nebula ballot that year. One of the major writers working in the field today, he has been nominated for at least one of the field's major awards in almost every successive year, and has won the Hugo, Nebula, World Fantasy, Theodore Sturgeon Memorial, and Locus awards. He has published six collections of short fiction, seven novels—*In the Drift, Vacuum Flowers, Stations of the Tide, The Iron Dragon's Daughter, Jack Faust, Bones of the Earth*, and *The Dragons of Babel*—and a Hugo Award nominated book-length interview with editor Gardner Dozois. His most recent book is major career retrospective collection, *The Best of Michael Swanwick*. Upcoming is a new "Darger and Surplus" novel, *Dancing with Bears.*

Rachel Swirsky holds an MFA in fiction from the Iowa Writers' Workshop and is a graduate of the Clarion West Writers Workshop. Her short fiction has appeared in a variety of venues, including *Tor.com, Subterranean Magazine, Weird Tales*, and *Fantasy Magazine.* Her story "Eros, Philia, Agape" was nominated for the 2009 Hugo and Sturgeon awards, while "A Memory of Wind" was a 2010 Nebula Award nominee. Her most recent book is a *Through the Drowsy Dark*, a short collection of feminist poems and short stories. She lives in Bakersfield, California, with her husband and two cats, and is seriously considering whether or not to become a crazy cat lady by adopting all four stray kittens which were recently born in her yard.

Jo Walton is a British fantasy and science fiction writer who makes her home in Canada. Her first published novel was *The King's Peace,* followed by *The King's Name*. In 2002 she won the John W. Campbell Award for Best New Writer, and subsequently published two more fantasy novels, *The Prize in the Game* and World Fantasy Award winner *Tooth and Claw*. She then went on to publish her "Small Change" trilogy—*Farthing*, *Ha'penny*, *Half a Crown*; and *Lifelode*. Her most recent novel is *Among Others*. She lives with her son and husband in Montreal, Quebec.